MUSICIANS COOK!

FROM THE PERFORMANCE HALL TO THE KITCHEN... QUARANTINED NYC MUSICIANS SHARE THEIR ARTISTRY

Recipes & Anecdotes Compiled by
REVA YOUNGSTEIN

Design & Layout
DEAN LEBLANC

Welcome

Welcome to Musicians Cook!

The idea to create a NYC-area musicians cookbook first came to me after seeing so many delicious food posts from my fellow musicians during the first months of the pandemic as we all quarantined at home. My friends were expanding their creative talents in their kitchens: some were mastering exciting new recipes, while others were discovering beloved old family recipes they'd never had time to prepare before. At this same time, I was moved by other posts from colleagues who were longing for camaraderie and sense of connection while having to remain isolated at home. We are highly trained performers, but we could not safely do what we love the most: playing with our cherished fellow musicians for a live audience. As educators, we could not enjoy the natural live exchange between student and master. Being part of this project would help us all connect with each other while also giving us a way to reach YOU, an audience of readers, for whom we missed performing so much.

Not only will *Musicians Cook!* bring pleasure and delight to your tables and taste buds, it will also provide financial support to keep our musical community healthy and safe. The proceeds of this cookbook will go towards the Local 802 Musicians' Health Fund. It has been a brutal time for our community while the performing arts industry was shut down, and New York musicians have been unable to get their regular health fund contributions, which is a great concern for many. My family and I have been lucky to enjoy good-quality affordable health coverage through our union's health fund over the years, as have so many of my colleagues, and support is sorely needed for everyone, because of the crisis. Even as performance venues reopen, our families and our union are suffering terrible deficits, and will continue to do so, for a very long time.

I partnered with the Save NYC Musicians fundraising campaign, which is raising money for musicians in need and boosting Local 802's Health Fund. Dean LeBlanc, Joanna Maurer and Louise Owen from the Save NYC Musicians committee were extremely helpful to me in getting the word out to a wide audience.

They wrote:

> *"We were quite excited when Reva came to us with the idea of raising money for our health fund by creating and selling a cookbook filled with recipes from NYC-area musicians. As members of the Save NYC Musicians campaign — which is raising money to help musicians in need and support our Local 802 Musicians' Health Fund — we knew right away that partnering with Musicians Cook! was a win-win situation. Save NYC Musicians could help solicit recipes and promote the cookbook, while the funds raised by Musicians Cook! would be an important infusion into our health fund. And with performance venues still closed, and so many arts organizations that will never recover, what better way for audiences to connect with NYC musicians than by enjoying their artistry in the kitchen!"*

So, my friends, crack open this cookbook, put on some beautiful music, enjoy our intimate anecdotes and delicious recipes, and get cooking!

Reva Youngstein

ISBN Paperback: 9781662916007

Edited by Reva Youngstein
Second paperback edition, June 2021

Front Cover Illustration by Sarah Hewitt-Roth
Back Cover Illustration by Marilyn Coyne

Design & Layout by Dean LeBlanc

Printed by Gatekeeper Press in the USA.

www.gatekeeperpress.com

Contents

 Visit our YouTube channel to see our recipe videos!

Glossary of Illustrations

Additional illustrations of food provided by Billy Hestand, freepik.com, and vecteezy.com.

*N*o one is loved like musicians. Musicians are loved by people. There's no other form that does that. I mean, I really think that musicians, probably musicians and cooks, are responsible for the most pleasure in human life.

~ Fran Lebowitz, from *Pretend It's A City* (Netflix Series)

Acknowledgements

I am extremely grateful to each and every musician who contributed a recipe. You shared your delicious recipes, and your heartfelt stories, an investment of your time, energies, and emotions. What an honor it was to read your contributions and get to know each of you a little better.

Karen Fisher, you suggested I present my cookbook idea in the union board meeting, which made it all possible. Janet Axelrod and all the other Local 802 officers, you were supportive and enthusiastic about my presentation. Mikael Elsila, your guidance throughout the creation process was instrumental. Lynne Cohen, your brilliant suggestions got this project launched. Thanks so much to Dianne Jacob (author of *Will Write for Food*) for all her time and her expert advice on recipe writing. Heartfelt thanks to Mariel Rodriguez-McGill for making her beautiful documentary on our cookbook, *From the Theater to the Kitchen.*

Dean LeBlanc, Joanna Maurer, Louise Owen, Rachel Drehmann, and the whole Save NYC Musicians crew, I can't thank each of you enough for all that you've

done to support my efforts and enhance this project. I couldn't have done it without you. Many thanks to Rachel for your expert help managing our social media. Louise, Joanna, I appreciated the great editing advice. Many thanks to Billy Hestand for assisting Dean in the layout and design of the book. Dean, you gave so generously of your talents, and your time designing, formatting, and laying out everything. You have made the cookbook so beautiful!

Sarah Hewitt-Roth, Marilyn Coyne, Joana Miranda, Marsha Heller, Emily Hope Price, Dana Lyn, Yevgenia Strenger, your artwork is exceptional, and I give you my heartfelt thanks. Jessica Troy, you connected me to some of these talented artists.

Kathy Cherbas, your ideas were an asset to this project. You were a huge help every step of the way; I am extremely grateful. My sister, Naomi Youngstein, you found numerous composer quotations, and assisted me in so many ways. Together, with your daughter, my niece, Mollie Wohlforth you created our fantastic recipe index. Tanya Dusevic Witek, thanks for your support; and your recipe was the first to come in. Deborah Saas, our family cookbook you created 15 years ago planted the seed for this musician cookbook. Diana Petrella, your expert editing suggestions were very helpful. Jim Neglia, your advice on using quotes was much appreciated. Cenovia Cummins, you found a stellar quotation and helped send artwork. Karin Dijkstra, my cousin, your artistic insights were amazing. Special thanks to my accountant Glenn Franke of *MusicTax.com*. Without your guidance I could not have established our non-profit status. Inbal Segev, your generous support is so greatly appreciated.

Dan Lipton, you gave generously of yourself, composing, recording, playing and rearranging our superb YouTube video jingle: I am deeply grateful to you and to the other fine Jingle Musicians: Joy Hermalyn, Daniel Spitzer, Jason Bitonti, and James Musto. Helen Campo and Danny Miller, your support was incredibly helpful. And your videos successfully launched our YouTube channel. Sincere thanks to all the musicians who made cooking videos; you are superstars!

To my smart and talented daughter, Natalie, I so appreciate your film editing expertise. And my whole family: daughters, Sarah and Natalie and my husband, Dan, you all had to tolerate my disappearing into my office for endless hours. Thank you for your love and support as I worked hard on the cookbook; I love you all very much!

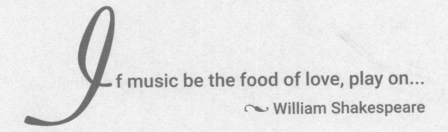

If music be the food of love, play on...
— William Shakespeare

BREAKFAST & ETC...

1-2-3 EASY SAUSAGE MUFFINS
～ Megan Shumate Beaumont

I work as a freelance clarinetist playing with various orchestras and Broadway shows. I also maintain a private teaching studio in New Jersey.

These easy-to-make muffins are a favorite in my family. They show up everywhere from camping trips to Christmas morning breakfast to mid-day snacks. They can be made in advance, are great to take on the go, and kid approved!

Special Prep/Equipment
A muffin pan or two

1 pound ground breakfast sausage	3 eggs
2 cups shredded cheese	1 can of 8 jumbo flaky biscuits

1. Preheat oven to 350°.

2. Brown sausage in a hot skillet and let it cool.

3. In a large bowl, mix sausage, cheese, and eggs.

4. Grease muffin pans. Divide each biscuit into two and flatten. Press each biscuit half into 16 muffin tin spots.

5. Fill each biscuit with a few spoonfuls of the sausage/egg mixture.

6. Bake in preheated oven for 10-15 minutes until cheese is melted and browned around the edges.

Yields 16 muffins

MAPLE BANANA MUFFINS
～ Yannick Nézet-Séguin

I am the Music Director for The Metropolitan Opera and The Philadelphia Orchestra, and the Artistic Director for the Orchestre Metropolitain in Montreal.

I adapted this from *detoxinista.com* and added a little Canadian touch with maple syrup.

Special Prep/Equipment
Muffin pan and liners

1 cup all-natural peanut butter	3 whole eggs
2 very ripe bananas, mashed	½ teaspoon sea salt
¾ teaspoon baking soda	¼ cup maple syrup
1 teaspoon vanilla	1 teaspoon cinnamon

1. Preheat your oven to 350º and prepare muffin tins with 12 muffin liners.

2. In a medium bowl, combine peanut butter, mashed banana, baking soda, vanilla, eggs, salt, maple syrup, and cinnamon, and mix until smooth.

3. Divide the batter among the 12 muffin cups.

4. Bake in preheated oven 20-25 minutes, until the muffins have risen and feel firm in the center.

5. Allow to cool for at least 30 minutes before removing from the pan.

Yields 12 muffins

DELECTABLE VEGAN BREAKFAST SOUP
Sandra Billingslea

I am a Freelance Violinist. I played in 15 Broadway shows including *Miss Saigon, The Life & Adventures of Nicholas Nickleby,* and the original *Dreamgirls.* I played with Queens Symphony, Scandia Symphony, and other freelance orchestras, in many movies, commercials, club dates, and played with countless popular artists including Aretha Franklin, Luther Vandross, Stevie Wonder, Frank Sinatra. I gave children's concerts and was a storyteller with Music Outreach West End Little Symphony, Westchester Philharmonic and many others.

This delicious soup is a great way to begin your day. The broth is naturally sweet & delicious from the root vegetables. It warms you up and gives you lots of energy. I often use the broth and some of the veggies to pump up other dishes later in the day adding spices for more punch as the day goes on.

Special Prep/Equipment
A nice heavy soup pot. Size depends on how much soup you want to make. I use Le Creuset because it holds the heat, but any heavy pot will work. I use a 2-quart pot so I have plenty of left-overs to add to other dishes.

¼-⅓ Vidalia or sweet onion

1-3 carrots, peeled and sliced on the diagonal

1-3 parsnips

1 butternut, acorn and/or delicata squash

1-2 heads of broccoli or a large bunch kale and stems

Herbs: Basil & Italian seasoning, black, white and a dash of cayenne peppers, (freshly grind into the soup from the pepper mill), except the cayenne pepper.

Note: I use organic or fair market veggies. They taste better & are healthier.

1. Fill half a pot with filtered or spring water. Bring it to a boil. Add black, white and a dash of cayenne pepper. You can vary the pepper according to your favorites, but not too much because it's a breakfast soup. Not too spicy.

2. Add four shakes of dried basil and three shakes of Italian seasoning. How much spice depends on how much water: a good amount but not overwhelming. Slice the Vidalia onion into half moons and add to the boiling water with herbs.

3. After 3 or 4 minutes, add chopped broccoli or kale stems, (just the stems not the florets or kale). Turn down the heat and add in order, carrots, (let them simmer covered for 2 minutes), then add parsnips, acorn and/or delicata squash, (I use them both although the acorn squash is hard to peel). If you are using kale instead of broccoli, add it here, wash, roll and sliced.

4. Let everything simmer covered an additional 2-3 minutes so everything is cooked but not mushy or overcooked. Veggies should still be firm. Turn the heat to low, add the broccoli florets heads up and skimming on top of the water.

5. Cover and let the pot's heat cook them for about 2 minutes. Turn off the heat. Move the pot off the burner to the back of the stove and let the soup sit about 20 minutes. Delicious!!! Broth is robust and sweet when you stir it and veggies are not overcooked.

Note
If you prefer pure sweet broth, you do not need to add the peppers or spices. I like to add basil because sometimes USA carrots are not as tasty as they should be. The taste varies greatly if you chose broccoli or kale but both are delicious. I like my vegetables medium sliced but not tiny either. Your soup, your choice. Be flexible and have fun making this recipe. No salt ever. You don't need it.

Yields 2-3 days of Breakfast Soup

RASPBERRY "CHEESECAKE WAFFLES" AND OVERNIGHT OATS

~ Rebekah Griffin Greene

Howdy folks! I'm a bassist, pianist, composer and teacher. I've been a bass sub on *The Phantom of the Opera* since 2017, and *Oklahoma* for a stint in 2019. I also run a (now virtual) pre-college music theory program at the Thurnauer School of Music, teach virtual bass lessons at Thurnauer and the Lucy Moses School, and have done orchestrations/arranging for film composer Christopher Wong in the past year.

My most exciting new project since the pandemic started was creating a cooking show with my kids based on my new gluten/soy free vegan lifestyle, which is helping to control my auto-immune disease without medication. Having been uber-inspired by British chef Nadiya Hussain's show *Time to Eat* and the cookbook of the same title, I decided to start adapting her recipes to fit my strict diet so I wouldn't feel deprived at all. This is the first recipe I adapted, and you can also see us cooking and eating it on our YouTube channel under my name. I also have a blog. This is a simple and economic recipe. Enjoy!

Special Prep/Equipment
Thaw out your toaster waffles in the fridge overnight.

6 thawed out gluten-free/dairy-free toaster waffles (Original recipe called for croissants)

2 cups + 1 tablespoon of plain coconut yogurt (Original recipe called for ricotta cheese. I used Anita's brand yogurt; thick, local and worth every penny!)

4 tablespoons coconut palm sugar, pulsed to a more fine consistency (our version of "caster sugar")

2 teaspoons vanilla

1¼ cups fresh or frozen raspberries

2 tablespoons gluten-free flour

¼ cup pumpkin puree (egg substitute, could also use applesauce)

For the overnight oats:

⅔ cup vegan milk (I used coconut milk)

⅔ cup gluten-free oats

1. Preheat the oven to 375°. Put cupcake cups underneath each waffle and then squish the thawed out waffles into the muffin pan. It won't be pretty!

2. In a bowl, whisk together the plain coconut yogurt (or ricotta cheese), sugar, and vanilla. Add the raspberries and break them up slightly "to give that lovely marbled effect", according to Nadiya. Set aside half of the mixture in a Tupperware to make the overnight oatmeal. Add the gluten-free flour and "egg" to the original bowl and mix it all up.

3. Use a measuring cup to scoop the filling into the waffles, and place the muffin tin in the pre-heated oven for 15 minutes. While you are waiting, prep the overnight oats by adding the milk and gluten-free oats to the raspberry-yogurt filling. Stick that in the fridge, and you'll have delicious breakfast waiting for you in the morning. You'll know the waffles are done if there is a slight jiggle in the middle.

4. Thanks for at least two days of breakfast, Nadiya!

5. Enjoy the allergen-free deliciousness, friends!

Serves 6

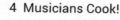

SLOTHROP'S MIRACULOUS BANANA CREPE-CAKES

~ Skye Steele

I am a songwriter, improvising violinist, and educator.

Inspired by an empty cupboard and the madcap "banana breakfast" scene in Thomas Pynchon's novel, *Gravity's Rainbow*, I improvised these banana crepe-cakes one morning in 2002 and have been making them ever since!

Special Prep/Equipment
Cast iron skillet or griddle

2 bananas

2 eggs

½ tablespoon butter

Dash of cinnamon

Dash of nutmeg

Dash of ground ginger

1 teaspoon honey (recommended only if your bananas are on the green side)

Note:
The biggest variable in this recipe is the ripeness of your bananas. A greener banana will yield a firmer, more pancake-like result. Riper bananas yield a wonderfully delicate texture and sweeter flavor, but can be difficult to flip without breaking.

1. In a plate, beat the eggs.

2. Peel bananas and use a fork to smash them into pulp on the plate.

3. Combine banana pulp and eggs with your fork, mixing vigorously until well combined.

4. Add spices and sweetener if using.

5. Heat up butter in a cast iron skillet or griddle.

6. Pour out batter in individual cakes, sized to your liking.

7. Flip when the edges begin to firm (they will not bubble like pancakes).

8. Serve 'em hot!

9. Eat plain or garnish to your liking. Try yogurt, crushed walnuts, and berries if you're feeling fancy. Add maple syrup or fruit preserves if you've got a sweet tooth.

Serves 2 (yields 4 - 6 crepe-cakes)

KORVAPUUSTI OR "SLAP ON THE EAR"
(FINNISH CARDAMOM/CINNAMON ROLLS)
Erik Ochsner

I am an orchestra conductor and play the flute, piccolo, and piano. I also sing as a tenor and collect requiems!

My mother is from Finland, and I grew up eating these. They are my comfort food! Many Finns eat this daily as part of their unofficial "coffee ceremony." Usually eaten with coffee in the afternoon. "Kahvi ja pulla" in Finnish or "coffee and pulla". "Pulla" is the larger category of pastry dough made using cardamom, of which korvapuusti is a subset.

NOTE: You really can and should eat these any time of day!! Since my partner is Japanese, I have successfully made a variant which substitutes Japanese matcha powder (Green tea) instead of the cinnamon! "OISHI" (Japanese = yummy!)

Special Prep/Equipment

Cookie sheet and rolling pin

Cardamom, and lots of it!

This requires a few hours of rising time.

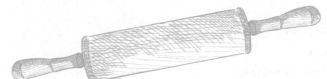

17 ounces milk	2 teaspoons salt	Ground cinnamon, 1 heaping teaspoon
5 envelopes yeast (as needed to make a "good dough")	2-4 tablespoons of cardamom (as desired, can be as little as 2 teaspoons)	*For basting:* 2 eggs
6 cups flour plus extra to flour the work surface.		Coarse sugar (like the size of sea salt)
14 ounces stick butter, warmed (plus additional butter for melting and "painting")	4 eggs	*Optional:* use slivered almonds when basting
	14 ounces sugar (plus additional sugar for sprinkling)	

1. Warm the milk to 110-115° (per yeast's instructions), and then add the yeast.

2. Add enough flour to yeast to make a good dough (2-3 cups) so the texture is no longer sticky. Let rise 1 hour.

3. Cream the warmed butter, and add to the mixture. Add salt, add cardamom.

4. Whip together eggs and sugar, add to mixture.

5. Now add enough flour to make a good dough (2-3 cups) constantly kneading so the texture is no longer sticky. Let rise 1 more hour.

6. Flour a flat surface. Remove ¼ of dough and put on the floured surface. Knead in more flour so the texture is no longer sticky.

7. Roll into a rectangle (see diagram on next page). "Paint" with melted butter and sprinkle with lots of white sugar and cinnamon.

8. Roll up as per diagram to make "a log" and then make the diagonal cuts seen in the diagram. Butter the cookie sheet.

9. Place cut pieces on the prepared cookie sheet. Pinch top of roll to create "slap on the ear" look.

10. Let rise approximately. 45 minutes.

11. Baste with beaten eggs. Sprinkle with coarse sugar.

12. Bake at 400° for 14 minutes, covering with loose foil to keep from over-browning.

13. Let stand to cool. Remove from the baking sheet and enjoy!

Yields 15-20 rolls

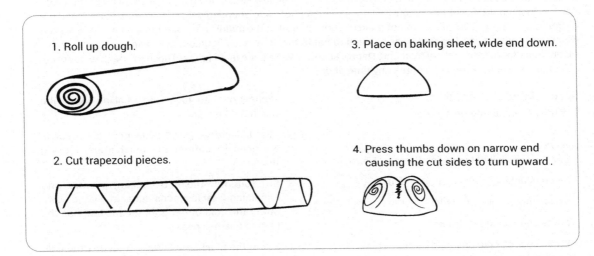

1. Roll up dough.

2. Cut trapezoid pieces.

3. Place on baking sheet, wide end down.

4. Press thumbs down on narrow end causing the cut sides to turn upward.

I am a pretty decent cook, actually, though I am much better at following recipes than opening the pantry door and saying, "wonder what I can make with corn flakes, Spanish olives, tomato paste and balsamic vinegar?"

~ Georgia Stitt, theater composer & pianist

BLUEBERRY SCONES WITH LEMON GLAZE

Karen F. Fisher

I was a professional clarinetist in bands, orchestras, and on Broadway. Currently I am the Financial Vice President of Local 802 AFM.

This was adapted from a recipe for strawberry scones I found in an email from *Enticing Desserts*. I get a lot of foodie emails because I love to cook and bake and I've somehow ended up on a ton of email lists. I usually don't even open them, but this recipe had an intriguing photo and sounded delicious. It was right around my birthday, which is in December. I'm not a fan of summer fruit in the middle of winter but we had some frozen wild blueberries on hand so there was no need to run to the store and I figured they would work just fine. I made these for myself and my husband, Danny, and they were gone in 24 hours. These scones are not overly sweet and are great with a cup of tea any time of day.

Special Prep/Equipment
Baking pan and parchment paper

Scones:

2 or 2½ cups wild blueberries (fresh or frozen)

2¼ cups unbleached all purpose flour

1 tablespoon baking powder

3 tablespoons sugar, divided

6 tablespoons cold unsalted butter, cut in small pieces

2 large eggs, divided

¼ teaspoon salt

⅔ cup milk

Lemon Glaze:

2 tablespoons fresh squeezed lemon juice

1½ cup powdered sugar

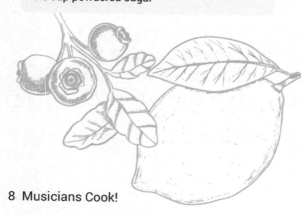

1. Preheat oven to 400°. Line a baking sheet with parchment paper.

2. Toss blueberries with 1 tablespoon of the sugar. No need to defrost the blueberries if using frozen.

3. Sift together the flour, baking powder, and remaining 2 tablespoons sugar in a large bowl. Cut in the cold butter until the mixture has the texture of small peas.

4. Mix in the blueberries. Whisk together the milk and 1 egg in a separate bowl and add to the flour mixture.

5. Flour a work surface, and turn out the dough, shaping into a 10" circle.

6. Place the circle on the baking sheet. With a sharp knife, cut the circle into 8 triangles. Don't worry if the pieces stick together.

7. Beat the second egg and brush over the top of the scones.

8. Bake for 20-30 minutes until the top is golden brown. Allow to cool on a wire rack.

9. Mix the lemon juice and powdered sugar together (you can adjust the amount of sugar to reach desired consistency and sweetness) and spread over the top of the scones.

Yields 8 scones

AUNT MARY'S WILD MAINE BLUEBERRY MUFFINS
⌇ Maureen Amaral Gay

I am a classical clarinetist/bass clarinetist and woodwind doubling theater and big band musician and a sometimes piano player and singer.

With this recipe I won 1st Place in the Machias, Maine Blueberry Festival Cooking contest. This was one of my favorite items that my Aunt Mary made and I am thankful she passed on the recipe. She would want it shared. *It's important to use Wild Blueberries, fresh or frozen to avoid the runny blue striped batter that occurs when using the large cultivated blueberries found on cream pie toppings. They are large because of the high water content and have much less flavor than wild. Also, I use organic ingredients when possible!

Special Prep/Equipment

2 regular sized muffin pans or oversized muffin tins

Paper baking cups, if possible

2 eggs

1½ cups sugar

1 teaspoon vanilla extract

8 tablespoons (1 stick) butter, softened, at room temperature

3 cups flour

5 teaspoons baking powder

1 teaspoon salt

1 cup milk

2 cups wild Maine blueberries

Optional: cinnamon or sugar to sprinkle on top

1. Let the butter soften at room temperature to truly cream the old fashioned way, instead of melting which changes the texture of the muffin batter.

2. Preheat oven to 425°. Cream eggs, sugar, vanilla and butter.

3. Slowly add and mix in the flour, baking powder, salt, and milk. Gently fold in the wild Maine blueberries.

4. Spoon mixture into muffin cups. I prefer to make 12 for oversized muffins but this recipe will make 18 standard sized muffins.

5. If desired, sprinkle sugar and/or cinnamon on top.

6. Bake 23-28 minutes for large muffins (or 21-25 minutes for the standard size muffins).

Yields 12 oversized or 18 standard muffins

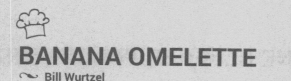

BANANA OMELETTE
Bill Wurtzel

I am the Jazz Guitarist with Count Basie Countsmen, Bill Doggett, Jimmy McGriff, Harlem Blues & Jazz Band, Gloria Lynn, Terri Thornton. American Folk Art Museum 12 years weekly concerts. Board member for the Jazz Foundation of America, and Local 802 member.

I learned about this recipe at a *Weight Watchers* meeting. Amazingly delicious and healthy with very few calories. It's perfect for breakfast, lunch or snack. But I've made this recipe my own with some very special garnishes at the end. It's fun to play with your food because it can get you into a creative zone. For more inspiration visit *funnyfoodart.com*.

Special Prep/Equipment
Small non-stick pan

Butter or oil for the pan

1 ripe banana

2 eggs

Drop of vanilla extract, optional

Garnish of fruit and low fat cottage cheese or yogurt

1. Heat butter or oil in a small non-stick pan.

2. Mash banana in a mixing bowl and stir in 2 eggs.

3. Pour into hot pan, and cover, to let evenly cook and retain moisture. Lift omelette out onto a plate when it's set and done.

4. It doesn't have to be a work of art because you are going to eat it anyway. Work quickly so it stays hot.

5. Place a teaspoon of low fat cottage cheese for each "eye".

6. Add 2 blueberries or raisins as "pupils" on the cottage cheese.

7. Put 2 blackberries or raisins as "eyebrows" above the cottage cheese.

8. 2 banana slices can be "ears" on both sides of the omelette.

9. A strawberry as a "nose" between the "eyes".

10. Arrange 3 raspberries as heart-shaped "lips".

11. Lettuce on top of the omelette can be "hair".

Serves 1

WHATEVER QUICHE
~ Yuko Naito-Gotay

I am a violinist and double as a violist. I am a member of the new production of the West Side Story orchestra.

In my opinion, quiche is such a versatile food you can eat any time of day. It could be for breakfast, lunch, snack, or dinner. I have been searching for a simple (but tasty!!) quiche recipe and finally hit the jackpot! This is a super simple recipe that anyone can make and it will come out delicious no matter the ingredients you choose! Ingredients and method are adapted from a recipe on *Food.com* called Basic Quiche by Mama Tia.

Special Prep/Equipment
9" springform pan, electric mixer

5 eggs, beaten

¾ cup milk

2 tablespoons grated Parmesan cheese (or Pecorino Romano cheese)

½ tsp salt

½ tsp pepper

1 tablespoon olive oil

2 cups vegetables, chopped (and/or protein)

½ cup grated or shredded cheddar cheese

9 inch pie shell, frozen

1. Preheat the oven 350°.

2. In a bowl, combine eggs, milk, Parmesan cheese, and salt and pepper. Whisk well.

3. In a frying pan with olive oil, saute the chopped vegetables and additional salt and pepper to taste. Put the sauteed vegetables on the bottom of the pie shell and spread evenly.

4. Add cheddar cheese on top of the vegetables and again spread evenly.

5. Pour the egg mixture into the pie shell.

6. Bake in the oven about 45-50 minutes until the mixture is set and the top is golden brown. Insert a knife and if it comes out clean it is done.

7. Take out from the oven and let it settle for about 20 minutes and serve.

Note
You can use any vegetables to mix and match. Here are some combinations you could try:

- zucchini, mushrooms, and bacon
- spinach, pepper, and onion
- cherry tomatoes, leeks, and sausages

I have used zucchini, mushrooms, shiitake mushrooms, peppers, hot peppers, leeks, onion, spinach, scallion, and more. As meat you can use some bacon, ham, and sausages to mix. To make it more cheesy simply add more cheese. You can even experiment with different kinds of cheese. Instead of cheddar you could use feta for Greek-inspired quiche, or gruyere for deep taste, or monterey jack for some hot spiciness!!

Serves 6-8

MOM'S PANCAKES/WAFFLES
～ Joe Fitzgerald

I am a bassist.

This is a slight alteration of my mom's recipe. I don't use quite as much butter as she did and I don't separate the eggs and beat the egg whites which she did quite happily. I'm not nearly as devoted as she was!

Special Prep/Equipment
Large mixing bowl
Whisk
Smaller bowl to melt the butter

4 eggs, well beaten

2 cups flour

3 teaspoons baking powder

1 teaspoon baking soda

1 teaspoon salt

2 cups milk

1½ sticks of butter, melted

1. Mix dry ingredients together thoroughly in large bowl. Add milk, eggs and melted butter in that order. <u>Mix thoroughly</u>!

2. If you're really ambitious you can separate the eggs and beat the egg whites to a light, fluffy texture and <u>fold</u> them in the mixture at the end. This will make a lighter texture but not really necessary to a successful outcome, and it's a lot more work.

Note
Feel free to add blueberries as I always do. But, be aware they can be a little messy if you're making waffles.

Yields about 2 quarts of batter

FRENCH CRÊPES
～ Anja Wood

I play cello, and am a musician in Hamilton.

My daughters' French grandmother makes them crêpes for special occasions, but my youngest daughter wanted to eat them regularly for breakfast. Admittedly, I was a little intimidated to attempt them, since their grand-mère is such a pro. But once you have the best recipe and the twirl of the pan down, they are fairly easy!

Special Prep/Equipment
This recipe is all about the pan. You want a flat, wide bottom with low edges. This is the full name of the pan: (on Amazon) New Ricovero Gourmet Copper Line. Hard Anodized 2.5mm Thickness Aluminum with two Copper Ceramic Nonstick Coatings, Crêpe/Pancake Pan 9½" diameter.

1 cup flour	¼ cup water
A pinch of salt	2 eggs
A pinch of sugar	
1 cup milk	1 teaspoon vegetable oil, + more oil to season the pan

1. Mix flour, salt, and sugar with a whisk to aerate. Add milk and water. Mix until there are no clumps. Whisk in the eggs and oil until blended. Let rest for a few minutes.

2. Place crêpe pan on the burner on medium high for about 30 seconds, then season your pan with a little oil on a paper towel. Spend time really greasing the entire surface in a thin coat of oil. The first crêpe wants to stick, so this will prevent that.

3. Let the pan heat up for another minute and pour a ladle of batter into the center of the pan. Tilt the pan so the batter is swirled in a circular motion towards the edges. The thinner the better!

4. Flip with a spatula once the edges come off the pan. The first crêpe takes the longest... possibly 2-3 minutes for that first side to be finished. After that, each side takes about 30-45 seconds. Flip when slightly golden brown.

5. Fill with Nutella, fruit, marmalade, whipped cream, lemon and sugar, etc. Fold in quarters.

6. Enjoy! You can stack crêpes on a plate covered by a tea towel to keep them warm.

Serves 4

DUTCH BABIES
〜 David Heiss

I am a cellist in the Metropolitan Opera, the New York Pops, and Little Orchestra Society.

As a sports-challenged lad in my junior high school, the after school "Boys' Chef Club" was just the ticket for me. Of the many recipes we tried, this one has stayed with me all these years – I've made it dozens of times for friends and family. The big reveal as it comes out of the oven is always a joy for my guests. Mangia!

Special Prep/Equipment
8" cast iron skillet

3 eggs

½ cup sifted flour

½ cup sugar

½ teaspoon salt

½ cup milk

½ teaspoon freshly grated nutmeg

3 tablespoons butter, melted

Maple syrup, warmed (for serving)

1. Preheat oven to 450°.

2. Break eggs in a medium sized bowl and whisk well.

3. Add flour, sugar, salt and blend.

4. Add milk and nutmeg and blend again.

5. Spread the melted butter around the bottom and sides of the skillet.

6. Add mixture and give it a quick stir.

7. Pop it in the middle of the oven for 10 minutes.

8. Dutch Babies are done when the elevated sides are golden brown and it is bubbling in the middle.

9. Top with syrup and enjoy!

Serves 2-4

SWEDISH HOLIDAY UGNSPANNKAKA
(A SAVORY BAKED PANCAKE WITH BACON)
~ Annbritt duChateau

I am a pianist/conductor/music director/music supervisor for multiple Broadway shows as well as a private teacher and vocal coach.

Growing up we celebrated the Swedish holiday St. Lucia Day on December 13th. December 13th used to be considered the shortest day of the year, and St. Lucia Day would celebrate the "bringing of the light" by the eldest daughter of the family (ME!) dressed in a white robe, a red sash and a crown of lit candles on her head. The daughter would rise early and bring breakfast to the family in the morning. My parents would celebrate the day by throwing a party and serving many edible Swedish favorites, but ugnspannkaka and glögg are mine! Ugnspannkaka is more of a breakfast food, and glögg is DEFINITELY a nighttime drink (includes alcohol) meant to warm you during the chilly winter nights! (My glögg recipe can be found on page 19 of this book.)

Special Prep/Equipment

9 x 9" pan is needed but you can double the recipe using a larger pan

Serve this with butter and Lingonberries! (Stock up at IKEA)

1 cup of flour
1 tablespoon sugar
½ teaspoon salt
2 eggs

2 cups of milk (can substitute non-dairy options)
1 teaspoon vanilla (optional)
½ pound of bacon

1. Pre-heat oven to 400°. Grease your baking pan.

2. Sift together the flour, sugar, and salt.

3. In a separate bowl, blend together the eggs, milk, and vanilla.

4. Add the milk, eggs and vanilla to the flour ingredients. Mix and set aside for an hour (optional, but makes it fluffier).

5. Pan broil ½ pound of bacon (I cut it into smaller pieces prior to frying for ease).

6. Stir bacon into batter and pour into the greased pan.

7. Bake at 400° for 40-45 minutes.

Yields 9 squares when using a 9 x 9" pan

HEALTHIER OPTION PANCAKES ("HOPS")
~ Kristin Bacchiocchi-Stewart

I own the Flute Academy in Bergen County, New Jersey. I am Co-President of the New Jersey Flute Society, principal flute with the New Jersey Wind Symphony and I play with the Lyra Ensemble and Classic V Winds.

I was trying to find a healthier pancake recipe for my kids because they LOVE pancakes and wanted to eat them every morning for breakfast. I went online and put a bunch of ideas together to come up with this one. They love this recipe and even prefer it to restaurant pancakes!

Special Prep/Equipment
Blender, Griddle

1. Mix all ingredients in the blender.

2. Heat the griddle on medium high heat, butter the pan and cook the cakes to your liking! Remember to only flip the pancakes once so wait until you see bubbles before flipping.

3. Serve with fresh berries and scrambled eggs!

1 cup oats	1 teaspoon cinnamon
1 cup whole wheat flour	2 eggs
2 tablespoons sugar in the raw	1½ cups milk
1 teaspoon salt	2 teaspoons vanilla
2 teaspoons baking powder	4 tablespoons butter, melted
1 teaspoon baking soda	Extra butter for greasing griddle

Yields about 12-16 pancakes, depending on how big you make them.

OAT NUT GRANOLA
 Sarah Carter

I am a cellist and play Broadway shows, in the Radio City Music Hall Orchestra, and in orchestras including American Symphony, Stamford Symphony, Oratorio Society, Westchester Philharmonic and American Composer's Orchestra.

I've adapted this recipe and can't even remember where I first found it. I have been making it for years for my family and it is a delicious way to start the day!

Special Prep/Equipment
2 baking pans with sides, lined with parchment paper

6 cups old-fashioned oats (not quick oats)

2 cups sliced almonds

2 cups of unsweetened coconut flakes

1 cup of chopped walnuts

½ cup coconut oil

⅓ cup honey

½ cup dried cranberries

½ cup golden raisins

1. Preheat oven to 350°.

2. Line the baking sheets with parchment paper. In a large bowl mix the oats, almonds, coconut flakes, and walnuts.

3. In a glass measuring cup, soften the coconut oil for 1 minute in the microwave oven, and then add the honey to the warmed coconut oil. Pour onto the oat mixture and mix well.

4. Distribute evenly onto the baking pans and place in the oven for 15-17 minutes, rotating pans halfway through for even baking. The granola should be a golden color when done. Allow to cool completely.

5. Put the granola back into the large bowl, breaking up large chunks as you go. Add the dried cranberries and raisins and mix thoroughly. Store the granola in airtight jars.

Yields about 18-24 servings

HEARTY GRANOLA
~ **Gary Fagin**

I am a conductor and composer.

My wife, Nancy Hume, makes yummy homemade crunchy granola. This is her recipe!

1. Heat oven to 325-350°.

2. Mix all dry ingredients together until well combined. Pour olive oil over the dry ingredients, then pour maple syrup, then vanilla and/or almond extract. Mix well. If you think you need more moisture to coat the oats, add a little more olive oil and/or maple syrup.

3. On the prepared baking sheets pour out the granola and flatten so that the mixture fills the sheet evenly.

4. Bake for 20-25 minutes, check, and shift location in oven. I do not mix up/break up the cooking granola, though some do.

5. Cook until golden brown and holding together. Let sit, to reach room temperature. Break-up, add dried fruit if you wish, and store in air-tight container.

Special Prep/Equipment
2 baking sheets lined with parchment paper

4-6 cups rolled oats

1+ cups raw pecans or almonds or walnuts or a mix

1 cup raw pepitas

1 cup raw sunflower seeds

1 cup unsweetened coconut flakes

½-⅓ cup brown sugar, to taste

1 heaping teaspoon cinnamon, to taste

1 teaspoon ground cardamom, to taste

Scant teaspoon kosher salt, to taste

¾ cup olive oil

½-¾ cup maple syrup

1 teaspoon vanilla

1 teaspoon almond extract, if desired

Note
Enjoy some pomegranate seeds with this delicious granola! Here's a great, easy way to get out those sweet delicious seeds from the pomegranate:

Cut the pomegranate in half.

Over a large bowl, hold the half pomegranate in one hand seed side down.

With a heavy wooden spoon in your other hand, repeatedly hit the top of the pomegranate. The seeds will spill out of the pomegranate through the fingers of your hand into the bowl.

Continue until all the seeds have spilled out. Repeat with the other half of the pomegranate.

Pick out any pith in the bowl. Eat and enjoy!

Serves 8-10

SOURDOUGH BREAD
~ Patricia Wolf Zuber

I am a flutist in and around New York City, playing at the Metropolitan Opera and on Broadway.

I started making sourdough bread in the spring of 2018 after watching Michael Pollan's four part series, *Cooked.* In the episode entitled "Air", Pollan explains the health benefits of sourdough bread which has had an overnight ferment. The nutrients in the grain are more accessible to our body, it is more easily digested. I thought I'd give it a try. I have not bought a loaf of bread in a store since!

Special Prep/Equipment
Kitchen scale, iron dutch oven, parchment paper, non-metal bowl, plastic wrap, cooking thermometer

1000 g organic wheat flour (or combination of various flours like rye, whole wheat, bread flour, etc. I sometimes grind my own flour from wheatberries using a blender)

750 g water, at a warm room temperature, filtered

30 g salt (I prefer Diamond Kosher Salt.)

200 g sourdough starter

Note:
I made my own sourdough starter following the recipe on the *KingArthurBaking.com* website. Starter can be ordered from that site, as well as many other sources on the internet.

1. Combine all ingredients in a non-metal bowl. Cover the bowl with a lid or plastic wrap. Set bowl in the oven with only the oven light on. This will create a warm environment for the dough.

2. After about an hour turn the edges of the dough into the center of the ball of dough. Repeat this 2 more times, waiting an hour in between each time. Each time the dough will feel gooier and more elastic. Put the dough in the refrigerator (or a cold garage!) overnight (up to 3 days).

3. Preheat oven to 550°.

4. Let dough rest at room temperature on a floured surface. After 15 minutes fold the edges of the dough into the middle of the dough ball. As you do this you can shape the dough so it will fit nicely into the baking vessel. An iron dutch oven lined with parchment paper is ideal. This recipe makes 2 loaves so if you only have one vessel you might want to bake the loaves separately.

5. Put half the dough (one loaf) into the dutch oven. Put the lid on. Place in center of the oven. Immediately turn the temperature down to 450°.

6. Bake for 45 minutes. Then, take lid off and bake for 15 more minutes. Bread is done when internal temperature reaches 211°.

7. Cool on a rack for at least an hour before slicing (this is the hardest step).

> **Note**
> This bread will last about a week at room temperature in a Ziploc bag.

Yields 2 loaves of delicious bread

OVERNIGHT PICKLES
~ Naomi Youngstein

I am a violinist in the New Jersey Symphony Orchestra since 1987, and coach/leader in the NJSO Academy youth orchestra program.

My Dad always made the sweet bread and butter pickles, but I could never get him to make the savory kind. I read a story in a magazine about how to make these, and they turn out great every time.

Special Prep/Equipment
1 quart mason jar

4 Kirby cucumbers

¾ cup white vinegar

¾ cup water

1-2 teaspoons sugar (I prefer the smaller amount)

2 teaspoons kosher salt

½ teaspoon peppercorns (I use black but other colors fine too)

½ teaspoon red pepper flakes (this makes a tangy spicy pickle, but if spice is not your thing use less)

3 cloves garlic, cut in a few big pieces

Optional items: fresh dill, mustard seeds, dill seeds, red onion slivers, or other seedy spices. Use your imagination.

1. In a small saucepan heat vinegar with ¾ cup water, and the other dried herbs and spices, until sugar and salt dissolve. No need to fully boil.

2. Meanwhile, cut the cucumbers into spears, lay the jar on its side, and stack cucumbers inside with a few cloves of garlic and fresh herbs, if using, interspersed. They should fit tightly and be standing upright once you right the jar.

3. Pour the hot liquid into the jar, and refrigerate with lid tightly on.

4. Wait a day for best flavor. You can also try jicama, carrot, and cauliflower cut small using this same method.

Yields about 16-20 spears

SWEDISH GLÖGG
~ Annbritt duChateau

I am a Pianist/Conductor/Music Director/Music Supervisor for multiple Broadway shows as well as a private teacher and vocal coach.

There are SO MANY variations to this recipe, but this is the one my family used from my grandmother who came from Veddige, Sweden.

Special Prep/Equipment

Dutch oven/stock pot needed (crock pot optional)

There is no need to purchase expensive alcohol as you are heating and "cooking" it.

1 bottle vodka or aquavit

1 bottle port wine

1 bottle burgundy

Peel of 1 orange

½ cup sugar

1 cup raisins

½ cup slivered almonds

3 sticks of cinnamon

1 small piece of ginger, peeled

8 cardamom pods

10 whole cloves

1. Combine the wines and vodka in the dutch oven.

2. Using a paring knife, remove the peel of the orange and add to liquid.

3. Add the sugar, raisins, slivered almonds, cinnamon sticks, ginger, cardamom pods, and cloves.

4. Bring the mixture to a boil. Reduce the heat and allow to simmer very low for an hour. You can leave the mixture on the stove on very low for hours, but make sure you keep an eye on it and aren't burning away the mixture (OR transfer to the crockpot and keep warm on low).

Note

If you want the glögg sweeter, use 1 cup of sugar. If you don't like a spicy taste, remove the ginger. Some people remove the cloves and cardamom right before serving so that guests don't accidentally eat them. You should serve in small mugs and definitely include the raisins and almonds when serving. Give your guests a small spoon so that they can eat those yummy glögg-soaked raisins and almonds!

Serves 8 (1-cup servings)

MUM'S MULLED WINE
Mairi Dorman-Phaneuf

I play cello pretty much anywhere anyone will hire me to play cello, but my first love is Broadway.

I'm from the UK where, like most northern European countries, mulled wine is very commonly drunk in the winter. We also used to drink glühwein in little ski huts in the Austrian Alps, and it's essentially the same thing. Perfect for Thanksgiving, Christmas, New Years, an outdoor firepit hang, or if the grown-ups need warming up on Halloween. I leave it on warm in a slow-cooker all day and it smells amazing. I call it Mum's Mulled Wine because I was looking for something that would remind me of home. This recipe is inspired by Michael Chiarello's recipe on the Food Network.

Special Prep/Equipment
Slow cooker, cheesecloth, tea-leaf holder or strainer

1.5 liters of red wine, or two regular bottles. (The cheaper the better! You'll add so much sweetness and spice to it you'll lose any fancy flavors regardless.)

1 cup of brown sugar

Half an orange peel

Splash of gin

1 large cinnamon stick broken in two, or two small sticks

1 small handful of allspice berries

1 whole nutmeg – if you don't have one, a sprinkling of nutmeg powder will work ok.

1. Pour ¼ of the wine in a saucepan. Add the brown sugar, orange peel, and gin. If you're using a cheesecloth place cinnamon, allspice and nutmeg in the bag and add to saucepan. (If you're using a tea-leaf holder, only put the allspice in the holder, and work around the cinnamon and nutmeg when serving. And if you have nothing to put the spices in, you'll need to strain out the allspice at the end.)

2. Bring to a gentle boil and simmer for 5 minutes, stirring to melt the sugar. Add the rest of the wine and bring back to a simmer. It's now ready to serve, and you can opt to remove the spices and orange peel, or leave them in if you want the flavors to intensify. Transfer to a slow cooker (set to warm) if serving over time.

Yields about 10 servings

MIDWEEK MARTINI
Tony Bruno

I am a composer/guitarist/MD. I worked with Rihanna, Enrique Iglesias to name a few. I am currently co-creating a show called *Rock Me Amadeus*.

This is my midweek answer to the blahs. I picked this up at my favorite restaurant in Isla Mujeres, Mexico called Olivia. Special thanks to Yaron, the owner.

Special Prep/Equipment
Shaker glass is helpful

1. Fill a shaker glass with ice. Add all ingredients and shake vigorously for a full minute so the sugar creates a froth, and add all the ingredients.

2. Serve in a proper cocktail or martini glass.

3. Enjoy!

Serves 1 - Double up for 2, but don't make more than 2 at a time.

1 shot vodka (I like Tito's)

1 shot espresso

1 shot Kahlua

Dash of Cointreau

1 teaspoon sugar

SHELAGH'S OPENING NIGHT JELLO SHOTS
∾ Shelagh Abate

I play the French horn, have opened more than one dozen Broadway productions including *South Pacific, Mary Poppins, Anastasia,* and *Frozen* and I perform with orchestral and chamber ensembles all over the United States. www.shelaghabate.com

First things first: these are NOT your college roommate's jello shots! These are delicious, classy, subtly flavored, and are a festive addition to any cocktail party spread! This recipe is tried and true, enjoyed by (forced upon) MANY a Broadway band. Feel free to experiment with garnish and presentation – so many possibilities!

Special Prep/Equipment
Medium saucepan

Setting pan: Tupperware, fancy mold, loaf pan, whatever works...but something close to 6 x 6" will result in a Jello shot with a nice height!

These shots need to set for several hours or overnight before consuming.

⅔ cup champagne or prosecco

⅔ cup grapefruit juice (I use Tropicana Ruby Red), strained of all pulp

1 teaspoon sugar

½ cup elderflower liqueur (St. Germain is the BEST!)

2 envelopes unflavored gelatin - vegetarians can substitute with agar agar!

1. Combine grapefruit juice and champagne in a medium saucepan, sprinkle with gelatin. Allow gelatin to soak for a minute or two. Distribute gelatin evenly, as clumping will slow things down in your next step.

2. Add the sugar to the saucepan. Using lowest possible heat setting, stir mixture carefully and constantly, until gelatin is completely dissolved (5 minutes). Be patient, because fizzy bubbles!

3. Remove from heat. Pour into a setting pan that will give your jello shots a nice height! Stir in Elderflower liqueur.

4. Refrigerate until fully set (several hours or overnight).

5. To serve, cut into shapes and garnish as desired.

Yields 25 shots (depending on desired size)

APPETIZERS & SNACKS

ASIAN VEGETABLE DIP
~ **Edith Stratton**

Since 1973, I have been a member of the Hudson Valley Philharmonic in the double bass section. I was an instrumental string teacher for over 30 years in the Hudson Valley in New York State, in the Hyde Park Central School District and the Arlington Central School District.

After finding this recipe decades ago, it has been my "go to" recipe to make for my family and friends!

Special Prep/Equipment
This dip needs to chill in the fridge for a few hours before serving.

1 cup Hellmann's mayonnaise	1 teaspoon ginger
2 tablespoons chopped scallions	1 teaspoon apple cider vinegar
2 tablespoons milk	4 teaspoons soy sauce

1. Combine all ingredients.
2. Refrigerate for 2-4 hours or overnight to allow the flavors to blend.
3. Prepare and serve with a variety of ready raw vegetables. Enjoy!

Yields 1 - 2 cups

DATE ALMOND BACON WRAPS
~ George Wesner

I am the organist for Radio City Music Hall.

No matter how many of these bacon wraps you make, they will all be eaten!

Special Prep/Equipment
Toothpicks, and a grill

1. Stuff the pitted dates with the almonds.
2. Wrap with bacon.
3. Secure with a toothpick and grill until done.

1 container pitted dates

1 bag whole almonds

Bacon

Serves 6-12 people as an appetizer

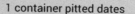

24 Musicians Cook!

PRALINE BACON
~ Allison Kiger

I'm a flutist in the Allentown Symphony and Garden State Philharmonic. In the summer I go to Maine to perform and work as Associate Director for the Bar Harbor Music School.

This is my go-to holiday treat bacon. It's also great to use chopped up in a spinach salad.

1 pound of thick cut, no nitrates added bacon

½-1 cup finely chopped pecans

¼-½ cup dark brown sugar

1. Pre-heat oven to 425°.

2. Line a large baking sheet with enough foil to lift the edges to make a 1" wall at the edges of the tray. This is to keep the bacon fat from leaking onto your sheet. Make sure there are no holes in your foil. This is for easier clean-up.

3. Arrange the bacon in a single layer. Pieces can touch each other slightly. Sprinkle the pecans and brown sugar over the bacon evenly.

4. Bake in the pre-heated oven for 15 minutes or more, checking frequently for desired doneness. Rotate the tray mid-way if your oven cooks unevenly.

5. Drain the bacon on paper towels before serving.

Serves 4-8

BACON ROLL-UPS
~ Marcia Gates

I am Principal Flutist of the Hudson Valley Philharmonic, chamber musician in the Hudson Valley, private flute teacher, instrumental music teacher, retired from Hyde Park Central School District.

I learned this recipe from a friend decades ago. It's a big hit with family and friends!

Special Prep/Equipment
Baking sheet is needed, a rolling pin is helpful

1. Preheat oven to 400°.

2. Trim crusts from bread slices.

3. Use rolling pin to flatten bread slices.

4. Spread cream cheese over bread slices.

1 loaf Pepperidge Farm white sandwich bread

2 containers cream cheese spread, with chive and onion

1 (12-ounce) package Oscar Mayer center cut bacon

5. Roll up bread slices and cut each roll into 2 equal parts.

6. Wrap ½ slice of bacon around each part, and secure with toothpick (wooden).

7. Place Rollups on baking sheet and bake in preheated oven for 15+ minutes, or until bacon is cooked.

Yields 30 roll ups

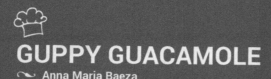

GUPPY GUACAMOLE
Anna Maria Baeza

I am a clarinetist and chamber musician. I teach all ages and levels, and I coach.

I grew up in California, outside of Los Angeles, and I learned to make this guacamole when I lived on the West Coast. This is a recipe from my family. It was named Guppy Guacamole by a college friend at USC in California due to the chunky nature and the various colors and textures within.

Special Prep/Equipment
Large mixing bowl, Juicer

3 ripe avocados	Half a bunch of cilantro
Juice of 1 lime	1 tablespoon of cumin
Several cloves of garlic, diced	Half a jar of spicy organic salsa
4-5 green onions	

1. Start with the avocados. Slice in half, remove the pits, scoop the interior flesh into a largish mixing bowl.

2. Juice one fresh lime and add to bowl.

3. Dice several cloves of garlic and toss in.

4. Find slim green onions (scallions on the East Coast), and slice thinly from the bottom to the top. I throw out the base of the root and the very top if it is not fresh.

5. Cilantro!! Separate the leaves from the big stems and chop up, but do not mince. Add a generous amount of the ground cumin.

6. Throw in the half jar of salsa.

7. Now all of the ingredients are together. Get a big spoon and start smashing and mixing. Leave some chunks intact. The better the quality of the Avocados, the better the result. I love Hass Avocados. The avocado is one food that does not need to be organic. They are amazing!

Note
You will make friends with this recipe! Goes great as a side for meat dishes, or a brunch or simply with blue corn tortilla chips.

YIELDS a quantity nice for a family

TEXAN PICANTE SAUCE
Maureen Strenge

I play the bassoon in many different groups in NYC and the surrounding area.

This picante sauce is too hot for me, but is just right for my trumpet playing husband and three sons! My husband is from Dallas and got this recipe from his Aunt.

3 jalapeno peppers, sliced	½ teaspoon cumin
½ onion, cut in chunks	½ teaspoon salt
½ carrot, chopped	¼ cup vinegar
1 clove garlic	1 (6 ounce) can tomato sauce

Special Prep/Equipment
Blender

1. Put everything in the blender and chop to your desired consistency.

Serves 6-8

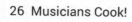

26 Musicians Cook!

BEST GUACAMOLE ON BROADWAY
~ Anik Oulianine

I am a cellist...famous for my guacamole, if nothing else! This has killer garlic – woodwind players beware!

Special Prep/Equipment
Serving bowl and two forks

1. In a large bowl, mush everything together <u>with two forks</u> (critical) until desired consistency.

2. Transfer to serving bowl. Enjoy with your favorite nacho chips.

2 (or 3 or 4) ripe Hass avocados, pitted, peeled, cubed

1 (or 2 or 3 or 4) garlic cloves, smashed and minced

1 (or 2 or...you get it) jalapenos, seeded and minced

1 bunch cilantro, minced

1 plum tomato, seeded and minced

Juice of ⅓ (or ½, or etc) of a lime

Salt and pepper to taste

SUSAN'S BEAN DIP
~ Michael Green

I've been playing Broadway shows since 1989. *Miss Saigon, Man of La Mancha, Woman in White, Porgy and Bess* and, of course, *Phantom of the Opera*.

This recipe is from a home published book named *Flounders Family Classic Recipes*. Half tongue in cheek, based on some of the food my mother-in-law, Jane, made while she raised her three daughters. Number two is my wife, Mary. She makes this every Christmas Eve and many Super Bowl Sundays. Served with plain corn chips. ~Susan, whoever and wherever and whatever else she is, is our hero.~

Special Prep/Equipment
We use a Corningware 2.8 liter baking dish
Cream cheese softened out of the refrigerator

1 can refried beans

1 (8 ounce) block cream cheese, softened

1 cup sour cream

15 drops Tabasco

2 tablespoons chili powder

2 tablespoons chopped parsley

½ cup chives (or scallions)

2 cups shredded Mexican cheese

1. Preheat oven to 350°.

2. Stir together all ingredients except for shredded cheese. Place mixture in greased baking dish, and top with cheese. Bake (uncovered) in preheated oven until bubbly.

3. Serve with tortilla chips.

This is simply a party appetizer. Eat until it's gone, and it will be gone.

JEN'S CHIP DIP
∾ Kent Tritle

I am Music Director and Organist at the Cathedral of St. John the Divine, and am Music Director of Musica Sacra, and the Oratorio Society of New York. I am also the organist of the New York Philharmonic and the American Symphony, and I am on the faculties of Manhattan School of Music and the Juilliard School.

This is my Mom's delicious Chip Dip recipe, updated by my sister Jen. Jen first got the recipe from Mom, and has been making it for the family for years. We always love it!

Special Prep/Equipment
Serving platter

This dip needs refrigeration for several hours before serving.

Layer all ingredients on a platter in the order listed below, and refrigerate for at least 4 hours before serving:

2 small cans of bean dip, or 1 (14½ ounce) can refried black beans

1 container Guacamole dip, or make your own using 2 large avocados, 1 teaspoon lime juice, pinch of salt.

2 cups sour cream, divided

½ cup mayonnaise

1 package taco seasoning

1 large bunch scallions

3 medium tomatoes, seeded, cut into chunks, patted dry with paper towel

2 small cans black olives, drained

Shredded Mexican blend cheese

LAYER 1: Bean dip or can of refried beans.

LAYER 2: Guacamole, spread over beans.

LAYER 3: Combine 1 cup sour cream, mayonnaise, and taco seasoning, mix and spread over guacamole.

LAYER 4: Remaining cup of sour cream. Stir to soften and spread.

LAYER 5: Chop scallions, and sprinkle over the top.

LAYER 6: Tomatoes, sprinkle over scallions.

LAYER 7: Olives, spread over the entire dish.

LAYER 8: Sprinkle shredded cheese over the entire dish, so that all the layers are covered.

Serves a crowd

TEQUEÑOS VENEZOLANOS
∾ Zamira Briceño

I play the Violin and Viola. I'm from Venezuela. Currently I'm a staff member at BGLIG charter School in South Bronx, New York, where I teach general music and strings.

As a Venezuelan, I am proud to share with you the recipe for one of our most traditional appetizers. Tequeños were born in a Venezuelan city called Maracaibo. This delicious appetizer is a special guest of our celebrations and has become enormously popular around the world. Tequeños are cheese sticks wrapped in a soft dough, which when fried are crunchy and tasty, as well as easy and quick to prepare. Tequeños are never lacking at home and my family loves them. Have fun preparing them too!

Special Prep/Equipment

A rolling pin and a large frying pan

1 pound semi-hard white cheese	1 egg, beaten
2 cups all-purpose wheat flour	½ teaspoon of salt
5 tablespoons butter, softened a little	2 tablespoons sugar
	4-5 tablespoons of cold water
	4 cups corn oil (for frying)

1. Cut the cheese into strips about 1 x 3" long.

2. On a large cutting board, place the flour in the shape of a crown with a hole in the middle, where you add the butter and the egg. Put butter and the beaten egg in the hole, and mix with your hands. In a small container mix the salt, sugar and cold water. Add the water mixture little by little to the flour and knead with your fingers until it is smooth and does not stick to your fingers. Roll into a ball and let it sit for at least 30 minutes on your counter. Do not refrigerate.

3. Sprinkle more flour on your cutting board, and with the help of a rolling pin, roll the dough out very thinly into a big square. Then cut into uniform strips with the help of a sharp knife.

4. Place the dough strip at one end of the cheese and wrap to the other end to completely cover the cheese. Pinch and seal the ends with your fingers so the cheese won't melt out when you fry it.

5. Heat the oil over high heat in a frying pan. When the oil is hot, lower the heat a little, to medium. Carefully deep fry the tequeños until crisp and golden brown. If you use less oil, and the tequeños aren't completely covered by oil, you'll need to turn them over in the middle, to cook the other side.

6. Place on a paper towel to drain excess oil.

7. Enjoy your Tequeños Venezolanos!!!

Yields 50 tequeños (serves about 10 people)

GREEK EGGPLANT DIP
∽ Olivia Koppell

I am a violist with a long career as a freelancer and member of the American Ballet Theater Orchestra. I like to say I have done every job in NYC from the most sublime to the most ridiculous – and loved them all, working with wonderful musicians and people.

This recipe is passed from generation to generation by Greek American matriarchs.

Special Prep/Equipment
Line a baking pan with foil.

1 large eggplant	1 tablespoon olive oil
1 slice of bread soaked in cider vinegar	Pinch of sugar
½ of a medium-large onion	
1 medium-large tomato or 2-3 plum tomatoes	*Note:* Amounts of onion, olive oil and sugar can be adjusted to taste.

1. Wash the eggplant, leave whole and pierce all over with a fork or knife. Place under broiler, not close to flame, in a foil lined pan. Keep turning until skin is black and really charred. You want that "burnt" flavor. Remove and let sit to cool off.

2. Carefully scrape meat of eggplant from skin (comes off easily). Put in a bowl and mash with fork.

3. Add the soaked bread; mash it in. Mince onion and tomato; add to eggplant with oil and sugar.

4. Mix well and serve cool, not cold; with crackers, pita or veggies.

Serves about 6

HUMMUS
〜 John Isley

I've been a saxophone player for most of my life. Alongside a multitude of other musical pursuits – writing, arranging, studio engineering, and general technology geekness – for the last ten years or so I've held down the saxophone chair with Southside Johnny & the Asbury Jukes, and occasionally touring with Diana Ross.

I'm biologically half Lebanese, though I was raised in a purely American household. Apparently I am genetically disposed to love Middle Eastern food, because ever since the first time I had fresh made hummus, i have been on a mission to make the best homemade hummus possible. This is an evolution of a recipe I got over 30 years ago from my upstairs neighbor when I lived in Brooklyn. I've been "perfecting" it ever since.

Special Prep/Equipment
Food processor

1 (15 ounce) can of chickpeas, drained and rinsed (reserving ¼ cup chickpea liquid)

½ cup tahini (invest the money in good tahini – it's worth it!)

½ cup plain greek yogurt, full fat

¼ cup lemon juice

2 cloves garlic, chopped

Dash of cumin (to taste)

Salt (to taste)

For serving: Olive oil, sumac

Note: Don't skimp on the tahini and most definitely use the full fat yogurt! That's the secret ingredient! The tartness from the yogurt adds another layer of complexity to the flavors.

1. Place all ingredients except salt, olive oil and sumac into the bowl of a food processor. Process on high speed until everything is broken down and the hummus is smooth and creamy, 3 to 5 minutes.

2. Add salt a bit at a time until the flavor is bright but not salty.

3. The hummus will be rather thin at this point. Refrigerate for several hours to thicken it. If it thickens too much you can stir in a tablespoon of water to thin it out.

4. To serve, drizzle the top with good quality olive oil and a dash of ground sumac. Serve with warm pitas.

Yields a bit more than 16 ounces

SALT & PEPPER TOFU
Zara Lawler

I am a flutist who combines music, dance and theatre, and in 2020 I released my 2nd album, *Clickable,* with percussionist Paul Fadoul on Parma Recordings. I studied at Juilliard with Carol Wincene and Sam Baron. *Zaralawler.com*

Around our household we call this "The Potato Chip of Tofu" because it is so salty and delicious that we end up eating it with our fingers right out of the pan, and cannot stop at just one bite! We make it with up to three blocks of tofu at a time, and keep it in the fridge for use throughout the week. It works well as a protein source in virtually any style of meal. We use it on salads, with noodles, with rice, with veggies — you name it. It's also about the easiest thing to make, requiring no skill and no measuring and only four ingredients. My wife invented this dish, inspired by Salt & Pepper Shrimp which she used to get at a favorite Vietnamese restaurant.

Special Prep/Equipment
Large fry pan

1 package Tofu, firm or extra firm

Canola oil

Salt

Pepper

Note:
Our young daughter loves the even easier, less spicy version of this: Salt Tofu. Follow the instructions below, but leave out the pepper.

1. Press the tofu, to remove excess water.

2. Remove the tofu block from the package. Place the tofu block on a plate or tray. Place another plate or tray on top of the tofu, and weight it down with something heavy like a cookbook or a can of beans.

3. Wait a while, 15 minutes minimum. (Maybe go practice your scales?)

4. Discard excess water from the tofu, and then cut the tofu into bite-sized cubes.

5. Heat a pan on the stove, and once the pan is nice and hot, pour in canola oil, and swish it around to cover the bottom of the pan. (How much is enough? A blob will do...you know you have enough if, by swiveling the pan around, the bottom of the pan is thinly covered.)

6. Put the tofu in the pan. Be careful — it is a bit wet so it may throw some oil droplets up at you if you do this with too much gusto.

7. Stir it around so it starts to get coated with the oil. Turn down heat if it seems too sizzly.

8. Sprinkle a generous amount of salt (about ⅛ cup to start), distributing it evenly over the tofu. (How much is enough? More than you think! But start with what seems like a medium amount, and then taste it. Then keep adding salt until it starts to remind you of potato chips. Then stop adding salt!)

9. Let it keep cooking. I like to let the tofu sit a while, until it starts to get a bit crispy on one side, then stir it so it gets crispy on another side, and keep going until I'm bored with that and just want to eat it already.

10. Add pepper to taste. (How much is enough? See number 8 above regarding salt.)

11. Eat and enjoy!

Serves 3-4

CRISPY TOFU WITH SPICY SOY SAUCE
Kiwon Nahm

I'm a violinist and violist. I am a teacher at The Calhoun School and looking forward to playing in the orchestra for *Flying Over Sunset* at Lincoln Center when theaters reopen.

You can use the sauce with a lot of different items, for example, steamed or fried dumplings, steamed tofu, steamed or fried zucchini, blanched spinach, steamed asparagus, etc.

Special Prep/Equipment
Large baking dish

1. Cut the tofu in half, then cut into ¼" slices.

2. Pat dry and then coat in cornstarch. Fry in a pan until slightly golden in color.

3. Meanwhile, make the sauce. Combine the soy sauce, sesame oil, gochugaru (add more if you like spicy), garlic, sesame seeds, and half the scallion in a bowl.

4. When the tofu is cooked add the sauce and then add the rest of the scallions on top.

1 cube of tofu	1-2 teaspoons of gochugaru (korean chili flakes)
¼ cup cornstarch	1 clove of garlic
Oil for frying - vegetable or canola	1 teaspoon of sesame seeds
4 tablespoons of soy sauce	1 scallion, chopped
1 tablespoon of sesame oil	

Serves 4 as an appetizer

TOFU BALLS
Stefani Starin

I play the flute and mostly have enjoyed exploring the world of current composers especially those interested in alternative tunings. I do a fair amount of teaching people of all ages.

These tofu balls mimic a classic meatball that I learned from my maternal grandmother and I made it work for vegetarians.

Special Prep/Equipment
A large fry pan is needed to fry the tofu.

2 cloves garlic	2 tablespoons fresh parsley
1 small onion	7 ounces firm tofu
½ teaspoon dried marjoram	2 eggs
¾ teaspoon each dried oregano and dried basil (if you use fresh herbs, use more)	⅔ cup finely ground italian breadcrumbs (or any kind of breadcrumbs)
¾ teaspoon salt	Red sauce of your choice
½ teaspoon pepper	Optional: a little parmesan, to your taste
2 teaspoons olive oil, plus 3 tablespoons to fry up the balls	

1. Mince the garlic and onion and place in a large bowl.

2. Add marjoram, oregano, basil, salt, pepper, oil, and parsley (and parmesan if using).

3. Add the tofu and break up with hands.

4. Crack eggs in the mixture, add breadcrumbs, and combine everything with your hands.

5. At this point, the mixture should hold together when rolled in your hands.

6. Let mixture sit for a bit (15 minutes).

7. Form the tofu into 1" diameter balls and flatten slightly with spatula. The balls will be about 2" wide and a little less than ½" thick.

8. Put the oil in the fry pan and heat.

9. Cook tofu on both sides till they are golden brown.

10. Add the browned tofu to a heated pot of already cooked red sauce and let it stew it there a bit.

11. Plate the mixture with more parmesan if desired.

Serves about 4

EASY MICROWAVE AVOCADO WRAP
~ Fritz V. Krakowski

I am a violinist, originally from Davis, California, and a graduate of Juilliard. I have done classical, Broadway and chamber music work since 1984.

I made this up after a doctor told me to eat more avocados to help raise my "good" cholesterol level (HDL). The ingredients just kept evolving until I found this yummy combo.

Special Prep/Equipment
A microwave or roll into foil to eat later (cold)

1 Toufayan Sundried tomato wrap (or Savory Spinach or Whole Wheat)	1 or 2 yellow, orange or red (1-2") sweet mini peppers, sliced in strips
1 teaspoon stone ground Dijon mustard	1 Campari tomato sliced or 3-4 grape tomatoes halved
1 small whole ripe organic avocado	1-2 slices Sargento Ultra Thin Swiss Natural Cheese slices

1. Place wrap on dinner plate.

2. Spread teaspoon mustard onto wrap. Slice avocado and place in center of wrap. Slice sweet peppers and place in between and on avocado. Slice tomato and place around edges of avocado. Put cheese slice(s) on top of avocado mixture.

3. Microwave on high for only 2 minutes. Cheese should be just melted; avocado warm but not cooked. Peppers crunchy. Tomato does whatever it does.

4. Remove from microwave and fold 2 opposite edges of wrap in and over melted cheese using a knife and fork. (I leave the fork resting on top of the folded wrap to keep it together and let it cool off a bit if it's too hot to eat right away.)

Cold version:
Place foil on dinner plate. Proceed as above before microwaving. Gently roll wrap as well as possible while bringing edges of foil together and pinch ends. Put in lunch bag or fridge.

Serves 1

CHEESE BOUREKAS
Jill Sokol

I am a Second Flute with the Hudson Valley Philharmonic and Garden State Philharmonic. I also substitute with the Allentown Symphony and teach at Kean University.

This recipe was developed by my husband, who does all the cooking in our household (yes, I am spoiled). This is one of our favorite mid-Eastern foods, and he developed the recipe for home cooks and to suit our tastes.

Special Prep/Equipment
2 sheet pans

2 packages of phyllo dough	Salt and pepper
3 pounds fine curd cottage cheese, drained	4 tablespoons melted butter + 1 cup olive oil, mixed together
1 pound feta cheese, crumbled	A little olive oil for greasing sheet pans
4 eggs	

1. Preheat oven to 325°. Coat two sheet pans generously with some olive oil.

2. Mix cheeses, add salt and pepper to taste, then add eggs and mix in.

3. Using a sharp knife or kitchen scissors, cut the shorter dimension of the phyllo dough into three strips, equal in size. Stack strips to make one pile.

4. Place 2 - 3 tablespoons cheese mixture at the bottom end of a phyllo strip.

5. Brush the strip with olive oil / butter mixture.

6. Fold the bottom left corner of the phyllo dough over the cheese, to the right-hand edge of the strip, creating a triangle.

7. Fold upward along top edge of triangle. Fold along diagonal edge of triangle. Repeat folding pattern until entire strip is folded (when done, cheese will be encased in a "triangular pocket" of phyllo dough).

8. *Note:* More phyllo strips will be added in the following step – don't worry if phyllo dough is soggy after completing the first strip.

9. Place triangle created in Step 7 at the bottom of a fresh strip.

10. Repeat Steps 6 thru 8 with four more strips.

11. Place bourekas on sheet pan.

12. Repeat Steps 5 thru 10 until all phyllo dough is used.

13. Generously brush top and sides of bourekas with olive oil / butter mixture.

14. Bake for 30 - 40 minutes, until tops of bourekas are lightly browned.

Yields 12-18

I f you combine good flavors, food turns into an orchestra.
Joey Fatone

STUFFED MUSHROOMS
~ Pamela Sklar

I am a flutist in ensembles, orchestras, as a soloist, studio recordings, and international tours. More recently I have been collaborating as a composer and flutist with my own and other groups.

I almost passed out when I first tasted my cousin's delicious stuffed mushrooms! Inspired by her cooking talents as well as fun options to change or substitute ingredients, this is a super easy recipe with a good variety of stuffing choices, especially for those who like to improvise. Thank you, Leslie!

Special Prep/Equipment
Baking tray

10-12 whole mushrooms (baby bella/shiitake/portobello)

¾ cup bread crumbs, or crushed croutons or Triscuits

Roughly 1 tablespoon of butter or oil or ghee

1-3 sticks of celery

1 medium-large or 2 small-medium onions

4-5 cloves of garlic

Spices: thyme, curry, and/or garam masala or oregano

Salt/pepper if desired.

Grated parmesan or chopped cheddar cheese or brie

Other stuffing options/substitutes: fresh basil, cream cheese, chives, cherry tomatoes, carrots, scallions, cooked eggplant, chopped string beans, dill, bacon bits, sausage, prosciutto, crab meat

1. Wash mushrooms, cut off stems, and set aside mushroom crowns. Measure out the ¾ cup of bread crumbs (or croutons or Triscuits) and set aside.

2. Melt butter/oil/ghee in a skillet/pan over low heat. Chop enough celery, onions, garlic, and mushroom stems to stuff 10-12 or more mushrooms. Add vegetables to melting butter/oil/ghee, turn up heat to medium, stir gently now and then for 3-4 minutes. Remove from heat.

3. Preheat oven to 400°.

4. Place mushroom crowns in the baking tray. Stuff the crowns with bread crumbs (or croutons, or Triscuits) and then add hot vegetables, and lastly the spices and cheese.

5. Bake in preheated oven 20-25 minutes.

Yields 10-12

IDIOT'S DELIGHT
Matt Goeke

I'm a cellist, and live in New York City. I'm very active in two chamber music groups – Eight Strings & a Whistle (21 years) and the Di.vi.sion Piano Trio (20 years) as well as being a member of the Stamford Symphony Orchestra for over 30 years.

This recipe was my mother's. She called them "Idiot's Delights" because they're so simple to make, they're almost idiot proof! These make a great appetizer or snack with cocktails.

Special Prep/Equipment
A baking pan or cookie sheet is needed

1 pound cheddar cheese, shredded

1 stick softened margarine

½ teaspoon Worcestershire sauce

1 tablespoon Tabasco sauce*

1 cup sifted flour

*The original recipe calls for Tabasco, but any hot sauce will be fine. Sriracha also works well. (And yes, 1 tablespoon.)

1. Preheat oven to 350°.

2. With a pastry cutter (or food processor) combine and blend together all the ingredients, except the flour. Then, add flour and mix with hands until the dough comes together.

3. Form dough into balls and roll out into "logs" about the diameter of a quarter. From here, you can wrap and store in the freezer.

4. When baking I've never needed to grease the baking sheet, although if one would like to use a non-stick sheet, they certainly could.

5. To bake, slice into approximately ¼" width pieces, and bake in preheated oven for 12-15 minutes. If the rolls have been frozen, let stand at room temperature for about 30 minutes, then slice and bake.

Yields about three 10" rolled "logs"

PERFECT DEVILED EGGS
Jessica Aura Tascov

I am a flutist in NYC.

This recipe has been adapted from *Best Deviled Eggs* on Epicurious who credits Gourmet Magazine from June 2002. I have streamlined the process a bit, plus I use much more mayo and mustard when I make it, with a 3/2 mayo to mustard ratio. I also go heavy on the Cayenne. I have experimented with organic versions of condiments and eggs, but the best flavor is with the brands that I have listed here.

Special Prep/Equipment
Egg platter

12 Eggland's Best Eggs	¼ teaspoon cayenne
¾ cup Hellman's mayonnaise	
¼ - ½ cup Grey Poupon Dijon mustard, to taste	*Garnishes:* chives, bacon, paprika, horseradish

1. In a large saucepan, cover eggs with cold water and bring to a boil, partially covered. Immediately remove from heat, cover the pot, and put aside for 15 minutes. Transfer eggs with a slotted spoon to a bowl of ice water for 5 minutes, which will stop the cooking. While the ingredient amounts are completely flexible, the timings should be precise so as not to over or undercook eggs.

2. Peel eggs and slice in half lengthwise. If the eggs are too hot at first, you can wait a few minutes, but don't wait too long, otherwise they are harder to peel.

3. Remove egg yolks from the whites, and mash in a separate bowl combining with the mayo, mustard, and cayenne. Find a consistency and taste that you like. It is better to have more filling than not enough. I don't use salt or pepper, but the original recipe calls for it at this point.

4. Use a spoon or fork to fill the egg halves. Top with Paprika and chives. I love horseradish and bacon pieces as well. Mix and match!

> **Note**
> I try to make these as close to the party as possible. They taste best slightly chilled but not too cold.

Serves 12 if you don't break or eat any eggs during prep (yields 24 egg halves)

LATKE BALLS
～ Larry Spivack

I am a percussionist and composer working in orchestras and on Broadway.

This is especially good at Hanukkah time. I had been making latkes (potato pancakes) for years using potatoes, onions, eggs, matzo meal, salt and pepper. I bought a salsa-maker (a hand-turned food mill) at a street fair and found it great for shredding the potatoes and onions. I would fry them in canola oil, turning them over with a spatula.

My son has been a vegan for 15 years and I wanted him to enjoy them, so I found a recipe that used applesauce instead of eggs. It didn't work too well because every time I turned them they broke apart. So instead of pancakes I made balls the size of golf balls and deep-fried them. They also are a hit at parties because you can eat them with a toothpick.

Special Prep/Equipment
I use a salsa-maker to shred the potatoes and onions.

4 medium potatoes (when peeled they weigh 18.5 ounces)	1½ cups matzo meal
1 medium onion (when peeled it weighs 8.5 ounces)	½ tablespoon salt
1 cup applesauce	½ tablespoon pepper
	32 fluid ounces canola oil

1. Peel the potatoes and cut them and the onions into pieces that will work in a salsa-maker.

2. Add applesauce, matzo meal, salt, pepper, and mix until the consistency is right (sticking together).

3. By hand, roll into balls, the size of golf balls.

4. Make sure the oil is hot enough before you put all the balls in. Deep fry in canola oil until brown.

Yields 24 latke balls, or 4 servings

KALE CHIPS
Anna Maria Baeza

I am a clarinetist playing chamber music and teaching all ages.

We failed multiple times to get the crispness right. It was our friends Lois and Mark from Eastport, Maine who actually gave us the key to success with this recipe.

Special Prep/Equipment
9 x 13" metal pan, pastry brush, salad spinner

Curly kale

Olive oil

Chili powder

Nutritional yeast (Bragg's is good)

Pinch Himalayan salt

Other seasoning options: Poultry seasoning, Italian herbs, curry, or mixed savory oriental seasoning. You just have to experiment with flavors and proportions.

1. Start with a generous amount of kale. I like the curly kale, but any will work. Wash the kale, strip it away from the thick stem and thicker veins. Spin in a salad spinner to remove excess water; pat dry with an absorbent kitchen cloth.

2. Preheat oven to 270°. Slow cooking at this low temperature makes the chips crispy.

3. Set kale aside and make the seasoning. Gather your ingredients of olive oil, chili powder, nutritional yeast, pinch of Himalayan salt. Mix these dry ingredients in a cereal or soup bowl, add olive oil. The consistency should not be thick, yet not so much oil that it separates.

4. Spread this mixture on the bottom of a 9 x 13" pan. Use a pastry or barbeque brush.

5. Place the Kale over this mixture and then keep turning with the brush and poking at the kale until it is all well coated and none of the mixture remains on the bottom of the pan.

6. Place in a preheated oven for an hour and twenty minutes to an hour and a half. You can turn the leaves during the cook time to help them cook evenly. They will come out crispy and yummy. Definitely not potato chips; you will want to make more!

Serves 2 hungry souls

CHICKEN WINGS
Martin Andersen

I am a violist in the New Jersey Symphony Orchestra and NYC-metro freelance musician for the last forty years.

My grandmother Arla showed me how to make these wings. Great for a party – my New Jersey Symphony Orchestra colleagues have always enjoyed them at our potluck lunches. I usually make at least a double recipe. So easy to prepare you can even use bagged frozen wing pieces (thawed) if making for a crowd.

Special Prep/Equipment
Large baking dish

12 chicken wings

⅔ cup soy sauce

½ cup brown sugar

¼ cup sherry (or any other wine)

3 green onions, chopped (I substitute one bunch of scallions.)

1. Preheat oven to 350 °.

2. Mix soy sauce and brown sugar; heat in pot to dissolve sugar. Add sherry and part of the green onions.

3. Disjoint chicken wings, discarding tips.

4. Arrange chicken pieces in baking dish in a single layer. Pour sauce over the chicken.

5. Bake for about 45 minutes, occasionally turning chicken wings. Top with the rest of the green onion.

6. Serve hot or at room temperature.

Serves 6 for hors d'ouevres

AUNT JANICE'S PARTY MIX
Emily Brausa

I'm a freelance cellist in the city – last spotted on March 11th, 2020 playing in the pit for *West Side Story*!

My taste buds were immediately tantalized when Aunt Janice gifted a bag of this many Christmases ago. I grew up in Kansas where we often measure snacks in "boxes", so I've modified her recipe to reflect the size of NYC kitchens.

Special Prep/Equipment
Brown paper grocery sack

2 cups Honey BBQ Fritos

1½ cups Nacho Cheese Bugles

1½ cups Wheat Thins

1½ cups Cheese Balls

1½ cups Hot & Spicy Cheez- Its

1½ cups Fritos

1½ cups Parmesan Goldfish

12 teaspoons ranch dressing mix (1½ packages)

1 teaspoon red pepper flakes

1 teaspoon mustard powder

¼ teaspoons cayenne pepper

¾ cup canola oil

Note:
You can substitute any other favorite crackers or pretzels!

1. Combine all snack crackers and chips in a brown paper bag. Incorporate all spices into the oil and pour over crackers.

2. Shake the bag for approximately 2 minutes and then transfer mixture to a large bowl.

3. Let the mix dry for a few hours until the oil evaporates.

4. Enjoy!

Yields 11 cups

FIDDLESTICKS
~ Denise Stillwell

I am a violin/viola doubler. I've played everything from symphony and operas to Broadway and pop music.

I don't even remember how I came up with this concoction but it's one of my favorite snacks or lunches.

Special Prep/Equipment
Frying pan, knife, cutting board, microwave

Olive oil

Italian seasoning

Salt to taste

1 bag shredded carrots

2 apples, julienned

2 small chayotes, julienned

2 tablespoons cashew butter

3-4 Swiss chard leaves

Note:
For the olive oil and Italian seasoning, you can substitute Italian dressing if desired.

1. Warm the oil in a frying pan and add the Italian seasoning.

2. When oil is hot, add carrots, apples, and chayotes. Saute until just softened .

3. Microwave the cashew butter until it's soft enough to pour.

4. Cut the stems off the chard leaves. Wrap the chard in a damp paper towel and microwave for a few seconds, just to soften them a little.

5. Spread the leaves out and spoon apple, carrot, and chayote mixture onto each leaf. Add a pinch of salt to taste and drizzle with melted cashew butter. Roll the leaves into tubes.

6. Eat and enjoy!

Serves 1-2 (about 3-4 roll-ups). Sharing is Caring!

SICILIAN CAPONATA
~ Lynne Cohen

I am an orchestral and Broadway oboist. I am also a bagpiper in St. Ann's of Hampton Pipes and Drums.

After viewing the series *Detective Montalbano* during the shut-in, we fell in love with all things Sicilian and we long to travel again. This easy antipasto will bring you right back to a sun-filled, seaside village, with all its colors and smells. This recipe is adapted from Caponata di Melanzane in the cookbook *Sicilia in Cucina*.

1 medium-large eggplant, 1" diced	Salt and pepper
Extra virgin olive oil	1 tablespoon capers
1 medium red or yellow onion, finely chopped	⅓ cup unsalted almonds, roughly chopped
1 celery stalk, diced	⅓ cup golden raisins
1½ carrots, diced	¼ cup black or green olives, roughly chopped
2 tablespoons tomato paste	1 tablespoon honey
½ cup of tomato sauce	1-2 tablespoons red wine vinegar
¼ cup chopped fresh basil	

Special Prep/Equipment

Large non-stick pan

1. In a non-stick pan, fry the diced eggplant in a small amount of oil. The eggplant will soak it up and seem too dry, but keep the heat at medium to just brown it. Set aside.

2. In another pan, saute the onion in oil and add the celery and carrot.

3. When the onion, celery, and carrot are golden, fry the tomato paste with them and add the tomato sauce and basil and cook for 10 minutes.

4. Add the cooked eggplant, salt, pepper, capers, almonds, raisins, olives, honey, and vinegar. Cook until the caponata is caramelized and the vinegar is evaporated.

5. Serve cold or at room temperature with good bread, on pasta, or as an antipasto with charcuterie and cheese.

Yields about 3 cups

MITCHELL'S SCAMPI
Cubby O'Brien

I am a drummer, an original Mouseketeer, and personal drummer for Bernadette Peters among many others through the years.

I have been making this recipe for years and it is always a big hit for family and friends. Easy too!

12 large raw shrimp	1 tablespoon shallot, chopped and/or ½ teaspoon garlic, minced
2 cups milk	
cooking oil	
1 cup flour	4 ounces softened butter
1 teaspoon salt, 1 teaspoon pepper	
2 cups sweet white wine	Lemon, cut into wedges
	Parsley

1. Make the scampi: Take off shells and remove veins from shrimp. Cover shrimp in bowl with milk and soak for 15 minutes.

2. In deep skillet, heat 1½" of cooking oil to 350°. Drain shrimp and dry on paper towels. Dredge shrimp in flour seasoned with salt and pepper.

3. Fry a couple shrimp at a time for approximately 2 minutes or until lightly browned. Remove and drain on paper towel. Keep warm.

4. Make the sauce: In 12" skillet add 2 cups sweet white wine (Sauterne is good). Add 1 tablespoon chopped shallots or ½ teaspoon minced garlic. Bring to a boil and saute until wine is reduced to 1 cup.

5. Add shrimp and boil for 1 minute. Add 4 ounces softened butter and toss with wine mixture and shrimp until the sauce is creamy and smooth. Do not cook sauce after butter has melted or it will separate. Remove from heat immediately.

6. Serve at once with lemon wedges and parsley.

Note

I like to fry the shrimp ahead of time. When guests arrive I saute them and serve them fresh and hot out of the pan!

Serves 4 as an appetizer

FRIED GEFILTE FISH
∽ Ina Litera

I am a freelance violist in NYC and teach at two local music schools as well as being on the CUNY adjunct faculty. I am a member of Eight Strings & a Whistle, a flute, viola and cello trio.

Many years ago I played an endless tour of *My Fair Lady* in Germany, Belgium and Holland. I was in Munich when Passover hit and was fortunate enough to be invited by a friend of my sister for a Passover Seder. There, for the first time, I had homemade Gefilte Fish. Who knew? All my life it had come from a jar. When I came home I said that was that, and homemade was the way to go. But traditional Gefilte Fish is a pain in the butt. This recipe for fried Gefilte Fish is adapted from *The Book of Jewish Food* by Claudia Roden (Knoff Publishing, 1996).

Special Prep/Equipment
Large fry pan or wok

1. Chop up your fish in a food processor till still chunky but not pasty. Remove and set aside.

2. Put onion, eggs, salt, pepper, and lemon juice in the food processor and blend till pretty smooth. (You don't need to clean the food processor in between – it's all ending up together.) Set this mixture aside in a bowl.

3. Now put some of your fish and some of your onion mix in the processor and blend really well. Put in yet another bowl and repeat till all done. Add ½-1 cup matzo meal and stir in well.

4. Refrigerate for 30 minutes or more.

5. When ready, form balls out of the mixture. Make sure to wet your hands. Form the fish mixture into balls – about ¼ cup each. Then roll them in the matzo meal. (Feel free to season it as you like – salt, pepper, anything you like.) Repeat till all are ready.

6. Now it is time to fry. Put about 2" of oil in your pan. We use a wok, but any big heavy fry pan will do. Heat your oil till it is hot! Then put a few of your gefilte fish balls in the pan. DON'T overcrowd them. Usually we can do about 6 at a time. If your

1 onion	And another cup of matzo meal for breading
2 eggs	
Salt to taste, but at least 2 teaspoons	2 pounds fish - You can use the traditional stuff like carp and haddock or bream, but if you want to go large, tilapia, cod, and even salmon work well. A mix of a few fishes is best.
Pepper	
About 2 tablespoons lemon juice	
½ - 1 cup matzo meal (If not for Passover, you can use Panko, I won't tell...)	Oil for frying (peanut, canola, olive)

oil is good and hot it will take about 6 minutes, flipping them over half way. They should be a good deep golden brown. Drain on paper towels and salt while still hot.

7. Repeat till all are done.

8. These are super delicious hot but good cold, too. Serve them with horseradish or, if you aren't worried about keeping kosher, wasabi.

Yields about 20 fish balls. Serves 2 balls per person.

RISOTTO WITH SAFFRON, MILANESE STYLE
Carla Fabiani

I play the viola and violin in Broadway shows and I co-founded the "Storytime Quartet" Concerts for Children.

This is a recipe my grandmother taught me when I would spend my summers in Northern Italy.

Special Prep/Equipment
3-quart saucepan
Wooden spoon to stir

1. Finely chop the onion and saute it in a pan with 1 ounce of butter, over a very low heat for about 5 minutes.

2. Add the rice and toast it over high heat for a minute while stirring.

3. Add in white wine, stir, until it evaporates.

4. Bring broth to a boil in a separate pot and pour in, little at a time, stirring occasionally.

5. Cook the rice for about 16-20 minutes as needed. Halfway through cooking, add the saffron. Add salt to taste.

6. Remove the pan from the heat, when rice is cooked to your preferred level of tenderness, and add the remaining cold butter and cheese; gently stirring, until blended and creamy.

7. Let it rest, covered with a lid for 5 minutes before serving.

Serves 4

⅓ cup diced onion

3 ounces butter (divided)

300g (1¼ cup) Arborio rice

¼ cup dry white wine

4.2 cups (33 ounces) beef broth

2 packets Saffron (about ⅛ teaspoon)

Salt to taste

⅓ cup grated Parmesan

SHRIMP & SCALLOP FRITTERS WITH CHIPOTLE MAYONNAISE

~ Wayne Fugate

I am a mandolin player and big fan of the back-beat. In the "before times" I played everything from Bluegrass to Bach in a variety of ensembles. I even played a bit on Broadway (Steve Martin & Edie Brickell's *Bright Star*) and did the first national tour of that show.

I used to make these for a near legendary Super Bowl party that I hosted for many years. Friends would try to outdo each other, with some pretty off-the-chain, delicious, culinary contributions. I made these fritters as an appetizer and I also grilled filet-mignons and served them with a gorgonzola scallion compound butter for the main course. Culinary nirvana!!

Special Prep/Equipment

12" heavy skillet

For the mayo:
½ cup mayonnaise

1 tablespoon canned chipotle chile peppers, finely chopped, plus 2 teaspoons of the adobo sauce from the can

a little fresh lemon juice (optional)

For the fritters:
½ pound sea scallops

1 large egg white

1 tablespoon chopped shallot

⅛ teaspoon black pepper

½ teaspoon salt

⅓ cup heavy cream

½ pound shrimp peeled, de-veined, and cut into ¼ inch pieces

1 cup plain fine dry bread crumbs (I use panko bread crumbs)

About ½ cup of oil – I use grapeseed oil to take advantage of its high smoke point.

1. Make the mayo. Stir together the mayonnaise, chopped chiles, and adobo sauce in a small bowl, then taste test for your desired level of spiciness. When chopping the peppers, use more of the seeds for a spicier mayo, fewer for a mayo that your guests won't hate you for. You can add the peppers in a little at a time, tasting as you go to make sure it doesn't exceed the desired heat-level. Once you get it "just right", you can add in a little fresh lemon juice, if you want.

2. For the fritters. Puree the scallops, egg white, shallot, salt, and pepper together in a food processor. Then, add the cream and pulse until the mixture is just combined.

3. Transfer mixture to a bowl and stir in the shrimp. Chill in the fridge, covered, for 10 minutes.

4. Put bread crumbs in a mixing bowl or on a pie plate. Drop 6 mounds of scallop mixture (about 2 tablespoons each) onto crumbs, then coat them with crumbs and shape the mounds into patties.

5. Transfer the breaded patties to a wax or parchment-paper-lined tray.

6. Make additional patties in same manner with remaining scallop mixture and crumbs.

7. Heat ¼" of cooking oil in your skillet over moderately high heat until the oil is hot but not smoking. Fry the patties in small batches, turning once, until they're golden brown and firm to the touch, about 4 minutes total. Drain the fritters on paper towels.

8. Serve with the chipotle-mayo and enjoy!

Note

Be super-careful handling the peppers and wash your hands well afterwards. You DON'T want to get any part of the pepper or the adobo sauce near your nose or eyes!!

Yields about 12 fritters – enough for 4 main courses or a larger number of servings as appetizers.

KOREAN TTEOKBOKKI
⌒ Alan Kay

I'm fortunate to be principal clarinet of New York's Orpheus Chamber Orchestra, Riverside Symphony, and Little Orchestra Society, and a teacher at Juilliard, Manhattan School of Music, and Stony Brook University.

My wife is Korean-born and an excellent all-around chef. With her help I've enjoyed learning some classic Korean recipes over the years. Tteokbokki is truly Korean comfort food and I highly recommend it!

1 pound tteok (a couple dozen 2-3" tube-shaped rice cakes)

1 sheet of odeng (flat form of fish cake)

4 ounces green cabbage (known as yangbaechu in Korean)

3 scallions

1 onion, sliced

3 cups (plus more, for more sauce) water or anchovy broth

1-3 teaspoon Gochugaru (Korean red chili pepper flakes – use just 1 teaspoon if you don't want it too hot!)

1 tablespoon soy sauce

1-2 tablespoons sugar (depending on how sweet you like it)

1 tablespoon minced garlic

1. Soak tteok (rice cakes) in water for about 20 minutes till soft (but not so long that they get mushy!) Meanwhile, cut the fish cake into 2" triangular pieces, and the cabbage and two of the scallions into 2" pieces. Chop the remaining scallion into small pieces for garnish.

2. Pour water (or anchovy broth) into a large saucepan. Bring to a boil. Add tteok, sliced onion, cabbage, odeng, Gochugaru, Gochujang, garlic, soy sauce, and sugar. Stir it all together; bring to a boil again. *Note:* You can add other vegetables if you like: mushrooms, carrots, etc.

3. Continue to boil, always stirring, for an additional 4 minutes or so. Check the tteok for softness - they might need a bit more time. There should be enough liquid in the saucepan to create a nice sauce for your rice cakes. Check for seasoning. If you like it hotter, add a touch more Gochujang or Gochugaru.

4. Serve immediately, garnished with the reserved chopped scallions.

Serves 3

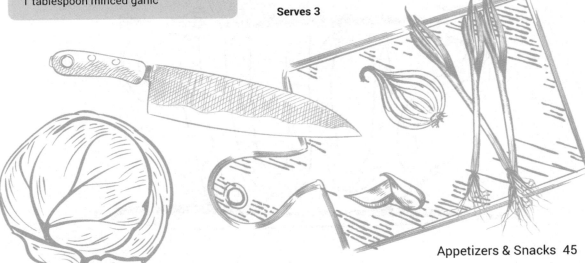

SOUP

KALE & SWEET POTATO SOUP
Wendy Richman

I am a founding member of the New York-based International Contemporary Ensemble. I am on the string faculty of New York University (NYU Steinhardt), where I teach viola, chamber music, and a class on extended string techniques. I have an album of commissioned works for singing violist, which you can see on my website *wendyrichmanviola.com*.

This soup is loosely based on two recipes I found on the NPR website. I sometimes make this soup in the Instant Pot, but the caramelized onions turn out much better low and slow on the stove. The onions and the arborio rice trick add great depth to this easy soup.

Special Prep/Equipment
Large dutch oven or stock pot

2 tablespoons olive oil

2 onions, chopped or sliced

Pinch sugar

Pinch salt

3 medium sweet potatoes, scrubbed and cut into 1" dice.

2 large bunches of kale or any dark greens, roughly torn or chopped.

Salt and pepper to taste

2-3 quarts chicken or vegetable stock, or water/bouillon equivalent

1 tablespoon - ¼ cup arborio or other high-starch rice.

Cayenne pepper to taste (I use a little under a teaspoon)

Fresh lemon juice to taste (I use about a tablespoon)

Notes
Sweet potatoes: There's no need to peel them, unless you want a super-smooth soup.

Rice: will add a creaminess to the soup and will blend in when you puree; if you're not going to puree and want to leave the soup chunky, you can omit the rice OR add about 2 tablespoons light cream.

Kale: There's no need to remove the stems, with the same caveat as the sweet potato skins.

Optional: Parmigiano Reggiano, Piave, or feta for grating/crumbling over soup

1. Caramelize the onions: heat a large dutch oven or stock pot for several minutes over medium-high heat, then add the olive oil. When the oil is shimmering, add the onions, coating them in oil and making an even layer.

2. Reduce heat to low and add a pinch each of salt and sugar. Let the onions cook very slowly, stirring every few minutes to prevent sticking. Adjust heat as needed, adding a tablespoon of water if they stick to the pan.

3. When the onions are soft and medium-brown — this will take about 30 minutes — add a quart of stock and the grains of rice (if using). Add the diced sweet potatoes and increase heat to high. When the stock begins to boil, reduce heat to medium. Cook the sweet potatoes until softened, about 15 minutes.

4. Add the greens in batches, allowing them to wilt on top of the potatoes. As each batch wilts, stir it into the potato/stock mixture and add another batch. Add more stock as needed.

5. Once all the greens are incorporated, taste the broth and season as desired. If you used unsalted stock or broth, you may need to add several teaspoons of salt.

6. Puree mixture with an immersion blender, food processor, or blender. Leave it as-is for a heartier texture. (Stir in cream, if using.)

7. Season each serving with cayenne and lemon juice, and garnish with Parmigiano-Reggiano, Piave, or feta.

> **Note**
> Refrigerate for up to one week or freeze in individual serving containers. Thin with water or more stock as needed.

Serves 8-10

TURKISH RED LENTIL SOUP (a.k.a. "BRIDE SOUP")

Sheila Reinhold

I play violin (and sometimes viola) and I have done all sorts of free-lance work in NYC and beyond: chamber music, Broadway, studio work, orchestral, solo performances, etc. and have also always loved teaching.

I found a recipe for this in a NY Times article many years ago. It is a traditional Turkish soup called Ezo Gelin Çorbası (Soup of Ezo the Bride), and I started comparing lots of recipes, developing my own vegetarian version which has become my go-to dish for lunch break with my colleagues during long chamber music rehearsals in my home, as well as a family favorite. The recipe has traveled to several cities by now! When I visited Turkey a few years ago I found that it is served in almost every kebab restaurant. If you use this recipe and perhaps use more water or broth it will taste pretty similar to what I ate there; I prefer to have it as a hearty main-dish soup so I make it thicker.

Special Prep/Equipment
Large soup pot

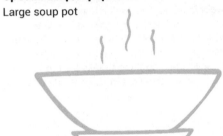

4 tablespoons olive oil

3 medium onions, chopped

2-3 tablespoons sweet (not hot) Hungarian paprika

1½ cups red lentils, rinsed well and drained

½ - ¾ cup bulgur wheat

1-2 bay leaves

Few shakes of thyme

10 cups water or any kind of stock/broth

3-4 tablespoons tomato paste

⅛ teaspoon cayenne, or red pepper flakes, to taste

2 tablespoons or more dried whole mint leaves

Lemon slices or wedges

1. Heat oil in large pot over low heat. Add onions and saute until golden, about 10 minutes. Add paprika, lentils, and bulgur, and stir. Add bay leaves and thyme.

2. Add water (or stock), tomato paste and optional cayenne/pepper flakes, and bring to a boil. Reduce heat and simmer until lentils are tender and soup is creamy, about 40 minutes or more. Add a little more water/stock if soup gets too thick. Crumble dried mint leaves and stir into soup.

3. Remove soup from heat, cover and set aside 10 minutes. Add salt and black pepper to taste. Serve with lemon slices/wedges.

Note
Original recipes often called for a lot of butter instead of olive oil and beef broth instead of water or other stock. I add the bay leaves and thyme especially when I use water to give the fuller flavor of broth. Non-traditional variations we have enjoyed include using rice or another grain instead of bulgur (if rice, can become gluten-free), using different sizes of bulgur (fine vs coarse), adding chopped tomatoes, carrots and celery after sauteeing the onions for a vegetable soup/stew version, adding garlic, serving with feta to crumble in, etc.

This recipe freezes well.

Serves about 8, less if it is a full meal

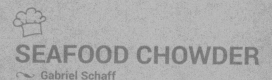

SEAFOOD CHOWDER
Gabriel Schaff

I am a violinist and an instrument and historical researcher.

I began to learn how to cook in my early teen years when my mom, struggling to balance a life of single parent, performer, composer, and university professor exclaimed to me and my brother, "if you don't like my cooking then learn to cook for yourself!" Challenge accepted.

Cooking allows me to enter a sacred and private space of self-reflection, experimentation, and communing with the abundant goodness and variety of edibles we are privileged to have access to in our community. I never use recipes beyond an occasional reference, and since accuracy and precision are not vital to my cooking, I almost never bake, as baking demands a healthy respect for physics and chemistry, which I happily respect outside of the kitchen.

Colder weather has me turning to my large soup pot for stews and soups. As I eat much less meat than before, I have increased my consumption of fish. This seafood chowder is hearty and well balanced and can serve as a side dish or a complete meal, and can be modified to be kosher and non dairy. Almost any kind of fish will work, and shellfish need not be added, but I now use filets to avoid bones/shells that are anticlimactic. Butter and cream/half & half are not required, but add a deeper dimension, and are included below. Unlike meat or poultry stews, this dish need not be prepared in advance as the longest cooking time is for the vegetables. Once the fish is added it needs only a few minutes to finish. As in all my cooking, contents and proportions are variable. Listen to your inner voice!

Special Prep/Equipment
Large, lidded soup or stock pot (5 quart or larger)

1- 2 tablespoons oil, enough to saute vegetables	1 quart chicken or vegetable stock, and additional water as needed
3- 4 onions, coarsely diced	1 pound of fresh fish, skin on, chopped into 1 inch cubes (more if not using shellfish below). I prefer a mix of salmon and cod (not tilapia).
3- 4 medium potatoes, pref. Yukon gold or red, cubed	
Fresh garlic, as much as you like, chopped	1 can clams in their juice (optional)
Carrots and celery to taste, chopped	2- 3 cups mixed seafood that can include shrimp (cleaned, tails off), scallops, or any other critters you like. Doesn't matter if fresh or frozen.
Mushrooms to taste, coarsely chopped	
¼ -½ stick butter (optional)	Salt and pepper to taste
½ cup half-and-half, or if you don't care, cream (optional)	½ cup fresh herbs: dill, cilantro, scallions, chopped. Use lesser amounts if using stronger herbs like thyme.

1. Heat oil on medium-high heat. Add onions and brown a bit, for around 5 minutes.

2. Add potatoes and agitate them with the onions. Add garlic, carrots, celery, and mushrooms letting them all get acquainted for another 5 minutes.

3. When they are all hot and sweaty, add butter if desired, and let them discuss for another 5 minutes.

4. Stir in cream (if desired) and once it is heated, add stock.

5. Once it all reaches a boil, turn heat down and let simmer another 5 minutes. (By now, I have said "5 minutes" several times, but I don't really keep track. The food will tell you.)

6. Poke a larger piece of potato. If it doesn't poke back, it is time to add the fish. Turn the heat back up to a boil, and add all of the fish products.

7. When the boil returns, turn heat down to a simmer for not more than 5 minutes.

8. Taste the broth, and adjust with salt and pepper.

9. Add the fresh herbs, stir throughout, turn off the heat and cover.

10. Wait 5 minutes and serve in medium bowls that are sure to be refilled!

> **Note**
> If you want a bit of heat, add some hot chili flakes or chili oil to taste, just before the fish goes in. For an added kick, fresh grated ginger adds a whole new dimension.
>
> The addition of one regular sized can of cannellini or other similar beans, drained, will transform this dish into a complete meal.
>
> Results may differ depending on what music you are listening to. I made this yesterday while listening to Mahler Symphony #6 with Leonard Bernstein and the Vienna Philharmonic. It was GREAT!

Serves alot people!

OLD-FASHIONED DUMPLING SOUP
ᴄ⌢ Helen Campo

I am the flutist of the Broadway show *Wicked*.

My mother taught me this recipe when I was a child. It is easy enough for a kid to make!

Special Prep/Equipment
Large soup pot

1. Place all ingredients except flour, carrots, and peas in a bowl and beat well with fork.

2. Add enough flour to make batter follow fork around the bowl.

3. Dump by heaping teaspoonful into boiling broth of your choice, or simply bouillon cubes in water.

4. When all dumplings are in, put lid on pot and cook for 3-4 minutes until they steam up and are done.

5. Add raw carrots and as in Version #1 peas, and serve immediately.

> **Note**
> A broth can be made by tossing together chicken, garlic, onion, carrot, celery, bay leaf, and salt.

Version #1:
1 or 2 eggs per person

1 or 2 tablespoons melted butter and a pinch of salt per egg OR

1 or 2 tablespoons parmesan or farmer's cheese

Enough flour to make batter follow fork around the bowl

Raw carrot thinly shaved with a peeler

A few peas fresh or frozen (optional)

Version #2:
Frozen square of finely chopped spinach, cooked slightly, water squeezed out (can also substitute same amount of radish or carrot tops prepared same way)

2 eggs per square of spinach

2 tablespoons of melted butter or parmesan

1/8 teaspoon freshly grated nutmeg

Enough flour to make batter follow fork around the bowl

Raw carrot thinly shaved with a peeler

Serves any number – 1 egg per person unless the person is a particularly good eater.

SAUERKRAUT & SAUERKRAUT, POTATO & BRATWURST SOUP
Julie Goodale

I play viola and I love food. I love all aspects of food: eating, cooking, growing it, sometimes foraging, and I love feeding other people. All my recipes are decidedly vague; I constantly experiment and adapt. Also, I think I'm not very good at following instructions.

Until I was up in the Finger Lakes region in late fall when cabbage was just coming in, I had never given much thought to sauerkraut, other than maybe, "no thank you." True, a few years before, I had marched in the Sauerkraut Parade in Phelps, NY, with my friends in the Hohenfels Trombone Quartet (I even bought a dirndl for the occasion!). I also won first prize in my age class in the Sauerkraut Festival 5K run. The prize was a can of sauerkraut. But when I couldn't resist filling my car with just-picked cabbages, including one that was bigger than my head, I needed to find cabbage recipes. I ate cabbage in soups, made acres of cabbage rolls, slaws, and simple sautées. Then I read a recipe for homemade sauerkraut and, after trying it out, my worldview changed. Homemade sauerkraut bears little resemblance in taste or texture to the canned stuff on grocery store shelves or hiding at the back of the cupboard in a cabin. Homemade is crunchy, zesty, sour – in short, it's delightful. Plus, you can endlessly tweak the recipe: try different salts for subtle taste differences, experiment with spices, add shredded carrots or other vegetables, or vary how long you let it ferment for more or less tanginess. Enjoy!

Sauerkraut

Special Prep/Equipment
Wide-mouth mason jars, sterilized by boiling in water for 10 minutes

1 medium cabbage, 2-3 lbs

1+ tablespoon <u>non-iodized salt</u> (1½ - 2 teaspoons salt per pound of cabbage)

1 tablespoon fennel seeds (or caraway seeds, juniper berries, turmeric and cumin...or nothing. For my latest batch, I used a Bengali 5-spice mix – delish.)

Note: The salt needs to be non-iodized salt. You can use pickling salt or Kosher salt. I've also used sea salt and pink Himalayan salt. Each produces a slightly different end result.

1. Weigh the cabbage. This is important since the amount of salt depends on the cabbage weight. Discard any damaged outer leaves. Cut the cabbage in quarters and slice out the core. Rinse the cabbage well and drain. Reserve one large outer leaf.

2. Slice cabbage into thin ribbons or shred in food processor.

3. Combine cabbage and salt in a large glass or stainless steel bowl. Use your hands to sprinkle the salt over the cabbage and work it in. Let it rest for about 15 minutes. The salt will begin to break down the cabbage. It will release liquid and start to look more like coleslaw than raw cabbage.

4. Massage cabbage again with your hands. If you want to add fennel or some other seed, mix it in now. Depending on how coarse you chopped the cabbage, you may need to let it sit longer. Shredded cabbage should soften up in about 15 minutes, a coarser chop could take up to an hour to soften and release its liquid.

5. Pack cabbage into sterilized jars. Pack it down firmly with your fist or wooden spoon. Leave an inch to inch and a half of room at the top. Pour any liquid left in the bowl from the softening cabbage over the top of the packed cabbage.

6. Cut out a circle the size of the jar opening from the reserved leaf. Nestle that down on top of the cabbage. There should be enough liquid to fully cover the cabbage. If you need more liquid, you can mix a 2% solution of salt water (1 teaspoon salt to 1 cup of water). The liquid must completely cover the cabbage.

7. Weigh down the cabbage to keep it submerged (the cabbage near the top will tend to float up). You can use kitchen weights, or you can use a Zip-loc baggie filled with stones or water as a weight. Any cabbage that's exposed to air can mold. (If that happens, not a big deal. Seriously. Just remove the moldy leaves and press the rest back under the liquid.)

8. Loosely cover the jar with its lid — loosely, do not tighten! Place the jar on a pan or plate. Set it on the counter or table, out of the way.

9. Do nothing. Really. It will start fermenting. You may see bubbles. It may bubble over the top; that's why the lid should be loose, and the jar placed on a dish. Fermentation takes anywhere from 1-3 weeks. The fermentation process varies depending on temperature, faster when it's warmer, slower if the air is colder. Taste it after about a week. If you would like it more sour, leave it to ferment longer. When you're satisfied with its tanginess, it's ready to go in the refrigerator. Scoop out any moldy bits, if there are any — really it is okay, the sauerkraut is NOT ruined, you will not die! Top off with more saline solution if needed to keep the cabbage covered. Screw the top on and refrigerate.

Yields at least a couple mason jars - enough to last a while.

Sauerkraut, Potato & Bratwurst Soup

A quick idea if you're looking for ways to use your wonderful sauerkraut: Potato Sauerkraut and Bratwurst Soup. This is all very approximate because I made it up recently when I was trying to use up a few things and really wanted soup.

1 medium onion, chopped	Bratwursts
Garlic, chopped	1 cup (or more) sauerkraut
3 or 4 potatoes, diced (I didn't peel them)	1 tablespoon flour
Broth or stock	Sour cream (optional)

1. Saute onions and garlic, add potatoes and cover with water (or stock — I used water because I was out of stock).

2. Cook until potatoes are tender.

3. Slice up the brats and saute them in a separate pan. Add the sauerkraut, cook through.

4. In a bowl, mix a ½ cup of the cooking liquid with a tablespoon of flour. Add some sour cream or heavy cream if you have it (I had some sour cream on hand). Stir that into the cooking liquid and potatoes. When the broth has thickened, add in the brats and sauerkraut.

> **Note**
> When I made this the first time, I was using up the last of an open jar of my sauerkraut with the Bengali spices, which added a subtle kick.

ALEXANDER HEROLD'S GAZPACHO (SOUTHERN SPAIN)
~ Sato Moughalian

I am the flutist and Artistic Director of Perspectives Ensemble, principal flute of Gotham Chamber Opera, Oratorio Society of New York, and several other NYC chamber and new music groups. In 2019, my biography of my grandfather was published, *Feast of Ashes: The Life and Art of David Ohannessian* (Stanford University Press). During this pandemic "pause," I'm writing a second book, about a group of early twentieth-century Ottoman-Armenian visual artists.

I learned this recipe in Valencia, Spain from Alexander Herold, descendant of the French opera composer Ferdinand Hérold, best known today for his three-act opéra-comique *Zampa*, whose overture remains in the classical concert repertoire. I make this gazpacho only in August, when East Coast tomatoes are luscious and meaty, with a tinge of mineral flavor, and watermelons are at the apex of juicy sweetness.

Special Prep/Equipment
Immersion blender or blender

2-3 pounds of ripe tomatoes, skins removed

1 ripe, medium Italian (or regular) green pepper

1 good-sized cucumber

½ a stale baguette of good quality white bread, preferably a bit stale – like a baguette from the organic baker at the farmer's market (if the bread is really stale, splash it with red wine vinegar)

A very generous fistful of basil leaves

2-3 cloves of garlic

Good pinch of sea salt

About 2 tablespoons cumin, to taste

A generous splash of red wine vinegar (to be used to soften the bread if needed, if not, straight into the pot)

½ a small round watermelon scooped out (no seeds) (or a quarter of the big seedless ones from the greengrocer, in season).

A good healthy few glogs of fruity extra virgin olive oil

Some freshly ground black pepper, to taste

A little water, if needed, to lighten the consistency (I almost never use this)

1. Combine all ingredients in a very good sized bowl or pot.

2. Blend with an immersion blender until smooth and lump free. If you don't have an immersion blender, you can put it into a blender in batches.

3. Chill very well before serving.

Serves about 6-8 as a starter dish, or 4 generous servings as a featured dish.

BLACK BEAN SOUP WITH LIME
~ Simone Dinnerstein

I am a concert pianist and on the faculty of the Mannes School of Music.

This soup will get you through an afternoon of practicing, no problem!

Special Prep/Equipment
You will need a large soup pot.
An immersion blender is helpful.

1. In your soup pot, heat the oil on medium heat. Saute the onion and the jalapeño and 1 teaspoon of salt until the onion is soft and almost turning brown, around 5-7 minutes.

2. Add the garlic, cumin and oregano and stir them all together, for around a minute. Add the bay leaf, broth, water and beans and bring to a boil. Then turn down the heat, cover the pot and let them simmer for around 30 minutes.

3. Add the juice of one lime and 1 teaspoon of salt and turn off the heat. Wait for it to cool and then liquidize it. I use the hand held immersion blender that can go straight into the pot, but you could also use a food processor or even a blender. After that, I usually store it in the amounts I would like to eat, so that I can have soup every day!

4. When you are ready to eat it, heat it up and while it is heating, make the yogurt topping. Combine the ½ of the lime juice and its zest, along with the ½ teaspoon of salt, with the yogurt. Then serve your soup with a dollop of yogurt and the cilantro and scallions. Yum! And if you have leftover yogurt, it makes a great dressing for cut up tomatoes and avocados. Extra yum!

Note
If you like your soup very thick, reduce the amount of water. Perhaps just 1½ cups. The yogurt topping seems to last for 3 days in the fridge. I didn't want to risk storing it after that, which was why I experimented with using it as a salad dressing. I bet there are lots of other things you could make with this very tasty and healthy topping.

1 tablespoon olive oil

1 large red onion, diced

1 jalapeño pepper, diced

2 teaspoons kosher salt, divided

4 cloves of minced garlic

1 heaping tablespoon of cumin

1 tablespoon of oregano

1 bay leaf

16 ounces vegetable stock

2½ cups of water

3 (28 ounce) cans of black beans, drained and rinsed

1 lime, juiced

½ additional lime, juiced and the zest of the entire lime grated

1 small container of nonfat, plain Greek yogurt

½ teaspoon of salt

Cilantro, chopped as topping, as much as you like

Scallions, chopped for garnish, as much as you like

Serves about 6-8

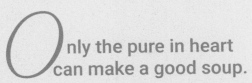

*O*nly the pure in heart
can make a good soup.

~ Ludwig van Beethoven

VEGETARIAN BORSCHT
~ Yevgenia Strenger

I am a violinist, and I have worked as the concertmaster of the New York City Opera, and am working in the New York City Ballet Orchestra.

I grew up in the Ukrainian city of Lviv. Borscht was a frequent part of our meals. When I came to New York City, I was interested in all the different cuisines and didn't make borscht at all. Then my husband ate some at my parents' home and not only wanted me to make it, but started making it too. The original recipe got tweaked a bit (cilantro was a new touch, and olive oil instead of sunflower oil). I don't put potatoes in, to keep it lighter, but no harm in adding some.

Special Prep/Equipment

Grater or food processor

5-quart pot

Big wooden spoon

Sharp knife for slicing onions and garlic

4 large beets

4 large carrots

1 parsnip or parsley root

2 small onions

4 cloves garlic

2 tablespoons vegetable oil

2 sticks celery

1 big sweet green or red pepper

Salt, to taste

A few sprigs of Italian parsley greens or cilantro

Some fresh dill

Juice of ¼ of lemon

Sour cream or Greek yogurt to serve at the table

Note: This is a vegetarian recipe, but I often add chicken broth into the water for richer flavor.

1. Wash and peel beets, carrots and parsnip. Take the skin off the onions and garlic, wash and de-seed pepper.

2. Heat the pot with oil coating the bottom. If using food processor, grate beets, carrots, and parsnip and add to the pot. While that is sauteed, chop the onions and garlic and add to the pot.

3. Add water (and broth if desired) salt and pepper.

4. While it's cooking chop sweet pepper and celery (both optional) and add to the pot. Let it cook until everything is soft, then add lemon juice and herbs, bring to boil and turn off the flame.

5. Serve hot or cold (if without broth) with a dollop of sour cream and some chewy dark bread.

> **Note**
> It seems there are many different recipes for borscht: Russian, Ukrainian, Polish, meat-based and not, using cabbage, tomatoes, tomato paste, mushrooms etc. My approach is to throw in "the kitchen sink", but beets are the immutable part.

Yields 4 quarts

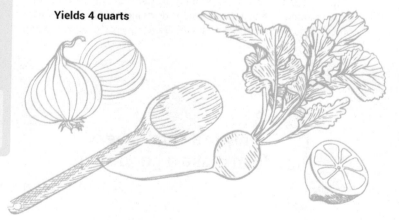

HEARTY CHICKEN SOUP
~ Sara Cyrus

I am a freelance French horn player.

This has a bit of a kick to it – great for when you have a cold! Super easy and inexpensive to make.

3 - 3½ pound chicken, cut up

8 cups water

2 onions, chopped

2 cups sliced celery

2 cups sliced carrots

2 chicken bouillon cubes

2 teaspoons salt

1+ teaspoon curry powder

2 tablespoon Worcestershire sauce

1 cup noodles

1. Boil chicken in water with all ingredients except noodles. Simmer 40-60 minutes.

2. Remove chicken from pot and let cool a little. Add noodles to the pot and boil according to package directions.

3. While noodles are boiling, remove skin and bones from chicken, cut into bite size pieces and return to pot. Heat through and enjoy!

Note
I use only dark meat (legs and thighs) to make a really rich broth. If you want a less oily broth include white meat.

Yields 3 quarts

ELAINE'S GREAT CHICKEN SOUP
~ Jeffrey Levine

I play the bass. I am a freelance classical and jazz player.

At the first sign of a cold...it's better than penicillin!

Special Prep/Equipment
A large heavy pot is needed

1 cut up chicken (bone in)

1 large onion

2 turnips

2 parsnips

2 leeks

2 carrots

2 celery stalks

5 garlic cloves

1 tablespoon (optional) of dry, powdered consomme mix (preferably OSEM)

Water to cover

1. Peel your root vegetables.

2. Put everything in a large pot, cover with water, bring to a boil, then simmer uncovered for 4 hours.

3. Add water when it starts to boil down, bring to a boil again, and then back to a simmer.

4. Salt and pepper to taste.

Serves 8-10

GARBANZO BEAN SOUP (SPANISH BEAN SOUP)
 Axel Tosca

I'm a Pianist from Cuba and currently have worked with George Clinton, BeBe Winans, The Clark Sisters, DJ/Producer /Remixer's Louie Vega and David Morales, Stretch & Bobbito, Mae-Sun, Steve Gadd, Ray Chew, Lenny White, Pino Palladino, Giovanni Hidalgo, Jocelyn Brown, Karren Wheeler, Monique Bingham, Godwin Lewis and J Balvin and Bad Bunny. I have had a 2-year residency at the New York City Jazz venue "Zinc Bar".

I'm sharing this soup recipe because for me it reminds me of being home in Cuba. Something my Grandma would make that always satisfied, like soup for the soul. It is healthy and hearty and can hold you for a while. This recipe is very close to my Abuela's and was created by Danny Gutierrez. I substitute the dry beans for canned beans, the pork for smoked turkey sausage or a smoked turkey leg, and the strands of saffron for powdered saffron.

Special Prep/Equipment
4-quart soup pot
The dried beans need to be soaked for several hours or overnight.

1 pound garbanzo beans, dried	2 large potatoes, peeled and quartered
1 tablespoon salt, to soak beans	4-5 cloves of garlic, minced
1 hambone, or smoked turkey leg or smoked turkey sausage	2 tablespoon olive oil
8 cups water or chicken broth or bone broth (low sodium)	6-8 strands of saffron
1 large onion, chopped	⅛ teaspoon of each; paprika, oregano, basil
½ large green pepper, chopped	2 bay leaves
1 pound ham, pre-cooked and cubed	2 spanish chorizo
	Salt & Pepper, to taste

1. Soak the dry beans overnight with salt in enough water to cover beans. Then, drain the salted water from the beans.

2. Next day – if you are using ham, start cooking beans with the ham bone or smoked turkey.

3. Place beans in a 4-quart soup pot; add 8 cups of water or broth and the ham bone, or smoked turkey sausage or smoked turkey leg, if you are using.

4. Bring to a boil, then reduce heat to low and cook for 1½ hours, skimming foam from the top with a large spoon. Cover the pot while cooking on low.

5. At the 1½ hour mark, remove the bone and if there is any meat on it, cut it off and set it aside.

6. Then, use a potato masher to gently push down on all the beans to aid in softening.

7. While the beans and ham bone or smoked turkey are cooking, chop onion and green pepper. Then, cube ham and peel and quarter potatoes and mince garlic.

8. In a skillet, preheat 2 tablespoons of olive oil over medium-high heat (making sure not to burn oil).

9. Add onion, green pepper, salt, and pepper, saute lightly for about 4-6 minutes, stirring frequently.

10. Add cubed ham (plus any off the bone) potatoes and garlic, cook for about 2 to 3 minutes, stirring frequently.

11. Add ham and vegetable mixture to the beans along with paprika, saffron, oregano, basil, and bay leaves. Stir well. Add more salt to taste and cook on low for about another 1½ hours.

12. Slice chorizo and add to the soup, about 30 minutes before removing it from heat.

13. When beans and potatoes are tender, remove from heat.

14. Serve hot in deep soup bowls with buttered Cuban bread on the side for dipping.

Serves 12

JUDY'S RICH & CREAMY PUMPKIN BUTTERNUT ONION SOUP
~ Janet Axelrod

I perform in studios, pits and stages with traditional flutes of the world, along with orchestral flutes. I also teach lessons and clinics to every level of flute students everywhere!

My sister, Judy, is like the improv musician of the kitchen. She can take a few ingredients and create a delicious new recipe. Here you have one! Since I don't eat dairy (or pumpkin pie spice) she always says that those are optional. She provides a variety of sweet and savory ingredients so this recipe is quite malleable to the preferences of your diners.

Special Prep/Equipment
Immersible blender or traditional blender

2 small onions

3 tablespoons olive oil

1 chopped apple

18 ounces butternut squash

1 (15 ounce) can pumpkin puree

A few tablespoons water for consistency

4 teaspoons apple cider vinegar

3 tablespoons molasses

2 teaspoons brown sugar

3 tablespoons maple syrup

2 teaspoons nut butter of your choice

Salt, pepper, powdered ginger, pumpkin pie spice to taste

Almond milk or half and half, at least ½ cup

Parsley, garlic, to taste

1 teaspoon bagel seasoning, if desired

Tabasco, if desired

1. In a large soup pot, saute onions in olive oil. Add apples, squash, pumpkin and enough water to create a thick soup consistency.

2. Add all ingredients, except for milk, bagel seasoning and tabasco.

3. Heat and simmer until apples are tender, around 30 minutes, then use immersible blender.

4. Finally add your choice of "milk" and blend again for your favorite consistency. Check in with your salt, pepper and spices to taste. If desired, top with bagel seasoning or Tabasco.

Serves 12

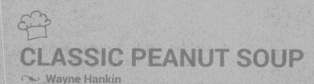

CLASSIC PEANUT SOUP
~ Wayne Hankin

I play early classical winds. I've conducted the Houston Grand Opera, performed with the Los Angeles Philharmonic, Glimmerglass Opera, and the Chautauqua Symphony, among others.

I encountered peanut soup when heading south to do workshops in North Carolina and Georgia. It's a simple recipe anyone can make and especially nice to warm your insides during colder months.

We have George Washington Carver to thank not only for his experiments with peanuts, but the promotion of alternative crops to prevent soil depletion. As an environmentalist, he was way ahead of his time and received numerous honors for his work. This recipe expands upon Carver's original recipe.

Special Prep/Equipment

Grater or food processor

5-quart pot

Big wooden spoon

Sharp knife for slicing onions and garlic

1. Pour milk/cream into a medium saucepan. Set to medium heat.

2. Sift flour into milk until smooth consistency is reached.

3. Add butter and peanuts and stir until desired consistency.

4. Add onion, celery and red pepper. Add salt & pepper.

5. Turn off heat. Let set for 10 minutes.

1 quart milk/cream

2 tablespoons flour

2 tablespoons butter

1 cup peanuts/organic peanut butter

½ cup of vidalia onion, chopped

½ cup of celery, chopped

¼ cup of sweet red pepper, chopped

Salt and pepper to taste

Note:
If you choose to grind peanuts you may do so. Be sure to grind them to fine consistency. Set aside.

Serves 6-8

SPICY PEANUT (OR NUT-FREE SOUP)
~ Katherine Cherbas

I work as a cellist in Broadway shows, several NYC-area freelance orchestras, and whatever chamber music opportunities I can find.

During a family vacation in California in 1988, my mother ordered spicy peanut soup at an otherwise forgettable restaurant and was blown away. She spent years trying to recreate the recipe or find a comparable soup in a cookbook. When she finally found a recipe for Senegalese Peanut Soup in James Paterson's book *Splendid Soups*, it became a frequent part of our family's repertoire. Over the years, we have modified the recipe by adding chicken or rice to bulk it up, and by substituting soy nut butter to make it allergy-friendly.

Special Prep/Equipment
Immersion blender, large soup pot

2 tablespoons canola oil

1 large onion, finely chopped

2 garlic cloves, chopped

1 teaspoon cayenne pepper

2 tablespoons curry powder

3 cups chicken broth (or vegetable broth)

28 ounce can of diced tomatoes

⅔ cup creamy peanut butter (or soy nut butter)

Salt and pepper

Optional:
Sour cream

Lime wedges

Shredded, cooked chicken

Cooked rice

1. Place a large pot over medium heat and add the oil. Cook the onion, garlic, and cayenne pepper until the onion becomes translucent, about ten minutes. Add the curry powder and stir for about 1 more minute.

2. Add the broth and the tomatoes and turn the heat down. Simmer for 10 minutes.

3. Remove from the heat and pulverize the mixture with an immersion blender.

4. Bring the soup back up to a simmer and whisk in the peanut butter or soy nut butter. Add salt and pepper to taste.

Note
If desired, serve with sour cream and lime wedges for garnish. Mix in some chicken and/or rice to make this a more filling meal. This recipe freezes well.

Serves 6

SALMOREJO
~ Eva Conti

I am a French horn player in the New Haven Symphony and the Stamford Symphony. I am a New York City freelancer and have played numerous Broadway shows.

This is a traditional cold tomato soup from the Andalusian province in Spain. This soup is traditionally served with chopped, hard-boiled eggs and/or chopped Serrano ham sprinkled on top. *P.S. This is not gazpacho!*

Special Prep/Equipment
Blender or large food processor
Allow 4 hours for chilling.

6 - 7 large juicy tomatoes (not plum)

2 medium cloves of garlic

¼ cup good quality sherry wine vinegar

1 cup extra virgin olive oil

3 - 4 ounces leftover bread or 1 roll torn and soaked in one cup of water for 5 minutes

1 teaspoon of kosher salt

1. Chop the tomatoes and garlic.

2. In a large bowl, mix all listed ingredients together. In small batches blend at high speed in a blender until smooth. Combine all batches in a large container and refrigerate at least 3-4 hours or overnight.

3. This soup is traditionally served with chopped hard-boiled eggs and/or chopped Serrano ham sprinkled on top.

Serves 6 - 8 appetizer portions

EVE ZANNI'S CALDO GALLEGO
Eve Zanni

I am a vocalist, composer, musician and author of *Eve Zanni's Jazz Superheroes*.

Caldo gallego is a simple, traditional, farmer's soup from Galicia, Spain. My first caldo gallego was from the famous Spanish bakery in San Juan, Puerto Rico, Panaderia España, where people line up for this hearty soup, served amongst the alcapurrias, cuchifritos, flans, sweets and savouries. It is a delicious, hearty, satisfying soup that keeps you nutrified all day but isn't heavy or highly seasoned; featuring broth, onions, potatoes, chorizo and greens with many different versions. This is a comfort soup for any season and is found all over Spain and the Spanish Caribbean. As ordinary as the ingredients are, Caldo Gallego always has a "special occasion" feeling to me. I love experiencing the different variations from Cuba to Jackson Heights and I hope to taste them all! My recipe can be done in different ways, which I will provide, so you have options. I am someone who is an improviser and cooks by ear, I describe amounts by handfuls or pinches. I hope that works for people.

Special Prep/Equipment
Large Pot, frying pan

Chicken or vegetable broth (big pot)

1 onion, 1 clove garlic, bay leaf

Olive oil (about 3 tablespoons)

3 white potatoes, peeled, cubed

3 handfuls or so Kale or collard greens, chopped fine

2 cups or so dried Great Northern White beans (Cannellini)

2 chorizos, chopped (or bacon or ham hock)

Salt and pepper to taste

Pinch smoked paprika

Note about the chicken: I buy organic half chicken breasts (skin & bone in) and freeze them singly in freezer baggies. Then when needed, I toss one into a pot of hot water and simmer away till done, seasoning with bay leaf, chicken or vegetable bouillon or miso, and garlic. Boil the half chicken breast/ simmer till falling off the bone. Remove the chicken breast, discard skin, bones, then use the meat for tacos, enchiladas, etc. Having these in the freezer is a great budget-booster and healthier than any can or box of broth you can buy. You can also control how much sodium to add.

Note about the beans: Soak the beans overnight in a pot of water or boil for 3 minutes, then let sit for one hour before cooking. Bring to a boil, then simmer till tender. Since one package of dried beans makes more than I need for a large pot of soup, I cool them then divide them into freezer baggies to freeze till needed for other recipes. Another budget boost.

1. First prepare the broth in a large pot. Put aside.

2. In a frying pan, saute onion and potatoes in olive oil, add bay leaf, and a little garlic.

3. Add onion and potato mixture to the broth, bring to boil, simmer until potatoes are tender. Mash them into the broth which makes the soup feel "creamy" but has no dairy. Add about 3 handfuls of chopped kale or collard greens, about 2 cups of cooked white beans, and simmer till greens are tender, about 10 minutes.

4. Chop, then sear chorizo in the frying pan. Add carats to soup and a pinch of smoked paprika, cook 5 minutes.

5. Serve with a sensual son Cubano, chilled white wine and crusty bread!

Serves 4 with seconds for all

CORN, CABBAGE, & KIELBASA SOUP
〜 Dean LeBlanc

I have been a clarinetist in NYC since 1994 and an Associate Musician with the Metropolitan Opera Orchestra for 23 years. I've also performed with the NY Philharmonic, Philadelphia Orchestra, numerous Broadway shows, and recordings for major motion film soundtracks.

This recipe is in memory of my stepfather, Ray Johnson, who made lots of different wonderful homemade soups and stews during my upbringing in Minnesota. There's nothing like a good soup when it's below zero outside! He made this particular soup once when I came home for the holidays about 20 years ago, and I've been making it ever since. This is my own version that I have developed over the past two decades. It freezes well and is great comfort food for the cold winter months. Enjoy!

Special Prep/Equipment
Large dutch oven or large soup pot

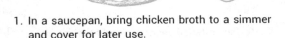

6 cups (48 ounces) low-sodium chicken broth

14 ounce kielbasa sausage, sliced about ¼" thick

¼ cup olive or vegetable oil

2 green peppers, seeded and coarsely chopped

2 medium onions, coarsely chopped

1 (12 ounce jar) of roasted red pepper, drained well and coarsely chopped.

1 large bay leaf

6 cups cabbage, shredded or chopped

Salt, black pepper, white pepper

2 cups corn kernels (fresh, canned, or thawed frozen)

3-4 medium red potatoes, unpeeled and cut into ½" cubes

½ cup milk

½ cream

Paprika

Note:
I always use low-sodium broth because kielbasa sausage can be very high in sodium and you can end up with a very salty soup if you're not careful. Adding salt as you go along will ensure you do not over salt.

1. In a saucepan, bring chicken broth to a simmer and cover for later use.

2. In the dutch oven (or soup pot), brown sausage slices over medium heat. Remove sausage and set aside. Drain most of the fat from the pan leaving behind about a tablespoon.

3. Add oil and saute green peppers, and onions until well caramelized. Add roasted red peppers and sausage while sauteing for another 5 minutes.

4. Add hot chicken broth, bay leaf, cabbage, 1 teaspoon of salt, ¼ teaspoon of white pepper, and ¼ teaspoon of black pepper. Stir well and bring to a boil. Reduce heat, cover, and simmer 30-40 minutes stirring occasionally until cabbage is cooked well.

5. Before adding potatoes, taste and salt as needed keeping in mind that the potatoes will absorb some of the salt. Add potatoes and bring to a boil. Reduce heat and simmer for 15 minutes.

6. Add corn and simmer for another 5 minutes or until potatoes are tender. Remove bay leaf.

7. Remove from heat, then stir in milk and cream. Add additional salt and pepper to taste. Paprika can be sprinkled just before serving, if desired.

Serves 4-6

HEALTHY GROUND BEEF SOUP WITH CABBAGE
Allison Kiger

I'm a flutist in the Allentown Symphony and Garden State Philharmonic. In the summer I go to Maine to perform and work as Associate Director for the Bar Harbor Music School

This was something my Dad's mother would make for us. We call it Georgie's soup.

Special Prep/Equipment
A large heavy pot is needed.

1. In the heavy pot, over medium heat, soften the carrot, celery, and onion in the butter or oil with Italian herbs, a sprinkle of salt and generous helping of black pepper.

2. In a separate, non-stick skillet, cook the ground beef completely over medium heat with more ground black pepper and drain off liquid.

3. To the softened vegetables add the remaining ingredients except the Parmesan, and simmer until the potatoes are soft. Add the drained ground beef and heat thoroughly.

4. Sprinkle with Parmesan cheese for serving.

2 tablespoons olive oil or butter

½ cup each: carrot, celery and onion - all finely chopped

Dried salt-free Italian herbs

Salt and pepper

12 ounces grass fed ground beef

1 (28 ounce) can of whole, low sodium peeled San Marzano tomatoes

1 carton of "no salt added" beef broth

1 large potato with skin, finely chopped

¼ head of green cabbage, finely chopped

2 bay leaves

Grated Parmesan cheese for serving

Serves 6-8

SWEET SOUP
Julie Goodale

I play viola and I love food. I love all aspects of food: eating, cooking, growing it, sometimes foraging, and I love feeding other people. All my recipes are decidedly vague; I constantly experiment and adapt. Also, I think I'm not very good at following instructions.

My ancestors were Norwegian and Irish immigrants, homesteaders on the Great Plains, from the mid-19th century, through the Great Depression and World Wars, to modern farms. I grew up hearing how my great-great grandmother cooked lefsa (thin potato crepes) on the wood stove. She kept her sugar locked in a cabinet in her bedroom in order to keep it safe, just in case one of the dust bowl hobos roaming the land tried to steal food. Many of those stories from the Depression came back to me when the music business was completely shut down from Covid. I made my grandmother's bread recipe, and learned about canning and pickling. This recipe (such as it is) was a favorite of my grandparents, and I've been told that Julia, my great-great grandmother, always had a pot of sweet soup stewing on her wood stove (which she kept stoked with wood that she chopped herself).

Special Prep/Equipment
Large soup pot

1. In a large pot, soak tapioca pearls in water overnight. Next day, add more water and cook very slowly on low heat. As the tapioca expands, you may need to add more water. When tapioca is almost translucent, add a couple cups of dried fruit. Add a cinnamon stick or a few cloves – I like to add a few cardamom pods. Pour in a splash of fruit juice if you have some.

2. When everything has softened up, add some fresh fruit. Peeled and sliced orange or an apple are nice. A bit of orange zest brightens it up. If it gets too thick, add more water or juice.

1 cup large pearl tapioca	Fruit juice
Dried fruit: prunes, raisins, apricots, cranberries, blueberries, cherries (whatever is available)	1 orange or apple
	Zest of 1 orange, optional
1 cinnamon stick or cloves, cardamom pods	Sugar

3. After a few hours of slowly stewing, it's ready to eat...with oatmeal, on ice cream, with a little cream. Yes, this is vague, use whatever you have or like, a little more or less won't matter. Add a pinch or two of sugar to taste if needed. As my grandmother wrote in her recipe book: "You just kind of make it by ear."

**This will feed a family and last a week.
It also freezes nicely.**

JOAN KENNIFF'S DANISH FRUIT SOUP
Christopher Kenniff

I am a classical guitarist - performer and instructor. I'm also in arts administration working as Dean of the Hoff-Barthelson Music School in Scarsdale, New York, home to some of the most wonderful faculty and students to be found anywhere!

This recipe is handed down from my maternal grandparents to my mother, Joan Kenniff (a superb pianist and teacher) and to me. It is commonly enjoyed at breakfast-time during winter months, particularly during the holiday season.

Special Prep/Equipment
Purchase only organic dried fruit (no sulfur added)

1. Place all ingredients, except tapioca and fruit juice, in a large pot, and cover all with water.

2. Bring to a boil then reduce to simmer until all fruit is soft. (Can also leave to soak until soft.)

3. Soften tapioca in 1 cup of organic fruit juice (any kind!) or water.

4. Once soft, add to the fruit. Stir in while simmering, until tapioca is distributed evenly.

5. Let cool overnight.

6. Serve cold!

Serves 8

5 ounces prunes

2 ounces dried apples

2 ounces dried peaches, (break big pieces in 3rds)

6 ounces dried Mediterranean apricots

5 ounces dried cranberries

2 ounces raisins (brown)

½ cinnamon stick

2 tablespoons tapioca

1 cup of organic fruit juice

Feel free to add or substitute other types of dried fruits such as oranges or cherries.

VEGETARIAN SPLIT PEA
Valerie Levy

I'm a violinist who freelances in the NYC area. I've performed countless times in venues from Carnegie Hall to Madison Square Garden, to quiet Jazz clubs.

Looking for a simple, hearty vegetarian version of this staple, I use smoked paprika to give it a bit of that smoky taste usually gotten from bacon or ham. This can be a hearty main course when served with some crusty bread and a salad.

Special Prep/Equipment
Fine grater or microplane for garlic, immersion blender to finish soup

1-2 tablespoons of olive oil	8 cups of water or vegetable stock
1 large yellow onion, finely chopped	small bunch of parsley, chopped
2 medium stalks of celery, chopped	Salt and pepper to taste,
2 medium carrots, chopped	about ½ teaspoon smoked paprika, or more to taste
1 large potato cut into half inch cubes	
1 pound dried split peas, picked over for any pebbles or debris, then rinsed and drained	3-4 cloves of garlic, grated finely

1 Cover the bottom of a large soup pot with enough olive oil to generously coat.

2. Add the chopped onion and saute for 2-3 minutes. Add the celery and carrots, and saute another 2 minutes, or until the onion is turning clear. Add the potato, split peas, cover with water or vegetable stock, and bring to a boil. Reduce heat, add parsley and salt and pepper to taste and cook, stirring occasionally, until split peas begin to soften, or about an hour.

3. Add smoked paprika and finely grated garlic. Add water, if necessary and simmer for another 30 minutes or so until peas are quite soft. Remove from heat. The soup will thicken as it rests and cools.

4. *Optional step:* Before serving, I like to smooth out the consistency by carefully using a hand-held immersion blender in the pot for a few seconds. Be careful to follow blender instructions to avoid splatters.

Note
Leftover soup will continue to thicken overnight. It may be thinned out by adding more water before reheating.

Serves 6-8

MEXICAN RICE & BEAN SOUP
~ Natalie D. Kriegler, violinist

This soup was our Thanksgiving Day appetizer!

Special Prep/Equipment
Large soup pot

1 onion, chopped	2 cups low sodium vegetable broth
A few garlic cloves, chopped/minced	2 cups vegan tomato broth
6 mushrooms chopped	2 cups of cooked brown rice
2 large fresh tomatoes	
1 or 2 small chipotle peppers	¼ cup cilantro
Olive oil	
A few teaspoons (2-2½) cumin	¼ cup fresh squeezed lime juice
Kidney beans cooked from fresh whole beans (use judgement on how much to cook)	Sliced avocado

1. Saute onion, garlic, mushrooms, tomato and chipotle peppers in large soup pot in a thin layer of olive oil. Add cumin, fresh cooked beans, vegetable and tomato broth and heat thoroughly.

2. Add the brown rice, cilantro, and lime juice and heat a bit more. Serve with a bit more cilantro and sliced avocado per bowl or cup and enjoy!

Serves 8-10

As a music student in Milan, Giacomo Puccini was largely broke.

"In the afternoon, when I have money, I go to the café," he told his mother. "But many evenings I cannot go, since a punch costs 40 cents. I do not starve. I stuff myself with thin broth of minestrone and the stomach is satisfied."

SALADS & SIDES

AVOCADO & PEANUT SALAD
∾ Pat Hackbarth

I play the french horn, in concerts, in ballet orchestras, in chamber groups, and on Broadway, etc...

This idea was inspired by avocado and peanut sushi, a variety offered by a couple of favorite Japanese restaurants.

Salad greens, your choice. I use baby leaf lettuce or red butter lettuce.

Olive oil, to taste. I use a blood orange-infused oil, and it works really well with avocado.

Balsamic vinegar, to taste

½ avocado per serving, sliced

Small handful of peanuts per serving, salted or unsalted

1. Mix oil and vinegar with greens.
2. Lay avocado slices on top.
3. Sprinkle peanuts over salad.
4. Hard to go wrong! Enjoy!

Serves 1 per ½ avocado

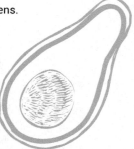

HERB SALAD DRESSING
∾ Jackie Stern

I'm a cellist and I freelance in a number of orchestras and play in two chamber groups. I'm also a teacher and conductor of young orchestras.

This is my friend Carolyn's recipe. It can be made with whatever herbs you have around (okay to leave out what you don't have). I also use some dried herbs instead of the fresh ones when I don't have them. (I use about ⅓ the amount indicated when I use dried herbs). This recipe is very forgiving!

½ cup apple cider vinegar

⅓ cup brown sugar

¾ cup olive oil

2 tablespoons chopped mint

2 tablespoons chopped thyme

2 tablespoons chopped rosemary

2 tablespoons poppy seeds

3 tablespoons mayonnaise

Salt and pepper

1. Heat apple cider vinegar in a small pot with the brown sugar. When sugar has dissolved, slowly whisk in the olive oil and bring to a slow boil. Season with salt and pepper.

2. Cool slightly and then stir in the chopped herbs, poppy seeds and mayo. Whisk until well mixed. Allow to cool.

Yields about 1½ cups of dressing, good for several large salads

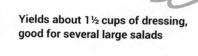

BEAN SALAD
Nancie Lederer

I work as a freelance violinist and have played with a number of orchestras and chamber groups throughout the Tri-State area. I also have a private teaching studio in West Caldwell, New Jersey.

My family enjoys outdoor get-togethers in the warmer months so I'm always on the lookout for easy, healthy dishes that can be prepared ahead of time. This is a recipe I adapted from Bon Appetit Magazine and it has been very well received over the years. It can easily be made for larger crowds, and tastes even better the next day.

Special Prep/Equipment

A whisk is helpful (although it's not totally critical!)

1 (15½ ounce) can black-eyed peas, rinsed and drained

1 (15½ ounce) can red or pink beans, rinsed and drained

1 (20 ounce) can chopped pineapple, drained

1 (7 ounce) jar roasted red peppers, drained and chopped

1 small red onion, finely chopped

⅓ cup of cilantro, chopped

2 tablespoons Dijon mustard

1 tablespoon cider vinegar

¼ cup olive oil

Pinch each of salt and pepper

1. Gently mix the first 6 ingredients in a bowl.

2. In a smaller bowl, whisk the Dijon and vinegar, then gradually whisk in the olive oil.

3. Pour the dressing into the bean mixture and season with salt and pepper.

4. This can be made a day ahead, just cover and refrigerate.

Serves 6

*G*iuseppe Verdi, after he became rich from operas, retired and bought a farm. "Now that I'm not manufacturing any more notes, I'm planting cabbages and beans."

BABA'S PEDOHAY (PIEROGIES)
～ Kate Spingarn

I am a classically trained cellist and have been happily sawing away on Broadway for about a decade.

My mom's mom, a.k.a. Baba, was born and raised in Ukraine, until she emigrated as a young mother to Canada in 1946. She was also one of the most extraordinary home chefs I've ever known. She cooked and baked delicious (often very complicated) foods all day, every day, in her cozy, colorful kitchen in Windsor, Ontario. Really, her food was her art form, and she was a true master.

This is my adaptation of one of her simpler dishes, her "recipe" for pedohay, which is my Anglicized spelling for Ukrainian potato dumplings, just like Polish pierogies. Baba never followed recipes, everything was stored in her brain, and so every dish she made had the same recipe: "You just put, and put, and put, until is ENOUGH… and then you stop!"

In my 20s, when Baba was still living at home and cooking up a storm, my husband and I started following her around her kitchen with a camera and a notepad to try to capture some of these "recipes". This is an adaptation of one of those, scaled down from her enormous portions. This will yield a bit more than 3 dozen pedohay, which is enough for two dinners for our family of three. I would think the recipe is easily doubled. Or if you want to make hundreds and hundreds at a time, as Baba did, multiply as you will.

Pedohay are a bit of a production to make, for sure, even in such a relatively small quantity. Perhaps because of that, they've been in fairly regular rotation since the shutdown – the process fills up a couple hours in these amorphous days, and then forming and lining up the rows of adorable dumplings is an engaging family project. My daughter is 13, and the pandemic shutdown has been especially hard on her (as it has on so many kids her age). But she perks up every time we've sat together and made these – a meditative and satisfying project that is also a small, yummy part of her heritage.

I use the dough recipe from the King Arthur flour website, because I find it easier to work with than Baba's more finicky dough. But the secret, extra-delicious ingredient in the filling is the milk-simmered onion – that's all Baba. We usually serve these alongside some slices of kielbasa, and a salad or other simple vegetable.

Special Prep/Equipment
Approx 12 x 16" enameled or glass baking tray

For Dough:
2 cups unbleached all-purpose flour

½ teaspoon salt

1 large egg

½ cup sour cream

4 tablespoons butter, room temperature

For Filling:
1 medium onion, diced small

¾ cup milk (I prefer whole milk)

½ pound potato, peeled and quartered (Yukon gold or Russets)

1 cup grated sharp cheddar cheese

4 tablespoons cream cheese, cubed

To Finish:
4 tablespoons butter

½ onion or 1 shallot, thinly sliced

Sour cream as garnish

1. *Make the dough:* Mix together the flour and salt. Add the egg to the flour and combine. The dough will be quite clumpy at this stage.

2. Work in the sour cream and soft butter until the dough comes together in a slightly rough, slightly sticky ball.

3. Using just your fingertips, knead and fold the dough without adding additional flour until the dough becomes less sticky but still quite moist.

4. Wrap the dough well in plastic wrap and refrigerate for 30-60 minutes, or up to 48 hours.

5. *Make the filling:* Bring milk and onion to a low boil over medium heat, then lower heat to simmer and stir occasionally until onion is very soft and fragrant and most of the milk has been absorbed, 20-25 minutes.

6. Meanwhile, boil potatoes in a large pot of salted water to cover until tender, about 15-20 minutes.

7. When potatoes are done, drain, return to pot, and mash thoroughly with the onion mixture and both cheeses. Generously season to taste with kosher salt and fresh pepper. (This filling is very tasty. Resist eating it all.)

8. *Fill the pedohay:* Roll half the dough ⅛" thick. Use a 2" round cutter or rim of small drinking glass to cut circles of dough. (Save the scraps; these can be re-rolled to make more pedohay.)

9. Repeat with the other half of the dough when needed.

10. Place 1-1½ teaspoons of filling on each round of dough. Gently fold the dough over, forming a pocket around the filling, and taking care that the filling doesn't get to the edge of the dough in order to keep the seal tight. Pinch the edges of the pedohay gently but thoroughly to seal, and line them up on a baking sheet or cutting board lined with a lightly floured dish cloth or piece of parchment paper.

11. At this point the pedohay can be frozen for up to 4 weeks (you can freeze them right on the lined tray, and then once frozen store them in a Zip-loc bag), or they can be cooked fresh in a large stockpot of boiling salted water. Only cook about a dozen pedohay at a time, so that they have room to float without sticking. When the dumplings float, they're done. The time will vary depending if they are fresh or frozen. Gently scoop them out with a slotted spoon.

12. To finish: Meanwhile, sauté the shallots or onion in the butter in a large skillet with a pinch of salt, until the onion is golden brown, about 15 minutes. Add the drained pedohay and gently stir to combine.

13. Serve hot with sour cream, or other condiments.

Serves about 6 as a side dish
(Yields 3½ dozen perogies)

*O*ne of the very best things about life is the way we must regularly stop whatever it is we are doing and devote our attention to eating.

∽ Luciano Pavarotti

ZUCCHINI WITH TOMATO SAUCE, CHEESE, & MIDDLE EASTERN SPICES

～ Diane Bruce

I am a freelance violinist with the American Symphony Orchstra, American Composers Orchestra, the Chautauqua Symphony and many other groups. Recently I've been teaching masked violin in my backyard when the weather is nice, and via Zoom as it's gotten colder. I'm also an Alexander Technique teacher.

When I'm in Chautauqua during the summer there's a lovely tradition of orchestra members hosting Sunday afternoon volleyball/potluck parties for the musicians, their families and friends. Luckily you don't have to play volleyball to attend! I don't remember the first time I made this dish, undoubtedly it was when there was a ton of zucchini at the local farm stand. I had fallen in love with ground coriander and cumin, and had some leftover pasta sauce in the fridge so I threw it in. The cheese on top started with a sprinkle and then evolved into a whole bag of shredded cheese. It's always been a hit – even the kids like it! You can halve the recipe if you're not planning to feed a lot of people, but I highly recommend the left-overs. Like so many dishes, it tastes even better the second or third day.

Special Prep/Equipment

Large heavy gauge frying pan/saucepan.
(I use non-stick, but it doesn't have to be.)

6 medium-large zucchinis, julienned (in the neighborhood of 2" x ⅓" x ⅓")

3 - 4 tablespoons EVOO (extra virgin olive oil)

2 medium-large onions, coarsely chopped

3 - 4 stalks celery, coarsely chopped

1 heaping tablespoon ground coriander

1 scant tablespoon ground cumin

5 - 6 large cloves garlic, chopped

24 ounce jar marinara sauce (you may not end up using the whole jar)

8 ounces, or more to taste, of a mildish shredded cheese (I use Cheddar, Colby Jack, Mexican blend or mozzarella)

1. Steam the zucchini for a few minutes to soften. Don't pack it too tightly in the steamer basket, so that it can evenly cook. You may have to do this in batches.

2. Let the zucchini cool to room temperature and then use your hands to squeeze out the excess water. It doesn't have to be perfect, but it will saute better if it's not water logged. Set aside this squeezed liquid and either save the rest for a future soup base, drink it (it's sweet and full of nutrients) or toss it (but I don't want to know about it if you do that).

3. While the zucchini is cooling, heat the EVOO in the pan. Add the chopped onions, celery and spices. Turn down the flame to medium; cook till soft, 5 - 7 minutes, stirring often so the mixture doesn't burn.

4. Add the cooled zucchini and stir to separate the pieces and let them mingle with the onions for a few minutes. Stir in the chopped garlic. If the mixture is drying out or sticking to the pan, add a little more oil and/or some of the reserved zucchini juice. You can also turn the heat lower.

5. After this zucchini mixture has cooked for a few more minutes add half the jar of marinara sauce. Add more, to achieve a moist but not soupy consistency. Turn down the flame to a low simmer, and cook for 10 min. or longer, till the zucchini is quite soft and even mushy. You can add the rest of the marinara sauce and/or more of the zucchini juice as it cooks if the zucchini is drying out.

6. At this point, if you don't intend to serve it immediately, you can turn off the flame, cover the pan and let it sit for a couple of hours. The flavors will meld and intensify.

7. Before serving, reheat, and when it's bubbling a bit, sprinkle the cheese over the top and cover so that the cheese melts. Serve hot or at room temperature.

> **Note**
> If you're vegan and not using the cheese you could add some chopped olives, and/or capers along with the marinara sauce to give it a little pizzazz. You can also add olives to the regular recipe.

Serves 10-12

EASY VEGETABLE FRIED RICE
ꙮ Sarah Badavas

I play violin, and I freelance and teach.

This is an easy, "throw in whatever you've got handy" recipe created in an effort to work more vegetables into lunch and dinner. If you have rice already made, and pre-shredded vegetables, it's a super quick dish to prepare. For some this might be too light on the rice and too heavy on the veggies. Adjust to your preference! Both my kids like it; a small victory.

Special Prep/Equipment

Large skillet

- 3-4 tablespoons avocado oil
- ½ cup leeks, white part, cut lengthwise and thinly sliced in half circles
- 5-6 cups loosely packed shredded cabbage (green or red or a mix); about 8 ounces
- 1 cup shredded carrots
- 1 cup frozen shelled edamame
- 3-4 cups cooked brown rice
- 3-4 tablespoons coconut aminos
- 1 tablespoon blackstrap molasses

Note:
Feel free to add or substitute other vegetables such as peas, snap peas, broccoli, cauliflower, etc.

1. Warm the avocado oil in skillet over medium heat. Add leeks and saute for 2-3 minutes.

2. Add cabbage and carrots and cook for 5-6 minutes, stirring occasionally, until tender-crunchy.

3. Heat edamame in microwave until barely done. (Subtract time from instructions on bag so they're not mushy.) Drain water and add them to the skillet.

4. Microwave the cooked brown rice 30-40 seconds and add to the skillet. Stir gently. Turn burner heat to low.

5. Drizzle the coconut aminos and molasses over everything. Stir, let cook for 3-4 minutes more, and serve.

Serves 4 as a side dish

RICE WITH OLIVES & PISTACHIOS
～ Dave Romano

I'm a double-bass player, and I've been playing in New York City since 1997. I regularly perform with the American Ballet Theater, the New Jersey Symphony Orchestra, the Metropolitan Opera Orchestra, as well as playing on various Broadway shows.

This was a totally improvisatory recipe that I threw together years ago when my friend, violinist Louise Owen, came over for dinner one night. I probably would have completely forgotten about it if Louise hadn't liked it so much and kept talking about it! Now it's in regular rotation in my kitchen.

This recipe is a guideline. Feel free to improvise in your own way — add crumbled feta or grated Parmesan, swap out some other favorite olives, etc. — but the pistachios and parsley are a must. It makes a great side dish to accompany a grilled steak or roast chicken, but it's terrific on its own.

1½ cups short-grain white rice

1 cup Castellevetrano green olives, pitted

¾ cup raw pistachios, shelled

A large handful of Italian flat-leaf parsley

3 tablespoons of olive oil, plus more as needed

1 lemon, zest finely grated and juice squeezed

Salt and pepper

1. Cook the rice according to package directions.

2. While the rice is cooking, prep the other ingredients. Roughly chop the olives, followed by the pistachios. Coarsely chop the parsley, leaves and about an inch of the soft stems.

3. When the rice has cooked, fluff it with a fork. Add the olives, pistachios, parsley, olive oil, lemon zest and 2 tablespoons of lemon juice to the warm rice. Toss the ingredients together and season with salt and pepper. Taste for balance, adding more olive oil, lemon juice, salt and pepper as needed. Serve warm.

Serves 4

MAPPINA (BITTER GREENS SALAD)
～ Steven Masi

I am a pianist. I have performed internationally and recorded the complete Beethoven Sonatas for Albany Records. My new recording for Navona is entitled Brahmsiana. I am on the faculty of the Thurnauer School of Music.

This is a salad that my great aunt Lucille says came from my great grandfather's restaurant, Capalbo's in Throggs Neck (Bronx). She called it "Mappina" and made it every Christmas. Italians love bitter greens and the heat from the pepper gives this real character. Please resist adding vinegar to the salad, especially balsamic vinegar.

Special Prep/Equipment
Once you assemble this salad, it needs to sit for 2-3 days

1. Chop the chicory leaves coarsely.

2. In a shallow, wide bowl mix the leaves with the other ingredients.

3. Put a plate on top and a weight on the plate. (A couple cans of tomatoes will do)

2 heads of chicory	1 mild chili pepper
3-4 tablespoons good quality olive oil	Some dried hot pepper
3-4 garlic cloves, chopped	Salt

4. Leave it unrefrigerated in a cool place for 2-3 days.

Serves 6-8

SUCCOTASH
~ Sarah Adams

I have been a violist, member of Local 802 freelance orchestras for more than 30 years, as well as on Broadway, at Lincoln Center, in recording studios, and as music faculty at Columbia University. I am a mom of 5, chamber musician, dog rescuer, and enthusiastic cook and gardener.

This recipe is at its best in the height of summer tomato and zucchini harvest, when your herb garden is also producing vigorously. But it is just as good when you are camping on cape cod or stuck in the house in a pandemic but don't want to go out for more veggies. My favorite memories of this dish are when my kids were small, and the taste of our garden was enough to make them swoon when I brought this bubbling pan to the table.

Special Prep/Equipment
Big saute pan with a lid

1½-2 tablespoons olive oil, to cover the pan bottom in a thin layer

2 small or 1 large zucchini, sliced

2 small or 1 large yellow squash, sliced

2 small or 1 large onion, sliced or chopped

Fresh tomatoes, chopped (as available, to taste)

Water, enough to cover, add more as necessary

Salt and pepper

Fresh thyme, oregano, basil, rosemary

1. The beauty is there is no particular order required. Put all ingredients in large saute pan, on high heat til it is bubbling, Cover with lid, turn heat down to simmer. Cook until zucchini and onions are tender. Add more water if it gets dry. You want a nice sauce.

2. Adjust salt and pepper to taste. Omit or add fresh herbs to taste. Dried herbs will be much stronger tasting, so go easy.

3. Add fresh corn, lima beans, or other fresh garden veggie according to availability or preference. If you don't have fresh tomatoes, you can use salsa, tomato sauce or paste.

Serves a family of 7 if you eat something else too

KALE WITH GARLIC & ONIONS
~ Matthew Goodman

I am the Clarinet/Eb Clarinet/Bass Clarinetist for *The Phantom of the Opera* Broadway Orchestra

Both my mother and grandmother were wonderful cooks. My mother would be fairly clear about how she made things, and would write down recipes. However, when I would ask my grandmother to tell me the ingredients of her wonderful Eastern European dishes, which often took days of preparation, she would invariably respond, "you use what you have in the house!" Inspired by this wisdom, I put together these ingredients, which I happened to have in the house.

Special Prep/Equipment
Large pot

2 bunches kale	4 anchovy filets, minced
2 garlic cloves	Salt and pepper
3 medium onions	*Note:* This recipe also works well with beet greens.
4 tablespoons olive oil	

1. Wash kale thoroughly. Separate the stems from the leaves. Chop the stems into 1 inch pieces. Break the leaves into smaller pieces, about 2 inches square. Chop the garlic. Chop the onions.

2. Heat the olive oil in a large pot (big enough to accommodate all the kale leaves) over medium low heat, and add the garlic. Stir for about 30 seconds, or until fragrant. Add the onions, and cook, stirring occasionally, until limp, about 5 minutes. Add the kale stems, and the minced anchovies. Add pepper to taste. Anchovies are salty, so additional salt may not be needed. Cook about 10 minutes, stirring occasionally, until the stems soften a bit. Add the kale leaves, and cover the pot for a few minutes.

3. Uncover the pot, and stir, so that the onions and garlic mix in with the kale.

4. Taste for salt and pepper, and add more if desired. Keep stirring until done, when the leaves have wilted but still have some texture. Do not overcook.

Serves 6

VEGAN STYLE MASSAGED KALE SALAD
~ Wendy Stern

I am a flutist and a teacher. This recipe is adapted from *Cookus Interruptus*...the original recipe included cheese.

Special Prep/Equipment
Large salad bowl and strong hands to massage the kale

⅓ cup toasted sunflower seeds	⅓ cup currants
1 large bunch kale	1 apple, diced
1 teaspoon sea salt	¼ cup olive oil
¼ cup red onion, diced	2 tablespoons apple cider vinegar

1. Toast sunflower seeds by putting in a dry skillet over low-medium heat and stir constantly for a few minutes until they change color and give off a nutty aroma. Set aside.

2. De-stem kale by pulling leaf away from the stem. Wash leaves and spin or pat dry.

3. Stack leaves, roll up, and slice into thin ribbons.

4. Put kale into a large mixing bowl. Add salt and massage salt into kale with your hands for 2 whole minutes. The volume of the kale should reduce by about ⅓.

5. Transfer kale to a fresh bowl, and discard any leftover liquid.

6. Stir onions, currants, apple, and toasted seeds into kale.

7. Dress with the oil and vinegar.

Serves 6

KALE & CANNELLINIS
～ Kirsten Agresta Copely

I am an international award-winning harpist, composer, and arranger, and am based in Brooklyn, NY.

Adapted from a Giada de Laurentiis recipe, this reminds me of my Italian heritage and is a simple main course or hearty side dish that I love!

Special Prep/Equipment
Dutch oven

2 cups dry white beans

6 cups water

1 fresh sprig of sage

4 smashed & peeled garlic cloves

½ cup + 2 tablespoons extra-virgin olive oil

¼ pound pancetta, diced

¼ cup pine nuts

1 large bunch kale (Tuscan or curly)

1¾ teaspoon salt

½ teaspoon crushed red pepper flakes

½ cup Parmesan Reggiano cheese

1. Combine the beans, water, sage, garlic and 2 tablespoons olive oil in your dutch oven or large pot. Bring to a boil and then simmer on medium-low for 1 hour and 20 minutes, stirring often until the beans are tender.

2. While the beans cook, heat a small skillet, and put in the diced pancetta. Stir and cook for a few minutes until cooked through, and starting to brown. Remove from pan, and set aside on paper towels to drain any excess oil.

3. Into this same skillet, place your pine nuts, and toss for a minute or two only, until fragrant and lightly toasted. Remove to a separate plate.

4. Add kale, salt, red pepper flakes to the beans and stir to combine. Add in the pancetta. Cover the pot and simmer for another 15 minutes. until the kale is wilted. Stir in the Parmesan and ½ cup olive oil.

5. Serve hot with pine nuts as a garnish.

Serves 4 as a side dish, 2-3 as a main course

ISRAELI SALAD
Jackie Schiller

I'm a pianist and teacher. I'm also an avid chamber musician and perform with the All Seasons Chamber Players and Alacorde Piano Trio.

When my kids were younger and we would go on vacations, they would always say how much they can't wait to get home so they could have my Israeli salad! It's an everyday staple in our home with lunch or dinner...actually sometimes with breakfast too!

2 cucumbers

2 tomatoes

1 red, green, or yellow pepper

A few scallions

Small amount of shredded lettuce (optional)

Olive oil, lemon juice, salt and pepper to taste

Note: Sometimes I add radishes, green olives, or even carrots – whatever is in my fridge.

Special Prep/Equipment
Large salad bowl for serving

1. Dice all the vegetables into small pieces.

2. Add olive oil, lemon juice, salt and pepper to taste, and mix.

Serves 5

SPICY CUCUMBER SALAD
Nadine Hur

I am an ex-New York flutist who loves to eat, explore and learn about food!

This recipe is from my flute teacher from Hawaii, Jean Harling. She was an amazing flutist who loved to cook and teach. If you like crunchy, spicy, and sweet, this salad will make a refreshing pair to many main dishes. This recipe is easy to modify the sweetness, acidity, and spiciness to your liking.

Special Prep/Equipment
This salad needs an hour or more to chill in the fridge before serving.

1. Thinly slice cucumbers and place them in a bowl.

2. Dissolve sugar in boiling water and stir in white vinegar and salt.

3. Pour hot liquid over cucumbers and add red chili pepper and garlic.

4. Mix well, chill for at least an hour or more and serve.

3 English cucumbers or 6 Persian cucumbers

5 tablespoons sugar

1 cup boiling water

½ cup white vinegar

1 teaspoon salt

1 or more (to your liking) fresh small red chili pepper, seeded and finely chopped

½ clove crushed garlic

Serves 4

RICOTTA POTATO CASSEROLE
〜 Tanya Dusevic Witek

I play flute and piccolo in the New York City Ballet Orchestra, the Mostly Mozart Festival Orchestra, and I am a freelance teaching artist.

This is a variation on a potato casserole my mother made when I was a child. During the COVID-19 pandemic, I often purchased large containers of ricotta from a local farm. I began to experiment with using ricotta in many recipes and these potatoes became a household favorite.

Special Prep/Equipment
Large casserole baking dish

This casserole can be assembled ahead and refrigerated until ready to bake. Alternatively, the casserole can be prepared and baked, and then reheated in a 375° oven for approximately 40 minutes.

3 pounds russet or Yukon gold potatoes (6-8 large potatoes) peeled and cut into ½" cubes

4 - 6 large garlic cloves

Kosher salt and pepper

6 tablespoons butter

1¼ cup ricotta

½ cup milk or half and half

1 cup grated cheddar cheese to mix in

¼ cup green onions, chopped

¼ cup fresh bacon bits (optional)

½ - 1 cup grated cheddar cheese to sprinkle on top of the full casserole (optional)

1. Preheat oven to 375°.

2. Boil the potatoes, garlic cloves and 1 teaspoon salt in a pot of water over high heat for approximately 25 minutes or until soft. Drain potatoes and garlic. Mash with a potato masher and place butter over potatoes to melt. Continue to mash in the butter. Add the ricotta cheese, salt and pepper to taste, and milk or half and half. Use a hand immersion blender (if available) or hand mixer to blend until creamy.

3. Stir in 1 cup grated cheddar cheese, green onions and bacon bits if desired. Spoon mixture into a large casserole dish and sprinkle with grated cheese.

4. Bake for 30-40 minutes in preheated oven.

Serves 8

WILD RICE SALAD
Rachel Drehmann

I play the french horn; I play on Broadway and freelance all over the city.

As a freelancer, I am always on the go and I usually try to bring food with me so I don't always have to eat out. I always like to feel good when performing, and that starts with eating good food. I enjoy eating salads but always try to find ways to make them a little more hearty for a meal on the go. This salad also works as a side at home.

Special Prep/Equipment
I use wild rice for the salad, since it's higher in protein and I grew up eating it in the Northern Midwest. Find good wild rice and cook per instructions.

1. Make the vinaigrette: mix shallot, lime, vinegar, salt/pepper and then whisk in olive oil.

2. Combine all salad ingredients together and add vinaigrette. Toss and serve.

Serves 2

1 cup cooked wild rice

A few handfuls baby spinach

1 ounce feta cheese, crumbled

½ red bell pepper, chopped

Handful of parsley, chopped

Shallot vinaigrette:
1 small shallot, finely chopped

Juice from half a lime

½ tablespoon red wine vinegar or apple cider vinegar

Salt and pepper to taste

1 - 3 tablespoons good olive oil

EASY CORN PUDDING
Russel Anixter

I am a music copyist and arranger. My music copying business specializes in preparing music for Broadway shows, regional theater, Radio City Christmas, live concerts and recording sessions.

This recipe came from a friend's family Thanksgiving dinner years ago. It's a real comfort food thing. I don't know if it originated on the back of a box somewhere or not.

Special Prep/Equipment
Blender or food processor

1 stick of butter

1 can of corn niblets

1 can of cream corn

1 small container of sour cream (reduced fat is ok)

1 egg

1. Preheat oven 350°.

2. In a casserole dish, melt the stick of butter in the oven.

3. When the butter is melted add the ingredients in the order above, and stir it up.

1 box Jiffy Corn Muffin Mix

Note:
You can add cheese or jalapeños if you want some variations. I've tried it with cheddar cheese, and I've also tried it with pepper jack.

4. Bake in the oven for about 45 minutes or until the top and edges get a little browned.

Serves 8 as a side dish

GRANDMA TESSIE'S EGGPLANT SALAD
～ Adria Benjamin

I am a violist, teacher, orchestra and chamber music musician, orchestra personnel manager and administrator.

This recipe is a family favorite, made for holidays and special dinners.

Special Prep/Equipment
Line a rimmed cookie sheet with parchment paper.

1. Preheat oven to 450°. (Don't put the eggplant and peppers in the oven until the oven has reached 450°).

2. Prick eggplant with a fork and bake with peppers on a parchment paper lined cookie sheet until eggplant and peppers are charred. This should take about 20 minutes, depending on your oven. Make sure to turn the cookie sheet around in the oven after 10 minutes for equal heat distribution.

3. After cooling, peel and seed the eggplant and peppers.

4. Chop by hand the eggplant and peppers with the onions and garlic. This salad should have texture to it.

5. Add the oil, vinegar, and salt.

6. Adjust seasoning and refrigerate, covered, for one day before serving.

1 large eggplant

1 green pepper

1 red pepper

2 medium onions, finely chopped

2 cloves garlic, crushed (or 3 if you love, love, love garlic)

¼ cup extra virgin oil

3 tablespoons red wine vinegar

1 teaspoon salt

Note: You can also add fresh herbs such as chopped parsley, dill or tarragon.

Serves 6 easily

ROSOLS (a.k.a. POTATO SALAD)
～ Una Tone

I play violin and viola. I have been concertmaster of *Miss Saigon*, *On The Town*, and have played many Broadway shows, tours, concerts and recordings. I love any projects that involve the amazing talent of NYC.

Rosols is the most important part of every celebratory table in Latvia. You won't find a single Latvian who has not made it or eaten it.

Special Prep/Equipment
The potatoes and eggs need time to cook and to chill in the fridge.

1. Boil potatoes, chill. Boil eggs, chill.

2. Chop bologna, pickles, potatoes, eggs. Drain the canned peas and add. Stir, and mix in sour cream and mayo, enough to make a creamy texture.

3. Pepper it. Mix it and refrigerate.

8 large potatoes	1 can of peas
6 eggs	½ - ¾ cup sour cream
20 slices bologna	½ - ¾ cup mayo
Small jar of kosher pickles	Black pepper

Serves 4

SPINACH FRITTATA
~ Barbara Merjan

I'm a drummer/percussionist. I play jazz, Japanese taiko, contemporary american music and show music.

My mom used to make this as one of the side dishes at family holiday dinners, so I make it now on those holidays.

Special Prep/Equipment
8 x 12 x 2" glass baking pan

1. Preheat oven to 425°.

2. Oil your glass baking pan generously. Sprinkle with matzo meal.

3. Squeeze excess water from spinach. Mix with 5 beaten eggs and pot cheese.

4. Add Romano cheese and remaining oil, salt and pepper. Stir lightly.

5. Pour over matzo meal. Sprinkle feta cheese on top and put the remaining beaten egg over all.

6. Bake in preheated oven for about 30 minutes.

7. Top should be nice and browned. Best served hot.

Serves 8 as a side dish

⅓ cup oil

½ - ¾ cup matzo meal

2 (10 ounce) packages frozen chopped spinach, defrosted

6 large eggs (divided)

8 ounces pot cheese, (cottage, ricotta or farmers are good substitutes)

¼ cup grated Romano cheese

Salt and pepper to taste

1 cup feta cheese crumbled

COLESLAW
~ Rebecca Harris-Lee

I am a freelance violinist, and a mother of three. I live in Montclair, NJ.

I am a member of the Madison String Quartet, and we did a residency with the Kenai Peninsula Orchestra every summer, giving us the opportunity to perform as a quartet and as mentors in the orchestra. We met some individualistic, amazing musicians in the towns of Soldotna and Homer. One friend, amateur violinist Linda Reinhart, made this killer cole slaw for one of the potluck dinners offered at rehearsal break. Anyone who has spent any time in Alaska knows that just about everything is eaten WITH SALMON, so this slaw was a perfect compliment! This recipe reminds me of Alaska, where gardening was taken very seriously. The vegetable gardens were amazing because of the extraordinarily long summer days.

Special Prep/Equipment

Blender or food processor

1. Make the dressing. Put all dressing ingredients (except the oil and greek yogurt) in a blender. Then, turn the blender on high, and add oil and yogurt.

2. Chop all vegetables, and mix with dressing. Add salt to taste.

Serves 6-8 as a side dish

Slaw:
One head cabbage

¼ sweet onion

4-6 leaves dark kale

3 shredded carrots

Dressing:
⅓ cup white vinegar

¾ cup white sugar (I use less; ½ cup)

1 teaspoon Coleman's dry mustard powder

1 teaspoon salt

a dash of paprika

⅔ cup vegetable oil

1 cup Greek yogurt

CHILE-LIME BRUSSEL SPROUTS
∾ Susan LaFever

I am a known freelance classical/church musician who performs regularly on horn, piano, and organ.

I developed this recipe especially for this cookbook. Citrus brightens any vegetable, and I decided on a Mexican twist using lime, chili and tequila! This bright and zingy dish is a nice change from highly seasoned "restaurant" recipes.

Special Prep/Equipment

Large non-stick skillet

1 (16 ounce) package of brussels sprouts de-stemmed, halved, and washed

1 tablespoon olive oil

2 cloves of garlic, medium chopped

Salt to taste

½ teaspoon of red pepper flakes

¼ teaspoon sugar

1 large lime, juiced

1 ounce tequila (optional)

1. Heat olive oil on medium heat in a large non-stick skillet and saute the sprouts until light yellow-brown in color.

2. Push sprouts aside and cook the garlic for 1 minute, stirring occasionally. While garlic sautees, add salt, pepper, and sugar.

3. After garlic is sauteed, add the lime juice and tequila, cover and reduce heat. Cook to desired tenderness (3-5 minutes), testing by inserting a knife into the thickest part.

4. Uncover, raise heat to high and simmer off any remaining liquid while stirring.

5. Serve at any festive and fun meal!

Serves 4 as a side dish

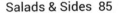

PASTA & NOODLES

AHI PASTA
～ Sasha Margolis

I'm primarily a classical violinist in orchestral, chamber and pit settings, but I also sing, play, and emcee in Big Galut(e), a Jewish music ensemble.

For a number of years, I played in the Honolulu Symphony. One of the almost countless wonderful things about living in Hawaii was how plentiful and cheap fresh tuna was. One way I took advantage was by making up very light, perfumey pasta sauce. It works great with olive oil-packed canned tuna as well.

Special Prep/Equipment
Large pot and a large skillet

1 pound spaghetti or bucatini

1-2 tablespoons olive oil

2-3 cloves of garlic, finely chopped

2-3 anchovy fillets, well-rinsed and roughly chopped

Zest of 1 lemon (probably best to use organic), finely chopped

1-2 handfuls of pine nuts, lightly toasted

1 handful of salt capers, well-rinsed (these work much better in this sauce than brined capers)

A lot of parsley, chopped

As much fresh tuna as you think is economically sound, cut into bite-size pieces; or 2 cans of olive oil-packed tuna, drained

1. Put up a pot of water to boil. When it boils, salt it well and put in the pasta. Follow cooking time on the pasta package.

2. Heat olive oil in the skillet, over low heat. Saute garlic. After a minute, turn off heat.

3. In your pot, make sure the pasta isn't sticking.

4. Add anchovy to garlic, and mash into a paste with a wooden spatula.

5. Turn heat back on for the skillet. Add lemon zest, pine nuts, and capers.

6. Once again, make sure pasta isn't sticking.

7. Add parsley and tuna to the sauce. If using fresh, cook to taste. If using canned, add at the last minute.

8. Drain pasta and toss with sauce in skillet. Serve!

1 pound of pasta should serve 4 moderate eaters.

BAKED MACARONI & CHEESE WITH PROSCIUTTO & PEAS
～ Charles McCracken

I am a long-time freelance bassoonist in NYC and beyond.

Basically, any Mac and Cheese recipe will work here, as long as you use really good, high quality cheese and pasta.

Special Prep/Equipment
Large pot
Medium size saucepan or high-sided skillet
9 x 13" baking pan
(A baking sheet can also be helpful.)

¼ - ½ cup grated Parmesan cheese

½ - ¾ cup bread crumbs

4 ounces fontina, grated

4 ounces sharp cheddar, grated

4 ounces gruyere, grated

4 ounces Romano, grated

1 pound penne pasta

2 tablespoons unsalted butter

2 tablespoons all-purpose flour

1½ cups milk (whole or skim)

½ teaspoon ground black pepper (or optional ½ teaspoon cayenne pepper to taste. Or use both!)

6 - 8 ounces prosciutto (chopped into 1" pieces)

1½ cups frozen peas

Note: I use whole wheat pasta and unflavored, whole wheat breadcrumbs. Packaged, pre-sliced prosciutto works okay, but if you can get it from a deli or butcher sliced a little thicker that's even better!

1. Preheat oven to 500°.

2. Combine Parmesan and bread crumbs in a small bowl, set aside. Combine 4 cheeses in a very large bowl, set aside.

3. Bring lightly salted water to boil in a large pot, add pasta and cook to two minutes less than package instructions.

4. While pasta is cooking, in your saucepan or skillet, melt butter over medium heat. When butter is melted, whisk in flour and stir until no lumps remain. Add milk and pepper, lower heat and stir occasionally until milk is heated through but not bubbling.

5. Drain pasta (do not rinse!) and leave slightly wet. Add pasta to bowl with the cheeses, stir to combine. Add the milk mixture, stir. Add prosciutto and peas, stir.

6. Transfer pasta/cheese mixture to a 9 x 13" baking dish, top with the bread crumb mixture, pressing down lightly with a large spoon or spatula. Bake for 7- 8 (possibly up to 10) minutes or until topping is golden brown. If it hasn't browned enough you can put it under the broiler for 1 or 2 minutes, but keep an eye on it for burning!

7. Let it cool for 10 minutes before serving.

Note
You might want to put a baking sheet on the rack under the pasta dish, in case it overflows. MUCH easier to clean the sheet than the oven!

As a main dish, serves 4. As a side dish, 6.

BUTTERNUT SQUASH LASAGNA

✎ Katie Kresek

I'm a violinist, arranger, and educator. Before the pandemic, I was concertmaster at *Moulin Rouge! The Musical* on Broadway, and working with many singer-songwriters. I also still teach for Lincoln Center and two universities.

I came up with this during the holidays when I was playing at Radio City in 2016. I was busy and tired and came home to cook dinner realizing I had no vegetables in the house except a butternut squash that had been lying around since Halloween, and some freezer spinach. The amounts are somewhat approximate, but that's the nice thing about Lasagna — you can adjust the amounts of vegetables, sauce, and cheese to your liking.

Special Prep/Equipment

Whisk

Wooden spoon

Parchment paper

Medium baking tray

9 x 13" lasagna pan

1 medium-large butternut squash (or 2-3 cups cubed)

2 tablespoons olive oil plus more for lining the lasagna pan

4 tablespoons of butter

4 tablespoons all-purpose flour

2½ cups of milk (2% or whole)

Salt, pepper

¼ teaspoon fresh grated nutmeg

¼ teaspoon paprika

2-3 teaspoons dried sage

2-3 cups of fresh or frozen spinach or other sturdy greens

Oven-ready lasagna noodles

2 cups of cottage cheese or ricotta (optional)

1-2 cups mozzarella

½ cup of grated Parmigiano-Reggiano

4-6 fresh sage leaves

Optional ingredients: garlic, peas, other herbs like Herbes-de-Provence. You could also substitute the butternut squash for other kinds of squash like delicata, or even roasted carrots.

1. Preheat oven to 400°.

2. Peel and chop squash into 1" cubes or discs, cover in olive oil, and sprinkle with salt and pepper and herbs, if desired. Roast until they are tender and golden, about 20 minutes.

3. While those are baking, make the béchamel. Over low-medium heat in a medium saucepan, melt the butter and whisk in the flour for about a minute. Whisk in the milk slowly until it's all added and there are no lumps. Then switch to a wooden spoon and let the mixture thicken until it coats the back of the spoon. Season the sauce with salt, pepper, nutmeg, paprika, and dried sage.

4. When the squash is done, brush the bottom of the pan with more olive oil and spread some (½ to 1 cup) of the squash and spinach, then add ¼ to ½ cup of the béchamel. Add your first layer of lasagna noodles. Top with a layer of cottage or ricotta, then repeat the layering with more butternut squash, spinach, and béchamel until you reach the top of the pan or run out of ingredients. For the top layer, spread the last of the béchamel and then a layer of mozzarella and the Parmigiano-Reggiano.

5. Bake in preheated oven in the middle upper section of the oven about 20-25 minutes. Cover with foil if it browns too quickly. Cool for 10-15 minutes before serving and top with fresh sage leaves.

Serves 4-6

BROCCOLI RABE & CHICKPEAS PENNE

~ Peter Seidenberg

I am a cellist living in Hastings on Hudson. I do a little bit of everything, freelancing, teaching, chamber music.

We've been enjoying this dish for many years. I do not know how it came about but I know it is an Italian vegetarian staple.

1 bunch broccoli rabe	½ teaspoon red pepper flakes
1 pound penne pasta	1 (15 ounce) can of chickpeas
3-4 cloves garlic	½ teaspoon salt
3 tablespoons olive oil	¼ cup Pecorino Romano cheese

Special Prep/Equipment
Large Pot for cooking pasta
Large pan or skillet

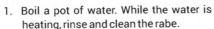
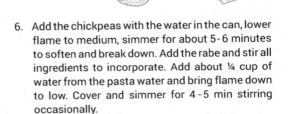

1. Boil a pot of water. While the water is heating, rinse and clean the rabe.

2. Rough chop and blanch the rabe in the boiling water for about 2 minutes. Rabe can be quite bitter so blanching it really reduces the bitterness and brings out the grassy, mild, flavor. Drain the rabe in a colander and then immediately shock the rabe with cold water or an ice bath to prevent it from cooking more. Set aside.

3. Bring another pot of water to boil for the penne. (Do not use the rabe water — it will be quite bitter.) Once the penne pasta is finished cooking reserve about ¼ to ½ cup of the water to mix into the garlic chickpea mixture.

4. Chop the garlic into a fine paste in order for it to kind of melt in the sauce

5. Heat the olive oil in a pan large enough to accommodate all the ingredients. Add garlic and pepper flakes and wait for the garlic to get just golden, about 2 minutes on high flame.

6. Add the chickpeas with the water in the can, lower flame to medium, simmer for about 5-6 minutes to soften and break down. Add the rabe and stir all ingredients to incorporate. Add about ¼ cup of water from the pasta water and bring flame down to low. Cover and simmer for 4-5 min stirring occasionally.

7. Add salt but keep in mind that pecorino cheese is quite salty.

8. Add more pasta water if you wish your sauce to have thinner texture. Sprinkle pecorino cheese on sauce.

9. Place penne in a large serving bowl and add the rabe sauce. Toss to cover the pasta. You can add a bit more cheese and perhaps some more olive oil, if you wish.

10. Salt and pepper to taste and enjoy!

Serves 4

TRADITIONAL LASAGNA
〜 Charles Descarfino

I play percussion and drums. I am a longtime member of Local 802 AFM, have been a regular member of the orchestras for twenty shows on and off Broadway, and I regularly perform with numerous classical and freelance orchestras and ensembles.

I call this Traditional Lasagna because it is the recipe for the lasagna that was presented for all the holiday gatherings of my extended family. It was first cooked by my grandmother, who came to America as a young woman from the small town of Menfi on the southern coast of Sicily, subsequently prepared by my mother, and now myself. It is traditional in the sense that it has been a long-established dish in my family, but different from Lasagna Classica, which is usually prepared in Italy with bechamel sauce rather than ricotta and mozzarella.

Special Prep/Equipment
Approx 12 x 16" enameled or glass baking tray

1 pound sweet Italian sausage

Extra virgin olive oil

3-4 med. cloves of garlic, finely minced

1 large yellow onion, medium diced

Fresh ground black pepper

3 (28 ounce) cans of San Marzano tomatoes

1 pound lean ground beef

10 ounce container of crimini or baby bella mushrooms

1 pound of imported Italian lasagna noodles

2 tablespoons of imported Greek or Italian oregano (dried on the stick, if possible)

32 ounces whole milk ricotta

16 ounce package of mozzarella, shredded

Grated Pecorino Romano cheese

1. Brown the sausage in a skillet on both sides until fully cooked. Discard the fat from the skillet and place sausage aside until cooled.

2. Pour a few tablespoons of olive oil, lightly covering the bottom of a large to medium saucepan, add the minced garlic followed by the diced onion to the oil and saute on low heat until translucent, but not browned. Add the oregano and some fresh ground black pepper to the pot with the garlic and onions and stir together.

3. Puree the entire contents of the canned tomatoes in a blender. Add the pureed tomatoes to the saucepan and simmer.

4. Brown the ground beef in the skillet, discard the fat from the skillet, and add the browned beef to the simmering sauce.

5. Rough cut and crumble the cooked sausage and add it to the simmering sauce.

6. Slice the mushrooms thinly, saute in the skillet with olive oil and add to the simmering pot of sauce.

7. Let the pot of sauce cook on the stove at a medium/low simmer for 45 minutes to an hour. Stir occasionally, allowing it to develop a thicker consistency.

8. Cook the lasagna noodles in a large pot of salted water to al dente as per instructions on the box. Drain in a colander and return the pasta to the pot and add some cold water to keep the noodles from sticking together.

9. When the sauce and noodles are cooked, you can begin to assemble the lasagna.

10. Preheat oven to 425°.

11. Ladle a thin layer of sauce into the bottom of the baking tray and arrange the lasagna pasta over the sauce, covering the bottom of the tray.

12. Next, evenly distribute generous dollops of the ricotta over the noodles and smooth out to cover the noodles best you can. Follow by evenly ladling sauce over the ricotta layer, then add a layer of the shredded mozzarella. Repeat this, starting with a new layer of pasta again followed by ricotta, sauce, and mozzarella layers, ending with a layer of pasta covered only by the sauce.

13. Bake in the preheated oven at 425° for 20-25 minutes. Remove from the oven, cover with foil, and allow to set for about 15 minutes.

14. Optionally, sprinkle with grated Pecorino Romano cheese and serve.

Note
The quality of ingredients will affect the quality of the recipe. Using bronze cut imported Italian pasta, certified San Marzano tomatoes, sausage from a local Italian butcher rather than the commercial supermarket variety, fresh made ricotta in the tin from an Italian specialty store, and imported wild oregano off the stick will improve the taste of this dish. I use packaged mozzarella for its lower water content, but fresh can be substituted. Also, for those not fond of mushrooms, the recipe can be made without them. The sauce can also be made the day before, which usually tends to enhance its flavor.

Serves 8

HALUSKY
〜 Marcia Hankle

I play flute and piccolo and have toured with National Ballet of Canada, Moiseyev Dance Company, and *Jesus Christ Superstar* Broadway tour. More recently, I've had the privilege of performing with some wonderful chamber groups, including the Bronx Arts Ensemble, Englewinds, UpTown Flutes, and the Phoenix Quintet.

This is a traditional Slovak dish.

Special Prep/Equipment
Large pot for cooking pasta
Large/heavy skillet

½ cup butter

1 small-medium head of green cabbage

Salt, pepper, garlic powder, to taste

12-16 ounce package of egg noodles

1. Bring pot of water to a boil for cooking noodles.

2. Brown butter in a heavy skillet. Add shredded cabbage and seasonings. Cook until tender and lightly browned.

3. Meanwhile prepare noodles — cook to al dente. Drain, and fold into cabbage mixture.

4. Adjust seasonings and enjoy!

Serves 4 as a side dish

PERRY'S LINGUINE WITH SHRIMP AND BROCCOLI RABE
Perry Cavari

I am a Broadway drummer.

This is a quick and easy pasta dish. There are variations of this served in most Italian restaurants.

1. Wash broccoli rabe, and cut into 2" pieces.

2. In a large pot, bring 5 quarts of water to a boil.

3. While water is heating, and 3 tablespoons of oil to a deep sided fry pan, or a saucepan. Add 2 cloves garlic and heat over medium heat until garlic is golden. Be careful not to burn garlic.

4. Add shrimp to garlic and cook until pink on both sides, about 2-3 minutes per side. Do not crowd pan. Fry it in 2 batches if necessary, adding additional oil and garlic as needed. When shrimp are fully cooked, remove to a plate and put aside.

5. By this time pasta water should be almost boiling. Salt the water and bring to a rapid boil. Add pasta.

6. While pasta is cooking, add 4 tablespoons oil and remaining 4 cloves garlic to the fry pan; again, cook until golden. Lower heat and add broccoli rabe and cover. After a minute, toss broccoli to coat with oil and to prevent it from burning. If you like a little heat, add red pepper now, and toss again. Re-cover and cook for about 3-4 minutes, or until broccoli is tender. Do not overcook. Broccoli should still be firm and have a little crunch. Add cooked shrimp and garlic.

7. Taste pasta. It should be "al dente". Drain, reserving 1 cup pasta water and return pasta to pot. Add the shrimp and broccoli to the pasta and toss. Simmer on low heat for about 2-3 minutes for flavors to combine. If noodles seem too dry, add some pasta water and/or drizzle in some more olive oil.

8. Serve and add black pepper and/or more red pepper flakes if desired.

9. Enjoy! Buon appetito!

Serves 2-4

1 bunch broccoli rabe, cut off about 1" of stems and discard.

6 tablespoons extra virgin olive oil

6 cloves of garlic, peeled and lightly smashed with the side of large knife

1 pound medium shrimp, peeled and deveined - at least 6-8 per person

1 pound linguine (or penne or your favorite pasta)

Salt and pepper to taste

Crushed red pepper flakes, to taste

SPINACH, RICOTTA AND MUSHROOM MANICOTTI AL FORNO
～ Patrizia Conte

I was the assistant concertmaster of the Saint Paul Chamber Orchestra, and left the orchestra after 30 years. I am currently a violin/violist freelance and chamber musician in Minneapolis, Minnesota.

This recipe is from a cookbook my Mom gave me, a collection of recipes from her church in Seattle.

Special Prep/Equipment

Large pot for cooking pasta

Skillet for making the filling

9 x 13" baking dish

1 box manicotti

½ pound of sweet Italian sausage or ground beef (optional)

1 garlic clove, chopped

12 ounces mushrooms, chopped

12 ounces chopped spinach

2 tablespoons extra virgin olive oil

12 ounces ricotta cheese

Salt and pepper to taste

1 cup Pecorino Romano cheese, divided

1 medium jar marinara sauce

Small handful of fresh basil, chopped

1. Bring a large pot of water to a boil. Preheat oven to 400°.

2. Cook pasta in boiling water for 9 minutes. Drain and cool on a sheet pan. Set aside.

3. If using meat, heat a skillet on medium-high heat, then add sausage or ground beef. Cook all the way through, stirring frequently to brown. Remove from pan and put aside. Drain fat, if desired.

4. Add a little olive oil to skillet, add garlic and mushrooms, then season with salt and pepper. Cook until browned.

5. Steam the spinach. Chop well. (If using frozen spinach, thaw, drain and steam.)

6. Mix meat, ricotta cheese, mushrooms, spinach, salt, pepper and half the Pecorino cheese. Fill the manicotti shells.

7. Grease (or spray PAM) a 9 x 13" baking dish. Add half the sauce and spread over pan bottom. Arrange the manicotti and cover with the remaining pasta sauce and Pecorino cheese. Cover with aluminum foil.

8. Bake manicotti in the oven, covered, for 30 minutes. Sprinkle with fresh basil to serve.

9. Mangia! Enjoy!

Serves 5

BI BIM GUK SU
Junah Chung

I am a violist in the *Lion King* on Broadway, and I'm on the viola faculty at CUNY Grad Center. I also perform with the American Ballet Theater Orchestra, record for movie soundtracks, and play chamber music and recitals.

My mom used to make this for lunch, usually on a hot summer day. From a Korean cook book published by the Korean Institute of Minnesota. I double a lot of the ingredients. So I use 4 tablespoons of soy sauce instead of 2.

Special Prep/Equipment
Blender or food processor

1 pound somen noodles (thin)

1 cucumber

¼ pound ground beef (leave out if vegetarian or vegan)

1 beaten egg

Meat & Cucumber Seasoning:
2 tablespoons soy sauce

2 teaspoons sugar

1 tablespoon chopped green onion

1 teaspoon sesame seed

Dash of black pepper

1 teaspoon sesame oil

Noodle Seasoning:
4 tablespoons soy sauce

2 tablespoons sugar

2 tablespoons sesame oil

4 tablespoons toasted sesame seeds

Dash of Korean red pepper flakes

¼ cup chopped kimchi and a little kimchi juice

1. Cook noodles, be careful not to overcook. Rinse in cold water. Drain and set aside.

2. Slice cucumber thinly, sprinkle with a little salt, set aside for 10 minutes before squeezing out liquid. Stir fry the cucumber in ½ tablespoon of sesame oil over high heat for about a minute. The fried cucumbers add a wonderful texture and flavor to the dish.

3. Add the ground beef and the Meat & Cucumber Seasoning ingredients, fry for a minute.

4. Make an egg pancake with the beaten egg. Slice thinly. The beef and egg can totally be omitted and it will taste just as good.

5. Place a portion of the cold noodles in a bowl, spoon over several spoonfuls of the noodle seasoning. Cover noodles with the meat and cucumber. Garnish with the sliced egg pancake. Mix well and enjoy!

> **Note**
> Put enough noodle seasoning to lightly coat the noodles but you don't want to put too much or it will be too salty and overly seasoned.

Serves 4-6

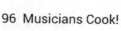

PASTA AL POVERO
∿ Ransom Wilson

I am a flutist, educator, and orchestral conductor. As a flutist I perform with the Chamber Music Society of Lincoln Center. As an educator I teach at the Yale School of Music, Idyllwild Arts, and SUNY Purchase. As a conductor with the Redlands Symphony, OK Mozart International Festival, London Symphony, LA Chamber Orchestra, St. Paul Chamber Orchestra, New York City Opera, and Metropolitan Opera.

This recipe for "Poverty Pasta" uses parts of vegetables that are ordinarily thrown away. I have always regretted that I couldn't use all of a head of cabbage, cauliflower, or broccoli, as I suspected that the tough outer leaves and stalk were very likely the most nutritious parts. I have at last found a way to serve them in a delicious sauce for pasta!

2 tablespoons olive oil

4 ounces breakfast sausage or any type link sausage (remove meat from casing) or bacon, or salami

1 large onion, sliced (About 1½ - 2 cups)

3 cups cabbage heart (the hard center) cauliflower greens and stem, broccoli stems, or a combination, finely chopped

4 small or 2 large garlic cloves, peeled and chopped

1 (14.5) ounce can diced tomatoes

1 pound pasta, any shape

2 tablespoons butter or plant butter

Grated cheese

1. Heat the olive oil on medium heat in a wide, deep pan (a wok works well).

2. Add sausage, breaking it up with a fork, until browned.

3. Add garlic, onion, saute until it starts to get soft (2-3 minutes). Add chopped cabbage heart or cauliflower stalk, saute until starting to get soft (4- 6 minutes). Add tomatoes, stir to mix.

4. Reduce heat to simmer, partially cover, and cook for 15-20 minutes.

5. Meanwhile, boil a large pot of well-salted water and cook the pasta only until al dente stage. DO NOT OVERCOOK, as it will continue to cook in the sauce.

6. When pasta is al dente, reserve ½ cup starchy cooking water, and drain pasta. Immediately add the pasta to the sauce and incorporate well, to cover every strand with sauce. Add reserved cooking water 1 tablespoon at a time, until a smooth, luscious texture is reached.

7. Add the butter and allow to melt. Stir to incorporate.

8. Separate into portions and sprinkle with grated cheese.

> **Note**
>
> A vegan version of this dish is easy to achieve. Just replace the sausage with chopped fresh mushrooms and saute until they start to release their moisture, before proceeding with the next step. Use the plant butter option and either omit the cheese or use plant-based cheese.
>
> If you like the Italian way of eating pasta (as I do) dress the sauce at the end with really good olive oil. It will improve the texture immeasurably! If you are watching your fat intake, you can reduce the olive oil and butter by half without doing damage to the dish.
>
> This recipe is designed to have a relatively small amount of tomatoes, as pasta sauces are made in Italy. If you prefer American proportions, just double the amount of tomatoes.

Serves 4 (or 6 who are watching their weight!)

ORECCHIETTE WITH RICOTTA SALATA
~ Thomas Verchot

I'm a trumpeter and play orchestral, solo, chamber music and occasional Broadway jobs. I also play a lot of new music in New York and internationally.

I received this recipe second-hand from an Italian assistant conductor while I was playing in the Spoleto Festival Orchestra in Spoleto, Italy.

Special Prep/Equipment
Put a large pot of water on to boil.

8 ounces Ricotta Salata (also called Ricotta Pecorino)

¾ cup of extra virgin olive oil

½ teaspoon red pepper flakes

1 pound dried orecchiette pasta

1. With your fingers, crumble the Ricotta Salata until it has a very fine, snowy quality. Make the crumbs as small as possible.

2. While pasta water is heating, combine olive oil and red pepper flakes in a small skillet (I prefer cast iron) over low heat to infuse the oil with the spiciness of the peppers. Keep an eye on this to make sure you don't burn the pepper flakes or the oil.

3. Cook the pasta in the boiling water to desired amount of doneness, either tender or al dente.

4. Drain pasta.

5. Place pasta in a large serving bowl. Using a strainer/sieve, pour the oil over the pasta, separating out the pepper flakes. Coat well the pasta with the oil. Stir in the crumbled Ricotta Salata. Combine well.

Serves 4

ORECCHIETTE PASTA WITH BROCCOLI RABE
~ Geoffrey Morrow

I am a freelancer on double bass and electric bass.

I have gradually developed this recipe from a previous one using regular broccoli with some tips from Lidia Bastianich on how to prepare the broccoli rabe.

⅓ - ½ pound orecchiette pasta (preferably DeCecco)

1 pound fresh broccoli rabe

2 tablespoons olive oil

3 large cloves fresh garlic, finely chopped (divided)

Kosher salt, crushed red pepper and ground fennel or dried fennel seeds

Romano cheese, grated (preferably Locatelli)

Fresh black pepper, to taste

Special Prep/Equipment
Large pot for cooking pasta

1. Cook pasta according to instructions on box.

2. While pasta is cooking, cut stems off broccoli rabe and for best results, remove veins from leaves and peel some skin from flowers. Rinse thoroughly.

3. In medium saucepan, heat olive oil and one clove chopped garlic over low heat for 1 minute. Add broccoli rabe and cover for 2 minutes. Add ½ teaspoon kosher salt, mix and cover (check in 2-3 minutes to ensure sufficient liquid, add a bit of pasta water if necessary).

4. Cook broccoli rabe another couple of minutes until tender. Don't overcook or it will be mushy and lose flavor.

5. Drain pasta and return to pan. Add ½ teaspoon of olive oil to coat. Add broccoli rabe to pasta and cover.

6. In small saucepan or skillet combine 1 table-spoon olive oil (or a little more if necessary), remaining chopped garlic, red pepper and fennel and heat on high until just before garlic turns brown. Either add entire mixture to pasta, or remove some of the garlic from oil and mix in.

7. Serve and top with Romano cheese and pepper.

8. Enjoy!

Serves 2

CHICKPEAS AND FRIED PASTA (GLUTEN FREE)
∽ Frank Donaruma

I am Principal Horn of the Queens Symphony, formerly Principal Horn of the Kansas City Philharmonic, New Jersey Symphony, American Ballet Theatre, Associate Principal Horn Baltimore Symphony, and 2nd Horn of the Metropolitan Opera.

I have celiac disease and decided to try to duplicate this southern Italian dish gluten free.

1 (15-ounce) can chickpeas

½ can water

2 garlic cloves, smashed with a knife

1 onion, cut in slices

2 bay leaves

1 stalk celery, chopped

1 dried chili crushed

Extra virgin olive oil

4 corn tortillas sliced into quarter inch strips

1 pound GLUTEN FREE linguine

2 tablespoons parsley, chopped

Pecorino Romano cheese

Black pepper

1. Empty chickpeas, including their liquid and half can of water into a small saucepan.

2. Add garlic, onion, bay leaf, celery, chili, and simmer for 20 minutes, making sure it has enough liquid.

3. Put enough oil into a small frying pan and fry tortilla strips until crisp, drain on paper towels.

4. Cook pasta and dress with chickpea sauce, parsley, cheese, and 2 tablespoons of the frying oil.

5. Top with tortilla strips. Remove bay leaves and serve.

Serves 5

DOROTHY'S NO-COOK LASAGNA
 Enid Brodsky

I've played timpani and percussion with many groups including the Queens Symphony Orchestra, the Goldman Memorial Band and various choirs in the New York and Philadelphia areas.

Dorothy Horowitz was my husband's aunt, who was a music teacher. She gave us this delicious, relatively easy recipe. I make it every year for a "car-pool" party. My husband sang with a Philadelphia chorus and would be driven home every week by other singers from our neighborhood. One of them still hosts a pot-luck party every January. This is the dish we bring.

Special Prep/Equipment

9 x 13" baking dish

1. Preheat oven to 350°.

2. Combine cooked spinach, ricotta, Parmesan, eggs, and parsley in a bowl.

3. Saute onion and garlic in a pan in some oil. When onions are tender, mix into spinach and cheese mixture.

4. Oil your lasagna pan. Then, layer in the uncooked lasagna noodles, cheese mixture, sprinkle with mozzarella, and cover with ¼ of the sauce. Make 4 layers of these ingredients in this order.

5. Cover with foil and bake at 350° for 1 hour or until

1½ pounds spinach, chopped (fresh, or if frozen, cooked and drained)	2 cloves garlic
2 pounds ricotta cheese	Oil for sauteing onions and garlic and for oiling pan
¼ pound grated Parmesan	1 pound lasagna noodles (regular, not precooked)
3 eggs, beaten	½ pound mozzarella, diced
5 tablespoon chopped parsley	Salt & pepper to taste
1 onion, chopped	1 quart tomato or marinara sauce

noodles are tender (usually another 15 minutes or so).

6. Uncover and bake another 10-15 minutes

Serves 8

SPINACH LASAGNA WITH DRY NOODLES
 Leslie Shank

I was the assistant concertmaster of the Saint Paul Chamber Orchestra, and left the orchestra after 30 years. I am currently a violin/violist freelancer and chamber musician in Minneapolis, Minnesota.

This recipe is from a cookbook my Mom gave me, a collection of recipes from her church in Seattle.

1 pint ricotta cheese	1 or 2 (10 ounce) packages chopped frozen spinach
2 beaten eggs	I also add some nutmeg
1 teaspoon oregano	1 quart meatless spaghetti sauce
8 ounces mozzarella cheese, grated	Lasagna noodles, uncooked
8 ounces cheddar cheese, grated	

Special Prep/Equipment

9 x 13" baking pan

1. Preheat oven to 350°.

2. Combine ricotta cheese, eggs, oregano, half each of the mozzarella and cheddar cheese, and the thawed spinach. You can add a little nutmeg, to taste.

3. Coat bottom of the baking pan with thin layer of spaghetti sauce and then a layer of dry noodles. Add half of the ricotta cheese and spinach mixture, then another layer of noodles, the remaining ricotta cheese mixture and then the last layer of dry noodles.

4. Pour spaghetti sauce over all and top with remaining mozzarella and cheddar cheese. Pour 1 cup of water carefully around edges, cover tightly with foil.

5. Bake for 1 hour and 15 minutes in preheated oven. Let stand for 15 minutes covered.

> **Note**
> This is especially good with whole wheat noodles but requires about ¼ cup more water and 15 minutes longer to bake.

Serves 8

SPAGHETTI AL LIMONE
꒰ **Anthony Scelba**

I am a performing double bassist and Professor of Music. I teach Music History, Form & Analysis, and Orchestration.

This is a classic Italian pasta that is not very widely known in the USA. Friends to whom I've given this recipe rave about it. Enjoy!

½ pound of pasta, spaghetti or thin spaghetti work best

⅓ cup extra-virgin olive oil

¼ cup fresh squeezed lemon juice

2 teaspoons grated lemon zest

Salt & pepper to taste

Optional alternatives (add any or all):
Press a tiny amount of fresh garlic into the sauce

Add 2 tablespoons fresh basil or parsley leaves on top

Dress with Parmesan cheese

Top with roasted asparagus or canned, drained artichoke hearts

1. Bring a large pot of water to a boil, and cook your pasta. While pasta is cooking you can make your sauce.

2. To make the sauce, simply whisk together the olive oil, lemon juice and zest, and the salt and pepper.

3. Put the hot pasta (cooked al dente and well drained) into the sauce. Toss and serve immediately.

Serves 2 (or 1 musician!)

CHIELI'S PASTA FRITA
⌒ Chieli Minucci

I am a guitarist, arranger and composer. I'm the bandleader for Special EFX since 1982, still touring!

This is a two part preparation, sort of, and so worth the wait to devour! If you cheat a little, and eat all of Part 1 of this recipe, I won't mind! This is a simple variation on a familiar meal which I grew up on, and continue to indulge in! My parents were both Italian, with my Dad actually from Sicily. We ate pasta regularly while I was a kid growing up. I've always loved pasta, and to me a restaurant is only as good as its simple tomato (marinara) sauce!

PART 1:

1. Cook your favorite pasta (Linguine, Mezzani, Elbow Macaroni, or whatever you like) in water boiled with some olive oil and a small palmful of salt. I wouldn't recommend putting more than 2 tablespoons of oil. Of course this is to your own personal taste. Don't forget to cook the pasta "al dente"! (slightly underdone)

2. The sauce can be made best from fresh tomato paste, however you like, cooked with a little garlic, salt, and just a touch of cinnamon. Add a little water, til your desired thickness is reached. I am modest about my sauce. I don't use much garlic, and only half the onion. The onion should be peeled in leaves, but not too small. (did you know that if you peel an onion near a burning flame there are no tears...? try it!)

3. In a separate pan, cook up ground sirloin, with a dash of teriyaki sauce on it (YES, I said Teriyaki!) adding a bit of olive oil as it nears the final stages of browning.

| 1 pound of your favorite pasta |
| Olive oil |
| Salt |
| 1 (6 ounce) can tomato paste |
| Garlic |
| Cinnamon |
| 1 small onion |
| Teriyaki sauce |
| ½ - ¾ pound ground sirloin |
| 6 sweet Italian sausages |

4. In a separate pan, cook up the sausages, turning them lovingly until they're brown all over. I prefer sweet Italian sausages for this meal.

5. Once all the ingredients are finished cooking, mix them together in a big serving bowl for a delicious meal. This is a full meal, and does not require anything else except a side salad perhaps.

PART 2:

1. Make sure there are leftovers! The "pasta frita" treat involves taking the leftover pasta meal and cooking it the next day in a frying pan, again, with some olive oil, and actually frying it up to a delicious, slightly crispy texture. This may vary for each of you. Personally, I like my pasta slightly burnt/crispy when I eat it this way. Unbelievably delicious – enjoy!

Serves 4

LINGUINE & COMFORT SAUCE

~ Patricia Ann Neely

I am an early bowed strings specialist (viola da gamba, violone vielle, baroque bass) I have worked with many early music ensembles here and abroad including Sequentia, Rheinschen Kantorei Köln, Washington Bach Consort, Opera Lafayette, Folger Consort, Boston Early Music Festival Orchestra. I am also the director of Abendmusik, New York's Early Music String Band (2 violins and 3 viola da gambas).

As a single parent with a day job and rehearsals and concerts, I had to fit in time to make meals. In my life multitasking was the norm. This is an easy to make recipe, fast, and disappears pretty quickly as well. Someday we will have gigs again!

Special Prep/Equipment
Large pot for cooking pasta

6 cloves garlic

½ large white onion

Olive oil

2 tablespoons Italian herbs and/or oregano

1 pound ground beef or sausage, or kidney beans

Pepper

1 (24 ounce) jar of marinara sauce

Linguine No. 7 (or any pasta of choice)

Fresh grated Parmesan cheese

1. Mince the garlic cloves. Dice half of the onion.

2. Heat 2 tablespoons of olive oil in a frying pan. Add Italian herbs and/or oregano.

3. Saute the garlic, onion, and herbs in the pan until brown.

4. Crumble ground beef, sausage, (or kidney beans) and cook until brown. Add pepper to taste

5. Add the entire contents of the marinara sauce, cover, bring to a simmer, cook for 5 minutes.

6. Boil water for pasta and cook pasta until desired tenderness.

7. Top with fresh Parmesan.

Serves 12 and allows for seconds

LOKSHEN KUGEL (NOODLE PUDDING CASSEROLE)
Erich L. Graf

I am a flutist, formerly with The Aeolian Chamber Players, Utah Symphony, and the former President of Local 104, American Federation of Musicians.

This is my father, Otto Graf's recipe and was a family staple for many years.

Special Prep/Equipment
Large pyrex baking dish

1. Preheat oven to 400°. Butter your baking dish.
2. Drop noodles in rapidly boiling water and cook until almost tender. Drain in colander and put into a large mixing bowl.
3. Add the salt, beaten eggs, cottage cheese, and butter or schmaltz. Mix well, preferably using hands but roll up sleeves.
4. Turn mixture into prepared baking dish.
5. Bake about 45 minutes in preheated oven.
6. Eat hearty!

1 pound broad egg noodles

Boiling water

1 teaspoon salt

4 eggs, well beaten

1 (12 ounce) container small curd cottage cheese

2 tablespoons butter or schmaltz

For the Galizianer version, Rumanian and Hungarian brothers prefer the following variant:

To the above mixture add:

3 tablespoon sugar

¼ teaspoon cinnamon

½ cup seedless raisins

¼ cup slivered almonds

Serves 12

VODKA SAUCE
Lee Ann Newland

I'm a french horn player and teacher. Throughout my career I've been blessed to work in NYC on Broadway, in the classical world, and with my quintet.

This recipe came to me from a friend's grandmother. It's one of our family favorites!

1 yellow onion, diced

1 garlic clove, chopped

1 tablespoon butter

½ cup vodka

1 teaspoon red pepper flakes

1 (28 ounce) can San Marzano whole tomatoes

1½ cup cream (I use heavy cream)

Blender

1. In a large skillet, saute the diced onion in butter. Add a chopped garlic clove for extra flavor. Cook until onions are soft.

2. In a saucepan, combine vodka and red pepper flakes and cook until the liquid starts to bubble. Remove from heat and set aside.

3. In a blender, chop the tomatoes in their liquid to the consistency you like. Pour tomatoes into the skillet with onion and cook on low, stirring often for 20 minutes. Add in the heavy cream and keep stirring until mixture is smooth and well mixed and starts to bubble around the edge of the pan.

4. You can strain the vodka and pour into the pan with tomatoes, or for some extra bite pour vodka with hot pepper flakes into the sauce.

5. Continue to stir over low heat for another ten minutes.

6. Serve with your favorite pasta!

Yields enough sauce for a box of pasta and can easily be doubled to serve more.

SPAGHETTI IN RED SAUCE WITH SQUID & MARROW BONES
 Helen Campo

I am the flutist in the Broadway show *Wicked*.

This is inspired by tasting Marea Restaurant's Octopus with Bone Marrow Sauce.

Special Prep/Equipment

Pot for cooking sauce

1. In a large pot, heat olive oil. Saute onion and sliced garlic until soft. Add carrot and thyme and saute another few minutes. Add tomatoes and salt to taste. Cook for 20 minutes or so.

2. Add the rest of ingredients except parsley and cook for an hour or so.

3. Put on boiled pasta and garnish with parsley.

Serves 3-4

¼ cup olive oil

1 small onion, chopped

½ bulb of garlic peeled and sliced

1 carrot, peeled and grated

Leaves from a few sprigs of thyme

1 (28 ounce) can of Italian plum tomatoes

½ bulb garlic peeled cloves, left whole

1 cup white wine

2 tablespoons red pepper flakes

1 pound squid cut in small pieces

½ pound marrow bones

Fresh parsley, chopped

¾-1 pound of pasta

BAKED RIGATONI
～ Sylvia D'Avanzo

I am a Broadway violinist for over 28 years and currently the concertmaster for the Lincoln Center Production of *Flying Over Sunset*. I have also toured with such artists as Barbra Streisand, Harry Connick Jr., and Madeleine Peyroux.

This pasta dish is a richer, denser version of baked ziti that NO ONE can resist!! Just ask my friends & colleagues!

Special Prep/Equipment
A large baking dish or 2 smaller dishes

For the Marinara (this should make at least 4½ cups):

½ cup olive oil

5 cloves of minced garlic

2 (28-ounce) cans of San Marzano Tomatoes

Large bunch of fresh basil, chopped

2 pinches of red pepper flakes

Salt and pepper to taste

For the Rigatoni:

16 ounce box of Rigatoni

4 eggs beaten

1 pound of ricotta

8-10 ounces of shredded mozzarella

⅛ cup grated Parmesan

4½ cups of the marinara sauce

1. *Make the Marinara:*
   Heat olive oil in large saucepan over medium heat, add garlic, and cook until golden. <u>Do not burn</u>, or the sauce will be bitter. Add tomatoes and increase heat to a boil for about 10-15 minutes. Break apart the tomatoes, add basil, red pepper flakes, salt, and pepper. Turn down heat and simmer for 30 to 40 minutes.

2. *For the Rigatoni:* Cook the noodles while making the marinara. Drain, and let cool.

3. Preheat oven to 375°.

4. Butter a baking dish, a large one or 2 smaller ones. Mix the cheeses, the beaten eggs and the 4½ cups of marinara with the cooked pasta in a huge bowl. Pour into baking dish. Bake for 30 to 40 minutes until bubbly and golden brown.

5. Buon appetito!!

Serves an army of hungry musicians

LINGUINE ALLA VONGOLE (LINGUINE WITH CLAMS)

Kate Dillingham

I'm a cellist, a producer, an executive director, and president of the Violoncello Society of New York. I love food almost as much as I love music!!

This is a simple and absolutely delicious recipe that I've made many times. It is pretty much my favorite! It's traditional New England fare. Yum!

Special Prep/Equipment

You will need fresh clams and a big, deep pot.

Serve with a green salad, fresh tomatoes, and crusty bread.

1 pound pasta fresh or dry

Pinch salt

2-4 cloves fresh garlic or to taste

A bunch of fresh Italian parsley

1-2 dozen fresh little neck clams

2 bottles of Gavi or Pinot Grigio (minerally wine white, 1 for cooking, 1 for drinking)

3-4 tablespoons olive oil

1 bay leaf

Fresh, coarse ground black pepper to taste

1. In a deep pot, (one that has a fitted lid) boil 8-10 cups of water. Add a pinch of salt, add pasta to boiling water, cook 6 minutes (just before "al dente"), and drain pasta. BE SURE to reserve 1 cup or so of starchy pasta water for sauce/soup!

2. Slice garlic thin, length-wise, don't crush or press. Remove stems from Italian parsley and roughly chop. Rinse clams under cold water, make sure they are all closed before cooking. If you find an open one, toss it! Clams are living creatures, so make sure to poke holes in the bag when storing in the fridge. They will keep for several days.

3. In the same deep pot, over medium heat, add 3-4 tablespoons of olive oil (I prefer unfiltered, but any good olive oil will do) add sliced garlic. When you start to smell the garlic, add clams in their shells, 1 cup of wine, 1 cup of starchy pasta water and bay leaf. Cover with lid, cook 5 minutes or until ALL clams open.

4. Carefully remove clams (still in shells) put aside.

5. Add the "al dente" pasta to the liquid in the pot. Cook until desired tenderness is reached. Add fresh Italian parsley and black pepper, put the clams back in the pot to warm. Serve in bowls, with plenty of liquid (soup). I like the shells in the dish as they look pretty, but you can remove them, if you prefer.

Serves 3-4

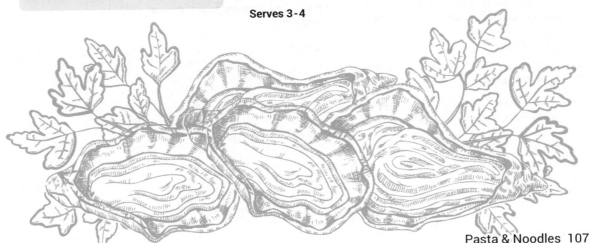

NO LEFTOVER PASTA
〜 Susannah Chapman

I am a cellist and I teach at Rutgers University and at Princeton University, and have younger students as well (now all on Zoom!)

I adapted a friend's vegetarian recipe into this version. I like it because each ingredient is one package, so clean up is easier! You can adapt with any vegetables you like.

Olive oil

Salt, pepper and onion powder

1 package cubed butternut squash (or you could use a few carrots)

1 package chicken (I like boneless, skinless thighs)

1 pound pasta

1 large red onion

A few cloves garlic

1 package fresh spinach

1 log of goat cheese (I like the kind rolled in herbs)

1. Preheat oven to 375°.

2. Boil water for pasta.

3. Toss the butternut squash with olive oil, salt, pepper, and roast in your hot oven on a sheet, tossing a few times, until golden brown, about 25 minutes.

4. Arrange chicken pieces on a broiling pan and sprinkle with salt, pepper and onion powder.

5. When squash is done, turn broiler on and broil one side of chicken pieces about 5 minutes until golden brown. Flip pieces, sprinkle new side with salt, pepper, onion powder, and broil new side until done. Chop the chicken pieces (I use scissors).

6. When boiling, add oil and salt to the pasta water and add pasta.

7. Saute the onion in a cast iron pan, and add the garlic after a few minutes. When onion is caramelized, add spinach for the final minute.

8. Unwrap goat cheese log and place in a very large bowl.

9. When pasta is done, reserve a cup of pasta water and drain pasta.

10. Add pasta and some of the water to the goat cheese in the large bowl. Stir to incorporate. The water will help soften and disperse the goat cheese, coating the pasta.

11. Add the spinach-onion mixture, the squash, and the chopped chicken (I cut the chicken with the scissors over the bowl.)

12. Toss everything together and serve!

Serves 4-6

CANNELLONI

Jim Neglia

I am an orchestra personnel manager, music coordinator, and author.

Coming from an Italian heritage, I grew up eating many delicious dishes! Homemade cannelloni is one of my favorites and I thought it might be something you all would enjoy. Although there are many versions of filling, my choice is spinach and ricotta. Bon appétit!

Special Prep/Equipment
I use a 8 x 10" baking dish that fits 20 cannelloni.

Basic Homemade Sauce:

1-2 tablespoons of chopped garlic

1 small diced onion

Roughly 2 pounds of crushed tomatoes

½ cup of water

Fresh basil, julienned

1 teaspoon of oregano

Salt and pepper to taste, but I use very little salt

Filling:

1 full bag fresh spinach

1 pound ricotta

½ cup of grated Parmesan cheese

1 cup of Gruyere or Swiss cheese

2 garlic cloves, minced

1 egg

Pasta:

20 cannelloni tubes

Grated mozzarella cheese, to your liking

1. First, the sauce: add oil to your skillet, and the garlic and onion, and cook until the onion is translucent. Add the tomatoes, and about a half a cup of water. Stir the sauce and reduce the heat to a simmer for about 5 minutes. If you would like a thinner sauce, you can add more water. Add in the fresh basil and oregano. Salt and pepper to taste.

2. Now for the filling: Wash the spinach, and then chop it. I roll up a handful at a time, so the chopping is easier. Place the spinach and all the other filling ingredients into a bowl, and mix them well.

3. Preheat the oven to 350 °.

4. Put a layer of sauce on the bottom of the pan. Next, fill each cannelloni with the incredibly tasty filling, arranging them snugly in the pan. I then use the rest of the sauce to cover the top of the waiting cannelloni.

5. Cover the pan with foil and bake for about 25-30 minutes.

6. Remove from the oven, and take the foil off. Shower the cannelloni with cheese, and back again into the oven for about 10 minutes, or until the cheese is melted. The sauce will have reduced further, but the cannelloni will have absorbed much of it in order to cook through.

**Serves 6 Italians or
8 Americans**

FUSILLI CON POMODORO FRESCO
~ Anthony Scelba

I am a double bassist who, in my career as a college professor, has specialized in chamber music. I have greatly increased the double bass chamber music repertoire.

My family has made pasta with fresh, raw tomatoes for decades. Flavorful, fresh, ripe tomatoes are the key to a great dish. This is a summertime treat. Great tomatoes are not easy to find even in late summer, but they are worth the hunt. High quality olive oil is a must. Oil cured olives are bitter and some don't like them. Kalamata olives can substituted.

Special Prep/Equipment
Large Pot for cooking pasta

The tomatoes need to sit for a couple hours before serving.

1. Mix all ingredients together (except the pasta) in a large bowl and let them sit at room temperature for 1-2 hours to let flavors meld.

2. Cook pasta according to instructions on box.

3. Combine the mixture with hot, freshly cooked, well-drained pasta cooked al dente. Serve immediately, or cold, as a pasta salad.

- 1½ pound fresh, ripe tomatoes at room temperature, medium dice (around 5 large tomatoes)
- ⅓ cup oil-cured black olives, pitted and slivered (20-25)
- 1½ teaspoons or 3 cloves garlic, finely minced
- ¼ teaspoon salt
- ¼ teaspoon crushed red pepper (peperoncino)
- ¼ teaspoon freshly ground black pepper
- ⅓ cup extra-virgin olive oil
- 3 tablespoons - ½ cup fresh basil, torn or julienned
- 3 tablespoons - ½ cup fresh Italian parsley, roughly chopped
- 1 pound fusilli or other pasta

Note
Mixing in a can or two of good Italian tuna would be delicious.

Serves 4 (and great when it's left over)

MACARONADA
～ Kim Laskowski

I am Associate Principal Bassoon in the New York Philharmonic.

I learned to make this meat sauce recipe from my husband, Local 802 member Zaharis Kalaitzis (percussion). It is a traditional Greek meat sauce served over spaghetti with plenty of grated dry mizithra cheese or any hard grating cheese of your choice. It is also the same meat sauce you would use in moussaka or pastitsio. On the side, serve a tomato and onion salad made with only salt and olive oil (no vinegar) and salted anchovies in olive oil as a condiment.

Special Prep/Equipment
Large Pot for cooking pasta
Medium saucepan for cooking sauce

2 pounds ground beef

1 tablespoon ground cinnamon

1 teaspoon salt

1 teaspoon pepper

2 tablespoons olive oil

4 large cloves garlic, cut in 1/16" wheels

1 large onion, diced

1½ small cans tomato paste

3 cups water, divided

½ cup red wine, preferably port or any Greek sweet wine (optional)

1. In a medium saucepan, place the meat, cinnamon, salt, pepper, and brown on a medium high flame until the meat is fully cooked. Throw the garlic and the diced onions into the pot.

2. In a medium mixing bowl, whisk the tomato paste with a cup of water with a wire whisk or a fork until smooth. Add to meat.

3. Add the 2 cups of water to the pan and mix all ingredients together on medium-high flame. The water level should be about an inch over the meat so add more if needed. Bring to a boil and then lower to a rolling simmer.

4. After about 20 minutes, taste to adjust salt and pepper.

5. After 45 minutes add the wine if desired. Cook another 20 minutes until garlic, onions and meat are tender. There should be an oily sheen on top of the sauce.

6. Turn off flame, cover, and cook some spaghetti!

Serves 4-5

PASTA BLT
~ Erika Boras

I am a cellist, teacher and performer, a chamber musician and orchestral player with recitals here and there.

My husband returned from a tour with Jerry Mulligan's Band (that included Italy) and cooked this for four generations of my family all gathered around a table in Chautauqua, New York. He recounted how he had this meal and learned how to make it as he loved it so much – and I still make it to this day.

Special Prep/Equipment
Large pot for cooking pasta

8 slices of bacon, cut into pieces

¼ - ½ cup extra virgin olive oil

3 cloves garlic, finely chopped (or more if you really like garlic)

1 cup cherry tomatoes cut in half

½ cup of basil leaves cut in thirds, or as you like

1 pound box of pasta – penne or other

Salt to taste

Parmesan cheese, grated

1. First we need to cook the bacon (well done) and set it aside. As the bacon is cooking, infuse the olive oil with the garlic by combining both into a bowl. This will allow the flavors to mix together. You can also add the tomatoes if you like. This can sit at room temperature for as long as you like - the longer the better!

2. Get a large pot of water boiling and cook the pasta (adding salt if you like and follow directions on the box). When the pasta is done, reserve a little of the water (½ cup) before draining. Drain the pasta into a colander, shake excess water out of it and then put it back into the pot adding the olive oil mixture, basil and bacon (and tomatoes if you didn't add before).

3. If it seems a little dry, use your reserved pasta water to spread the deliciousness around.

4. Shake Parmesan cheese and voila! You are ready to enjoy this oh so good meal! Feel free to experiment with quantities of ingredients to your taste – in my world, more bacon is better!!!

Serves 4

PASTA PROVENÇALES
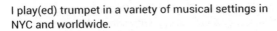
~ Dominic Derasse

I play(ed) trumpet in a variety of musical settings in NYC and worldwide.

Growing up in Nice, South of France, this has been a "staple" dish for me for years!

2 yellow onions

Olive oil

1 pound box of pasta of your choice. I like tri-colored Rotini with this.

1 (12.5 ounce) can of chicken (can be substituted with a can of tuna)

1 red pepper

1 green pepper (these can also be substituted with a jar of roasted peppers)

Herbes de Provence (can be replaced by basil, oregano and thyme powder if you cannot find the Herbes...)

Olives, to liking

Parmigiano cheese

Salt to liking

2-3 tablespoons pesto sauce, optional

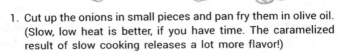

1. Cut up the onions in small pieces and pan fry them in olive oil. (Slow, low heat is better, if you have time. The caramelized result of slow cooking releases a lot more flavor!)

2. Bring a large pot of water to a boil, and cook your pasta al dente.

3. While the pasta and the onions cook, chop your peppers. Once the onions start to brown, add the peppers, if using fresh ones. Then, add your can of chicken. If using a jar of pre-roasted peppers, add these after you add the canned chicken or tuna.

4. Sprinkle herbs and add a bit more olive oil, always keeping the mixture moist in the pan. Add olives. An added extra is to add a couple of tablespoons of pesto sauce. Mix sauce into your pasta.

5. Add a bit of olive oil if it looks too dry. Sprinkle the cheese as desired.

6. This dish goes well with garlic bread and Rosé wine.

Serves 3-5 depending on appetite!

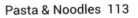

NEW YEAR'S BOLOGNESE
Alex Mastrando

I've been a freelance French horn player for the last 30 years, with roots in South Philly/South Jersey, settling in North Jersey in 1999. Since then, I've had the pleasure of working (and cooking) with some of the finest musicians in and around New York City.

This recipe is the culmination of many wine-filled New Years Eve celebrations at the New Hope, Pennsylvania home of a dear friend, and wonderfully talented musician. It became a tradition to have a big pasta dish to ring in the new year, and I always ended up being the chef du jour.

Special Prep/Equipment
5-6 quart saucepan

2 tablespoons vegetable or canola oil

6 tablespoons unsalted butter

1 cup onion, ½ inch dice

1 cup celery, ½ inch dice

1 cup carrot, peeled and ½ inch dice

½ pound ground beef (85% lean)

½ pound ground pork

½ pound ground veal

Salt and pepper

2 cups whole milk

¼ teaspoon nutmeg, freshly grated

2 cups dry white wine (Sauvignon Blanc, or dry vermouth in a pinch - Dolin Dry is nice in this)

1 (28 ounce) can Whole Peeled San Marzano tomatoes, crushed by hand (if you can find crushed San Marzano tomatoes, great. Just make sure they're San Marzano. Don't skimp!)

1. Heat oil and unsalted butter in pan over medium heat. Once the butter has melted, immediately add the onion and cook until soft, approximately 5 minutes.

2. Add celery and carrot and cook for about 2 minutes, stirring.

3. Add meats and a pinch of salt and pepper. Cook until browned. Do not drain off fat!

4. Set the heat to low, pour in milk and simmer about an hour. Stir in the nutmeg at the end of the hour.

5. Add the white wine (or vermouth) and simmer for 1¼ hours.

6. Add the crushed tomatoes and stir. Bring to a gentle simmer.

7. Cook uncovered for 3 hours, until reduced. Stir occasionally. Season to taste with salt and pepper at the end of the 3 hours.

Note
This Bolognese goes best with homemade pappardelle and a really nice Carménère, though, the Australian wine with the kangaroo logo can be surprisingly adequate (Yellow Tail).

Serves 6

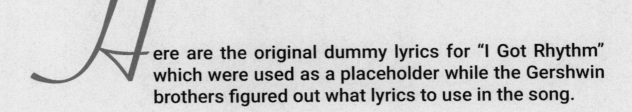

Here are the original dummy lyrics for "I Got Rhythm" which were used as a placeholder while the Gershwin brothers figured out what lyrics to use in the song.

Roly-Poly,
Eating solely
Ravioli,
Better watch your diet or bust.

Lunch or dinner,
You're a sinner.
Please get thinner.
Losing all that fat is a must.

Main Courses

MEATS

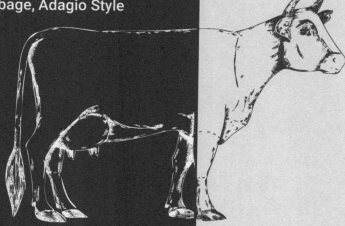

BEEF STEW

～ Patricia Johnson

I am a violinist and owner of Encore Music.

My beef stew includes the flavors I love and sometimes I change the herbs around a bit, so you should feel free to change some of the herbs to your liking, as well.

Special Prep/Equipment
I soak the beef cubes in wine overnight, or at least for several hours.

2½ - 3 pounds of beef chuck, cubed for stew	4 carrots, cut into 2" pieces
2 cups dry red wine, divided	¼ cup kalamata olives (halved, and spiced, if you can find them)
3 tablespoons of olive oil	1 sprig of rosemary
1 pound mushrooms, halved (cremini or white button mushrooms)	2 bay leaves
Salt, pepper, and herbes de Provence, to your taste	3 cups beef broth
3 thick slices of pancetta, roughly chopped	1 can crushed tomatoes
½ large vidalia onion, roughly chopped	3 medium red or Yukon Gold potatoes, halved
2 cloves of garlic, smashed and chopped	

1. Place the beef in a freezer bag and pour a cup of the wine over the meat. Place in refrigerator for 4 hours to overnight. Reserve the other cup of wine. (Of course, you can pour another cup for yourself to enjoy as you are cooking.)

2. Remove the meat from bag and pat dry with paper towels. Make sure it's really dry so the meat will brown.

3. In a large pot, heat olive oil. Season meat with salt and pepper. Place the meat in the pot and brown. Remove the meat and set aside.

4. Lower heat to medium. You may need to add a little more olive oil. Add herbes de Provence. Add pancetta and mushrooms. Cook for at least 5 minutes. Add onion. Cook for a couple of minutes. Add garlic, carrots, olives. (Add red pepper flakes if the olives are not spiced.) Cook for a couple of minutes.

5. Pour in reserved wine and deglaze the pot bottom. Pour in just a little bit of the beef broth. After deglazing, turn down the heat a bit and let the flavors blend for a couple of minutes.

6. Return the meat and all of its juices to the pot. Pour in all the wine and beef broth. Bring the heat up and bring to a boil. As you add the tomatoes, turn down the heat. The liquid should almost cover the stew. Simmer for 1 hour before adding the potatoes. In all, the stew should simmer for 3½ hours, or until the beef falls apart.

Note
If you can't find spiced olives, add red pepper flakes. Experiment with the herbs. For example, instead of herbes de Provence, I sometimes use Italian herb blend.

Any hearty red wine will work. Choose the wine you will drink as you eat this stew.

Remember to take the bay leaves out before serving. Serve with crusty bread.

Serves 5-6

6 CAN CHILI
~ Katie Steinhauer

I am a drummer/percussionist. I played in *Hamilton: An American Musical* (Philip Tour).

This was my mom's go-to chili! Easy, fairly quick, and delicious! I remember her making this in the fall and winter months. It makes your house/apartment smell great and is a total crowd pleaser!

Special Prep/Equipment
A medium-large size pot or dutch oven

1 pound ground meat (I use ground turkey)

1 onion, chopped into bite sized pieces

½ package of taco seasoning

1 small can tomato sauce

1 can diced tomatoes

1 can sweet corn

1 can kidney beans

1 can pinto beans

1 can black beans

Salt/pepper to taste

If you want heat, add any pepper you enjoy!

1. Brown ground meat, add chopped onion and taco seasoning and let them cook together for a few minutes.

2. Add all the canned ingredients and bring to a boil. Let simmer for an hour or so and serve with cornbread!

3. You can also add avocado, cheese, sour cream, green onions, and Fritos as toppings, if you like!

Note
You can drain the juice out of the cans of beans if you like, depending on if you want a dry chili. This recipe also lends itself for perfect serving adjustments so you can make a HUGE pot of it for a crowd by doubling the recipe or use half the recipe for a smaller gathering. The chili could also be made in a crock pot/instant pot, just brown the meat first and add everything else. Cook on low for a few hours.

Serves about 10

TOMMY'S TEXAS CHILI
~ Mary Schmidt & Elizabeth Thompson

Mary is a flutist and Elizabeth is a cellist. And we are also the librarians for the Princeton Symphony Orchestra.

This is Elizabeth's father's chili recipe. Elizabeth's father owned a cattle ranch in Texas. He loved making this chili and Elizabeth continues the tradition to this day.

Special Prep/Equipment
Large pot or dutch oven

1 tablespoon olive oil

1 large yellow onion, chopped fine

1 large bell pepper, diced, seeds removed

2 pounds ground meatloaf mix (mix of equal parts ground beef, veal, and pork)

½ teaspoon (rounded) cumin

¼ cup (rounded) chili powder

½ tablespoon (rounded) salt

½ teaspoon (rounded) pepper

1 (14.5 ounce) can diced peeled tomatoes

1 can organic chili beans (kidney or pinto beans, or a combo of both)

1 cup chicken broth

1. In a dutch oven or large cooking pot, saute onions and pepper in olive oil.

2. In a large skillet, brown the meat. Midway through browning the meat, add the cumin, chili powder, salt and pepper.

3. Add the entire can of tomatoes and any liquid from the can to the meat. Cook for 10-15 minutes.

4. Scoop the meat and tomato mix into the dutch oven.

5. Add the beans. Mix it all up.

6. Stir in 1 cup chicken broth.

7. As the chili cooks, add water as needed for desired consistency (start with ½ cup).

8. Simmer for an hour or more.

Serves 6-8

ROULADEN
～ Christine Coyle

I am a cellist and teacher.

My mother taught me this recipe and her mother taught her. A favorite of mine.

Special Prep/Equipment
Several toothpicks or skewers

4-8 braciole beef slices

Mustard – enough to spread on each slice of meat

1½ cups finely chopped onion

¾-1 cup thinly sliced slab bacon

4-8 small gherkin pickles

Salt and pepper, to taste

2 tablespoons butter

2 tablespoons olive oil

Chicken broth or water, a few cups

2 tablespoons flour, for thickening sauce

1. Lay out slices of braciole and spread with mustard. Sprinkle each with onion and bacon. Place a pickle on each and roll up, not too tightly, and secure with a toothpick or skewer. Don't worry if a bit of the stuffing falls out, just toss it in the pan, it makes the gravy better. Salt and pepper each roll.

2. Place oil and butter in a deep pan which can hold all the rolls and has a cover and heat to medium high. Sear all sides of the meat. Approx. ten minutes. Lower heat and add water or chicken stock to half way up the sides of the rolls. Cover and simmer for two hours. Add more water if necessary.

3. Before serving, thicken the sauce by mixing the flour with 1 tablespoon of water or sauce from the pan. Stir this slurry into the sauce. Cook for 3 minutes more or until sauce thickens.

4. Serve with red cabbage and dumplings or spätzle or egg noodles.

Serves 6

ROCKY HORROR "EDDIE" MEATLOAF
~ Samantha Nahra

I am a soprano who is the creator of *A Dramatic Soprano Tries Cooking...* on YouTube and Opera on Tap NYC!

This is an original recipe I created for my Rocky Horror episode of *A Dramatic Soprano Tries Cooking...* for last Halloween!

2 pounds ground turkey

4 eggs

2 cups breadcrumbs

2 tablespoons rosemary

1 tablespoon cilantro

1 cup sour cherry jam

1 hunk of brie cheese

Special Prep/Equipment
Rimmed pizza sheet

1. Preheat oven to 375°.

2. Mix turkey, eggs, breadcrumbs, rosemary, and cilantro together.

3. Grease a pizza sheet and form "Eddie's Body" wrapping jam and Brie inside.

4. Bake for 45-50 minutes or until meat thermometer reads 165° in the thickest part of your "Eddie".

5. Let cool and serve.

6. Don't tell Columbia!

Serves a small party of sweet transvestites

MISO PORK BELLY
~ Paul Wonjin Cho

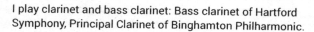

I play clarinet and bass clarinet: Bass clarinet of Hartford Symphony, Principal Clarinet of Binghamton Philharmonic.

Courtesy of my dear friend Gi Lee, this modified pork belly (called sahm-gyup-ssal) has long become my family's go-to meat dish.

Special Prep/Equipment
An air fryer works best, but I would guess you can oven roast.

1 pound pork belly

1 tablespoon miso paste

1-2 teaspoons honey
(adjust amount for your taste)

2 tablespoons cooking liquor
(soju, mirin, etc. – no wine)

Salt and pepper for taste

1. Cut pork belly into bite size pieces. I usually cut it to 1 x ½ x ½" pieces.

2. Mix miso paste, honey, cooking liquor, salt, and pepper, at room temperature.

3. Put the paste on the meat, mix thoroughly.

4. Let chill for 30 minutes in the fridge (you can omit this step).

5. Cook it in the air fryer for 15 - 20 minutes at 325°.

Serves 10-12

SWEDISH MEATBALLS

~ Annelie Fahlstedt

I am a freelance violinist and teacher.

These meatballs are traditionally served on Christmas Eve, along with lingonberry sauce, small buttered potatoes which have been boiled in water with fresh dill, accompanied on the side with buttered crispbread topped with sliced Jarlsberg cheese. My mother's recipe did not include sauce, so I have modified it using a recipe found in an old magazine with this note added underneath: Institute/Food/Mildred Ying, Director. *(Source: Good Housekeeping Magazine)*

Special Prep/Equipment
Large skillet

Meatballs:

¼ - ½ stick butter

½ large onion, chopped

2 pounds ground beef

1 egg

½ cup dry or fresh bread crumbs

¼ cup half-and-half

1 - 2 teaspoon salt

1 teaspoon ground pepper

¼ teaspoon each: allspice, mace, and nutmeg

Splash of soy sauce

Sauce:

¼ cup flour

1 teaspoon sugar

Ground pepper and salt to taste

½ teaspoon allspice

½ - ¾ cup water

1 cup half-and-half

Parsley, chopped, to garnish

Lingonberry sauce

1. Finely cut up onion and cook in a big skillet in butter until tender.

2. In a large bowl, mix the fried onion with ground beef, onion, egg, bread crumbs, half-and-half, salt, pepper, allspice, mace, nutmeg, and splash of soy sauce.

3. Roll into small balls and cook on medium heat in the same skillet as you did onion, adding more butter if needed. Don't pan-fry on too high heat or the meatballs will burn on the outside before they are cooked on the inside.

4. Remove meatballs as they finish and place in big bowl.

5. Once all meatballs are cooked and removed from pan, make the sauce.

6. Add about ¼ cup flour, a little at a time into drippings in skillet, whisking vigorously so flour does not clump. Add teaspoon sugar, ground pepper and salt to taste along with ½ teaspoon allspice. Gradually stir in ½ - ¾ cup water and up to 1 cup of half-and-half, stirring constantly until mixture is thickened and boils, adding more liquid if necessary.

7. Return meatballs to skillet, simmer and cover to blend flavors for 5 - 10 minutes, stirring occasionally.

8. Spoon meatballs into serving dish, garnish with chopped parsley and cover to keep warm. Serve with lingonberry sauce.

Yields about 20 meatballs depending on size

SHANGHAI RED-COOKED ANISE PORK
～ Paul Woodiel

I'm a Broadway violinist/fiddler. I started 30 years ago as the *Fiddler in the Pit* for the 25th anniversary production starring Topol, and now I'm concertmaster of the nascent smash hit *Mrs. Doubtfire*. During the pandemic, I've been playing a lot of Swedish nyckelharpa and cooking!

My mom was born in Shanghai, as a part of the American community there in the 1930s. Her dad was born and raised there, bilingually, by my great-grandma. He also learned how to cook native dishes there from local cooks. They would have stayed in China forever, but that war got in the way, and so my grandfather sent his wife and kids to the US, while he himself was captured, and spent the Pacific war as a guest of the Emperor, in a prison camp in the Philippines. My mom and family had no clue about his fate until his liberation years later. Happily, he then rejoined his family in Tennessee, where he had a long career as a surgeon and accomplished Chinese chef, passing along his authentic recipes to my mom, who taught them to me.

This dish is my favorite of all, for my entire life. The heady redolence of this braise fills the house, and reminds me of my late mom and grandfather, like anyone's favorite recipe should! Getting the glaze right requires attention, but otherwise, it's throw it all in the pot and wait.

Serve this very rich dish with plenty of steamed rice and a simple green like steamed bok choy or Chinese (Napa) cabbage. It's decadent, but worth it. Eat vegan for a week before, if it makes you feel better, but otherwise, ENJOY!

Special Prep/Equipment
A good iron dutch oven or large cast iron enameled pot

2 pound slab of skin-on pork belly	4 whole star anise
2-3" hunk of ginger root, cut into a dozen or more "coins"	8 ounce can bamboo shoots (or larger can, if you like...I do!)
2 bunches scallions, divided	2 tablespoons light soy sauce
3 tablespoons vegetable oil, total	2½ tablespoons dark soy sauce
3 tablespoons sugar	3 tablespoons Shaoxing rice wine
5 cloves of garlic, smashed	

1. To begin, bring a stock pot of water to a boil.

2. Take your slab of pork belly and scrape the skin side with a knife to remove any hairs or other matter that may remain on it. Put it in the boiling pot to blanch, along with a few coins of the ginger and three scallions tied in a knot. Let it boil for 5-7 minutes, using a slotted spoon to skim off any gray scum which may rise to the top.

3. Remove the pork, then strain and save 3 cups or so of the blanching water for the braise, discarding vegetables. Let it cool for a minute or so, and then with a sharp knife, slice the slab into cubes, about 1½-2" wide. The idea is to have a square piece of skin and fat on every piece. Pat them as dry as possible with paper towels.

4. Heat about 3 tablespoons water in a dutch oven or a large enameled iron pot at medium heat. Put about the same amount of sugar in and stir constantly to dissolve. This is the only tricky part of the dish. Let the sugar caramelize to a brown color but don't burn it! It can go from brown to burned quickly in a heavy pan. When it reaches the deep amber color, add a tablespoon of oil and mix vigorously together as it bubbles.

5. Keep the heat at medium while adding the pieces of pork. You want to coat and brown all sides of each piece, turning them with tongs, if possible. Try not to break the pieces of fat/pork apart, and again, don't let your heat get too high and burn the sugar.

6. Now throw in 4 whole stars of anise, a whole bunch of scallions cut in half, 5 cloves of smashed garlic, bamboo shoots, and the rest of the ginger coins which you've smashed with the back edge of your knife to release their flavor. Push them around in the pan to give them a head start cooking among the pork pieces for a minute or two.

7. Now, add dark and light soy sauce and the rice wine, and gently mix for a few seconds. Now you want to settle everything in the pan, and add the HOT water to the pot, enough to just cover the pork. Bring to a boil, and then immediately turn the heat to a low simmer. Cover and leave it for at least 90 minutes, even 2 hours or so!

8. Clean up your kitchen and check your email. You can even start your steamed rice and green side dish while it cooks!

9. When it's done, you can serve the pieces on rice with the very succulent sauce spooned over, with a chopped scallion as garnish. If you have the patience, though, you can reduce the sauce for a bit, and put it ALL in the fridge overnight. The next day, you'll have a thick layer of fat which you can discard (most of), leaving the delicious jellied sauce below. It reheats perfectly on the stovetop and if anything, is even BETTER the next day, and the day after that!

> **Note:** If you like, you can wrap the star anise in a bit of cheesecloth before adding it, so it can be removed at the end - chomping down on a piece of a star can be unpleasant.

Serves 6

AUNT MARGIE'S HAMBURGER CASSEROLE
(AMERICAN GOULASH) ～ Keith O'Quinn

I am a NYC freelance and Broadway trombonist.

My Aunt Margie from Missouri, who is 97 years old, gave us this easy recipe that is a great weekday comfort food.

Special Prep/Equipment
A large skillet with a cover

1. Heat a large skillet over medium heat. Add ground beef, and break up and stir until just browned. Drain excess fat off.

2. Add the diced onion, garlic, and mushrooms, and cook until soft, about 5-6 minutes.

3. Add the basil, bay leaf, crushed red pepper and stir to combine. Then add the tomato sauce, elbow noodles and enough water to cover everything by about an inch, stirring to combine. Bring to a boil, cover, reduce heat to a simmer and cook until the noodles are tender, about 10 minutes longer.

4. Remove lid and stir to let excess liquid reduce if necessary.

5. Add Parmesan cheese, and salt and pepper to taste and stir to combine.

Serves 5-6

1 pound ground beef

1 medium onion, peeled and diced

2 - 3 cloves of garlic, diced

3 - 4 large mushrooms, sliced (or other vegetables)

1 teaspoon dried basil

1 bay leaf

¼ teaspoon crushed red pepper (optional)

1½ cups favorite tomato sauce

6 - 8 ounces dried elbow pasta

2 cups water to cover

Parmesan cheese (optional)

Salt and pepper to taste

2 DELICIOUS RECIPES FOR LEFTOVER ROAST BEEF
~ Allison Brewster Franzetti

I am a pianist. I'm still teaching, recording and doing some live stream performances.

I made up these recipes on a couple evenings, when I needed to use up leftover roast beef! Enjoy!

Beef Stir-Fry

1 large onion, finely chopped

4 cloves of garlic, peeled and chopped (or use a garlic press)

Vegetable oil to coat the bottom of a large pan, or wok, if you have one

1 tablespoon of sesame oil

½ of a leftover roast beef, cubed

Salt, pepper, soy sauce, teriyaki sauce and powdered curry to taste

2 cups of cooked white rice

1. Chop onion and garlic. In a large pan or wok, heat vegetable oil with 1 tablespoon of sesame oil.

2. Add onion and garlic and cook until browned, not burnt!

3. Add the cubed roast beef and add in salt, pepper, soy sauce, teriyaki sauce and powdered curry to taste (basically to lightly coat the meat, onion and garlic).

4. Stir and then cover until thoroughly heated through.

5. In a separate pot, follow the usual recipe for preparing white rice. When both are ready, place rice on a plate and top with roast beef/onion/garlic mixture.

Tomato-Beef Melange

Olive oil to coat the bottom of a pot

1 large onion, chopped

4 cloves of garlic, chopped (or use a garlic press)

½ of a leftover roast beef, cubed

Salt, pepper, garlic powder, and oregano to taste

1 large jar of tomato sauce

2 - 3 potatoes, peeled and cut into cubes

1 can of mixed vegetables

1. In a large pot (typically one you'd use for pasta, etc.), heat oil. Add onion and garlic and cook until browned.

2. Add the cubed roast beef and stir together, heating the meat through. Add salt, pepper, garlic powder, and oregano to taste.

3. Add jar of tomato sauce to cover, making sure meat is thoroughly covered. If there is some leftover sauce in the jar, add water, shake it up and add the contents to the pot. For those who like more sauce, add another ½ jar of tomato sauce instead.

4. Add the potatoes and mixed vegetables and cook for about 1 hour or until potatoes are thoroughly cooked and meat is tender.

Serves 4 for each recipe

MEAT LOVERS' BUTTERNUT SQUASH LASAGNA
～ Steven M. Alper

I am a composer, arranger, music director and copyist.

This is, hands down, the best noodle-less "lasagna" recipe I've come up with, and it's really just a pretty standard lasagna recipe with squash slices substituted. I spent an afternoon reading similar recipes and then just made this up.

Special Prep/Equipment
9 x 13" baking dish

1. Preheat oven to 350°.

2. In a large pan, saute the onion and garlic in the olive oil until fragrant (maybe 5 minutes).

3. Brown the ground beef with the onion and garlic. While it is browning, season with salt and pepper.

4. While beef is browning, cut the ends off the squash and peel. Cut the bulb end off and reserve for other use. Using a mandolin or vegetable peeler, cut the squash the long way, making long, thin lasagna-like slices. The thinner the better.

5. After the beef has browned, remove from pan to a bowl. Drain the fat and discard.

6. In the same pan, cook the sausage according to directions. When the sausage is cooked, cut into ⅛" slices on a slight diagonal. Add slices to the bowl with the beef mixture.

7. Add the tomato sauce to the beef-sausage mixture and thoroughly combine.

8. In a separate bowl, combine ricotta, ¾ of the mozzarella, half the Parmesan, the beaten egg, and half the oregano. Add the spinach and thoroughly combine.

9. Grease a 9 x 12" baking dish and then spread a thin layer of the meat sauce. Jigsaw a layer of squash slices.

10. Onto the squash layer, spread about ⅓ of the remaining meat sauce, then ⅓ of the cheese mixture. Top with a layer of squash.

11. Repeat the previous step.

12. Onto the squash layer, spread the remaining ⅓ of the meat sauce. Sprinkle with the remaining 2 ounces of mozzarella and the remaining 4 ounces of Parmesan.

13. Bake for 45 minutes. Allow to rest for 15 minutes and sprinkle the remaining oregano.

Ingredients

1 medium yellow onion, chopped

4 cloves of garlic, minced

1 pound ground beef

1 large butternut squash (neck only)

1 pound sweet Italian sausage

24 ounce jar of your favorite (low carb) tomato sauce

16 ounce container of ricotta cheese

8 ounces shredded mozzarella

8 ounces grated Parmesan cheese, divided

1 large egg, beaten

1 tablespoon fresh oregano

12 ounce package of frozen spinach (thawed, with liquid squeezed out)

1 tablespoon fresh basil

Olive oil

Salt & Pepper

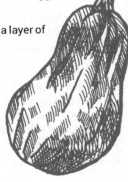

Serves 4-6

BRAISED LAMB SHANKS

∾ Karl Kawahara

I am a violinist. I've played with the Orchestra Of St. Luke's and in numerous Broadway productions since 1983.

This is a basic recipe for lamb shanks braised in the oven. I've taken inspiration from Daniel Gritzer's recipe on *Serious Eats*.

Special Prep/Equipment
A dutch oven with cover

If lamb shanks seem very fatty, trim excess fat leaving a thin layer.

3-4 lamb shanks, about 2½ pounds	2 tablespoons tomato paste
2 tablespoons neutral oil, such as grapeseed oil	1-1½ cups red wine
1 medium onion, diced	1½ cups chicken stock (homemade preferable)
2 medium carrots, diced	
2 stalks of celery, diced	1 sprig fresh rosemary (or 2 teaspoons dried)
4-5 cloves of garlic, crushed and roughly chopped	2 bay leaves
2 anchovy filets (optional)	Salt and pepper

1. Preheat oven to 300° and move rack to middle position.

2. Heat 1 tablespoon oil in dutch oven over medium high heat. Season lamb shanks liberally with salt and pepper. When oil is shimmering hot, brown shanks on all sides, about 10-12 minutes total. Don't overcrowd the pan or meat will not brown properly. It's better to do it in shifts if they don't fit. Remove lamb to a plate. If there are any blackened bits in the pan wipe with a paper towel or remove with a spoon.

3. Add additional tablespoon of oil and add onions, carrots, and celery to dutch oven. Season with salt and pepper and saute, adjusting heat to prevent burning. Cook until softened and just beginning to brown, about 5-7 minutes. Add garlic and continue cooking for about 1 minute.

4. Make a well in the middle of the dutch oven and add anchovies (if using) breaking them up with a wooden spoon. Add tomato paste and stir. Pour wine into the pan and bring to a boil and cook for about 3 minutes to boil off alcohol. Add chicken broth. Place lamb shanks into the liquid. Add the rosemary sprig (or if using dried, crumble into the pan) and bay leaves. Bring to a simmer.

5. When the liquid is simmering, cover the dutch oven with lid leaving it slightly ajar and move it to the oven. Cook for 3 to 3½ hours, turning the shanks about halfway through. Meat should be very tender and almost falling off the bone.

6. When the lamb is done, remove shanks from oven and onto a plate. If gravy seems very fatty, degrease by skimming off layer of fat. Test for seasoning by adding more salt and pepper if you think it needs it.

7. Serve the lamb with the gravy over mashed potatoes, polenta, or side of your choice.

Note: This recipe can be modified by using white wine instead of red, beef broth instead of chicken broth. Different seasonings can also be used and rubbed onto the meat before browning, such as ground coriander and cumin. Also, different herbs can be substituted like thyme or oregano. Feel free to experiment with mushrooms or dried fruit, like figs or prunes.

Serves 3-4 (one shank per person)

SOUTH AFRICAN BOBOTIE

 Alexandra Knoll

I am an oboist, and I play in the American Symphony Orchestra.

South Africa, like the US, is a melting pot of cultures; African, European and Southeast Asian influences are very much reflected in its cuisine. Bobotie (bah-BOO-tee) is a South African dish with Indonesian and Malaysian roots. It's a slightly sweet curried meatloaf with an egg custard on top. It's traditionally served with sambals, which are side-dishes of fresh salads or greens. I adapted this recipe from Getaway magazine. I spent my first 20 years in Zimbabwe and South Africa and this is a dish that always brings me back to a happy childhood place.

Special Prep/Equipment

9 x 9" baking dish, or any shape dish of your choice

3 slices crustless bread (white or brown)

375 ml milk (about 1½ cups)

2 tablespoons olive oil

2 medium onions, diced

2 large cloves of garlic, crushed

2 inch nub of ginger, finely chopped or grated

2 tablespoons curry powder

1 teaspoon turmeric

1 teaspoon ground cumin

1 teaspoon ground coriander

(You can substitute the 4 dry spices with 2 tablespoons of Patak's Mild or Madras Curry Paste)

2 teaspoons salt

2 pounds ground beef

2 tablespoons apricot or peach jam

1 cup crushed tomatoes

⅔ cup raisins

½ cup water, if needed

2 eggs

8-10 bay leaves

1. Preheat oven to 375°. Soak bread in milk.

2. Heat oil in large pan and fry onions, garlic and fresh ginger. When this mixture is soft, add spices and salt. Cook another minute.

3. Add ground beef and cook until it's lost its pink color.

4. Add jam, crushed tomatoes and raisins. Cook until incorporated, and add water if too thick.

5. Drain and mash the bread mixture, reserving milk. Add bread to meat mixture and turn off heat.

6. Spoon meat and bread into your baking dish, and press it down.

7. Beat eggs with reserved milk (you should have 1⅓ cups or so) and pinch of salt and turmeric.

8. Pour eggs over meat mixture and stick the bay leaves into the meat.

9. Cook in hot oven for 45 minutes to 1 hour, or until egg topping is set.

10. Serve with basmati or your favorite rice, toasted slivered almonds, raita (grated cucumbers, yoghurt, cilantro) and salsa (finely chopped tomatoes, green peppers, red onion, oil and vinegar).

Serves up to 8

DEIRDRE'S "CORNER SCONE" BABY BACK RIBS

∿ Cliff Roberts

I play the Great Highland Bagpipe. I am the Pipe Major of St. Ann's of Hampton Pipes and Drums and I have taught bagpipes to many ages and abilities. I also teach traditional Irish Drum (The Bodhran). I play the 9/11 Service each year in the afternoon at St. Paul's Chapel in Manhattan for First Responders and Medical Staff who have died from exposure to the 9/11 debris field recovery and clean up.

My sister-in-law Deirdre and her husband Darren ran a small cafe and eatery in the Woodlawn section of the Bronx. This recipe is the result of many years of experimenting with the best way to make Baby Back Ribs without a smoker. While the "Corner Scone" is no longer there, the recipes live on from the sharing of great food with family. I have adapted it with my own "special dry rub", and it can be modified further to taste depending on how spicy or mild you prefer it. I think my recipe is a nice balance of the two.

Special Prep/Equipment

In order to really make baby back ribs work – you need to remove the thin film of connective tissue that is on the rib side of the baby backs. For step by step instructions on how to do this go to: *www.weber.com*. If you don't do this you really will not know it, but it will help the dry rub penetrate the meat a bit deeper.

> 1-2 full racks of baby back ribs
>
> Ground sea salt
>
> Fresh cracked black pepper
>
> Smoked paprika
>
> Chipotle or chile powder
>
> Cayenne powder
>
> Homemade BBQ sauce...or my favorite: Sweet Baby Ray's Hot and Sweet Sauce

1. Place 2 racks of ribs on a flat cookie sheet covered by a long sheet of heavy duty aluminum foil. Fold an equal length of foil over the top of the ribs. Allow some of the foil to be a "bit" longer on one end of the cookie sheet. This creates a rib cooking pocket that holds in the heat and the juices. This is important because this is how they become fall-off-the-bone tender.

2. Place the ribs meat side up, and cover all areas of meat with the dry spices, which is your "dry rub".

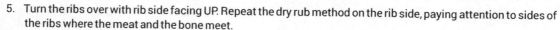

3. Apply a light dusting of salt and pepper, and a generous dusting of paprika. Put chipotle or chili powder in half the amount as the paprika, and a light dusting of cayenne, but more, if you like it spicy.

4. Push the dry rub down into the meat with your hands (wash hands to avoid rubbing the spices into your face or eyes).

5. Turn the ribs over with rib side facing UP. Repeat the dry rub method on the rib side, paying attention to sides of the ribs where the meat and the bone meet.

6. Create a foil tent over the ribs, crimping the foil carefully on all the sides. Make sure you leave one end of the tent with some foil overhanging (but crimped closed). You will use this as a drip edge when you have to pour off the juices after the first 2½ hours of cooking.

7. Cook the ribs in the oven at 250° for 2½ hours.

8. After 2½ hours, remove the ribs from the oven. Open the foil "drip edge" you created when you crimped the foil around the ribs. Using oven mitts, pour off the juices in a sink or vessel. Discard juices. Be careful to tilt the tray and not have the ribs slide out.

9. Take the top layer of aluminum foil completely off the ribs. Apply a generous amount of barbecue sauce over every part of the bone side of the ribs

10. Turn the ribs over, so meat side is up. Apply a generous amount of BBQ sauce on the meat side. Cook the ribs with the top foil OFF, meat side up for another 30 minutes with the oven at 325°.

11. Take the ribs out of oven and cut the rack to ½ rack or ¼ rack size for serving.

12. Serve with your favorite sides. If your ribs are very spicy, fresh cole slaw is a good addition to the plate.

Serve a half rack per person

GRILLED PORK CHOPS
Ming Yang

I am a violinist in the New Jersey Symphony Orchestra.

Easy to make and everyone loves it. I first saw the original recipe on Pinterest. But I changed some of it and added a few Chinese ingredients.

Special Prep/Equipment
The chops will need to marinate for at least couple of hours before preparing the dish.

Pork chops, enough for 4 people (I like to get at least ¾" thick chops with bone, but any cut pork chops will do.)

¼ cup soy sauce

½ cup Worcestershire sauce

⅓ cup brown sugar

4 cloves of minced garlic (amount depends on your taste)

½ cup extra virgin olive oil

Sesame oil, couple of drops

Salt & pepper to taste

1. Cut a small slit on the edge of each chop so it will stay flat and cook evenly.

2. Mix well all the remaining ingredients together in a bowl and then add your chops. Marinate for at least 2 hours, or you can make it overnight and put in the fridge. I put them in a big Ziploc bag and flip the bag half way through the marinating, so the chops are covered well with the marinade.

3. Grilling is the best way for this recipe, but you can pan fry it, too. Turn the grill on high and cook about 3 minutes on each side, but cook time depends on your grill and the thickness of the chops.

4. Serve with your favorite rice. Done!

Serves 4

GRANDMA'S SAUSAGE & POTATOES

~ Harry G. Searing

I play the bassoon, contrabassoon AND the almost extinct Heckelphone. I've been freelancing in the NYC/New Jersey area for about 50 years, so I'm old.

A very hearty and filling dish, Sandy's mom made it plain and simple, and delicious – just sausage, potatoes and onions. I couldn't leave well enough alone, so over the years it has morphed into this still easy to make casserole.

Special Prep/Equipment
Large and deep casserole
(I use a large Le Creuset)

1 pound Italian sweet sausage

1 pound potatoes – those little creamers are pretty popular right now, but Grandma would have made a face!

1 large yellow onion

4 or 5 cloves of garlic

1 green bell pepper, 1 red pepper, 1 yellow pepper, 1 orange pepper

Olive oil

Spices: salt, pepper, oregano, parsley, paprika (optional)

Note: You can also do a mix of sweet and hot Italian sausage. My preferred sausage has been Premio for more than several years, although I will try other brands from time to time in search of the ultimate sausage, kind of like trying bocals.

1. Preheat oven to 425°. Spray your casserole dish with canola oil.

2. Cut each sausage link into 6 pieces. You don't have to be perfect here, but then you probably never are anyway. Leave the casings on.

3. If using those little creamer potatoes, just wash 'em off. If you want to use red or russet, whatever, peel and cut into smaller chunks about the size of those pieces of sausage. Wash them off.

4. Slice the onion on the thick side, then make a cut from the center out so that you end up with long wide strips. Chop the garlic, or slice it, I don't care. Just don't fuggedaboutit.

5. *Peppers:* I cut the tops off, sometimes I discard them, if there's enough stuff there, I throw them into the mix. If the peppers are a good size, I cut them into quarters, remove the seeds and that fleshy stuff, then try to get 3 or 4 strips out of each quarter. In other words, with both the onions and peppers, you don't want to make the pieces too small or they'll cook away. Wash both the peppers and onions in a large bowl, add the washed potatoes.

6. In a measuring cup, pour in ¼ cup of olive oil and ¼ cup of water. Add your spices, go easy the first time, especially with the paprika and oregano as they can overwhelm the flavor. You wouldn't want to add them later, either. Salt and pepper you can add after cooking, no problemo. You'll figure it out, cuz you're gonna make this shit again! Mix the oil, water and spices together. Pour over the vegetables. Stir so they're well coated. You might think that this isn't enough but as the sausage cooks it will create, er, additional juices to keep it all moist, for awhile.

7. Transfer to your casserole. Add the sausage, stir it all again, if you like. Cover. Cook, stir things up at 45 minutes, scrape the bottom of the casserole, cover again and cook for at least another 15-20 minutes. Check. The sausage should be starting to brown. If it's starting to look a little dry or there's not much liquid left, add some oil and water. Cook another 10-15 minutes uncovered. Watch it, don't go make a reed or practice or something. PAY ATTENCH!

8. Serve with nice crusty Italian bread and a good Montepulciano di Abruzzi. $7.99 a bottle sounds about right.

Serve 2-3

LAMB MEATBALLS
～ Daryl Goldberg

I am a cellist. I am a member of The New York Pops, and perform with many other orchestras at Carnegie Hall, Lincoln Center and on Broadway.

I am partial to middle eastern cooking and experimented until I found a satisfying option to ordering out!

Special Prep/Equipment
Parchment paper and a rimmed baking pan or cookie sheet is needed. These meatballs freeze well.

1 small onion, diced

1 pound ground lamb

½ cup parsley, chopped

½ teaspoon ground coriander

½ teaspoon ground allspice

½ teaspoon cinnamon

½ teaspoon garlic powder

1 teaspoon cumin

1 teaspoon salt

¼ teaspoon nutmeg

¼ teaspoon pepper

½ cup bread crumbs

1 egg, beaten

Plain yogurt, sour cream or ketchup for serving, if desired

1. Saute onion until almost brown, set aside briefly to cool.

2. Preheat oven to 375°.

3. Put lamb, parsley, and spices in large bowl and mix well.

4. Add onion, breadcrumbs, and egg, incorporate gently.

5. Form mixture into golf size balls and place on parchment lined, rimmed b aking sheet.

6. Bake for 20 minutes.

7. Serve with plain yogurt, sour cream, or ketchup according to preference.

Serves 4 (about 16 meatballs)

MOM'S BULGOGI
～ Hansaem Lim

I am an Associate violinist in the Met Orchestra.

This is a traditional Korean BBQ dish. The word Bulgogi is directly translated as fire + meat. This recipe has been passed down from my grandmother to my mother to me, and one day I'll teach my daughter.

3 pounds rib eye, thinly sliced

1 mid size onion

20 cloves garlic

1 Asian pear, optional

¾ cup soy sauce

¼ cup cooking sake or mirin

¾ cup sugar

1 tablespoon pepper

2 tablespoons sesame seeds, or ground sesame

¼ cup sesame oil

Desired vegetables

Special Prep/Equipment
Blender, frying pan. Before cooking, the beef needs to marinate in the sauce for a day.

1. Dab the beef with a paper towel to clean the meat.

2. Make the sauce. Grind onion, garlic, asian pear, soy sauce, cooking sake, and sugar in a blender.

3. Add ground pepper, sesame seeds, and sesame oil to the mixture.

4. Marinate the meat in this sauce for one day.

5. Cook in a pan with desired vegetables such as scallion, broccoli, and sliced carrots.

Serves 5

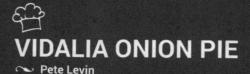

VIDALIA ONION PIE
∽ Pete Levin

I'm a keyboard player, composer and arranger, mostly jazz. After 35 years in NYC studios, I'm now living upstate near Woodstock, NY, still recording and playing live – looking forward to touring again someday, when it's possible.

This is a sweet onion pie with chopped ham, eggs, cheese and cream. I can't remember where I picked this up. I've modified it several times. It's a very unusual side dish that almost always meets with applause. In season, definitely use Vidalias. If you can't find them, use the sweetest onions available. Variations: Substitute small cooked bacon pieces for the ham, or pancetta - or skip the meat entirely. Seafood might be possible, although I haven't tried that yet. Sprinkling in some chopped chives is nice. Substitute blue cheese for cheddar, or use your favorite melty cheese.

WARNING: Serious cholesterol content! Ask your doctor if it's ok to have a second helping. Vegans, stop reading here.

Special Prep/Equipment
Not being very good at making pie dough from scratch, I use store-bought pie crusts.

3-4 medium sized Vidalia onions

3-4 tablespoons butter

¼-½ cup chopped ham (optional)

*Ham alternatives: crumbled bacon pieces, pancetta

Small handful chopped chives

Chilled, store-bought unbaked pie shell for a deep-dish, 2-crust pie

¼-½ cup crumbled blue cheese, or shredded Cheddar cheese

3 egg yolks plus 1 whole egg

½ cup heavy cream

Salt, freshly ground black pepper

Dash of nutmeg (optional)

Optionally – 1 more egg to make an egg wash for the crust

1. Preheat oven 450°.

2. Halve the onions and slice thinly. Saute in butter until tender; don't let them brown. Add ham, then salt and pepper to taste. Optionally, add a small handful of chopped chives. Pour into a chilled pie crust. Fill it almost to the top and spread evenly. Sprinkle the onion mixture with the shredded cheese. Whisk together the egg yolks, whole egg and cream, then pour over onion mixture. Fill to just short of the top. With a spoon, press down on the onions here and there to get the cream mixture to soak in. Sprinkle with a pinch of nutmeg (optional).

3. With a rolling pin, roll the 2nd pie shell dough flat and fit it over the filling for a top crust. Pinch all around the edges to seal it and trim off the excess. Cut a ½" hole in the center. You can use those extra bits from the trimmed edges to make fancy little thingies on top of the crust; birds, leaves, stars, whatever turns you on. Optionally, brush the top crust and fancy thingies with an egg wash, if you like that kind of crust.

4. Bake the pie at 450° for 10 minutes. Reduce heat to 350° and continue baking until the custard is set and the crust is browned – about 30 minutes more. Serve warm or cool.

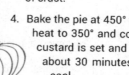

Serves 6-8

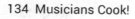

HERB-Y CRUSTLESS SAVORY PIE
~ Miriam Lockhart

What a privilege it has been playing clarinet, Eb clarinet, bass clarinet, and basset horn in orchestras, chamber music, and shows (some flute and sax too) in New York and surrounding areas. Really missing it!

This recipe started out as a refrigerator cleanout/kitchen sink recipe. It's never quite the same twice. It has become a favorite, and now is even served to guests! Great texture. Serve with a piece of nice chewy bread. This is the only recipe I use frozen vegetables in, and you can use previously cooked leftover vegetables instead. Also good as a vegetarian dish. Just leave out the meat. I hope you enjoy it as much as we have!

Special Prep/Equipment
Pie plate

2 tablespoons olive oil

1 onion, chopped

2 or more cloves garlic, minced

Salt and pepper to taste

½ teaspoon dried thyme,

1 teaspoon dried marjoram

1 teaspoon dried crushed rosemary

Freshly ground pepper

½ pound ground turkey or ground beef

1 cup frozen lima beans or other beans on hand

1 cup frozen corn, or other leftover vegetables

2 cups frozen spinach or other leafy green vegetables

8 ounces cottage cheese

1 cup grated cheddar

3 beaten eggs

½ cup milk

1. Preheat oven to 350°. Butter or oil your pie dish.

2. If using frozen vegetables, measure them out into a colander and let them defrost a bit first.

3. Heat olive oil and add chopped onion. Saute, stirring occasionally, for 3 minutes, then add garlic, and cook 3 minutes more. Add the salt, freshly ground pepper, thyme, marjoram, and rosemary and cook 1 or 2 minutes more, until the herbs are fragrant. Transfer all this to a mixing bowl.

4. Brown the meat in the same pan, adding more salt if desired. Transfer to mixing bowl and stir around. Add frozen lima beans or leftover beans, frozen corn, frozen spinach or other leafy green vegetable. Stir around.

5. Add the cottage cheese, grated cheddar, eggs, and milk. Stir around. Pour into prepared pie dish and cook in preheated oven for 60-70 minutes. It will still be a little jiggly.

6. Cool for 20 minutes or until set before serving.

Serves 4

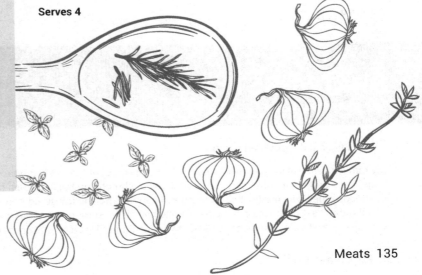

WHITE BEAN AND SAUSAGE STEW
~ Debbie Sepe

I am a freelance cellist in the Broadway, orchestra and chamber music fields. I also teach at Adelphi University.

This recipe is adapted from a Pampered Chef recipe book entitled *29 Minutes to Dinner*. I purchased this recipe book along with several kitchen gadgets at a Tupperware style house party. This recipe has become a family favorite. The original recipe calls for 1 medium bulb of fennel, but I use onion instead. You can use ground pork instead of the Italian sausage and roll it into small meatballs instead of peeling the casings off of the sausage links, which is more time consuming. I also use sweet sausage instead of hot sausage. It calls for fresh basil, but I don't always have that on hand and it's fine without it.

Special Prep/Equipment
Large pot for stew

1 package of sweet Italian sausage links or 1 pound of ground pork	2 cups chicken broth
2 medium carrots	2 garlic cloves, pressed
½ onion, diced	2 (15 ounce) cans cannellini beans, drained and rinsed
1 (14½ ounce) can petite diced tomatoes, undrained	Parmesan cheese grated
	Fresh basil

1. If using sausages, remove casings and cut in half and then cut cross-wise into small pieces. If using the pork, roll pork into small balls. Place your chosen meat into a 4-quart casserole. Cook over medium heat for about 5 minutes or until golden brown. Move the pork or sausage around so it doesn't burn. When done, remove from pot and drain grease.

2. As sausage or ground pork cooks, peel and chop carrots and onions. In same casserole, cook carrots and onion (add a touch of olive oil if needed) 3-5 minutes. Return meat to casserole and stir for 1 minute.

3. Stir in tomatoes, broth, garlic, and beans to casserole. Simmer stew, uncovered for 10-12 minutes or until carrots are tender. Remove from heat and serve immediately.

4. It's best served in bowls with Parmesan sprinkled on top and fresh basil, if you like.

Serves 6

BRATWURST
~ Bruce Tammen

I am a singer and choral conductor.

My family farmed in western Minnesota. They grew most of their own produce, raised chickens and a few hogs and a couple of calves. My grandfather would butcher in the Fall when the weather turned cool. Sausage of various types was made of all the scraps. I suppose he and my grandmother used recipes; I never knew about them. I set out to learn, or relearn, how they did it. Started with a basic formula for pork sausage, fiddled with spices and herbs I know they used at various times. This is what I came up with...

Special Prep/Equipment

If you want to stuff the sausage in casings, you'll have to invest in equipment for that. Otherwise, you'll just need some way to grind the meat.

1. The meat should be nearly frozen. Cut in small pieces (to save wear on your equipment) and grind it. I prefer a coarse grind.

2. Grind the spices coarsely (I use a coffee grinder), and add, along with salt and cold water, to the meat. Mix by hand until it melds together.

3. If stuffing in casings, find out how to do that elsewhere (it is technology, not recipe). Otherwise, form in burger or sausage shapes, and fry.

5 pounds pork butt, 70% lean	1 teaspoon dried marjoram
½ teaspoon allspice, ground	1½ teaspoon white pepper, ground
1 teaspoon caraway seed	4 teaspoon salt (be generous)
1 teaspoon juniper berries, ground	1 cup cold water

Yields 5 pounds of brats.

CORNED BEEF AND CABBAGE, ADAGIO STYLE
∽ Micheale Ryan

I am a clarinetist/woodwind player who freelances with various orchestras and Broadway shows along with teaching students privately. During the pandemic, my family formed a non-profit, *metamorphicentertainment.org*, which brings entertainment to seniors and underserved communities.

This is a traditional Irish recipe passed down through my family. I adapted it to make in the slow cooker as I am usually working on St. Patrick's Day, yet I still wanted to celebrate with a traditional meal. After a trip to Ireland, I found that using corned beef is an American tradition. In the 1800's many Irish refugees settled in lower Manhattan along with other ethnic groups. Corned beef was an economical staple found in local butcher shops.

Special Prep/Equipment

Large slow-cooker

1. Peel carrots and cut into 3" sections. Peel potatoes and cut in large chunks.

2. Place corned beef brisket fat side up in bottom of slow cooker.

3. Place carrots and potatoes on top.

4. Add water, beer and seasoning packet.

5. Cook on low heat for 6 hours.

6. Cut cabbage into large wedges, and add on top of meat in slow cooker. Cook for 2 more hours.

7. When done, slice corned beef against the grain, dish up vegetables and serve with soda bread and Irish butter.

Serves 4

3-5 pounds corned beef brisket with seasoning packet	2 cups water
4-6 carrots	1 bottle Guinness Draught beer
6-8 Yukon Gold potatoes	½ head of green cabbage

Note
You can use any brand/type beer, except extra stout. If you don't want to use beer you can substitute water or beef broth. If you substitute baby carrots or baby potatoes, adjust cooking time for them. You can add all vegetables at the beginning if you like them well cooked. Conversely you can hold off putting carrots and/or potatoes in until around 4 hours if you like them firmer.

Bonus meal
We take the juice, vegetables, bits of meat left in the slow cooker and puree them in the blender to make a soup. You can adjust thickness by adding water or broth. For a healthier soup, refrigerate leftovers and skim fat off before blending.

POULTRY

ITALIAN CHICKEN CAMPAGNOLA

Jonathan Weber

I am a NY freelance violinist/violist who has worked regularly on Broadway. I was a former orchestra member at *Kinky Boots the Musical,* and am a faculty member at the Aaron Copland School of Music at Queens College (CUNY).

Growing up, I used to frequent two sister restaurants in Westbury, Long Island called the Baci Cafe and Cafe Spasso. Whenever I would dine there, I would always order the same thing: Pollo Campagnola. (The dish was on the menu in both establishments.) I believe the last time I was there was in the early 90's.

During the past ten months of lockdown, with all of the cooking my family has been doing at home, I found myself feeling nostalgic for that dish so one night, I decided to recreate it myself with some modifications. I have never actually seen a written recipe for this dish so I cooked it from memory inspired by my experiences at the restaurants mentioned above.

Special Prep/Equipment
Large chef's pan or saute pan with a cover

3 large boneless chicken breasts

3 Idaho potatoes, peeled or unpeeled

1 whole red pepper

1 whole yellow pepper

1 whole spanish onion

1 cup of flour with pinches of cornstarch

2 tablespoons za'atar spice blend, divided

12 whole cloves of garlic

12 pieces of sun dried tomatoes

1 cup olive oil, divided

1 tablespoon salt

2 teaspoons crushed black pepper

2 teaspoons dried crushed dill weed

2 teaspoons dried crushed parsley

1 cup tomato sauce

1. Cut up chicken breasts, potatoes, red and yellow peppers, and onion, all into 1" chunks.

2. Place chicken chunks in a large freezer bag along with the flour, cornstarch and 1 tablespoon of za'atar. Shake until the chicken is covered in the flour and za'atar.

3. Brown the chicken on all sides in a large chef's pan with 2 tablespoons of olive oil over medium heat. Add more oil as needed.

4. Remove chicken from chef's pan to a bowl and let rest.

5. Add to chef's pan the potatoes, yellow and red peppers, onion, sun dried tomatoes, and garlic cloves. Saute in oil until it vegetables soften – about 6 minutes, give or take.

6. Return chicken to the pan, along with salt, black pepper, dill weed, parsley, the remaining za'atar, and tomato sauce.

7. Cover and let cook for about 40 minutes, while continuously checking, stirring and adding oil as needed to keep everything moist. Taste and stir as you go, and add more of the spices listed above to your liking.

Serves 4

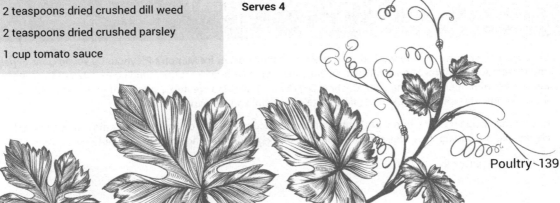

BAKED CHICKEN WITH OLIVES, TOMATOES, LEMONS & CAPERS

Joanna Maurer

I've lived and worked in NYC as a violinist for 27 years. I'm an Associate violinist of the Metropolitan Opera Orchestra, the violinist of the chamber ensemble, American Chamber Players, and I've worked as a studio recording musician as concertmaster on numerous film soundtracks and pop albums.

This recipe is adapted from *New Food Fast* by Donna Hay. It's a family favorite that I've cooked countless times over the past 15 years. We love this dish with rice or pasta, and green beans. My husband and I love to spend quality time with our kids over a nice meal before heading out to play an opera at the Met, and this one is always a hit!

Special Prep/Equipment

9 x 11" baking dish

1. Preheat oven to 425°.

2. Combine the tomatoes, olives, zest, juice from ½ of the lemon, capers, olive oil, salt, and pepper in small bowl. Stir.

3. In the baking dish add some of the mixture to coat bottom of dish, place chicken breasts on top, then cover with rest of mixture. Cover with aluminum foil.

4. Bake in preheated oven for 20 minutes, then uncover and add crumbled feta. Bake for an additional 15-25 minutes until chicken is done.

Serves about 4

1 pint cherry or grape tomatoes, halved	2 tablespoons olive oil
½ cup of Kalamata olives, chopped	Salt & cracked black pepper
Zest & juice from 1 lemon	4 chicken breast fillets
2 tablespoons capers	3-4 tablespoons of feta, crumbled

WEST INDIAN CHICKEN CURRY

Eladio Rojas

I am a drummer, a writer of songs and an activist. I was the booker for Minton's Playhouse's *Young Lions Series*, and Project Assistant for Migiwa Miyajima's big band album *Colorful*. I am the founding member of Drinking Bird, and current member of the John Cushing Big Band. I have also created a system of rhythmic analysis and am currently writing a book about flow state and social engagement.

I found this recipe on the internet at theblackpeppercorn.com. I have modified it by browning the marinated chicken before adding the water, shallow frying the chicken skins, and adding extra ginger!

Special Prep/Equipment
Blender, large pot, frying pan

The chicken needs to marinate for 24 hours before cooking.

1 onion

1-2 Inch piece of fresh ginger, peeled

4 cloves of garlic

½ bunch cilantro

1 habañero pepper

2 tablespoons curry powder

12 chicken thighs/drumsticks

Oil (for pan)

½ cup of water

Salt to taste

1. Place the onion, ginger, garlic, cilantro, habañero pepper, and curry powder in a food processor or blender. Blend into a paste.

2. Peel the skin off of your chicken. Save the skin in a small Tupperware container.

3. Place skinless chicken in a Ziploc bag. Pour the curry paste over the chicken, seal the bag, and mix the curry paste around each chicken piece. Place both the chicken and the chicken skins into the fridge. Let the chicken marinate for 24 hours.

4. Heat the oil in a large pot, and add the marinated chicken. Cook the chicken and the marinade and brown the sauce. Then add water. Bring to a boil, then simmer for 45-60 minutes.

5. When the chicken is almost done (easily falls off the bone), Heat oil in a frying pan, and shallow fry chicken skins until golden brown. Serve golden chicken skins on a separate plate.

6. Salt to taste. Serve with rice or roti bread. Eat!

Serves 4-5

THAI CHICKEN THIGHS
≈ Jackie Schiller

I'm a pianist and teacher. I'm an avid chamber musician and perform with the All Seasons Chamber Players and Alacorde Piano Trio.

I made up this recipe after trying Trader Joe's Thai Style Curry sauce. My family loves it. It's super easy and delicious.

Special Prep/Equipment
Oven-safe pot

1. Preheat oven to 425°.

2. Clean chicken and put in an oven safe pot. Cover chicken with one jar of Thai sauce. Bake covered for 15 minutes.

3. Add carrots, celery and potatoes. Bake another 15 minutes covered, then bake another 30 minutes uncovered. It should brown a little on the top.

4. Add spinach towards the end and mix in.

5. Serve over white basmati rice.

1 package boneless, skinless chicken thighs

1 jar Trader Joe's Thai Style Curry Sauce (either yellow or red)

2-3 carrots, cut up

2-3 stalks celery, cut up

2-3 small potatoes, cubed

Fresh spinach

Note
You can add peas, zucchini or cauliflower or any other vegetables you like.

Serves about 4

CHICKEN CHILI-ISH
🎵 Ryu Cipris

I am a freelance flute player. I've worked with the New York Pops at Carnegie Hall and on Broadway in the *Lion King,* and have degrees from the Amsterdam Conservatory in The Netherlands and the Peabody Institute in Baltimore.

I worked on a touring show for years, which was as wonderful and monotonous as you would imagine. One thing I missed most on the road was cooking and its adjacent activities — browsing local grocers, buying esoteric kitchen gadgets, hoarding cookbooks etc. I moved back to New Jersey in 2013 and have cooked most days since — this is a recipe I made up around that time.

This is not standard chili, so to avoid offending chili cognoscenti, I'm calling it "chili-ish". There are a lot of ingredients, but any surplus dried chiles and whole spices can be stored indefinitely for other uses, and everything can be found at a well stocked regular supermarket or Latin grocery. It is even better the next day, so any leftovers can be refrigerated and reheated.

Special Prep/Equipment
Dutch oven (5.5 quarts works great), meat thermometer, blender, mortar/pestle or spice grinder

Chili-ish spice mix (makes just over ½ cup):
2 tablespoons whole coriander

2 teaspoons whole cumin

1 teaspoon whole achiote (annatto seeds)

1 teaspoon whole black pepper

2 inch piece canela (or 1 teaspoon ground cinnamon)

5 whole cloves

3 tablespoons sugar

1 tablespoon kosher salt

1 tablespoon cocoa powder

1 tablespoon oregano

Blended whole chile mix (can substitute with milder chiles if you wish):
3 cups boiling water

3 dried ancho chiles

3 dried morita chiles

3 dried bird's eye chiles

2 tablespoons vinegar (apple cider or white)

1 bunch of cilantro stems (reserve leaves for serving)

2 tablespoons of Chili-ish ground spice mix (see above)

Chili:
2 tablespoons neutral oil (canola, grapeseed, etc)

1 pound ground chicken

2 large onions (red or white), chopped

½ teaspoon kosher salt

3 fresh small green Thai chiles (substitute 1 jalapeno or omit depending on heat tolerance), sliced

2 inch piece of ginger, peeled and grated

5 cloves garlic, minced

Remainder of Chili-ish spice mix

1 cup medium-bodied red wine

2 bay leaves

2 large chicken breasts, cut into thirds crosswise

1 bell pepper (I use red, yellow, or orange), chopped into approximately ½ inch squares

1 (15 ounce) can of beans (kidney or black), drained

Lime, cilantro leaves, chopped scallions

1. Make Chili-ish spice mix by toasting and grinding whole spices, then mixing with the already powdered ingredients.

2. Pour 1 tablespoon of oil into a dutch oven and put over medium high heat. When oil is hot, add ground chicken and 2 tablespoons of Chili-ish spice mix. Cook thoroughly, stirring often until it has brown, crispy bits. Remove ground chicken to a bowl.

3. While ground chicken is cooking, make the blended whole chile mix: Pour 3 cups boiling water over the de-stemmed dried chiles and let sit submerged for about 10 minutes (if you don't like spicy foods, you can use milder dried chiles and remove all veins/seeds after soaking). After the chiles become pliable, blend the chiles and soaking water along with the cilantro stems, 2 tablespoons of vinegar, and 2 tablespoons of the Chili-ish spice mix. The product should be completely smooth and liquefied.

4. In the same dutch oven (after you remove the ground chicken) pour 1 tablespoon of oil over medium heat, and when hot add the chopped onions and ½ teaspoon of salt. Stir and cook until onion is translucent and starting to brown on edges (5-6 minutes), then add sliced fresh Thai chiles (or omit according to your taste), garlic and ginger. Stir and cook for a minute, then add the rest of the Chili-ish spice mix. Stir and cook for an additional minute, then deglaze with 1 cup of red wine. Scrape up the burned bits from the bottom of the pan and let boil until the raw wine smell dissipates. Turn heat down to low and pour in the blended whole chile mix and two bay leaves. Once mixture is simmering, add chicken breast pieces (mix to submerge the meat), cover, and cook on low for 20 minutes. During this time you can chop up the bell pepper and open/drain your beans if you haven't done so already.

5. After 20 minutes, check chicken breasts for temperature (at least 160°); if they're ready, remove chicken breast segments from liquid and set aside to cool. Add half of the beans and half of the chopped bell pepper to the liquid and let simmer covered for 10 minutes. When chicken breasts are cool enough to handle, shred/chop into bite-size pieces. Put chicken breast pieces back into the pot along with the rest of the beans and bell pepper, and simmer for 5 more minutes (uncovered). Add the cooked ground chicken to the pot, stir, and turn off heat. Remove bay leaves and serve in bowls topped with a squeeze of lime, chopped cilantro leaves and chopped scallions.

Serves 4

DAVE'S STUPID CHICKEN
∾ Dave Achelis

I am a guitar user and have my own band, 8 ACE, in which I sing and play original material.

This is for when you have only 20 minutes to make dinner.

Special Prep/Equipment
Large pan or skillet

1 pound chicken thighs

Mushrooms

Trader Joe's frozen artichoke hearts

1 can Campbell's chicken soup

A little half and half or sour cream (optional)

1 box Uncle Ben's Rice

1. Cut up the chicken. I prefer tasty chicken thighs. Slice up some mushrooms.

2. Dump chicken in a large pan with some olive oil. As the chicken cooks, dump in some artichoke hearts and mushrooms.

3. Add the can of soup and stir. Add a little half and half or sour cream and get extra points.

4. Prepare Uncle Ben's rice. When the chicken is cooked, serve over rice.

Serves 2 hungry musicians with a little left over for soup the next day.

CHICKEN HALAL
~ Harold Stephan

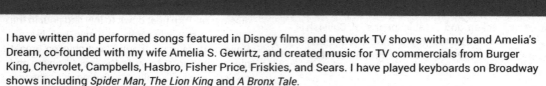

I have written and performed songs featured in Disney films and network TV shows with my band Amelia's Dream, co-founded with my wife Amelia S. Gewirtz, and created music for TV commercials from Burger King, Chevrolet, Campbells, Hasbro, Fisher Price, Friskies, and Sears. I have played keyboards on Broadway shows including *Spider Man, The Lion King* and *A Bronx Tale*.

We have been riding out the pandemic in the Catskills, about 90 minutes outside of Manhattan. My son Adam, who is 13 years old, asked if I could make him Halal-style chicken. It is one of the most distinctive dishes you will find served up fresh from street vendors in every borough of NYC. It is one of those dishes that says "Welcome to NYC!" I found a great recipe on the seriouseats.com website, which I bring to you in a slightly modified form. I have made this recipe many times since March 2020, and I streamlined several of the processes to make it a bit simpler. I also added fresh cilantro to the chicken marinade, which is like adding cowbell to your favorite song...it just makes it better!!!

Special Prep/Equipment
Blender

For the chicken:
Juice from 1 freshly squeezed lemon

1 tablespoon freshly chopped cilantro

½ teaspoon each: oregano and ground coriander

3 garlic cloves, roughly chopped

¼ cup organic olive oil

Freshly ground sea salt and black pepper

2-3 pounds boneless, skinless chicken thighs, trimmed (8 thighs)

1 tablespoon avocado oil

For the rice:
2 tablespoons unsalted butter or avocado oil

½ teaspoon turmeric

¼ teaspoon ground cumin

1 ½ cups long-grain or basmati rice

2 ½ cups chicken broth

Freshly ground sea salt and black pepper

For the sauce:
¾ cup mayonnaise

1 tablespoon sugar

2 tablespoons white vinegar

Juice from 1 freshly squeezed lemon

¼ cup chopped fresh parsley

Freshly ground sea salt and black pepper

To serve:
Shredded iceberg lettuce (1 head or 1 small package)

Optional: Toasted pita bread cut into 1 × 3" strips

Optional: harissa-style hot sauce, for serving

1. Make the marinade. Squeeze the juice from 1 lemon into a small bowl. Remove the pits, and pour juice in a blender. Finely chop 1 tablespoon of fresh cilantro and place it in the blender. Add oregano and ground coriander to the blender. Chop up 3 garlic cloves and place it in the bender. Add ¼ cup of olive oil to the blender. Place the blender on the pulse setting and mix up your marinade.

2. Apply the marinade. Place 3 pounds of deboned chicken thighs into a large Ziploc bag and pour the marinade over the chicken thighs. Shake it like you would shake the maracas for a revival of *West Side Story*. Set the bag aside, and let the marinade soak into the chicken breast while you work on the rice.

3. Make the yellow rice. Set your stove to medium heat, and get your dutch oven ready to heat up 2 tablespoons of butter or avocado oil. Add turmeric and cumin over the butter or avocado oil. Mix the these spices around so that it dissolves and becomes aromatic. Add the basmati rice mix it all together. It should look evenly spread and you will want to let the rice sit for a few minutes and brown up, being careful to not let it burn. Pour chicken broth over the rice, turn the heat down to low and set your timer for 15 minutes. Cover the pot.

4. Prepare the chicken. Grab the chicken from the marinade bag and slice it into thin pieces. Add avocado oil to a medium size pan and add the sliced chicken and any leftover marinade. Stir it up. Turn the heat up a little higher and let the chicken cook until the juices start to seep out. When the chicken begins sizzling, stir the pan to ensure that the chicken slices cook evenly. Repeat this process as necessary while moving onto the sauce, and turn down the heat to low once all the slices are evenly cooked.

5. *Make the sauce:* Place the mayo, sugar, white vinegar in a medium size serving bowl. Squeeze the juice from 1 lemon into a small bowl and remove the seeds. Add the juice to the mayo, sugar and white vinegar. Chop up fresh parsley and add it to the sauce. Use a whisk to whip up the sauce, and add salt and pepper to taste.

6. Serve it up! Start with the shredded lettuce and add some yellow rice to your plate. Place some chicken over the top of the rice. Use a lacerated spoon to allow the drippings from the chicken to drop back into the pan. If you like, you can slice up some fresh pita for serving. Don't forget to toast it. Add white sauce and hot sauce to taste, and enjoy a delicious chicken halal meal while imagining your favorite NYC art, entertainment and culture!

Serves 4

CHICKEN MARSALA WITH MUSHROOMS
⌒ Jenny Hill

I am a freelance saxophonist/flautist. Pre-pandemic I was gigging and touring with the Easy Star All-Stars, Denis Leary, Lioness and Broken Reed Saxophone Quartet.

I modified a NY Times recipe. I have made this for over 10 years and all my friends love it (except not the vegetarian ones!)

Special Prep/Equipment
Large skillet or saute pan, large pot for cooking pasta

½ cup flour, plus 1 tablespoon for thickening sauce.

¼ teaspoon salt

freshly ground black pepper

1 pound chicken breasts or chicken tenders

1-2 cloves garlic

Olive oil to cover bottom of pan

8 ounces baby bella mushrooms, sliced

¼ - ½ cup Marsala wine

Fusilli pasta and Parmesan, for serving

1. Mix the flour, salt and pepper in a bowl. Coat the chicken breasts with the flour mixture.

2. Meanwhile, chop the garlic cloves and heat them in the olive oil in a skillet or saute pan for 2-3 minutes. Add the chicken into the garlic and oil and cook for approx. 4 minutes on each side; do not overcook. The chicken should be golden brown on each side. During the last 2 minutes, add the chopped mushrooms into the pan. You may need a little more oil at this point.

3. When the mushrooms and chicken are almost done, raise the heat and pour the Marsala wine over everything. Wait until most of it evaporates (about 1-2 minutes) then add 1 tablespoon of flour to thicken the reduction into a gravy. Serve immediately with fusilli pasta (with butter and Parmesan cheese).

Serves 3-4, depending on how much chicken is used.

BOTTOMLESS COSTCO CHICKEN RECIPE THEME & VARIATIONS

 Martha Mooke

I'm an electro-acoustic violist/composer/improviser/educator, with a long and winding career that's taken me from Broadway to Carnegie Hall to The Cutting Room, tours with Barbra Streisand, Star Wars in Concert, collaborations with David Bowie, Philip Glass, Laurie Anderson and legendary beatboxer Rahzel. I created and produced ASCAP's genre defying New Music Showcase *Thru the Walls* and am currently developing the first ever Multi-Style Strings Program at New Jersey City University.

Costco roasted chickens are inexpensive, delicious and versatile! Enjoy with guests in one sitting, or stretch the bird for a whole week while stretching your creativity!

Special Prep/Equipment
Go to Costco and buy a roasted chicken.

1 Costco roasted chicken

Anything else in your kitchen (especially leftovers and things you forgot in dark places)

Monday:
Buy Costco roasted chicken (eat legs for dinner).

Tuesday:
Eat wings and dark meat (with mashed potatoes and lightly steamed broccoli).

Wednesday:
Make chicken salad (any variation).

Thursday:
1. Simmer sliced onion in olive oil in a pot, add 2 cups of water and chicken bouillon cube, let cook while you do social media and answer emails.

2. Add whatever is left of Costco chicken (including bones, skin, etc). Add 2 more cups of water. Add a capsule or 2 of Turmeric (good for inflammation).

3. Add any other leftovers from the refrigerator or dark storage area.

4. Practice and/or compose for an hour.

5. Add more water and bring to boil, add a cup of rice and half a bottle (or more) of hard cider. Simmer.

6. Watch the sunset or play a game (do not watch the news).

7. Enjoy with a 2nd bottle of cider! Bon appétit!

One chicken serves 1 - 2

CHICKEN THIGHS
WITH MUSTARD TANGERINE SAUCE

Judy LeClair

I play Principal Bassoon in the New York Philharmonic, and teach at Juilliard and Manhattan School of Music.

This easy recipe, inspired by a recipe I saw in the Washington Post, has become one of our favorite meals. The tangy tangerine juice adds a great deal to the overall taste. You can find it with all the specialty juices at your grocery store. If you cannot find it, use orange juice or fresh squeeze some tangerines!

6-8 skinless, boneless chicken thighs (breast tenders can also be used)

Salt and pepper

3-4 tablespoons olive oil

¾ cup tangerine juice

¾ cup chicken stock

¼ cup whole grain spicy brown mustard

1 tablespoon honey

1 teaspoon hot pepper sauce

¼ cup onion, sliced

2 cloves, garlic, sliced

2 portobello mushroom caps, slice

Note:
As far as side accompaniments to this dish, I am partial to Japanese sushi rice – I like the stickiness of it – but any rice will do. For vegetables, I always use roasted brussels sprouts or broccoli florets. Mix them with olive oil and kosher salt, perhaps fresh ginger if you have it. Set oven for 425° and roast for about 25-30 minutes in upper third of oven. The sauce is nice with all these roasted veggies!

Special Prep/Equipment
Large cast iron skillet
Smaller fry pan

1. Rinse chicken thighs, pat dry, season with salt and pepper.

2. Heat olive oil in a cast iron skillet till it shimmers, add thighs, and cook undisturbed over medium-high heat until browned, about 5 minutes. Turn over and do the same on second side. Transfer thighs to a large plate.

3. While chicken and sauce are cooking, heat oil in a small pan, and add chopped onion, garlic and portobellos. Saute until tender. Keep warm on very low heat on your back burner.

4. Pour tangerine juice and broth into the chicken skillet and cook over medium-high heat for at least 5 minutes. Whisk in mustard, honey, and hot sauce. Once it comes to a boil, cook for 7-10 min or until it thickens. Reduce heat to low and return chicken to the skillet. Cook for a minute, until heated through.

5. To serve, add sauteed vegetables to sauce, and then pour over chicken.

Serves 3-4

CHICKEN TAVANI
～ Sasha Margolis

I am mostly a violinist in the classical world. I also play, sing, arrange, and emcee for Big Galut(e), a Jewish music ensemble. And I write regularly for Strings and Chamber Music magazines.

Beginning in 1989, and continuing for some years, one of the joys of my life was traveling to Italy to play at the Spoleto Festival. We always enjoyed the restaurants in Spoleto, and also getting to cook in our little apartments with beautiful Italian ingredients. One summer, I got to be friends with a pianist playing for the festival, named Elisabetta Tavani. She taught me this simple but wonderful chicken alla cacciatora. (The figs are my addition.)

1. Rinse chicken thoroughly. Dry, then salt and pepper the chicken.

2. Heat oil in a large skillet over medium-high heat.

3. Add chicken. Brown on both sides.

4. Pour in a good splash of wine. Let reduce for a minute or two.

5. Lower heat, add garlic. Don't let the garlic brown.

6. Add rosemary, olives. Add figs, if you use them.

7. Add tomatoes and partially cover.

8. Continue cooking for 30-45 minutes.

Serves 4-6 when served with roasted potatoes.

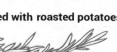

6 chicken thighs, or ideally, a whole chicken cut into 2" pieces

Salt and pepper

Olive oil

Dry white wine

2-3 cloves of garlic, minced

2-3 sprigs rosemary

1-2 handfuls oil-cured olives

Optional: a handful of dried figs, slivered

4-5 plum tomatoes, skinned and chopped (parboil to skin more easily)

BEER BUTTER CHICKEN
～ Adela Peña

I am a violinist, and toured and recorded with the Eroica Trio for 20 years as a founding member. Currently I teach violin and chamber music at Mannes Prep, University of Pennsylvania, InterHarmony International Festival, and when performances rev up again, I'll return to my position as Principal Second Violin of the Opera Saratoga Orchestra.

If you like to swig a beer while cooking, this one's for you! I recommend an India Pale Ale or something similar, and to be honest I have never measured the beer when I pour it in. This recipe "happened" because I was trying to poach chicken according to a Julia Child recipe. I used a little less butter than she called for – trying to be healthier, I guess... When I was ready to put it in the oven, I feared it would dry out. What to do? Naturally, I had an open beer in my hand. I poured a little in the pan, and the rest is history.

Special Prep/Equipment

Ovenproof skillet, strainer, tin foil

2-4 tablespoons olive oil, or whatever amount will cover your pan bottom.	Fresh ground pepper to taste
	2 lemon wedges
2 large boneless, skinless chicken breast halves	3 tablespoons unsalted butter
Kosher salt to taste	⅓-½ cup beer, approximately!

1. Preheat oven to 400°.

2. In an oven-proof skillet (I use cast iron) heat olive oil on high heat until it shines – a drop of water should sizzle if you want to test it that way.

3. Place chicken breasts flat side down (like they were placed in the package). While they're sizzling in the pan, shake salt and pepper (I recommend generously) on chicken, then squeeze 1 lemon wedge on each piece of chicken through the strainer, lightly covering the surface with juice.

4. When the bottom side is nicely browned (just a couple of minutes, so keep an eye on it) flip the chicken over and season cooked side with salt and pepper.

5. When the flipped side is also browned (another couple of minutes) add the butter. Roll the chicken over and back for a minute or two, to make sure both sides get good butter on them. Then add the beer, and turn off the heat. This should all be sizzling like crazy. Make sure now that the chicken breasts are round side down (opposite of how you started) cover the pan with tin foil, and place in the oven.

6. Cook for 8-9 minutes (should feel springy but not rubbery). Carefully (please, dear fellow musicians, use heavy-duty pot holders!) remove pan from oven. Immediately transfer chicken to a cutting board, flipping it back to flat side down.

7. Cover lightly with tin foil, and let sit for 10 minutes. Slice (about ¾" thick), and serve!

8. There will be juice in the bottom of your pan. It's rich and salty, and I love to spoon it on the sliced chicken. But the chicken itself is still nice and juicy even if you forego these extra zillion calories.

9. It goes great with rice and a green salad.

Serves about 3-4 hungry people

SANDRA'S HONEY CHICKEN
〜 Amelia Gold

I am Director of the Arts at The Elisabeth Morrow School, Founder and Artistic Director of the Eastern Music Festival Summer String Festival, and violin faculty, and the Manhattan School of Music Pre-College division.

This is my mother's recipe which she made almost every Friday night for our family's Shabbat dinner.

Special Prep/Equipment

Large glass baking dish

½ stick of margarine	½ cup mustard	2 teaspoons salt
1 cup honey	2 teaspoons curry powder	8-10 pieces of chicken, skinned

1. Preheat oven to 350°.

2. Melt the margarine and whisk in the honey and mustard. Add in the curry powder and salt.

3. Put the chicken in a glass baking dish and cover it completely with the sauce. Bake covered in aluminum foil in preheated oven for 30 minutes. Then, remove the foil and bake for another hour until browned and tender.

4. While it is baking it is a good idea to continue to cover the chicken with the sauce.

Serves 8-10 depending on how many pieces of chicken you use.

BOURBON THANKSGIVING TURKEY

~ Daniel Spitzer

I am a classical clarinetist, performing in orchestras, chamber music and on Broadway, where I also play saxophones.

This recipe was handed down to me by my brother-in-law, and I've prepared this turkey for many Thanksgivings over the years. I've also passed it along to several musician-colleagues, who've reported great success, enjoying this moist, juicy bird.

Special Prep/Equipment
The dried fruit should be soaked the night before preparation.

Large roasting pan with rack, cheesecloth, poultry string, needle and thick thread to sew up the bird, baster, meat thermometer (cordless, battery powered one is great)

1. The evening before cooking, put your dried fruit in a large mixing bowl, pour bourbon over fruit, until submerged. Cover, and leave the fruit to absorb bourbon.

2. The next day, bring bird to room temperature on your counter for an hour, and then fill the cavity with the lemons, vegetables and fresh herbs.

3. Preheat oven to 350°.

4. Close up the cavity with your needle and thread, and truss the bird with poultry string to keep the legs secure.

5. Thoroughly coat all the bird surfaces with a generous amount of olive oil or butter, depending on your preference. Sprinkle with salt and pepper. Place on a rack that sits in but above the roasting pan bottom. Place the soaked fruit all over the breast, to cover it as much as possible, then place cheesecloth over the whole top of the bird. Baste it with a generous amount of bourbon.

6. Put the turkey in the hot oven. After 45 minutes start basting every half hour with bourbon. You will need to roast the turkey for 15 to 20 minutes per pound. It should take 3 - 4 hours until done, when the internal temperature is 165°. After 2½ hours of cooking, start checking internal temperature, using a meat thermometer. The main concern is not to overcook it, so the white meat doesn't get dry.

7. For the last 45 minutes remove the cheesecloth and any fruit still stuck to skin, to allow the skin to brown. Any fruit that is still intact can be served as a garnish to the sliced meat.

Serves at least 8-10.

2-3 cups dried, mixed fruit (apricots, prunes, apples, raisins, etc)

Bottle of bourbon (at least 750 ml, or more, to get your bird good and drunk!)

14-16 pound kosher (brined) turkey

2 lemons, sliced in quarters

1 Vidalia onion, sliced in quarters

10+ whole garlic cloves

1-2 carrots

1-2 stalks celery

Fresh herbs, such as parsley, sage, rosemary, thyme

Olive oil or butter

Salt and pepper

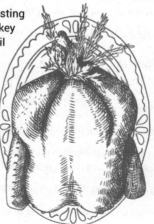

CHINATOWN CHICKEN

Keith Bonner

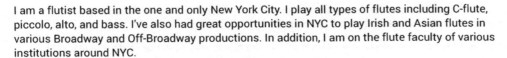

I am a flutist based in the one and only New York City. I play all types of flutes including C-flute, piccolo, alto, and bass. I've also had great opportunities in NYC to play Irish and Asian flutes in various Broadway and Off-Broadway productions. In addition, I am on the flute faculty of various institutions around NYC.

I've always enjoyed going to Chinatown in NYC and feasting on various Chinese dishes. One of my favorites is a simple chicken dish that remains juicy, flavorful and very satisfying on the palette and in my belly! I adapted a recipe from *The Frugal Gourmet* by Jeff Smith called Chow Yow Gai that comes very close to what I often eat on my Chinatown excursions.

I love the simplicity of this recipe. The chicken sits in boiled water for much of the time which allows you to get back to practicing the music you so love!

Special Prep/Equipment
Large pot for cooking chicken

A steaming bowl of rice compliments this dish perfectly.

½ cup sesame seeds and/or crushed peanuts

1 (3-3½ pound) chicken

2 bunches green onions

1 tablespoon tamari soy sauce

1 tablespoon sesame oil

2 teaspoons salt

½ cup peanut oil, heated to smoking point

Sambal oelek (ground fresh chili paste) for serving

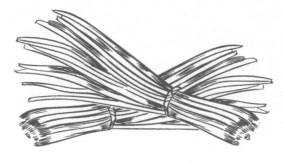

1. Toast the sesame seeds and/or peanuts on the stove top. First, heat a small pan over a medium-high setting, and then place seeds or nuts in pan, to toast for 3-5 minutes, tossing and stirring to prevent burning. Keep a careful eye on the pan while toasting. Once the sesame seeds or peanuts become fragrant and begin to brown they are done. They will continue to cook a bit off the heat.

2. Fill a pot big enough for your chicken with water to fully cover. Bring to a boil. Place the chicken in the boiling water. When the water stops boiling take out the chicken. Cover the pot and when the water begins to boil again put the chicken back in the pot and cover. Turn off the burner, leave the chicken in the pot and let sit for an hour. When the hour is up, remove the chicken from the pot and allow to cool.

3. Once the chicken is cooled you can go ahead and debone, then tear the meat into small strips. Place the meat on a large plate or in a large bowl. Clean the green onions, cut into ¼" rounds and place on top of chicken. Pour the tamari soy sauce, sesame oil and salt over chicken – yum! When you are ready to serve, pour the hot peanut oil over the onions and chicken, then toss.

4. At this point I like to put the toasted sesame seeds and/or peanuts on top for an extra crunch. I also love to dip pieces of chicken into the chili paste when my taste buds crave that extra kick.

Serves 4-5 comfortably.

CENOVIA'S PUERTO RICAN CHICKEN
～ Cenovia Cummins

I'm a violinist. I'm the concertmaster for the New York Pops and for *West Side Story* on Broadway. I'm also a composer and play in rock and bluegrass bands.

I grew up with a Puerto Rican mother, and my father's side of the family was from the south. I really feel I got such great culinary exposure by experiencing two diverse cultures in one family. This is a recipe my mom used to make.

I rarely measure anything in the kitchen unless I absolutely have to. (This is very much in keeping with my musical preferences, which is to improvise as often as possible!) I made this dish for my violinist friend, Louise Owen, who must have been taking notes because she kindly adapted my recipe for her food blog, *www.kitchenfiddler.blogspot.com.* Now there is official documentation, with measurements! The stars of this recipe are the raisins and olives. Make sure you use golden raisins and olives with pimentos. The combination of sweet and salty is so very tasty, the combination will have you exclaiming "qué rico!"

Rice:
2 tablespoons olive oil

1 small yellow onion, finely diced

2 cups basmati or jasmine rice, rinsed

4 cups of water

1 packet Goya Sazón seasoning

Chicken:
8 boneless thin-sliced chicken cutlets

1 cup all-purpose flour, for dredging

Goya adobo and freshly ground black pepper

½ cup golden raisins and 1 heaping cup Spanish green olives stuffed with pimento

Olive oil, for cooking the chicken

Sauce:
3 tablespoons olive oil (use more if you need it)

1 medium yellow onion, diced

1 small green pepper, diced

4 cloves garlic, minced

1 tablespoon dried oregano

2 (28 ounce) cans crushed tomatoes

½ cup dry white wine

1 bunch cilantro, leaves and soft stems, coarsely chopped (reserve ½ cup for garnish)

1. Make the rice: heat 2 tablespoons olive oil over medium heat in a medium-sized heavy pot. Add the small onion and sauté till the onion begins to soften, about 5 minutes. Add the rice and stir well, cooking for a minute until all the rice is coated with the oil. Pour in the water and the packet of Sazón, turn up the heat and bring to a boil. When the mixture comes to a boil, turn the heat down to low and simmer, covered, until rice is done. (This will take about 30+ minutes.) Remove the pot from the heat and fluff the rice with a fork.

2. For the sauce: while the rice is cooking, heat 3 tablespoons olive oil over medium-high heat in a large heavy pot. Add the medium-sized onion and sauté for 5 minutes. Turn the heat down to medium-low and add the green pepper, garlic, and dried oregano. Cook another 5 minutes until the veggies start to soften, stirring frequently. Add the crushed tomatoes and white wine, and stir in the chopped cilantro. Turn the heat down to low and let the sauce simmer while you prepare the chicken.

3. Make the chicken: put the flour on a shallow plate. Give both sides of the chicken cutlets a nice sprinkling of Goya adobo and black pepper, then dredge in the flour. Cover the bottom of a large skillet with olive oil, and set over med-high heat. When the oil is hot, add as many chicken cutlets that fit comfortably in the pan. (Do this in batches if you need to.) Brown the chicken about 3 minutes per side, turning at least once, until they begin to turn light golden brown. (Don't overcook them as they will finish cooking in the tomato sauce). When the chicken pieces have turned light golden brown, remove them from the skillet and set them aside on a plate. Continue cooking the chicken in batches, adding more olive oil as needed.

4. When all the chicken has been lightly browned, add the cutlets to the tomato sauce. Stir in the green olives and raisins. Let it simmer, partially covered, about 15 minutes.

5. Serve the chicken and tomato sauce over the rice, garnished with additional cilantro and olives.

Serves about 6-8

COCONUT CURRIED CHICKEN & RICE
~ Sarah Hewitt-Roth

I am a professional cellist and a member of the New York Pops, New York City Chamber Orchestra, and a frequent performer on Broadway, currently holding a chair on the revival of *West Side Story*.

This is a family favorite! I especially love it because it is so easy and quick to make! It can be done in just over a half an hour. For vegetarians, the chicken can be substituted with tofu.

1½ pounds boneless, skinless chicken breast, cut into bite sized pieces

1 tablespoon curry powder

3 tablespoons vegetable oil, divided

1 red bell pepper, cut into thin slivers

2 cloves of fresh garlic, finely minced

1 can (13.5 ounce) of coconut milk

¼ cup mango chutney

1 teaspoon soy sauce (or to taste)

⅛ teaspoon ground pepper

1 teaspoons cornstarch

1 teaspoon water

4 cups cooked white rice (*optional:* cook in broth instead of water for extra flavor)

Optional: Handful of chopped fresh cilantro, or finely chopped scallion greens, to sprinkle on top before serving

1. Sprinkle the chicken, coating it with the curry powder. Heat 2 tablespoons of the oil in a large skillet over medium heat. Add the chicken and saute it for about 5 minutes until it is lightly browned, and then remove it from the pan.

2. Put the remaining oil in the pan and saute the pepper and garlic for about 2 to 3 minutes until the pepper is crisp-tender. Return the chicken to the pan, add coconut milk, chutney, soy sauce, and ground pepper. Bring to a boil, reduce heat, and then simmer for 12 minutes, stirring occasionally.

3. Combine cornstarch and water, stirring until smooth and then add it into the chicken mixture. Boil over medium heat until it thickens, about 1 minute. Serve the chicken over rice, sprinkled with fresh cilantro or scallions.

Serves 4

CHIPOTLE CHICKEN & BLACK BEAN CASSEROLE
~ Katherine Hannauer

I've played the violin all over town! Out of town, too, come to think of it.

As a classical violinist, I don't get to improvise much. I make up for it in the kitchen, though! This is my riff on the many versions of "Mexican lasagna" that I have had at various parties and potlucks over the years, all of which were tasty, but often tended to be on the heavy side. If, like me, you are so inclined, this recipe lends itself to personal touches. You might want more heat; try adding a diced jalapeno or canned chipotle in adobo to the beans. You could add frozen corn, or those leftover sauteed greens that are sitting in your fridge. If you don't eat chicken, try sauteed chunks of butternut squash instead. Or maybe that plant-based "chick'n" I've heard so much about. Use your imagination!

Special Prep/Equipment
8 x 12" baking dish

2 boneless, skinless chicken breasts

1 medium/large onion, divided

Juice of 1 lime, divided

½ of a medium green pepper

1 (15.5 ounce) can of black beans, drained

1 cup of your favorite salsa

6 corn tortillas

4-5 tablespoons canola (or other neutral) oil

½ teaspoon each: garlic powder, chipotle powder, cumin powder, oregano, salt and pepper

4 ounces grated pepper jack cheese (or more to taste)

Optional for garnishing: chopped cilantro, chopped scallions, sour cream, guacamole, crushed tortilla chips, another squeeze of lime.

1. Coat the chicken breasts in the spices and salt & pepper. Coarsely chop ½ of the onion and put into a small slow cooker with the seasoned chicken. Top with half the lime juice and 1 or 2 tablespoons of oil, and cook on high for 1½ hours (alternatively, bake in the oven, covered, at 350° for 30-40 minutes). Shred the meat with 2 forks.

2. Dice the remaining half onion and the green pepper. In a medium-large skillet, on medium heat, soften the veggies in a tablespoon of oil. Add the beans and salsa, season with a dash of salt and the remaining lime juice, and continue to cook over medium heat until hot through.

3. Preheat oven to 400°. Cut the tortillas into small squares, toss with 1 tablespoon of oil, and lay them in a single layer on a baking sheet, then bake until crisp, about 10 minutes. (you can use bagged tortilla chips, if you want to skip this step).

4. Reduce oven temperature to 350°. Coat the inside of a 8 x 12" baking dish with the remaining oil. Add the ingredients in layers as follows: tortilla chips, shredded chicken/onion mixture, bean mixture, grated cheese. Cover and bake for 40 minutes, removing the cover for the last 5 minutes of cooking time to let the cheese get nice and bubbly.

5. Let stand for 10 minutes or so before serving, if you can wait that long. Cut into squares and serve with garnishes, if desired.

Serves 6 (2 in my house with delicious leftovers)

CHICKEN-QUINOA-VEGGIE PATTIES
〜 Dorothea Figueroa

I am the Associate Principal Cellist at the Metropolitan Opera for nearly two decades, and I have a Master's from Juilliard. I originally grew up in Leipzig, former East Germany.

Many years ago I made meatballs simply out of beef, onion and some soaked bread. With two kids now, I wanted to change it into a healthier version and they love it being made out of ground chicken and don't even "notice" that it's loaded with wholesome quinoa and carrot/broccoli slivers. In fact it's one of their favorites foods to take for school lunch.

Special Prep/Equipment
Food processor (optional, cuts prep time to a few minutes)

1. At first, boil quinoa per package instructions (½ cup dry quinoa will yield approximately 1 cup cooked).

2. Meanwhile mince the onion, carrot sticks and /or broccoli (I use a food processor until it is all as small as oats or rice).

3. Mix all remaining ingredients (except the cooking oil) together in a big bowl, best to use your clean hands (careful if quinoa is still hot) until very well blended.

4. Heat nonstick pan with the oil over medium-high heat.

5. Form patties the size of half your palm and place into pan. When brown on one side, turn with a fork one by one. Turn heat down to medium-low and let the second side brown.

6. Best served warm, or store in fridge and enjoy cold or reheated up to a week later.

Yields about 12 patties. I usually make three times the amount and it serves our family of four at least two meals and school lunches.

1 cup cooked quinoa

1 small-medium onion, diced

1 cup carrot and/or broccoli, shredded

1 pound ground chicken

1 egg

¼ teaspoon salt (bit more if you like salty)

¼ teaspoon caraway seeds (optional)

2 tablespoons of high heat cooking oil (grapeseed, sunflower etc)

Note
These patties are a mini meal by themselves, since they have meat, grains, egg and veggies. You can also use any cooked rice instead of quinoa or add any other (leftover?) veggies you may have. I recently added uncooked butternut squash, also dicing in the food processor, which gave a nice, sweet, nutty flavor. So go ahead and make it your own family staple by further experimenting.

CURRY ROASTED CHICKEN
 Tereasa Payne

I am a flutist, world flutist, and woodwinds player who freelances, teaches, subs on Broadway, and performs a solo show which promotes flutes from around the world.

I always find myself with leftover jelly in the fridge (apricot, apple, grape, etc). Believing that curry is the world's most perfect food, I designed a curry recipe that would make use of these leftover jars of jelly!

Special Prep/Equipment
Oven-proof skillet

½ cup curry powder

1 teaspoon salt

1 teaspoon black pepper

1 tablespoon turmeric

8 pieces of bone-in chicken thighs or drumsticks

¼ cup olive oil

¾ cup jelly (apricot is my favorite...apple works well too!)

Rice or quinoa for serving

1. Preheat oven to 375°.

2. Combine the curry powder, salt, pepper, and turmeric in a bowl. Add the chicken and toss to coat.

3. Heat oil in an ovenproof skillet over medium heat. Brown the coated chicken for 4-5 minutes on all sides (Reserving the leftover spice mix in the bowl).

4. Transfer the skillet to the oven and roast for 25 minutes, uncovered. Remove the chicken to a plate. Stir the jelly and the remainder of the spice mix into the skillet and heat over medium heat until the jelly melts.

5. Return the chicken to the skillet and toss to coat. Place back in the oven and let chicken roast for an additional 10 minutes.

6. Serve over rice or quinoa.

Serves 4

CHICKEN PAPRIKAS
 Michelle Hatcher

I am a violist, teacher, and conductor of youth ensembles.

This is a family recipe handed down from my Hungarian grandfather. It has been modified by my son, Tim, to be made for 2 or 4 people. The original recipe was for very large gatherings.

Special Prep/Equipment
Hungarian sweet paprika is really important!

A large dutch oven/pot that can go from stove to oven is helpful.

3 pounds boneless, skinless chicken, cubed (white or dark meat, approximately 10 thighs)

10 sweet onions, chopped

2+ cups oil (either olive, coconut or vegetable), oil must cover onions!

Hungarian sweet paprika, approximately ⅛ cup

Salt and pepper

1 pint sour cream

1. Preheat oven to 350°.

2. In a large pot, heat oil over medium heat. Add chopped onions and make sure they are covered by the oil. Simmer until brown. Add paprika.

3. Add chicken to onions and oil and put in hot oven, cover and simmer until cooked through and flavors have melded, about 45 minutes.

4. Strain out some oil, discard. Or if you strain it before you add the chicken, put it in a container in the fridge for future use.

5. Add sour cream, stir quickly. Adjust paprika as necessary. Salt and pepper to taste.

6. Works nicely over egg noodles, rice or nokedli (dumpling).

> **Note:**
> When my mother makes this, she often keeps the bones and skin in the hot oil for extra flavor, and then removes them before adding the sour cream.

Serves 4-6

HUNGARIAN PAPRIKA CHICKEN & RICE
∾ Dorothea Figueroa

I am the Associate Principal Cellist at the Metropolitan Opera for nearly two decades, and have a Master's from Juilliard. I originally grew up in Leipzig, former East Germany.

Growing up in East Germany, we spent several summers of my childhood in Hungary and I think that is where my parents got to know Hungarian Paprika Chicken. We have been eating this at home since I can remember, and I just started to make it again during the pandemic here in NYC.

Special Prep/Equipment
Best to use a heavy pot, such as a dutch oven

1. Take skin and excess fat off the chicken legs. Sprinkle all over with salt.

2. Brown diced onion in oil in dutch oven over medium high heat. Add chicken legs and brown from both sides, turning each once.

3. Mix crushed tomatoes with paprika powder and sour cream in a separate bowl, whisk until well blended. Add to dutch oven, covering the chicken with the sauce.

4. Let simmer on low heat with lid on for about 1 hour. It's ready when meat is tender and almost falls of the bones, if you poke it with a fork.

5. Add salt to taste if needed.

4-6 chicken legs

Salt

3 tablespoons high heat oil (grapeseed, sunflower etc)

1 large diced onion

1 (28 ounce) can crushed tomatoes

2 tablespoons sweet paprika powder (or add a pinch of hot paprika for a kick)

4 tablespoons sour cream

Note
I usually serve this over my homemade pasta (mix 2 eggs, 1 cup cold water and 1 tsp salt with about 4 cups flour until thick sticky dough forms, let sit for half an hour and push droplets through special pasta sieve into boiling water, cook until floating for 2 minutes), but any pasta would be fine with it. Also great with cucumber salad on the side.

Serves 3-6 (1 or 2 legs each)

CHICKEN WITH PRUNES & OLIVES
 Miho Weber

I am a cellist and a teacher.

A dear friend made this in Vermont after a chamber music festival. She described it as a wonderful communal meal, easy, warming, and the perfect mix of sweet and savory. I used a NY Times recipe, and tweaked it to make it my own.

Special Prep/Equipment
Roasting pan, parchment paper

1. Preheat oven to 400°.

2. In a small bowl, mix olive oil, vinegar, white wine, olive paste, brown sugar, and capers.

3. Lay out parchment paper in a roasting pan. Place the crushed garlic, sliced onions, green olives, and prunes on parchment, and put cut chicken into the pan on top.

4. Pour marinade (liquids) around and over the chicken. Salt and pepper the chicken to taste and add za'atar and smoked paprika.

5. Roast for 45 minutes (and up to 1 hour). Baste every 15 minutes with liquids.

6. Serve with basmati or saffron rice.

Serves 2-3

¼ cup olive oil

¼ cup red wine or apple cider vinegar

½ cup white wine

1 tablespoon green olive paste

½ cup brown sugar

½ cup capers, with a bit of juice

6 cloves garlic crushed

1 onion, cut up thinly

1 cup pitted prunes

½ cup pitted Spanish green olives

1 whole chicken, quartered

1½ teaspoons of salt or garlic salt

¼ teaspoon freshly ground pepper

2 tablespoons Italian seasoning or za'atar spice

2 tablespoons Spanish smoked paprika

THEA'S CHICKEN
~ Terry Eichler Wager

I am a flutist, but my career has been music school administration at Manhattan School of Music Preparatory Division and Hoff-Barthelson Music School.

My mother crafted this recipe which is a family favorite. It's quite rich, though, so we only make it for special occasions.

6 boneless skinless chicken breasts cut into large pieces (about 6-8 ounces per breast)

4 large cloves or more fresh garlic, crushed, divided

Butter, for sauteing

Mayonnaise (one soup can worth)

2 cans cream of chicken soup

Juice from 2 Lemons

Curry powder

8 ounces of cheddar cheese, shredded, divided

1 pound Orzo

1 big head of broccoli with stems removed, cut into florets

Special Prep/Equipment
Large baking dish (9 x 13")

This dish goes well with a crusty Italian sesame seed bread.

1. Preheat oven 350°.

2. Saute chicken pieces in butter and half of the garlic until mostly cooked.

3. In a separate mixing bowl, combine mayo and undiluted cream of chicken soup. Add curry powder to taste and the rest of the fresh crushed garlic and the lemon juice. Add about 2 ounces of cheddar cheese. Let mixture sit for 15 minutes.

4. Prepare the orzo by following the instructions on the box. Cook until al dente.

5. Cook the broccoli florets by steaming them.

6. In a large pan spread the orzo evenly, then lay the broccoli florets over the bed of orzo. Add the chicken pieces and cover with the sauce. Add lots of cheddar on top.

7. Cook for 30-40 minutes in preheated oven until top is bubbly and browning.

Serves 6-8

GARLIC POT TERIYAKI CHICKEN
❧ Atsuko Sato

I am a bassoonist at the Queen's Symphony and at *Phantom of the Opera*.

This recipe is for Shawn Edmonds and the members of the Queens Symphony.

1 cup sake or dry sherry	Handful of garlic cloves peeled, whole
½ cup mirin, or 3 tablespoons sugar mixed with ½ cup sake	1¼ pound package chicken thighs, with or without skin and bones
½ cup soy sauce	Add any hot flavorings, if you want spicy taste
½ cup water (optional)	

Special Prep/Equipment
Large, heavy pot is needed.

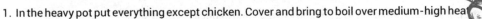

1. In the heavy pot put everything except chicken. Cover and bring to boil over medium-high heat.

2. Put chicken thighs in the pot, cover and simmer until chicken is done. Keep turning the chicken.

3. Take chicken out, cut up, and put on the serving dish. Boil and reduce the remaining juice, becoming great Teriyaki sauce. Pour over cut up chicken.

Serves 3

INSTANT POT CHICKEN CHILI

 Amy Wright

I am a violinist-freelancer and teacher.

This is adapted from a recipe I found on the *Williams-Sonoma.com*. Several adaptations came into play in March when I was terrified to go shopping and it turned out my family liked it even better! It is also worth noting that this is a very flexible recipe and could also be made on the stove top.

Special Prep/Equipment
It's an Instant Pot recipe, but with a few minor adjustments you could make it on the stove top in a dutch oven.

2 pounds boneless, skinless chicken breasts

Kosher salt and freshly ground pepper

2 tablespoons extra-virgin olive oil

1 yellow onion, diced

4 garlic cloves, thinly sliced

1 jalapeño chile, seeded and finely chopped

1 teaspoon dried oregano

1 teaspoon ground cumin

1 teaspoon salt, ½ teaspoon pepper

1 cup frozen corn kernels

4 cups chicken broth

1 jar of tomatillo salsa

Juice of one lime

Fresh cilantro leaves, avocado slices, and lime wedges for garnish

1. Season the chicken breast generously on both sides with salt and pepper. Set Instant Pot to "saute", heat the olive oil and sear the chicken, in batches, browning till golden brown on both sides. Transfer the chicken to a plate.

2. Add the onion to the pot and cook until tender and translucent (about 3 minutes). Add the garlic, jalapeño, oregano, cumin, salt, pepper and cook, stirring until fragrant, about 1 minute. Add the corn, chicken broth and tomatillo salsa to the pot and stir to combine. Add the browned chicken and the juices from the plate back into the pot.

3. Cover the pot with the lid, lock the lid into place, and turn the valve to "sealing". Set the Instant Pot to cook on high pressure for 20 minutes.

4. When the cooking is finished, turn the valve to "venting" to manually release the steam. When all the steam is released, carefully remove the lid and transfer the chicken to a large bowl. Let it cool for a bit and then shred it with a fork.

5. Return it to the pot and add the lime juice. Season with salt and pepper.

6. To serve, garnish with avocado, cilantro, and lime wedges.

Serves 6, but my son is a big eater so maybe don't count on leftovers!

TURKEY LEG WITH VEGETABLES STEW
 Inbal Segev

I am a cellist. I play mostly solo and chamber music. I commission and record new works for cello, most recently a cello concerto by Anna Clyne that I recorded with Marin Alsop and the London Philharmonic Orchestra.

This is my mother's recipe. She lives in Israel and is a pianist herself. She loves cooking and eating healthy food and is always researching ingredients that can benefit our health.

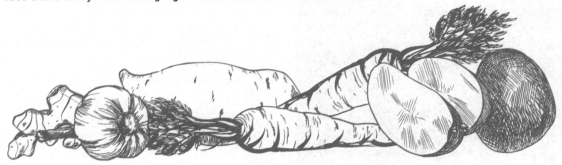

2 turkey legs	1 celery root	*Optional:* coriander, saffron and nutmeg
3 medium potatoes	1 yam	
4 carrots	½ teaspoon each: cumin, hawaij (middle eastern spice), salt	3 celery stalks
2 tablespoons fresh ginger root, diced	¼ teaspoon each: black pepper, red pepper	2 zucchini
		3 cloves garlic

Special Prep/Equipment
Large pot

1. In a large pot cover the turkey legs with water, cook for 45 minutes until the meat is soft. You can discard any foam that rises to the top.

2. After the 45 minutes are up, add the hard root vegetables, and the herbs and spices. 15 minutes after that, add the softer vegetables. Cook for another 15-20 minutes.

3. Turn off the heat and enjoy.

**Serves 4
(less if you're really hungry)**

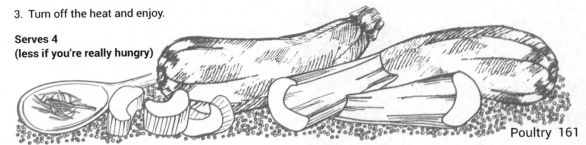

SEAFOOD & FISH

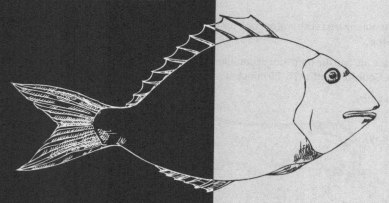

FRIED WHOLE SEA BASS

Danny Miller

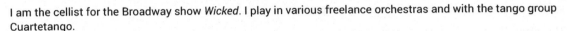

I am the cellist for the Broadway show *Wicked*. I play in various freelance orchestras and with the tango group Cuartetango.

As a fisherman and an Asian food fan, I wanted to come up with a way to replicate with my catch at home the delicious fried whole fish I have eaten in restaurants.

Special Prep/Equipment
A wok is helpful.

Approximately 2 pounds black sea bass, porgy, snapper or grouper (you can use fish filets also if you wish)

½ cup flour

½ cup water

½ cup panko bread crumbs

1½ teaspoons salt

1½ - 2 cups of peanut oil

3 tablespoons chopped cilantro

For the sauce:

3 tablespoons garlic, minced

3 tablespoons ginger, minced

1 hot Thai or finger pepper, minced

1½ tablespoons hot chili paste

1 tablespoon soy sauce

3 chopped scallions

1½ tablespoons Chinese cooking wine

1. Take the scaled, gutted, gilled fish and remove all fins with kitchen scissors. Rub a pinch of the salt in the cavity and lightly score each side of the fish twice with a knife.

2. Make a batter with the flour, water and approximately one teaspoon of salt. It should be the consistency of thick gravy. (Note that if you're avoiding gluten you can use rice flour combined with cornstarch).

3. Dip the fish in the batter and then dredge it in the bread crumbs. Put it in the refrigerator for ten minutes to help coating to adhere.

4. In the meantime, heat the peanut oil in a wok to 350°-375°.

5. Take the fish and carefully lower it into the hot and popping oil. Cook for 5 minutes, monitoring the heat so that the fish cooks through, but does not burn or stick to the bottom of the wok. You may need to lower the heat a bit after the fish starts cooking.

6. Carefully turn the fish (you may need tongs and a spatula) and cook for another 5 minutes, once again, being careful not to burn the bottom.

7. Remove fish to a rack to drain and then put it on a platter.

8. Make the sauce: remove wok from heat and dispose of all but 2 ounces of the peanut oil, removing any pieces of batter, crumbs or fish with a slotted spoon.

9. Place wok with remaining oil on heat; add garlic, ginger and hot pepper. Scald, but don't let them get brown, then add the chili paste, soy sauce, scallions, and cooking wine.

10. Heat for a minute then pour sauce over the fish on the platter. Garnish with chopped cilantro and serve.

Note
This recipe is versatile and can be adapted. Ingredients and proportions can be altered to taste. If using a fish filet, it is good to leave the skin on for enhanced flavor. You can also experiment with different combinations of non-glutinous flour, rice, cassava, etc.

Serves 3-4

SALMON WITH FENNEL & ORANGE
~ Denise Cridge

I play viola and I freelance and teach in and around NYC.

This recipe keeps turning up. It's pretty and tastes fresh! I've seen many like recipes, but I cook this in a tin foil tent like Erin Clarke who writes *Well-Plated*, and she credits the Barefoot Contessa (Ina Garten) as her inspiration. My sister likes my version with shrimp too!

Special Prep/Equipment
Aluminum foil and parchment paper

1 teaspoon butter	1 teaspoon extra-virgin olive oil
1 medium red onion, peeled and quartered	1 navel orange
2 lemons, 1 for cooking and 1 for serving	1½ pounds of salmon fillet
1 medium bulb of fennel	Salt and pepper
½ cup white wine	Pinch of red pepper flakes
¼ cup water, or orange juice	Thyme (a few sprigs)

1. Pre-heat oven to 375°. Take salmon out of refrigerator, at least 10 minutes before cooking.

2. Prep baking sheet with tin foil. Take a piece of tin foil twice the width of the pan plus 6-8" for tenting. Center foil so equal amounts overhang the two sides. Place piece of parchment paper in center of baking pan, on top of foil. If no parchment paper, just put some olive oil on the foil.

3. Melt butter in a saucepan on low heat. While butter melts, slice the red onion and put in pan.

4. While onion cooks wash lemons and orange thoroughly. Make nice, even slices of 1 lemon and the orange.

5. To prep the fennel bulb, remove the tough outer sections. Chop off the stalk and save the feathery fronds for plating. Then, cut the bulb in half. Looking inside, cut out the solid white core. It can be bitter. Then, quarter the bulb and thinly slice the fennel.

6. Put fennel and sliced citrus into onion pan with the ½ cup white wine. I like to cover with a lid and turn up to med-low flame. Only cook until the fennel starts to become tender.

7. Set the salmon on the parchment paper. Put just a small amount of olive oil on top. If you're not using parchment, be sure to put olive oil on both sides of the fish. Salt and pepper the fish. Sprinkle a pinch of red pepper flakes on fish. Peel thyme leaves off a couple stalks and put on fish. Then put fennel, onion and citrus mixture on top of fish. Reserve a few of the bigger orange slices to go on top. Add an additional ¼ cup of white wine or orange juice to the pan. Water is also fine. (The orange juice is too sweet for me.)

8. Fold side pieces of tin foil in. Fold together to seal.

9. Pop into oven for 15-20 minutes. Cook longer if fillet is thick. Be sure to carefully check for doneness as end of cook time approaches.

10. Serve on a platter with fresh lemon slices and the fennel fronds arranged around the edge! Serve with a strong green like broccoli rabe, or have an arugula salad.

Serves 2-3

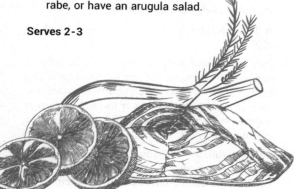

GRAVLAX
～ Pete Levin

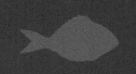

I'm a keyboard player, composer and arranger, mostly jazz. After 35 years in NYC studios, I'm now living upstate near Woodstock, NY, still recording and playing live - looking forward to touring again someday, when it's possible.

I think of this recipe as a Scandanavian version of Lox, although they probably see it the other way. Cured salmon, not smoked. Sliced thin, it's heavenly on toast, a bagel, on a salad, or just noshing by itself.

Special Prep/Equipment
1-gallon resealable storage bag, plastic wrap, very sharp knife

This gravlax will take 3 days to cure in the fridge.

3 pounds salmon filet, skin on

1 ounce vodka

4 tablespoons sugar

4 tablespoons salt

Fresh dill, a big handful

Note: Get the salmon from a butcher. Have them cut the skinny parts off each end; you want the thick center part. Farm-raised salmon works, although it can be difficult to find it thick enough. If you're willing to spend the extra bread, wild-caught salmon will raise the level of your final product.

1. Cut two 3-foot strips of plastic wrap. Lay them in a cross, like a + on your workspace.

2. Lay the salmon out on a cutting board, skin side down. By feel, check it for bones the store may have missed. (Use long-nosed pliers for removing them.) Cut the filet into two equal pieces. Place one piece on the plastic wrap on the cross juncture, skin side down, fatter edge toward you. Leave the other piece on your cutting board.

3. Moisten the flesh side of the two fish halves with the vodka. Use only enough to moisten, but if some drips off the edges it's ok. Spread with your fingers rather than pour it on.

4. Put the salt and sugar in a small bowl and mix thoroughly with a spoon. With the spoon, spread the sugar/salt mixture evenly over the pieces of fish. The mixture will absorb the liquid and turn into a paste.

5. Loosen up the fresh dill and pack it evenly on the fish that's on the plastic wrap. Use plenty, stems and all. One inch thick at least. Don't worry if it overlaps.

6. Rotate the second piece of fish so the thick side is away from you. Put it flesh side down, on top of the dill. The two thicker edges should be opposite, so they fit together like a jigsaw puzzle. Press down to make it snug, but not too hard. Fold the pieces of plastic wrap up over and around the fish to make a tight packet. Place the packet in the resealable bag; squeeze gently to get most of the air out.

7. Refrigerate for 3 days, turning it over once a day. It will create a lot of liquid; that's normal. Just make sure the bag is sealed shut when you put it in the fridge!

8. After 3 days, take the fish out. Discard the plastic wrap and the dill. Save the resealable bag. The sugar/salt will be gone. Using very little water, rinse the flesh to remove little bits of dill.

9. Lay the fish flat, skin side down, and using an extremely sharp knife, cut thin slices. Work your way down to the skin, then discard the skin. Use the resealable bag for the discards to contain the odor.

Note
Try liquid smoke with or in place of the vodka. Adds a bit of smoky flavor to the fish. 3 days in the fridge is perfect for a nice, delicate flavor. For stronger flavor, leave it in longer. If you're partial to salty lox, change the ratio of the salt/sugar mixture.

Serves 12 easily with bagels and cream cheese for breakfast.

HEALTHFUL HALIBUT
Lisa Alexander

I am a freelance bassoonist/teacher in the NYC metro area since 1986.

When I was a student of Loren Glickman's on a lesson day at his house, his wife Dobbie would always be cooking up something yummy in the kitchen. Once I saw her make an Asian fish dish with halibut. I got inspired and tried a variation of it. Voila!

Special Prep/Equipment
Large baking dish

- 1-2 pounds of halibut, skinned
- 1½ tablespoons olive oil
- Fresh garlic, chopped
- Fresh ginger to taste, chopped
- 1 teaspoon five spice powder
- Sea salt & pepper to taste
- Juice of 1 orange
- ¼ cup teriyaki sauce

1. Preheat oven to 350°.
2. Place the halibut in a baking dish and drizzle the olive oil over both sides of the fish.
3. Squeeze the orange over the fish, sprinkle chopped garlic, ginger, five spice powder, salt and pepper to taste.
4. Cover baking dish and bake in preheated oven for 20 minutes.
5. Add teriyaki sauce just before taking out of the oven. Enjoy!

2 pounds of fish serves 4

DALMATION FISH STEW
(BRODET NA DALMATINSKI NAČIN)
Svjetlana Kabalin

I am the flutist of the Sylvan Winds and have also performed on Broadway, at Radio City, with the New York City Opera and the New Jersey Ballet Orchestra. I also enjoy teaching flute now at Diller-Quaile, and previously at Hofstra University, the Juilliard MAP program, and Simon's Rock of Bard College.

This recipe has been in my family for years, but it was most appreciated on a trip with my husband and our son when he was a toddler. It would be our second trip to Europe where we were to visit England and Italy, as well as Yugoslavia. My husband wasn't sure about going to a communist country, but since it was next door to Italy, I wasn't going to miss a chance to visit my family. We travelled by car from Venice, through the Istrian peninsula, down the Dalmatian coast to Split and then inland to Zagreb, before returning to Venice. Each successive day was spent exploring a new town on the Adriatic coast, then hiking in the Plitivice Lakes, and finally visiting my cousins in Zagreb. As we were about to leave Zagreb we got a phone call from my cousins in Kraljevica, an Adriatic village, insisting that we stop for lunch! We didn't understand why, but weren't going to miss the opportunity to see them, so we set off arriving in time for the first catch of tuna in this brodet served on piping hot polenta! It was an unforgettable meal, devoured most appreciatively by my husband and son. Enjoy!

Special Prep/Equipment
This dish is served on polenta or rice.
A large skillet is needed.

3 pounds of firm, white fish	1 cup dry red wine
Juice of a lemon	⅓ cup white vinegar
¾ cup olive oil	4 tablespoons tomato paste
Salt and pepper to taste	1 teaspoon salt
2 onions, sliced, divided	½ teaspoon pepper
1 clove garlic, minced	Parsley, finely chopped

1. Cut the fish into 12 pieces, approx 2 x 3" strips. Sprinkle with lemon juice.

2. In a large skillet, heat olive oil and saute one sliced onion until transparent. Add the fish, flesh side down, a minced clove of garlic, and one additional sliced onion.

3. Lightly brown the fish, turning, to finish skin side down. Add the red wine, the white vinegar, tomato paste, and a scant amount of water. Salt and pepper the fish.

4. Simmer uncovered for one hour, occasionally spooning the pan liquids over the fish and shaking the pan to prevent the fish from sticking. Do not stir.

5. Sprinkle with finely chopped parsley and serve on polenta or rice.

Serves 6

CLASSIC FENNEL WITH SARDINES
 Hugo Moreno

I play the trumpet. I am a New York City freelancer, and played in *West Side Story* on Broadway.

Someone very close to me showed me this recipe. It is delicious, perfect for any day of the week and it's so simple to make.

Special Prep/Equipment
Large pan or skillet

Approx. 2 tablespoons olive oil	Plenty of salt (Diamond Kosher preferred)
1 fennel bulb with shards, chopped.	1 - 2 servings of pasta, ½ - ¾ pound
1 can or jar of sardines (pref. packed in oil)	1 handful of raisins (approx ⅓ cup)

1. Heat olive oil in a medium to large pan or skillet on medium-high heat. When oil is hot, add fennel bulbs and stalks, sauteing until soft, about 15 minutes.

2. Add sardines (and the oil they came in) on top. Continue to sauté for another 10 minutes. You can break up the sardines or leave them whole, both are good.

3. In a separate pot, bring several cups of water to boil. Season with plenty of salt – make it taste like the sea.

4. Add the fennel shards to the fennel mixture, and cook for another 10 minutes, until everything is cooked together.

5. Add pasta to the boiling water. Cook until al dente, or 98% done (to get that "bite").

6. Turn off the heat, and toss the handful of raisins onto the fennel mixture. Drain the cooked pasta, but save a few teaspoons of the seasoned water and stir into the mixture.

7. Serve fennel and sardines over pasta.

Serves 2

TUNA NUNA CASSEROLE
Karen Blundell

I play oboe and english horn in and around NYC. I'm a member of the Northeastern Pennsylvania Philharmonic and the Double Entendre Music Ensemble.

As a child, this was one of the few things I would willingly eat. It's a family recipe passed down from my grandmother. My sister couldn't say the word noodle when she was little so "Tuna Nuna" stuck. As an adult, I've found it's a fabulous pre-performance food. It's very easy to make and has a good balance of protein and carbs for focus and energy.

Special Prep/Equipment
Large, heavy pot is needed.

1. Preheat oven to 350°.

2. Cook elbow noodles as directed on the package, and drain.

3. While the noodles are cooking, drain the tuna and mix in a casserole dish with the soup and peas.

4. Add noodles and milk to casserole, mixing thoroughly. Make sure the noodles are coated and there are no glops of the sauce left in the casserole.

5. Sprinkle the top with crushed Ritz crackers and four to five pats of butter.

6. Bake in preheated oven for one hour.

Serves 3-4

1 cup elbow noodles

1 small can tuna

1 can cream of celery soup

½ cup frozen peas

¼ cup milk

Ritz crackers

Butter

Note: I now use buttered whole wheat breadcrumbs instead of the crackers.

MOM'S TUNA CASSEROLE
Joan Reveyoso

I am a lyric soprano, doing mostly oratorio, recital and cabaret work. I am also an aspiring flutist, who picked up the instrument again after high school.

I ate this a lot as a kid. The recipe was taught to me when I was a teenager by my mother, Marty Barnhill. I am happily married to a wonderful guy who cannot stand cooked tuna or macaroni and cheese. So, the only people who get to eat this dish are my friends and myself. The potato chips are the "secret" ingredient.

4 (5 ounce) cans tuna, albacore preferred, drained

1 (15 ounce) can of sweet peas, drained

1 large bag of potato chips

1 (10½ ounce) can of Campbell's Cream of Mushroom soup

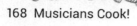

Special Prep/Equipment
2 quart casserole dish with lid

1. Preheat oven to 350°. Lightly spray casserole dish with Pam.

2. Into your casserole dish, place tuna and peas.

3. Take the bag of chips, and empty into the dish, squishing with your fingers, to break up the chips and mold into the casserole.

4. Add your soup, mix thoroughly. If there are any remaining chips, sprinkle over the top.

5. Cover casserole, and place into preheated oven for 30-35 minutes. Serve immediately.

Makes 4 healthy portions.

GRANDMA MITSUKO'S SUSHI
Rie Schmidt

I play flute with the American Symphony and Westchester Philharmonic Orchestras. I am a frequent sub in the NYC Ballet Orchestra.

My grandmother, Mitsuko Akimoto came to Hawaii at age 17 as a picture bride from Japan. This is her recipe for sushi as remembered by my mother. Grandma liked her sushi very sweet! You can cut down the amount of sugar to your taste.

Special Prep/Equipment
Bamboo sushi rolling mat

1. Wash and cook rice.

2. Combine vinegar, ginger juice, salt and sugar in a large, flat dish. Reserve and put aside a ¼ cup of this liquid for making sushi. Add cooked rice to dish; stirring quickly to season rice. Cool rapidly with a fan. Grandma recommends a paper fan.

3½ cups uncooked short-grain white or sushi rice

5½ cups or more water for softer rice

1 cup rice vinegar

1 tablespoon of fresh ginger juice (grated and squeezed grated ginger)

3 tablespoons salt

1 cup sugar

1 package flat seaweed in square sheets (package of 10)

Various other filling ingredients to your taste:
Imitation crab and avocado, raw fish, cooked vegetables (carrots, mushrooms, bamboo shoots, etc.) raw or pickled cucumber, cooked egg, wasabi-spicy green mustard, unagi (eel). All fillings should be cut into long thin strips to spread evenly in a roll.

3. Lay bamboo sushi rolling mat on table. Put one sheet of seaweed on the mat, shiny side down. Take approximately 1 cup of the rice mixture and flatten onto the bottom of the seaweed sheet. Leave ½" margins on the right and left sides. Flatten the rice. Add the filling of your choice. Dip fingers into liquid and moisten the upper edge of the seaweed. Roll from bottom to top. Use mat to compact roll. Seal upper edge.

4. Let rest and then cut into bite-size pieces. Wipe knife with wet rag between cuts to keep the knife from sticking. Serve with soy sauce, wasabi mustard and pickled ginger.

> **Note:** It's important to cool the rice down so it doesn't keep cooking after it's seasoned. Use a large flat pan like a lasagna pan to spread and cool the rice. Dip fingers in water and shake excess liquid off, if they get sticky with rice.

Yields about 8 rolls

SALMON BE-BOK CHOY
~ Cheryl Pyle

I am a flutist, composer, jazz, classical, experimental.

I conjured up this recipe, after many years of cooking dinner.

Special Prep/Equipment
Skillet for salmon and veggies

1. Cook the brown rice, set aside. Brush top of fish with some teriyaki sauce.

2. Put sesame hot oil, garlic, ginger, pepper, spices in a skillet. Start to brown, and then place your fish with sauce in the pan and throw all the veggies into the skillet with a bit of water.

3. Cover for a few minutes until cooked.

4. Serve over brown rice.

Servles 1-2

Brown rice	Organic herbs (I use Graggs Organic Spice mix, it has everything)
1 small piece salmon	
Teriyaki sauce	
A few shakes of hot sesame oil (for the skillet and to dress top of fish)	One small bunch bok choy, chopped
2 cloves garlic, or more to taste	2-3 brussel sprouts, chop in quarters
2 slices fresh, organic ginger	1 stalk celery
Ground pepper, to taste	Yam, a few thin slices

THAI RED SHRIMP & VEGGIE CURRY
~ Bette Sussman

I am a keyboard player, singer and musical director.

My last trip to Thailand was a game changer...the food, the street food, and asking questions and reading to learn what the essential ingredients in Thai food are..once you learn what they are...the Thai food world is your oyster!

Oil (not olive) grape seed, or peanut, or canola	A few kaffir lime leaves, sliced	1 cup chicken stock or broth
1 small onion, sliced	½ teaspoon of light brown sugar	½ pound raw shrimp, cleaned and deveined
½ can of Maesri (my favorite) red curry paste	1 cup chopped broccoli	2 tablespoons fish sauce
1 can of unsweetened coconut milk (try and get a Thai brand like "Chaokoh" which is just better. Do NOT get "lite coconut milk")	1 small sweet potato, cut into bite size chunks	1 small bunch fresh cilantro, chopped
	A few thai eggplants cut in quarters or Japanese eggplant cut into smallish pieces	1 lime
		Jasmine rice

Special Prep/Equipment
I use a wok, but a small dutch oven is good, too.

1. Heat pan or dutch oven and add 1½ tablespoons of oil.

2. Add onions and saute for a minute. Add a heaping tablespoon of red curry paste (or to taste). Coat the onions and cook for about 2 minutes.

3. Shake can and add the coconut milk. Add a touch of water to clean can, and pour into pan.

4. Let simmer a minute or two, then add kaffir lime leaves and brown sugar.

5. Add veggies and cover.

6. Cook for 5 minutes and add a little stock or broth.

7. Add shrimp and cook another 5 or 10 minutes, til all seems cooked through.

8. Add fish sauce and cilantro. Stir, let sit for a minute.

9. Serve over jasmine rice. Squeeze lime juice over all.

> **Note**
> If you live in NYC, these ethnic items can be found at: Kalustyan's (123 Lexington Avenue) or H Mart (110th and Broadway).

Serves 2

ATÚN GUISADO
Evelyn Estava

I am a violinist/quartetfolk/teacher/cook. Music is love. Food is love.

This is a recipe I developed when I was still in Venezuela and couldn't get to the market for whatever reason. It makes use of mainly pantry staples, and it's not only super easy to make, but CHEAP! I've made this recipe quite a bit, but much more since the start of the lockdown. It has been a surprising hit among anyone I've served it to, and in the last months, it has become much more of a comfort food than ever before.

Special Prep/Equipment
Serve with whatever kind of rice you prefer.

1. In a medium size pan, heat olive oil to medium high, throw in diced onion and a pinch of salt. Let it sweat for about 3 minutes, or until they are somewhat translucent and giving off their fragrance.

2. Add the minced garlic and let sweat a bit with the onion--at this point you need to babysit it for a couple of minutes so that the garlic doesn't burn. Add tomato paste, let it cook for a minute, add olives, tomatoes, Worcestershire, salt, pepper.

3. Bring the heat down to medium low, and let it simmer a bit while you're opening and draining the cans of tuna. Add the tuna to the mixture, and let it cook for another 10 minutes.

4. Adjust seasonings before serving. If you have fresh cilantro, mince some and add at the end. Serve along with whatever kind of rice you prefer. Avocado slices make it extra special.

Serves 4

1 teaspoon olive oil

1 big onion, or 2 small

2 cloves of garlic, finely minced

1 teaspoon tomato paste

½ cup of salad olives (the ones that have the pimento in the middle and come already sliced)

1 can of diced tomatoes, or 2-3 fresh diced tomatoes

1 dash Worcestershire sauce

Salt and pepper to taste

3 cans of tuna. I use tuna in olive oil. (If you choose the one with water, increase the amount of olive oil by a tablespoon.)

Optional: garnish of chopped cilantro, sliced avocado

SPICY MONKFISH
Gretchen Pusch

I am a flutist in NYC.

I found a recipe similar to this long ago from the NY Times, and over the years have made it my own by changing both the ingredients and the preparation method.

Special Prep/Equipment

Ceramic baking dish, large enough to hold the fish in one layer

Sheet of aluminum foil

The peanut oil is key, as it imparts a nice, nutty flavor to the pasta/rice.

1. Preheat oven 350°.

2. Make the sauce. In a heavy saucepan, place first seven ingredients, and cook over medium heat until reduced by half. Add capers.

3. Brush olive oil to coat your baking dish, and put in the monkfish. Cover fish with the tomato sauce, and then cover dish with foil. Bake 30-40 minutes in preheated oven, until the thickest part of the fish is almost cooked through.

4. Sprinkle with Ouzo and feta cheese, and bake until cheese has melted, another 10 minutes or so.

5. *While the fish is cooking, make your rice and pasta:* In a medium saucepan, saute dry uncooked pasta in peanut oil, stirring constantly until golden brown (this happens quickly, so watch closely). Add uncooked white rice to pasta, and cover with an appropriate amount of water (a bit more than a two-to-one ratio, to accommodate the pasta) and cook, covered, until water is absorbed and rice is tender, but not mushy.

6. Serve fish and its sauce on the rice and pasta. Sprinkle generously with chopped parsley. Bon appétit!

Serves 4

Sauce and Fish:

1 (28 ounce can) Italian plum tomatoes

½ head garlic, or to taste, thinly sliced

Hot red pepper flakes, to taste

Dried oregano, to taste

Tomato paste, to taste

Salt and pepper, to taste

A handful of pitted black Greek olives, sliced

Capers, several tablespoons

Olive oil

1½ pounds monkfish filets

Ouzo (Greek anise-flavored liqueur)

½ pound feta cheese, crumbled

Flat leaf parsley, chopped

Bed of long grain white rice and pasta:

Peanut oil

½ cup long grain white rice

12 ounces angel hair pasta

SOUTHWESTERN SALMON
Jeanne Wilson

I am Solo Piccoloist with the Hartford Symphony, and freelance flutist in the NYC area.

The recipe is from Cookingprofessionally.com. It was originally titled Tuscan Salmon, and I modified it, changing it to a southwest flavor, as I did not have the ingredients on hand.

Special Prep/Equipment
Broiler pan, large skillet

1. Preheat broiler.

2. Place fillets on broiler pan, sprinkle with chili powder and broil until cooked through, about 10 to 12 minutes.

3. While fillets are broiling, melt the butter in a large frying pan. Add the garlic and cook for about one minute. Add the onion and cook for several minutes. Add the salsa, and can of chilies (if using) stir frying for another several minutes. Add the broth and let the sauce thicken.

4. Lower the heat, add the milk and simmer. Stir occasionally. (If desired, add more milk to sauce, along with salt and pepper to taste.)

3 salmon fillets

½ - 1 teaspoon chili powder

2 tablespoons butter or margarine

5 cloves garlic, finely diced

1 small onion, diced

5 ounces salsa

1 can of diced chilies, optional

⅓ cup chicken or vegetable broth

1 cup milk, plus more if desired (any percentage is fine including skim, or for a richer sauce, cream)

Salt and pepper

3 cups baby spinach leaves

½ cup grated parmesan or pepper jack, if you like more spice.

Couscous or rice

5. Add the spinach, allowing it to wilt. Add the cheese and simmer until the cheese is melted.

6. Add the fillets to the pan, covering them with the sauce.

7. Serve over couscous or rice.

Serves 2 - 3

SALMON CAKES
Lisa Hansen

I'm a Juilliard grad, former Principal Flutist of the Mexico City Philharmonic, and current member of North/South Consonance, NY Scandia Symphony, All Seasons Chamber Players. I am on the faculty of Kean University Conservatory. I've recorded many solo and chamber music works for flute — my passion is Latin American, Spanish and contemporary repertoire.

I'm not the greatest cook and am always too busy to prepare elaborate meals, so I like easy, quick recipes! I love salmon cakes and adapted this easy recipe from *Joy of Cooking* by spicing it up a bit with garlic, minced celery, and additional spices.

Special Prep/Equipment
Large fry pan

1. Mix ingredients and then shape into salmon cakes.

2. Fry in olive oil (or butter if you're feeling sinful) until golden brown.

Yields 2-3 salmon cakes

2 cans of salmon, or one large can — you can use boneless & skinless for greater ease but the wild caught salmon has more flavor.

½ cup bread crumbs

3 eggs, beaten

½ teaspoon salt

¼ teaspoon paprika

Add pepper, as you like

2 cloves garlic, finely chopped

1-2 stalks celery, diced

1 teaspoon prepared mustard

Seafood & Fish 173

GRILLED WHOLE BRANZINO

～ Orlando Wells

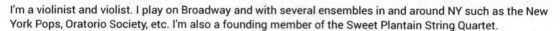

I'm a violinist and violist. I play on Broadway and with several ensembles in and around NY such as the New York Pops, Oratorio Society, etc. I'm also a founding member of the Sweet Plantain String Quartet.

This recipe was suggested by our local fishmonger in Sharon, Connecticut. It also works well with snapper. I've added garlic to the recipe because, garlic!

Special Prep/Equipment
Propane or charcoal grill, fish basket for grilling, non-stick cooking spray (optional)

1-1½ pounds whole branzino fish gutted and cleaned, with head on	Several cloves of minced garlic
Neutral high heat oil such as avocado, sesame (not toasted) or olive oil (not extra virgin)	Fresh herbs such as fennel, dill, parsley, etc.
	1 lemon, sliced
	Salt and pepper

1. Preheat your grill to around 400°.

2. Cut 3 or 4 slashes on both sides of the fish in the direction of the bones. Rub or brush the fish with oil. Take half of the minced garlic and work it into the slashes in the fish, then season with salt and pepper.

3. Stuff the fish cavity with the remaining garlic, herbs and lemon. If using a fish basket use a non stick cooking spray before closing the fish in it.

4. Grill with the lid closed for about 10 to 12 minutes per side, and you're done.

Serves 2 if it's a large fish

MONKFISH WITH FENNEL
～ Eriko Sato

I am a violinist, and co-concertmaster of Orpheus and Orchestra of St. Luke's.

This dish is inspired by Monkfish with Savory Cabbage from Le Bernadin many, many years ago, and Shrimp with Fennel from Brooklyn Fair.

Special Prep/Equipment
Heavy skillet

1 pound monkfish	1 medium fennel bulb
Flour or cornstarch to dust the fish	Salt and pepper
Several tablespoons olive or vegetable oil	Fish stock or clam juice to cover the fish
1 medium yellow onion	1 bay leaf

1. Salt and pepper the monkfish, coat with cornstarch or flour, dust off any excess. In the heavy skillet, heat the 2 tablespoons of any olive oil or vegetable oil, brown the fish on all sides.

2. Remove fish from pan. Thinly slice the onion and fennel.

3. Add 1 tablespoon of oil to the pan, add thinly sliced onions and fennel, saute for a few min. Salt and pepper to taste, put the fish back, add the stock to cover the fish, add bay leaf, adjust the seasoning.

4. Cover and cook on low heat for about 20-30 min. until the fennel is soft.

Serves 2

I am sure my music has a taste of codfish in it.

∽ Edvard Grieg

VEGETARIAN

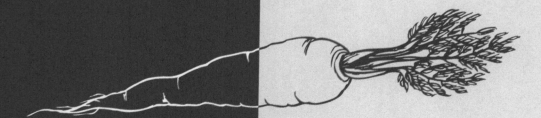

BAKED STUFFED PORTOBELLO MUSHROOMS

~ James Biddlecome

I have been a trombonist with the NY City Opera for 42 years.

I had this at a luncheon place in Ithaca, NY. I could only get the ingredients, so I improvised.

Special Prep/Equipment
Rice cooker or saucepan
Baking sheet
Parchment paper or aluminum foil

The Risotto:
¼ cup butter

¾ cup onion, diced

1 cup arborio rice (risotto)

3½ cups chicken stock

¼ teaspoon dried sage

Pinch of saffron (optional)

⅓ cup dry red or white wine

⅛ teaspoon white pepper

The Stuffing:
(You can be creative with these)
4 mushroom stems, chopped (add a little more chopped mushrooms if available)

2 cloves of garlic, minced

½ cup tomatoes, diced

Fresh spinach, coarsely chopped (This will cook down so be generous)

¼ cup sweet red pepper, chopped

4 large portobello mushrooms caps (to be stuffed)

1 tablespoon balsamic vinegar

Parmesan cheese to taste

1. Make the risotto. Place butter in rice cooker or saucepan and turn on. When melted, add onion and saute 3-4 minutes until soft. Add rice and saute 2-3 minutes until coated with butter and rice has turned milky white. Add remaining ingredients. Cover and cook until rice cooker turns off.

2. Just before rice is done, preheat oven to 375°.

3. Make the stuffing. Remove stems from the mushrooms and chop. In a medium saute pan, over medium-heat, heat the cooking oil and saute mushroom stems, garlic, tomatoes, spinach, and sweet red pepper. Add a dash of salt and pepper.

4. Cook for about 10 minutes, stirring until the spinach is wilted.

5. Place mixture into a bowl and add cooked rice. Add Parmesan cheese and 1 tablespoon of balsamic vinegar. Mix thoroughly and adjust seasoning.

6. Assemble and bake. Prepare baking sheet with parchment paper or aluminum foil and spray with non-stick spray.

7. Lay washed and dried mushroom caps out on baking sheet and drizzle with olive oil and sprinkle with salt and pepper. Carefully stuff each mushroom cap with rice mixture and bake in oven for about 20-25 minutes.

Serves 4

GRANDPA IRVING'S LATKES
⌇ Owen Kotler

I play clarinet and reeds on Broadway, in orchestras, recordings and chamber music.

Traditional in my family and one of the few things grandpa Irving cooked. He mostly did the shopping! He bought a mean bagel :-)

Special Prep/Equipment
Grater, large bowl, frying pan, spoon or fork, spatula, paper towels

About 1 pound Russet potatoes

About ½ pound onion

Few pinches salt, freshly ground black pepper

1 extra large egg

About ½ cup matzo meal

Oil for frying — Irving used Crisco, I would use olive oil, or non-GMO vegetable oil.

1. Peel potato, peel onion. Into a large bowl, grate potato on large holes of grater and grate onion on smallest holes of grater. Potato should be in small strips and onion should be almost liquid.

2. Add salt and pepper to taste, 1 whole egg and stir.

3. Add enough matzo meal to hold the other ingredients together into a kind of batter that would hold together when fried.

4. In a frying pan, heat about ¼ - ½" oil over medium heat. When hot, start adding about a tablespoon/or forkful (more or less depending on the size you prefer) of potato mixture to the oil. Pancakes should be about ¼" thickness.

5. Cook until it's the amount of brown you prefer on first side, and flip and repeat on second side.

6. Remove and drain slightly on paper towels. Salt and pepper as needed and eat.

Serves 4 as an appetizer or side dish.

AMAZING GREEN SAUCE FOR ANYTHING!
⌇ Carol Sudhalter

I play flute, tenor, baritone and alto saxophone. I moved to NYC in 1978 to join the first all-female Latin band, Latin Fever. I founded and led the Astoria Big Band. Our most exciting gig was at the Kennedy Center for the Mary Lou Williams Women in Jazz Festival. I lead the monthly Jazz Jam at Flushing Town Hall.

I had Covid in April and May. I could still taste and smell my food, and I had a decent appetite; but the virus left me with months of "long-hauler" after-effects that challenged my appetite: chest pain, stomach aches, intestinal problems and even pancreatic inflammation. To keep from losing any more weight, I had to find foods that were very tasty. This sauce truly makes anything taste better. The original version was a complement to quinoa. It goes well as a sauce on pasta, a dip with bread, a savory side sauce with fish, you name it. The recipe is adapted from *www.citronetvanille.com*. The original version included mint, but since I'm in the care of a homeopath, and mint is considered antagonistic to homeopathy, I just go without it. I use the salsa but not the quinoa part. Sometimes I add parmesan cheese or a drop of yogurt or lemon or both. It works in a variety of ways and will never let you down. Tangy!!

Special Prep/Equipment
Food processor or blender

1. Process or blend the ingredients to make it into a smooth mixture. Enjoy!

Serves 5 (fills a 10 ounce jar)

2 scallions	1 tablespoon balsamic vinegar
2 garlic cloves	½ teaspoon cumin
½ bunch parsley	½ teaspoon paprika
½ bunch cilantro	Pinch chili powder
bunch mint (optional)	Salt and pepper, to taste
5 tablespoons olive oil	

CHANA MASALA (CHICKPEA CURRY)
∾ Richard Einhorn

I am a composer of concert, theater, dance, and film music.

This recipe was given to me by my friend Karen who watched her friend Janaki make it in her kitchen. It has been a favorite in our house for well over 10 years.

Special Prep/Equipment
Serve this dish with basmati rice or with Indian bread such as naan.

1. Heat oil in saucepan over medium heat.

2. Add chopped onion and continue to cook over medium heat until caramelized and charred.

3. Lower heat. Add minced garlic, cumin seeds, ground coriander, ground ginger, garam masala, and cardamom pods. Cook for about 30 seconds, until fragrant.

4. Add 1 cup or less water and scrape the pan. Cook until water evaporates

5. Add can of tomatoes, including juice, and break them apart. Add 1 teaspoon salt, bring to a boil.

6. Reduce heat to low, add cilantro and pinch cayenne. Simmer until thickens.

7. Add 2 cans of chickpeas and stir well. Cook about 5 minutes over low heat.

8. Add 2 Tablespoon water. Cook about 5 minutes longer, until water is absorbed.

9. Add lemon juice and garnish with fresh ginger slices.

Serves 4

- 2-3 tablespoons canola oil
- 1 medium onion, chopped
- 2 cloves garlic, minced
- 1 teaspoon cumin seeds
- ½ teaspoon ground coriander
- ¼ teaspoon ground ginger
- 1 teaspoon garam masala
- 3 cardamom pods, crushed
- 1 cup plus 2 tablespoons water
- 1 (28 ounce) can tomatoes, including the juice
- 1 teaspoon salt
- 1 tablespoon cilantro, chopped
- 1 pinch cayenne
- 2 (15 ounce) cans chickpeas
- Juice of ½ lemon
- Fresh ginger, sliced thinly with a vegetable peeler

DAL CHAAWAL (LENTILS & RICE)

~ Rachel Golub

I'm a freelance violinist. In addition to a lot of sidewoman and session playing, I perform on Broadway (currently *Moulin Rouge*), and I'm an Associate first violinist at the Met Opera. I play my own music whenever possible and I might be the only Afrobeat violinist in New York City.

I imagine every freelance musician has some secret cooking weapon that has gotten them through the times when money was tight. For many years, I lived in Astoria, Queens, back when there were Punjabi and Bangladeshi grocery stores that sold VHS tapes and desi sweets on every corner. I was, at the time, steeping in South Asian music, playing tabla and sitar, singing and teaching. And roommates and friends, students, even the folks who ran the local internet café all knew they could count on me for regular helpings of dal.

I am not much of a precision cook — I am an improviser, I like to feel things — but here is a basic dal-chaawal recipe. I learned this over several years of studying sitar with the mighty Ustad Shahid Parvez. We would all cook together, usually five or six of us, and gradually he delegated the prep tasks, but when he made the baghaar/tarka (the hot oil and spice process) we would all stand on tiptoes to watch him do it. Thus we learned many of the recipes he had learned from his mother. One can play with this, experiment with different spices and oils and types of lentils, but it's fairly foolproof when the lentils are cooked through, the oil is hot enough, and the timing lets the baghaar hit the dal with a satisfying sizzle. The steam inside the closed pot creates the flavor. It's also easy to make in quantity for a last-minute party, when people are coming in and out all night, alongside a few vegetable dishes. For special occasions, skip the oil and just make it in straight ghee for a richer version.

Special Prep/Equipment
A pressure cooker helps

Salt, to taste

1+ teaspoon turmeric

Asafoetida or ginger (optional, a pinch or 2 slices)

1-2 tablespoons neutral vegetable oil, like safflower

1 tablespoons ghee

Basmati rice, cooked, a big pot

About a cup dry lentils (this quantity for 3-4 people)

1 tomato, chopped

Big handful cumin whole seeds (to cover a 6" pan)

1 clove garlic, chopped very fine (optional)

1 onion, chopped fine

4-5 dried whole red chillies (depending on spice tolerance)

Small bunch of cilantro leaves, to season

Your favorite achaar (south asian pickle)

1. Pressure cook or cook fine a pot of lentils. Any kind will do! I mostly use split yellow pigeon peas (toor) and occasionally mix in some split red masoor. Use about ⅓ dal to 1 pot water ratio. 2 cups of dal will go a long way.

2. Add turmeric powder, a small handful of salt and a little hing (asafoetida) or sliced ginger to the pot before cooking. A couple of whistles should do it in the pressure cooker, let it depressurize on its own.

3. Meanwhile, cook basmati rice. I rinse before cooking, then strain it when it is al dente and steam it a little.

5. Cook the lentils fine and when they are done, stir the dal — it should have few or no pieces left, and a fairly watery consistency that will boil off.

6. Add chopped tomato. Keep simmering and fairly liquid. Check the salt at this point.

7. In a small 6" saucepan, heat enough oil to cover most of the onion. I use safflower oil with a teaspoon of ghee. When the oil is hot enough that a cumin seed dropped in sizzles immediately, add a handful of cumin seeds. When the smell blossoms, add the chopped garlic if using, and when it starts to smell, add the onion. When the onion starts to just begin to brown, break 3-4 red chillies in half and put them in the oil, which should remain quite hot.

8. Keeping the lid of the pressure cooker or pot with lentils/dal in it in one hand, pour the hot oil and spicing with quick motion, into the dal and close the lid. It should steam up and sizzle. This flavors the dal.

9. Let it sit for a bit on medium heat, and serve hot over rice.

10. Garnish with cilantro and a spoonful of pickle, to be mixed in in tiny dabs. Eat with yogurt and chopped fresh vegetables, or a vegetable dish with contrasting spice.

Serves 3-4

LAURA'S IKARIAN LONGEVITY STEW
Laura Bontrager

I'm a freelance cellist in NYC. I graduated from Juilliard and have been performing and teaching and enjoying life here for almost 30 years, thanking my lucky stars that I'm a professional musician.

I found this recipe from an article about the Blue Zones of the world, the places where people have the longest, healthiest lives. I love fennel, and I like this soup warm and also chilled. Sometimes I ladle a warm scoop over a kale and radicchio salad.

Special Prep/Equipment
Large soup pot

The black eyed peas need to be partially cooked and soaked.

1 cup (8 ounces) dried black eyed peas (bring to a boil, boil for 1 minute, remove from heat, cover and let sit for an hour. Drain, rinse, and use.)

½ cup extra virgin olive oil

1 large red onion, finely chopped

4 garlic cloves, finely chopped

1 fennel bulb, chopped

1 large, firm ripe tomato, finely chopped

2 teaspoons tomato paste, diluted in ¼ cup water

2 bay leaves

Salt and pepper to taste

1 bunch dill, finely chopped

1. Heat some of the olive oil over medium heat and cook the onion, garlic, and fennel, stirring occasionally until soft, about 12 minutes. Add the black-eyed peas and toss to coat in the oil.

2. Add the tomato, tomato paste and enough water to cover the beans by about an inch. Add the bay leaves.

3. Bring to a boil, reduce heat and simmer until the black-eyed peas are about half way cooked. (Check after 40 minutes, but it may take over an hour.)

4. Add the chopped dill and season with salt.

5. Continue cooking until the black-eyed peas are tender, add more water if needed. Remove, pour in remaining olive oil and serve.

Makes 4 big bowls, 8 smaller bowls

RICE OF ORIGINAL QI
~ Andrew Sterman

I play saxophones, flutes, clarinets. I play extensively on Broadway, in recordings, and for 30 years with the Philip Glass Ensemble.

This recipe is from book 2 of my set *Welcoming Food: Diet as Medicine for the Home Cook* (2020, Classical Wellness Press, NYC). These recipes support health and healing as well as being great to eat and easy to make. This is a rice salad combining black rice with vegetables and red beans to support Constitutional Qi in a delicious and flexible manner.

1. Cook the black rice using steam absorption method: bring water and rice to a boil, reduce to a simmer, cover, cook for 40 minutes (20 in an electric pressure cooker), do not stir. Allow rice to rest and cool a bit.

2. In a large bowl combine the cooked adzuki beans, peas, and broccoli florets with the mushrooms, cashews, arame, and scallions.

3. In a smaller bowl, mix the dressing (the oil, tamari, vinegar and toasted sesame oil). Pour the dressing over the vegetables, stir to mix. Gently mix in the rice. Taste for balance, adjust as needed.

4. Stir in the chopped parsley or cilantro, reserving a bit for on-top presentation. Serve at room temperature.

Serves 8

2 cups black (forbidden) rice

3½ cups water

1 cup adzuki beans, cooked (canned or home-cooked)

1 cup peas, cooked (frozen okay)

1 cup broccoli florets, steamed

1 cup dried black mushrooms, soaked, drained, sliced (substitute porcini or other mushrooms, fresh or dried, if desired)

1 cup cashews (substitute sliced walnuts, chestnuts or sunflower seeds, if desired)

½ - 1 cup arame seaweed, soaked and drained

½ cup scallion, finely sliced (raw)

Dressing:
1 cup grapeseed oil

1 cup tamari

2 tablespoons black vinegar (Shanxi black vinegar is a barley-sorghum vinegar from central China. Substitute rice vinegar and balsamic, 1 tablespoon each, if Shanxi vinegar is hard to find)

2 tablespoons toasted sesame oil

Sea salt, to taste

1 bunch parsley or cilantro, washed, chopped

A Note on the Food Energetics
Original Qi is a term from classical Chinese medicine packed with meanings and connotations, all pointing to the status of our deepest health. In other words, how are the strengths and weaknesses of our constitutional health? Some squander strong constitutions, others are constitutionally fragile but do much better. There is an art to life.

The Rice of Original Qi plays with these ideas. Black rice is a wonderful kidney support food. In earlier times the entire crop of black rice was reserved for the Imperial Chinese court that resided in the Forbidden City, prized for its value for health and longevity (this is why it is marketed today as "forbidden rice").

Adzuki beans support kidneys, build blood, calm emotions and aid liver function. Arame seaweed is cleansing and nourishing; being black and from the sea it is also a kidney food. Cashews are one of the nuts used for kidney health, but cashews easily add to dampness if digestion is weak (use walnuts or chestnuts in place if you like, or the much more easily digested pumpkin seeds). If you can have them, cashews are wonderful — they even look like little kidneys.

Black mushrooms are also an important kidney supporting food. Mushrooms help clear dampness while supporting original qi and good immune function. The raw scallions give a gentle nudge to energize the digestion process. Vinegar stimulates digestion as well, but more importantly helps the liver hold the healthy blood that is being made from such good food. When the message from our deep health organs is that we have enough of what we need (not too much, that's a different issue), then the internal organs can relax. Black Shanxi vinegar is available in Chinatown markets or online, but be sure to read the ingredients — the real stuff has no added sugar or coloring and is made from sorghum or millet. It's beautiful: deep, very mildly acidic, and full of flavor.

For your Rice of Original Qi add salt, other vinegars, spices... the dish is essentially a rice salad and the sauce can be seen as a dressing. Toasted sesame seed oil also speaks to the kidneys, said to be the home of original qi. Mustard seed or prepared mustard is a nice addition — mustard warms the belly for good digestion. Make the dish your own, but be careful that your improvisations follow the theme — it's your original qi we're feeding here, it's good to be respectful of what you are made of.

NANA'S LATKES
∾ Deborah Buck

I'm a violinist who was a member of the Lark Quartet for 17 years. I was the tenured Concertmaster of the Brooklyn Philharmonic and currently Acting Concertmaster for Stamford Symphony. I am Assistant Professor of Violin and Head of Chamber Music at SUNY Purchase Conservatory, and Co-Executive Director of the Kinhaven Music School.

Need a nana and lots of love to make these with!

Special Prep/Equipment
Large skillet, a box grater or food processor

1 pound potatoes, peeled

½ cup finely chopped onion

1 large egg, lightly beaten

½ teaspoon salt

½ - ¾ cup olive oil

Accompaniments: sour cream and applesauce

1. Grate the potatoes using your box grater, or in a food processor. Place potatoes in a colander.

2. Chop the onion, and mix with egg and salt. After about 20 minutes, the grated potatoes will turn pink/purple with the starch coming out. Spray them with a hard spray of water. They will be white again.

3. Squeeze the potatoes out with a kitchen towel, blotting out as much moisture as possible. Then, mix with the egg, onion, and salt.

4. Heat the oil in a skillet, and when good and hot, drop mounds of the potato mixture in. Flip when the potatoes are crispy and golden brown. Let the other side cook. Then, serve with applesauce and sour cream.

Yields 12-16 latkes

ZUCCHINI BOATS

~ Susan Rotholz

I am a flutist: performance of solo, chamber music and orchestral music of all genres, recordings, flute professor at Vassar College, Columbia University and Barnard College, ACSM Queens College CUNY.

This recipe is from my mother. It is a Middle Eastern recipe from her upbringing that is a favorite of ours. Growing up with her surrounding us with Mediterranean meals, my mother would stuff zucchini, tomatoes, eggplant, peppers and artichokes with either meat and rice, or cheeses and eggs. We would often have a tahini sauce over the dishes with meat and rice giving them a delicious lemony flavor. This dish is very versatile and considerate for vegetarian and gluten free eaters.

Special Prep/Equipment

Large frying pan
Pyrex baking pan
Tin Foil

5 organic zucchini	Organic flour, or gluten free option (about ½ cup)
2-3 eggs, divided	
2 packages of Friendship farmers cheese	Organic canned whole tomatoes and/or 1 jar of Rao's marinara sauce
Fresh Parmesan cheese (about ½ cup)	Olive oil.

1. Start by cutting the zucchini lengthwise in the center of the zucchini and again in half creating 4 pieces or "boats". Take a teaspoon and scoop out only the center of the zucchini pieces leaving the outer edge in tact, creating a boat or canoe. Keep the inner parts of the zucchini. This will be used as a bed in the baking dish. Set the boats aside.

2. In a mixing bowl, put all the farmers cheese, 1 egg, and shredded Parmesan cheese together and mix.

3. With a spoon, take a spoon full of cheese and fill the zucchini boats. If you need more cheese, take from some of the overfilled boats to make the rest have cheese. Use all the cheese to fill the boats.

4. In another flat bowl, beat an egg, and on a separate plate, put about ½ cup of flour.

5. Preheat oven to 375°. On the stove, medium temperature, heat the pan with olive oil. You may be happier with a non-stick pan.

6. Prepare to fry the zucchini by first dipping the filled zucchini in the flour (a step you can skip for gluten free eaters) and then turning the floured zucchini in the egg. (If there's not enough egg for all the zucchini, add the third egg.) Put face down in the heated pan with olive oil. Be focused on browning both sides of the boat, but not letting the cheese melt and become unruly. Attend to the boats with a spatula, and take out the boats when you feel they are brown enough.

7. In the baking dish, line the bottom with the extra zucchini taken out to make the boats and start to line up the browned zucchini boats face up in the pan. You will have 20 boats.

8. When all the boats are in the baking dish, either take the can of organic plum tomatoes and blend in blender for 5 seconds, and pour over the zucchini boats, or you can use a jar of Rao's instead, if you prefer.

9. Cover the baking dish with tin foil to bake.

10. Bake in preheated oven for one hour. Check to see if it needs more time. The sauce should be like jam but not dry.

11. Remove from oven and serve with a big salad and other things on your colorful plate!

Serves 5 (20 pieces)

STUFFED AVOCADOS
~ Amy Goff

I am a singer. I toured with the artist Meatloaf, performed in several NY based club date bands, and sang on hundreds of jingle sessions in NYC.

I found this recipe in an old 1980's cookbook of Rose Elliot's called *The Complete Vegetarian Cuisine*. I tweaked most of the ingredients, and added the water chestnuts and cooked farro. Rose Elliot bakes these in an oven, but you can also use a microwave. I just add a salad and some roasted potatoes or garlic bread. Super easy, vegetarian, and elegant to serve to dinner guests!

Special Prep/Equipment
Baking sheet

1. Preheat oven to 400°.

2. Saute the onion in the butter or oil until just tender. Set aside to cool slightly.

3. Cut each of the avocados in half and remove the pits. Carefully scoop out the flesh with a spoon, reserving the skins. Cut the avocado into large dice.

4. Gently toss everything together until just combined, seasoning with salt and pepper to taste. Don't over mix so as not to crush the diced avocado.

5. Pile the mixture into the reserved avocado skins.

6. When ready to serve, heat the avocados on a sheet pan in preheated oven, just until the cheese is melted, about 10-15 minutes. You can also heat them in the microwave for 5 minutes or so, on high, until heated through and the cheese is melted.

Serves 6

1 large onion, peeled and chopped

2 tablespoons butter or oil for sauteing

3 large avocados, ripe but not too soft

1 cup of finely diced Gruyere cheese. (Or Jarlesburg, Cheddar, or even Monterey Jack will work well.)

⅓ cup grated Parmesan cheese

1 cup chopped, toasted walnuts. (or use cashews, pine nuts, pistachios, or Brazil nuts.)

1 can water chestnuts, finely diced (optional)

1 cup cooked grain, like farro

¼ cup chopped fresh parsley

¼ cup medium sherry

Salt and pepper to taste

Note
I once had a guest start to eat the avocado skin. You might mention not to do that!

*B*ela Bartok, upon the first time eating an avocado: "This is a fruit somewhat like a cucumber in size and colour," he carefully recorded. "But it is quite buttery in texture, so it can be spread on bread. Its flavour is something like an almond but not so sweet. It has a place in this celebrated fruit salad which consists of green salad, apple, celery, pineapple, raw tomato and mayonnaise."

VEGETARIAN MOROCCAN STEW

~ Jo-Ann Sternberg

I am a clarinetist, music educator and people-person! I feel profoundly grateful to be a part of the truly inspiring and remarkable musicians/artists/humans of Local 802 and miss collaborating with them all!

My dear friend, the beautiful violinist Anna Lim, cooked up this flavorful Vegetarian Moroccan Stew at our cabin in Maine a few summers ago. I was her sous-chef, chopping, peeling, mincing and sauteing. As soon as the aroma of the onions, garlic, cumin and cinnamon began to mingle, I was hooked. The flavors continued to evolve – becoming more pungent with every passing second. I felt like I could taste the air!

This is a vegan recipe adapted from the tried and true *Moosewood Cookbook*. I have made some changes to the original recipe, altering some amounts, and adding ginger, maple syrup, celery and vegetable broth.

Special Prep/Equipment
Large pot or dutch oven

1 cup olive oil	1 teaspoon smoked paprika (regular paprika works fine, too)	2 mid-size bell peppers, chopped (any variety)
3 cups onions, chopped	1 tablespoon maple syrup	4 cups zucchini, cubed
3 garlic cloves, minced	¼ cup chopped fresh parsley (to be added just before serving)	2 large tomatoes, chopped
1 tablespoon fresh ginger root, minced	1 cup carrots, chopped	1 cup chopped celery
1½ teaspoons each: cumin, turmeric, cinnamon	2 cups sweet potatoes, cubed	1 (15 ounce) can chickpeas (including liquid)
¼ - 1 teaspoon cayenne pepper (temper according to your personal heat index!)	2 cups butternut squash, cubed	½ cup vegetable stock
	3 cups eggplant, chopped (1 small-medium)	Pinch of saffron (optional)
		1 cup raisins

1. In a large pot, heat olive oil and saute the onions until transparent. Add garlic, ginger, spices, and maple syrup, stirring continuously. In the order they are listed, add one vegetable at a time, sauteeing each new addition until its color deepens before adding the next.

2. Stir in the chickpeas and raisins. If the stew seems dry, add more vegetable stock.

3. Cover the stew and simmer on low heat until all vegetables are tender.

4. Add chopped parsley and any other desired topping just before serving.

Note
My family's favorite way of enjoying this stew is to set up 6 or 7 small bowls of toppings/sides to be passed around the table so everyone can personalize their plate and create their own masterpiece. Toppings in highest demand have been: roasted pumpkin seeds, sesame seeds, sliced almonds, chopped chives, slivers of fresh ginger, wedges of hard boiled egg, pita bread or pita chips...

Have at it to create your own bowl of aromatic deliciousness!

Serves 4-6

VEGAN WINTER STEW
~ Louise Dubin

I am a cellist. Check out my website at *louise-dubin.com*.

When you're in the mood for a sweet, non-spicy curry, this vegan one is great to eat before going out to work on a cold evening. It will sustain you through a symphony, opera or Broadway show without putting you to sleep as a steak would. It's adapted from a recipe from one of my favorite cooking blogs, *chocolateandzucchini.com*, which was inspired by a recipe by Beena Paradin (*franceinter.fr/vie-quotidienne/curry-de-legumes-d-hiver*). It's a flexible recipe so pandemic substitutions are good. For example, if it's hard to find ginger then garlic works. Turnips and yams are interchangeable with butternut and potatoes. You could also use broccoli instead of cauliflower if you add it later.

Special Prep/Equipment
Thick bottomed pot with a lid, such as a dutch oven

¾ pound large cauliflower florets (about ⅓ of a large cauliflower)	1 teaspoon fine sea salt
¾ pound butternut squash, cut into 1 inch chunks	1½" thumb of ginger, or more, peeled and cut into matchsticks.
½ pound kale leaves, stripped from stems and shredded to bite-size pieces	4 cloves
	¾ teaspoon ground cinnamon
½ pound carrots, preferably rainbow, for color, peeled and cut into 1" chunks	1 (13½ ounce) can of coconut milk
2 tablespoons cooking oil	Freshly ground black pepper
1 medium onion, chopped	Brown basmati or brown long grain rice to serve stew over

1. Cut veggies into cubes/chunks/florets as described above.

2. Heat oil in a thick-bottomed pot with a lid, such as a dutch oven.

3. Add onions and salt, cook for 3 minutes, stirring frequently, until softened. Add ginger, cloves, and cinnamon and cook for about 1 minute more.

4. Add your cauliflower, butternut squash and pour in ⅔ of the coconut milk and ½ cup water. Add the kale leaves on top.

5. Stir, cover, bring to low simmer, and cook for 10 minutes. After 10 minutes, kale will be wilted and reduced. Add carrots and cook 20 more minutes, until veggies are soft.

6. Stir in remaining coconut milk, cook for another minute or two (you can turn off heat and just use the heat left in the pot) and serve over brown rice.

Serves 4 (unless you're married to my husband)

AMRAM'S DESPERATION CROCKPOT STEW
~ David Amram

I am a composer/conductor/multi-instrumentalist.

Rather than microwave instant meals which are filled with corn syrup and other nefarious ingredients, I took fresh vegetables and tofu and let the Crock-Pot work in order to have time to compose, practice and know that I would be nourished!

Special Prep/Equipment
Crockpot and a strong stomach

1. Put can of tomato soup in crockpot and wait 5 minutes. Then add cabbage, mushrooms, tofu, onion, cauliflower, and honey roasted peanuts. Then add curry powder.

2. After 45 minutes add spinach and a ½ cup of water.

3. After 10 minutes, stir from the bottom up and wait 20 more minutes.

4. Season with salt and pepper to taste.

5. Then put all in a large bowl (or two bowls) and ENJOY!!!

Serves 2 hungry people (or 3 who are scared of this recipe)

1 small can of tomato soup

1 half head of cabbage, sliced

1 small box of mushrooms

1 box extra-firm tofu, sliced into cubes

1 large white onion, sliced

1 half head of fresh cauliflower, sliced

1 handful of honey roasted peanuts

1 tablespoon of red curry powder

1 small carton of spinach

Slight sprinkle of black pepper and sea salt

SPINACH & RICE, GREEK STYLE
~ Greg Thymius

I am a woodwind player (flutes and single reeds); the usual freelance stuff.

This rice dish ("Spanachorizo", pronounced, "Spah-nah-CHO-ree-zoh"; "ch" as in "Challa") is a simple, vegetarian/vegan friendly recipe that makes for a good side dish, or even a main course if you want something on the lighter side. It was one of those things that always seemed to be present whenever extended family was visiting or staying with us. For me, it's always been easy, eat-in-front-of-the-television, comfort food.

½ cup olive oil

2 cups onion, minced

1 tablespoon tomato paste

1 pound spinach (or 2 frozen packages, thawed)

½ cup raw rice

1 teaspoon dried dill

1 teaspoon dried parsley

Salt and pepper, to taste (A shake or two of each should do it)

1 cup hot water

Special Prep/Equipment
Medium-sized saucepan

1. On medium-high, or medium heat (it depends on your stove and your pan), saute the minced onion in the olive oil until wilted - usually, that takes about 5 minutes.

2. Add the tomato paste, spinach, and rice, and saute until everything is well mixed.

3. Add the dill, parsley, salt, pepper, and water.

4. Cover and allow to simmer until the rice is cooked, and most of the liquid has been absorbed.

> **Note**
> If the rice has completely absorbed all of the water, but still isn't cooked completely, simply add some more water - you will have to use your judgment as to how much, as it will depend upon how much longer the rice needs to be cooked. Again, allow to simmer until the water has been absorbed.

Serves 4-6

SPANAKOPITA
~ Greg Smith

I play French horn. I play at *Lion King* and also play the piano.

I first found this recipe in the *Moosewood Cookbook* by Mollie Katzen, and have streamlined the method significantly, making it my own. This is a healthy, energizing meal any time of year.

Special Prep/Equipment
9 x 13" baking dish

1 onion, chopped	1 teaspoon basil
Olive oil	1 pound cottage cheese
2 pounds spinach, fresh or frozen	Oregano, basil, salt and pepper to taste
4 eggs	2 cups feta cheese
2 tablespoons flour (optional)	12-15 sheets of phyllo dough, preferably no. 7

1. Preheat oven to 375°. Butter the baking pan.

2. In a large frying pan, saute onion in olive oil and when brown add spinach.

3. Meanwhile, in a large bowl mix all other ingredients (except feta and phyllo dough).

4. Chop feta into small pieces.

5. After spinach and onion are sauteed and all excess moisture cooked off, mix with other ingredients.

6. Layer 4-5 sheets of phyllo dough on bottom of prepared baking dish. Pour half of spinach mash onto dough and spread 4-5 more sheets. Pour remaining spinach mash and pour a large glass of red wine. Finally, again, top with again 4-5 sheets dough and lightly spell your name with olive oil on top.

7. Bake UNCOVERED in preheated oven 35-40 minutes. It's done when fork poked in is dry.

8. Goes well with steamed rice and much more red wine.

Serves at least 4

Vegetarian 189

TOFU WITH MUSHROOMS
Bill Trigg

I am a percussionist/timpanist. Performed and recorded with Brooklyn Philharmonic, American Composers Orchestra, Orchestra of St. Luke's, Steve Reich & Musicians, and numerous chamber ensembles. I am a Broadway sub, and was timpanist for *Man of La Mancha* 1992.

This is my wife's favorite stir-fry recipe. We are not vegetarians, but we love vegetarian meals. My grandfather was a Chinese chef, and this is inspired by him.

Special Prep/Equipment
Big wok or skillet

14 ounce package of extra firm tofu, pressed & cubed

1 tablespoon canola oil

8 ounces mushrooms (I use Wegman's Gourmet Blend of oyster, crimini, & shitake)

Soy sauce

1 cup vegetable broth

1 tablespoon cornstarch

¼ cup water

1. Press the water out of the tofu before cubing.

2. Heat wok for 30 seconds. Add canola oil and heat for 20 seconds.

3. Place mushrooms and a splash of soy sauce into the hot oil. Stir fry for 3 minutes, adding additional soy sauce, as desired.

4. Add tofu and stir fry for 2 minutes. Then, remove tofu and mushrooms to a serving dish.

5. To the wok, add broth and bring to a simmer.

6. In a separate little bowl, whisk cornstarch into the ¼ cup water. Slowly whisk this mixture into broth.

7. Once sauce has thickened, return mushrooms & tofu to the pan. Stir and simmer for 2 minutes until everything is heated and well mixed.

8. Serve over rice with steamed or sauteed vegetables.

Serves about 3-4

RISOTTO WITH WINE, CHEESE & APPLES
Diana Petrella

I am a clarinetist and have performed in Great Britain as a member of the Cambridge Philharmonic and toured internationally as a member of the Campbell Clarinet Quartet. I am frequently a chamber music collaborator here in the US and am on the music faculty of the Brearley School in New York.

This risotto recipe uses apples, which sounds odd, but the pairing of wine and cheese is a classic. The rice stands in for the bread. This is the first dish my husband Steve ever cooked for me. He got the recipe from a woman in Italy, who made it for him in the 1980's. It's a traditional dish in northern Italy.

190 Musicians Cook!

4 cups chicken or vegetable stock	1 onion, finely chopped	A handful of Parmesan cheese, more or less, to taste
4 tablespoons unsalted butter, divided	2 crisp apples, peeled and cut into thin slices	Flat leaf parsley, chopped
2 tablespoons olive oil	2 cups Arborio rice	Fresh basil (optional)
	1 cup white vermouth	Salt and plenty of pepper

1. Have a saucepan with the stock simmering over low heat.

2. In a separate 12″ pan, heat half of the butter and the 2 tablespoons of oil until the butter melts. Add the onions. Cook over medium heat until the onion is soft.

3. Add the apples and the rice to the onion and cook until you hear the rice "popping". Add the vermouth and cook until it evaporates.

4. Add a cup of the simmering stock. Stir and cook making sure that the mixture is active, but not boiling. When the stock is incorporated into the rice add a cup more and continue this process until all the stock is used. This should take about 20 minutes or so. The rice should be al dente.

5. Off the heat add the remaining butter, the cheese, parsley, and basil.

6. Salt and pepper to taste.

Serves 4

MUJADRAH (LEBANESE LENTILS & RICE)
◦ Sara Milonovich

I am a violinist/fiddler and a singer-songwriter. I lead my own alt-country band, Daisycutter, and also work as an accompanist, recording artist, and Broadway sub.

I learned to cook from my mother and her mother, who are of Lebanese descent, and found a refresher of the old family recipes from a community cookbook (not unlike this one) printed in Greenville, SC in the 1940s. This is my own adaptation of a traditional Lebanese recipe. I prefer sauteeing the onions rather than frying them, as is usually done. The substitution of Nishiki Japanese brown rice instead of white rice adds an extra nuttiness (and fiber) to the finished recipe, and it can easily be made vegan by using veggie broth. Easy, hearty, and healthy!

1 tablespoon olive oil	4 cups water
1 onion, diced	2 bouillon cubes (chicken or veggie - enough to make the 4 cups water into broth)
1-2 cloves garlic, minced	
1 cup brown lentils, rinsed and sorted	
	Salt and pepper to taste
1 cup brown rice (I love Japanese brown rice)	Dash of cumin

Special Prep/Equipment: Stock pot

1. Heat olive oil in a stock pot and saute onions and garlic until soft. Add lentils, rice, and water. Bring to a boil.

2. Add bouillon cubes, cumin, salt, and pepper. Reduce heat to low, cover pot, and simmer for 45-50 min, until lentils and rice are done.

3. Using brown rice evens out the cooking time. If using white rice, let lentils cook for 20 minutes before adding rice. The Japanese brown rice adds a very nice nuttiness to this!

BAKED PARSNIP SWEET POTATO GRATIN

〜 Annaliesa Place

I play violin/viola. and I am the Director of Strings at the Dwight-Englewood School, a founding member of the East Coast Chamber Orchestra, and do freelance work including Broadway and movie soundtracks.

My cousin, Amber, introduced me to this recipe. She is a wizard at whipping up truly savory and decadent dishes that are vegan and gluten-free. This dish is so rich and the creaminess comes from cauliflower and nutritional yeast. You can check her out at *Instagram*.com/*chefamberla* for more fab recipes!

Special Prep/Equipment
9 x 9" casserole dish

1. Pre-heat oven to 400°.

2. In a pot, add the veggie broth, garlic, and cauliflower. Bring to a boil. Lower heat, cover, and simmer for 5 minutes. Remove from heat. Blend the hot cauliflower mixture with yeast, salt, pepper, olive oil, paprika, and almond milk until creamy.

3. In a large bowl, toss all of the veggies (including sage) with the cauliflower cream.

4. Lightly spray your casserole pan with coconut oil. Add the gratin.

5. To make the crumble: Combine all ingredients and mix with your hands to create a crumble. Top the gratin with the crumble. Bake in preheated oven 1 hour.

Serves 6

1½ cups veggie broth

2 garlic cloves

½ head large cauliflower, chopped (2 cups chopped)

1 tablespoon nutritional yeast

1 teaspoon salt

½ teaspoon black pepper

2 tablespoons olive oil

½ teaspoon paprika

1 cup almond milk

1 large sweet potato, sliced thin

1 large parsnip, peeled, sliced thin

1 onion, sliced thin

3 tablespoons sage, chopped

Crumble:
1 cup almond flour

2 tablespoons nutritional yeast

2 tablespoons olive oil

½ cup chopped almonds

4 leaves sage, diced

1 teaspoon sumac (optional)

¼ teaspoon mustard seed powder

Pinch of crushed red pepper

TOMATO TARTE
〜 Dave Phillips

I have the honor of playing the bass. For the past 9 years I worked in the pit of *The Book of Mormon* while continuing to compose and release original material.

This recipe comes from a chef friend in the South of France where I spent 5 years before arriving in New York.

Crust:
2½ cups flour

2 sticks salted butter (1 cup) chilled

⅓ - ½ cup vodka, chilled, or ice water

Tarte filling:
2 pounds tomatoes, sliced inch thick

1 pound mozzarella, sliced into rounds

¼ cup Dijon mustard

2 cups shredded cheese, I like Gruyere and Comté, but any cheese will do

1 teaspoon herbes de provence, or whatever herbs you like

2 tablespoons olive oil

Special Prep/Equipment

Tart pan or a sheet pan with edges. The tart would work on a flat cookie sheet, as well, you can roll up the edges.

1. Preheat oven 350°.

2. Make the crust: add the flour to a food processor. Cut cold butter in ½" slices and add to food processor. Pulse gently until butter and flour resemble rice (a meal of sorts). Slowly add chilled vodka (or ice water) and continue to pulse until dough begins to form big clumps.

3. Remove from food processor onto plastic wrap and form into a disk , 1 disc if you are making a large tart, or 2 small ones.

4. Wrap in plastic and refrigerate for 1 hour.

5. *Assemble the tarte:* Roll pastry disk out on a lightly floured surface.

6. Put rolled out dough into pan, using your fingers to distribute evenly, bring dough up to the height of the pan edges.

7. Spread layer of Dijon mustard with the back of a spoon into crust.

8. Add tomato slices, rounds of mozzarella, and grated cheese, distributing evenly.

9. Sprinkle herbs, and drizzle olive oil over all.

10. Bake in oven for 35 - 45 minutes or until crust and tart are light brown.

Serves about 6-8

SOUTH ASIAN FOOD NIGHT
NEPALESE POTATOES, DAHL, STIR-FRIED CABBAGE
⌒ Alisa Wyrick

I am a violinist/violist free-lance member of New York City Opera Orchestra.

This is a hand me down from my brother-in-law who learned to make these dishes from his roommate at Harvard. This is my interpretation of the recipes. It is a compilation of three different dishes to make a full menu!

Special Prep/Equipment
Spice grinder or small food processor

Nepalese Potatoes:

1. Boil potatoes whole until just knife tender, drain and let cool. Peel and quarter.

2. Toast sesame seeds in cast iron skillet, shaking pan until evenly dark and they start to pop.

3. Grind up sesame seeds with a small food processor or spice grinder. Place in large bowl with turmeric salt and cayenne. Mix in potatoes.

4. Cut 2 onions into thick rings. Cook in oil until wilted but crunchy. Pour hot onions over potatoes, add lemon juice and mix. Salt to taste.

Dahl:

1. Rinse yellow peas and just cover with water. Add salt, cayenne, and turmeric. Boil and reduce heat. Simmer for about 40 minutes or until tender, checking water level. Add salt to taste.

2. Add spinach. Cover the dahl pot.

3. *Make garnish:* Fry garlic in oil on low heat. Add all spices until fragrant; remove large spices (cinnamon, cardamom, cloves) and add chopped tomato. Pour over hot dahl.

Cabbage:

1. Chop cabbage in ½" pieces.

2. Heat oil and add mustard seeds. Quickly cover. When popping subsides, add cabbage, turmeric, and cayenne. Stir until wilted. Add salt, lower heat, cover.

3. Steam for about 10 minutes until cabbage is buttery. Toss in coconut and cilantro, if using.

> **Note**
> You can boil the potatoes ahead of time. Use the same pan you used to fry the onions. Less cleanup!

Potato dish (intense dish!):
2-3 pounds yellow waxy potatoes

½ cup of sesame seeds

1 tablespoon turmeric

2 teaspoon salt

2 teaspoon cayenne (or less, or use mild paprika)

1 tablespoons oil

2 onions

Juice of 1 lemon

Dahl:
1 pound yellow peas

1 teaspoon each: salt, cayenne, turmeric

6 ounces baby spinach (optional)

Cabbage:
1 small cabbage

2 teaspoons oil

2 teaspoons mustard seeds

½ teaspoon each: turmeric, cayenne

½ cup shredded unsweetened coconut

½ cup cilantro

Dahl garnish:
¼ cup oil

4 cloves of garlic, sliced

5 tablespoons cumin seeds

3 whole cloves, 2 cardamom seeds, cinnamon stick

3-4 whole dried red peppers

2 large tomatoes chopped

Serves 6 plus leftovers

TORTILLA DE PATATAS
(AS TAUGHT TO ME BY CLARA DE LA PEÑA)
David A. Berger

I've been a professional drummer living in NY since 1987 with a magical sidestep to New Orleans for several years in the 1990's. In the before times, I toured extensively, recorded sessions often, wrote, arranged and produced music and taught. Once music got shut down, I taught myself home recording and have been seriously pursuing electric guitar, because drums are heavy and I'm tired of sitting in the back!!!

Tortilla de Patatas, or Potato Omelette is an old Spanish recipe. It isn't known exactly where it originated, but I learned it from one of the two Spanish women who lived in my loft in Long Island City with me. They both made tortilla, however Clara's was always more subtle and flavorful...and so of course it was Clara who I eventually fell for. Years later, a good friend and musical colleague named Daniel Isengart, a gifted singer, performer and professional personal chef, wrote a memoire/cookbook stringing together life experiences and the art of cooking and eating called *The Art of Gay Cooking, A Culinary Memoire*. Daniel asked friends from his life to contribute recipes for a section of his book, from which I've excerpted the recipe that I learned from Clara, which can be found at the top of page 265 in the Egg Dishes category. I texted Daniel, and asked if it would be okay to excerpt my recipe from his book, and he replied back, "of course!"

Special Prep/Equipment
8" frying pan with sloped edges, and 2 large plates that will fit easily over the edges of the pan. A hand towel (slightly larger than the plates) for protection when you flip the mixture. A large strainer, 2 medium sized mixing bowls, whisk, spatula, and wooden spoon.

1 large Spanish onion
1 large Russet potato
About 2 cups of good quality extra virgin olive oil
Salt, freshly cracked black pepper
6-7 large eggs

1. Peel and coarsely chop the onion. Wash, peel and very finely slice the Russet potato.

2. Heat the frying pan (regular or non-stick) on a low-medium flame, add about two cups of olive oil (or enough to cover the vegetables). Scatter first the onion, then the potatoes into the oil, and cook everything until the potato starts to crumble and the onions are lightly caramelized.

3. Place a strainer over a mixing bowl and pour the entire content of the pan into it. Allow the oil to fully drain (10 minutes or so). Season the potato mixture with salt and cracked black pepper. Crack 6 or 7 large eggs into a mixing bowl and beat them lightly. Fold the seasoned, still warm potato/onion mixture into the beaten eggs.

4. Wipe out the pan, heat it over a medium flame and add a couple of tablespoons of the infused oil. Increase the flame to high and pour the egg potato mixture into the pan. Shake the pan as it cooks to prevent sticking. Once a crust has formed, cover the pan with a large plate and boldly flip the mixture onto it in one swooped motion. You don't want to flip too soon or it'll be too wet to hold together, but at the same time, you don't want to flip too late and risk the egg burning itself onto the pan, which will leave half of your crust behind when you flip.

5. Once flipped, jiggle the pan slightly to allow the tortilla to sit fully on the plate. Lift off the pan, wipe it out, replace it on the burner, flame on high, and add another 1-2 tablespoons of the oil. Now slide the half cooked tortilla back onto the pan and cook the second side, shaking the pan to prevent sticking. When done, invert it once again onto a large plate.

6. Serve warm or cold. My personal preference is to cook it just long enough so that the tortilla is still creamy inside. Store the excess oil in a jar, to be used for the next tortilla event.

> **Note:** When the tortilla has finished cooking, it's a good idea to cover the plate it's on to keep the tortilla warm and moist.

1 tortilla serves 2

SWEET POTATO & BROCCOLI RICE BOWL

 Amy Zoloto

I play bass clarinet in the New York Philharmonic.

This is from my favorite food blogger Deb Perelman's website *Smitten Kitchen*. Every single thing I have made from her blog is delicious! I have adapted the recipe slightly by increasing the amount of sweet potatoes and including Eden Shake. This recipe is easy and fast and my daughter requests it!

Special Prep/Equipment
Blender or food processor
Parchment paper

1. Turn on oven to 400 °.

2. Turn on rice cooker (easiest!) or prepare rice on stove top.

3. Peel sweet potatoes and slice into bite-sized pieces. Cut the bottoms off the broccoli and cut florets into small pieces.

4. Start by roasting well oiled sweet potatoes for 20 minutes. Line your baking sheet with parchment paper.

5. After 20 minutes, flip them, and add well oiled broccoli to the baking sheet. Roast for another 20 minutes. Flip around making sure the pieces are nice and browned.

6. *While you are roasting vegetables, make the dressing:* combine all ingredients from the

1 cup jasmine rice

3 sweet potatoes (I like to use the Korean "sweet" sweet potatoes from H Mart)

Large bunch broccoli

Olive oil (enough to pan roast vegetable)

Salt/pepper to taste

Furikake seasoning (I use *Eden Shake*)

Ingredients for dressing:
1 tablespoon fresh chopped ginger

1 clove chopped garlic

2 tablespoons white miso

2 tablespoons tahini

1 tablespoon honey

¼ cup rice vinegar

2 tablespoons sesame oil

2 tablespoons olive oil

dressing list together in a blender or food processor and blend well.

7. Layer your bowl with rice, vegetable and dressing on top.

8. Sprinkle with Eden Shake and enjoy!!

Serves about 4

*G*ustav Mahler, on a vegetarian diet: "The moral effect of this way of life, with its voluntary castigation of the body, is enormous. I expect nothing less than the regeneration of mankind. I advise you to eat suitable food (compost-grown, stone-ground, wholemeal bread) and you will soon see the fruit of your endeavors."

FAVA BEAN PUREE WITH VEGETABLES
~ Frank Donaruma

I am Principal Horn of the Queens Symphony, formerly Principal Horn of the Kansas City Philharmonic, New Jersey Symphony, American Ballet Theatre, Associate Principal Horn Baltimore Symphony, and 2nd Horn of the Metropolitan Opera.

I have celiac disease and decided to try to duplicate this southern Italian dish gluten free.

Special Prep/Equipment
Buy dried, skinned fava beans. Soak the dried fava beans overnight.

Serve this antipasto on a platter.

½ pound dried, skinned fava beans soaked overnight.

½ cup olive oil

1 teaspoon salt

More salt and pepper to taste

2 large heads of chicory

2 poblano peppers

2 green Italian peppers (sometimes called cubano)

1 red bell pepper

1 clove garlic

⅔ cup Kalamata olives

½ cup tomato sauce

Pinch oregano

1 large red onion, sliced and soaked in red wine vinegar

Italian bread

1. Drain soaked beans, place in a pot, cover with 2" of fresh water and bring to a boil. Turn down, simmer for 45 minutes. Add 1 teaspoon of salt. While they simmer, make sure to check that there is always enough water to not burn.

2. Cook until beans are soft enough to mash to the consistency of mashed potatoes. You can also mash them in a blender. Then, stir in ½ cup olive oil. Add any additional salt and pepper, to taste.

3. Chop chicory and put in boiling water for 4 minutes. Drain, squeeze out water. Dress greens with a little additional olive oil, salt, and pepper

4. Cut the different peppers into 1" strips. Saute peppers in a fry pan with the clove of garlic. Cover and cook on low, until soft.

5. Cook olives in a little olive oil on medium heat until hot. Add tomato sauce and a pinch of oregano.

6. Remove onion slices from the red wine vinegar.

7. Lay out each of these delicious components on your serving platter. The bean puree, the greens, the peppers, the olives, and the onion slices. Serve with your favorite Italian bread, toasted. Enjoy!

Makes 8 servings as an antipasto and 4 as a main course.

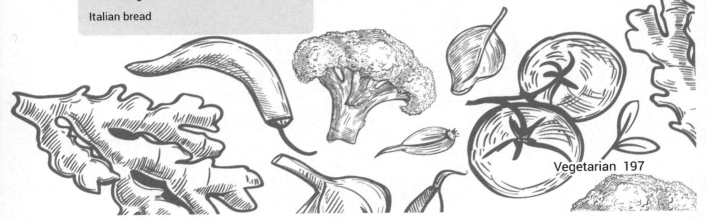

DESSERTS

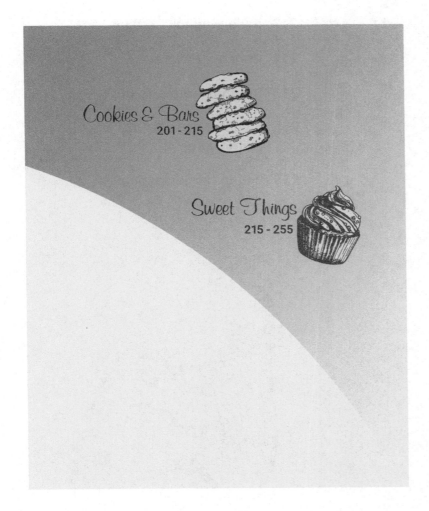

Cookies & Bars
201 - 215

Sweet Things
215 - 255

COOKIES & BARS

CHOCOLATE TOFFEE ALMOND COOKIES
～ Emily Bruskin Yarbrough

I am the violinist of the Claremont Trio. I sub with the Orpheus Chamber Orchestra, the Metropolitan Opera Orchestra, and the American Ballet Theatre Orchestra. I was the concertmaster of the Broadway shows *Frozen*, *Anastasia*, and *Cinderella*.

I'm very fussy about how I bake my cookies. A minute or two extra in the oven can produce a completely different type of cookie! I like mine firm enough to hold together but soft and chewy in the middle. The chunks of toffee candy in these cookies help to give them structure so they don't flatten completely while baking. This recipe is adapted from an Epicurious recipe called Chocolate Toffee Cookies.

Special Prep/Equipment

Leave the butter out at room temperature to soften.

Use an ungreased cookie sheet (not the kind with the layer of air inside).

The cookie dough will need to chill in the refrigerator for at least an hour before baking.

10 full size toffee candy bars (like Heath Bars or Skor Bars)	2 eggs
	4 teaspoons vanilla
1 cup roasted, salted almonds, finely chopped	2 cups flour
2 sticks unsalted butter, room temperature	1 cup unsweetened cocoa powder
	1 teaspoon baking soda
2¼ cups sugar	½ teaspoon salt

1. Use a knife to cut the candy bars into small chunks roughly the size of raisins. Use a food processor or blender to chop the almonds finely. Put these aside.

2. Preheat the oven to 350°.

3. Mix butter and sugar until they are soft and easy to stir. Add eggs and vanilla, and mix thoroughly. In a separate bowl, mix the flour, cocoa, baking soda, and salt. Gradually mix the dry ingredients into the wet ingredients. Add the candy and almonds, and mix well.

4. Refrigerate the dough for at least an hour.

5. Form the dough into perfectly round balls about the size of apricots. Place the balls on the ungreased cookie sheet. Try to avoid having too many candy chunks right on the bottom of the dough balls because they can make the cookies stick to the pan.

6. Bake for 8 minutes. Then let the cookies cool on the sheet for another 8 minutes. Remove the cookies from sheet and let them cool completely on a rack or plate.

Yields about 30 cookies

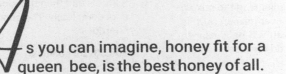

*A*s you can imagine, honey fit for a queen bee, is the best honey of all.

～ Igor Stravinsky

GIG COOKIES
∽ Gabriela Rengel

I'm a Venezuelan-American violinist and violist. I'm a member of the Albany Symphony, and I freelance with a number of groups in New York and New Jersey. Ever since the pandemic, I've continued my work with the symphony, and I'm currently homeschooling my six year-old twins. I most look forward to being in a room with my friends and colleagues making music and performing for a live audience again!

These cookies are the snack I reach for when I'm running out the door to an early morning "gig", or for a long day of work and commuting. I love that they're packed with good-for-you ingredients that help you feel satisfied. This recipe is an adaptation of the Jumbo Oatmeal Raisin cookies in Isa Chandra Moskowitz's *Isa Does It*. I was on the lookout for a cookie that would be nourishing and satisfying, something that I would feel good feeding to my then toddler twins.

This recipe is highly adaptable: you can replace the almond flour and the spelt flour with all-purpose flour, or whole wheat flour, or use mashed banana instead of applesauce, or raisins/nuts & seeds instead of chocolate chips. But this is by far our favorite version.

Special Prep/Equipment
Blender or food processor

3 cups rolled oats, divided	½ cup canola oil (or other high smoke point, neutral tasting oil)
½ cup all purpose flour	⅔ cup coconut sugar
¼ cup spelt flour (or use all purpose flour)	½ cup organic sugar
¼ cup fine ground almond flour	½ cup unsweetened applesauce
1 teaspoon baking soda	2 tablespoons ground flaxseeds
1 teaspoon ground cinnamon	2 teaspoons vanilla extract
1 teaspoon sea salt	1½ cups chocolate chips

1. Place 1½ cups of rolled oats in your blender or food processor and grind the oats into a fine powder (it should take 10-15 seconds) and reserve the rest of the oats.

2. Add to the blender the dry ingredients: all purpose flour, spelt flour, almond flour, baking soda, cinnamon, and sea salt, and run it for another 10-15 seconds. Just long enough to combine all the ingredients

3. In a large bowl combine, the oil, coconut sugar, sugar and applesauce, and mix vigorously with a whisk for about 2 minutes, until it resembles a thick caramel sauce.

4. Add the ground flax seeds to the bowl and mix thoroughly one more time.

5. Dump the dry blend from the blender or food processor unto the wet ingredients in the mixing bowl, and combine (without over mixing). At this point the texture of the dough will be similar to that of traditional cookies. Add the reserved oats and the chocolate chips.

6. If you can, let the cookie dough rest in the refrigerator for at least 20-30 minutes (sometimes we wait until the next day – most cookies benefit from a little time in the refrigerator!)

7. When ready to bake, preheat your oven to 350°, line a baking sheet (or two!) with parchment paper, and drop spoonfuls of the cookie dough on the baking sheets. Bake for about 14 minutes, until they start to look golden on the outside.

8. Let the cookies cool on the sheets for about 5 minutes and then transfer to a cooling rack to let cool completely. The cookies will firm up as they cool down.

Yields 30-32 cookies

PEANUT BUTTER FUDGE
✎ Kathleen Ditmer

I play the French horn in the Greenwich and Queens Symphony, as well as Broadway shows, movie and TV recordings, and have subbed just about everywhere.

Only my dad made it like this!

Special Prep/Equipment

Sauce pan

1 cup whole milk

1 pound brown sugar

1 small jar peanut butter, around 10-12 ounces. These days the jars of PB are bigger than when I was a kid.

1. Heat milk, and then stir in and dissolve brown sugar.

2. This is the hard part... stir occasionally and boil until a few drops of it in cold water form a hard ball. When this happens, stir in the PB as quickly as possible and fold onto a buttered plate.

3. If you don't get it onto the plate and cut it into bite sized portions fast enough, it will harden and break into little pieces when you try to cut it.

4. After cutting, let cool a few minutes then cover with plastic wrap so it doesn't crystalize. YUM!

Yields about 20 pieces

MOM'S CHOCOLATE CHIP COOKIES
✎ Steven W. Ryan

I am a pianist with The Dessoff Choirs, The Baldwin Festival Choir and a professor at Montclair State University

Mom always made the best cookies and everybody wanted a tub of them. She passed in 2020. Thankfully, I got her recipe for these in one of our last conversations.

Special Prep/Equipment
Cookie sheets, parchment paper (optional)

1. Preheat oven to 350°.

2. Prepare cookie sheet with parchment paper, or a light coat of the lard.

3. Mix the lard and sugars until they are whipped and creamy. Then add the other ingredients. When adding the flour, put in one cup at a time. Mix thoroughly, scraping off the edges of the bowl frequently. Lastly, add in the chocolate chips.

4. When placing on the cookie sheet, I use my ice cream scooper. Get a scoop of the dough into a ball about the size of a very small lemon. Six cookies per pan.

5. Bake for 13 minutes.

1 cup of good lard, or Crisco

¾ cup of brown sugar

¾ cup of white sugar

1 teaspoon soda

1 teaspoon water

2 eggs

½ teaspoon vanilla

1 teaspoon salt

2¼ cups flour

1 (12 ounce) package chocolate chips (I use 2 packages of the dark chocolate chips)

Yields 24 good-sized cookies

SNICKERDOODLES
Jeffrey Venho

I'm a trumpet player currently teaching as an Adjunct Trumpet Professor at Hofstra University. Also, I am a longstanding member of the music department at the Rudolf Steiner School.

This is an easy recipe with delectable results.

Special Prep/Equipment
Cookies sheets

1. Preheat oven 350°.
2. Cream butter. Add sugar and eggs. Beat until light and fluffy.
3. Sift first four dry ingredients together and stir in. Chill dough.
4. Roll into balls the size of walnuts and roll in the mixture of sugar and cinnamon. Place about 2" apart on ungreased cookie sheet.
5. Bake in preheated oven until lightly browned but still soft, 8-10 minutes. These cookies puff up at first and then flatten out with crinkled tops.

Yields about 3 dozen cookies

1 cup soft butter

1½ cups sugar

2 eggs

2 teaspoons cream of tartar

½ teaspoon salt

2¾ cups sifted flour

1 teaspoon baking soda

2 tablespoons sugar and 2 tablespoons cinnamon, mixed together

ANNIE'S THUMBPRINTS
Meg Zervoulis

I was serving as the Associate Music Director at *West Side Story* on Broadway before the shutdown and I am an educator..

My mom's first cousin Annie Brunton's lifelong hobby is baking cookies. She is hands down the family baker. Right before Christmas every year, all of the ladies in our family gather to bake her famous recipes – it's something we look forward to every year. I am significantly culinarily challenged so I am so happy to have cousin Annie in my life for some guidance. This is her recipe.

Special Prep/Equipment
Electric mixer

You will also need to chill your dough for 1 hour before baking.

1½ cups flour

¼ teaspoon salt

⅔ cup margarine or butter

⅓ cup sugar

2 egg yolks

1 teaspoon vanilla

2 slightly beaten egg whites

¾ cup finely chopped walnuts

⅓ cup strawberry preserves (or apricot)

1. Stir together flour and salt in a small bowl and set it aside.

2. In a separate bowl, beat margerine/butter for 30 seconds, then add the sugar and beat.

3. Add egg yolks and vanilla and beat.

4. Add the dry ingredients and beat until well combined.

5. Cover and chill for 1 hour.

6. Place your slightly beaten egg whites (you can whisk them) into a shallow dish and place your walnuts in a separate shallow dish (Hint: you will need to dip your dough balls into this dish!)

7. Preheat your oven to 350°.

8. Once chilled, shape your dough into 1" balls, roll them in egg whites, then in the walnuts. Place on an ungreased cookie sheet (Cousin Annie recommends using parchment paper on your cookie sheet).

9. Repeat Step 8 until the sheet is full. (FYI, the cookies will expand when you do the next step, so don't make them too large, and don't place them too close together on the sheet.)

10. Press down the centers of each dough ball with your thumb (hence the name of this recipe) and fill the centers with the preserves.

Yields approximately 36 cookies

GINGER OAT COOKIES
∾ Gili Sharett

I play bassoon and contrabassoon. I play on Broadway and in several area orchestras.

I love these cookies! You can modify with whatever nuts you like. It's a recipe from my beloved aunt, Nurit.

1 cup all-purpose flour/whole wheat flour

1 tablespoon baking powder

1 cup rolled oats

1 cup sesame seeds

1 cup of any ground nuts you have: almonds, sunflower seeds, or coconut flakes, etc

6 ounces melted butter

1 cup brown sugar

2 tablespoons honey

2 tablespoons water

Spices, to taste: 1 tablespoon ginger (I add a chai spice), 1 tablespoon cinnamon, 1 tablespoon nutmeg

Special Prep/Equipment

9 x 13" baking pan, parchment paper

1. Preheat oven to 350°.

2. Mix all the dry ingredients in a bowl.

3. In a larger bowl, mix melted butter, brown sugar, honey, water, and spices.

4. Mix the dry ingredients into the butter mixture.

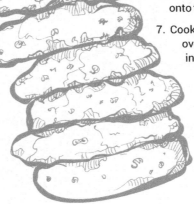

5. Line a baking pan with parchment paper.

6. Pour all the ingredients onto the parchment paper.

7. Cook for half an hour in the oven. Cut it immediately into squares and when it gets cooler, place them nicely in a tin/box.

Yields a couple of tins of cookies

GRANDMA V's ITALIAN MEATBALL COOKIES
Gina Cuffari

I am a bassoonist, singer, and teacher (also wife, mother and amateur baker!). I have had the good fortune to work with many NYC orchestras and chamber groups over the past two decades, and am currently Co-Principal Bassoonist with the Orpheus Chamber Orchestra, and a member of the Riverside Symphony, Sylvan Winds and Jupiter Symphony Chamber Players.

My grandmother, Caroline Valvano, would always make loads of these cookies during the holidays, freeze them, then pull them out throughout the year. Whenever I eat these cookies, I am transported back to my grandmother's kitchen in Canandaigua, NY. My father has now taken over the tradition of making too many of these delicious treats for the holidays!

Cookies:
1 cup vegetable shortening

1½ cups sugar

3 eggs

1 cup milk

1 teaspoon vanilla extract

5 cups flour

5 teaspoon baking powder

1 tablespoon cinnamon

1 tablespoon cloves

1 tablespoon nutmeg

¾ cup unsweetened cocoa powder

1 cup walnuts, chopped

1 cup chocolate chips

1 cup raisins

Glaze:
4 cups powdered sugar

½ cup milk

Mint extract (optional)

Special Prep/Equipment
Cookie sheets, parchment paper

1. Preheat oven to 365°.

2. Cream shortening and sugar, then add eggs, milk, and vanilla. In a separate bowl, combine flour, baking powder, cinnamon, cloves, nutmeg, and cocoa powder. Mix dry ingredients into the wet ingredients. Stir in walnuts, chocolate chips, and raisins (it's ok to use your hands!).

3. Prepare cookie sheets with parchment paper or cooking spray. Roll dough into balls (teaspoon-sized portions work well).

4. Bake in a preheated 365° oven for 10-12 minutes. Let cool completely.

5. For glaze, combine powdered sugar, milk, and mint extract (optional). Add more milk if thinner consistency is desired. Pour small amount of glaze over each cookie.

Yields about 4 dozen cookies

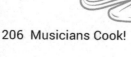

MAUD BALLARD'S COOKIES
Frederick Alden Terry

I am a music copyist/librarian who also plays cello, bass, and electric bass.

This spicy cookie recipe is from my great-great grandmother. It's delicious.

Special Prep/Equipment
Cookie sheets, butter must be at room temperature

1. Preheat oven to 350°.
2. Combine flour, spices, and salt in a bowl, and set aside.
3. Put soda in warm water and dissolve.
4. In large mixing bowl, cream butter and eggs. Add brown sugar. Add soda mixture. Gradually beat in dry ingredients. Stir in nuts and raisins.
5. Drop by teaspoonful onto cookie sheet.
6. Bake for 17 minutes in preheated oven.

3 cups flour	¼ cup warm water
1 teaspoon cinnamon	1 cup butter, soft
1 teaspoon nutmeg	2 eggs
¼ teaspoon cloves	2 cups brown sugar
½ teaspoon mace	½ cup nuts
1 teaspoon salt	1 cup raisins
1 teaspoon baking soda	

Note
I use chopped walnuts or pecans, but you can use whatever nuts you like with spice. I also chop the raisins a little bit, to open up their flavor, but you can use whole raisins, and it works fine.

Yields around 6 dozen, unless you make them large.

VIRGINIA'S OATMEAL COOKIES
Mitch Kriegler

I am a clarinet player with New York Pops, City Opera, and the Bronx Arts Ensemble.

This was my mother-in-law's cookie recipe, a favorite in our family. It goes great with our eldest son's freshly-roasted coffee from Explorer's Beans (available on Amazon).

Special Prep/Equipment
Cookie sheets

1. Preheat oven to 350°.
2. Mix the all of the ingredients together.
3. Drop onto cookie sheets and bake in preheated oven 10-12 minutes. Eat and enjoy!

Yields approximately 2 dozen cookies

2 cups brown sugar
1 cup melted butter
2 eggs
1 teaspoon baking soda, dissolved in 1 cup of hot water
2 cups oats
2 cups flour
1 teaspoon cinnamon

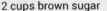

FORGOTTEN COOKIES
~ Melanie Baker

I play violin and have worked in theaters and concert halls in New York and beyond.

I don't remember where this recipe comes from, but it is a go-to recipe when I am short of time and/or have extra egg whites hanging around.

Special Prep/Equipment
Mixer or hand beater would be helpful

2 egg whites

¾ cup sugar (I usually use only ¼ cup)

1 cup chocolate chips

1. Preheat oven to 375°.
2. Beat egg whites until stiff. Gradually beat in sugar.
3. Fold in chips.
4. Drop by teaspoon onto greased cookie sheet.
5. Put the pan in the oven and immediately turn off the oven. When the oven is cool, the cookies are done.

Yields about 2½ dozen cookies

GRANDMA'S PFEFFERNÜSSE (PEPPERNUT) COOKIES
~ Maureen Hurd

I am a clarinetist, head of the woodwind program and member of the clarinet faculty at the Mason Gross School of the Arts, Rutgers University. I am a free-lance clarinetist, appearing in NYC and the area, nationally, and internationally as soloist, chamber musician and orchestral clarinetist.

Our grandmother, Jane Ummach Lipton, was a wonderful cook. I'm still amazed at what she did with relatively limited ingredients, and I wish I had apprenticed with her. We grew up enjoying foods that she made from our combined Irish and German traditions. Grandma Jane created the most magical Christmas celebrations in front of a big brick fireplace, around a cozy kitchen table, and at her elegant dining table in my tiny hometown in Iowa, and her cookies (especially the pfeffernüsse) were a central part of this experience. Her mother, Jenny Mitchell Ummach, had a peppernuts recipe, too, which we also have in the family collection. My foodie cousin, Jena Lipton, has recently updated Jane's recipe which also credits Gertrude Houlihan as collaborator. Gertrude and her husband, Dr. Houlihan, were previous homeowners of my grandparents' beautiful arts and crafts style house. Jane's (and Gertrude's) recipe had almost no instructions (probably since it was made so many times). Our grandma's recipe had molasses, no egg, and baking soda dissolved in water, and required standing overnight plus an hour to chill. Jena combined our family recipe with some ideas from this recipe, so the end result was also adapted from *www.bakerbettie.com/holiday-party-made-easy-part-1-pepper-nuts/*. Jena updated our grandma's recipe to add eggs and cinnamon, retaining the molasses, and eliminating the dissolving of baking soda and overnight time. Modifying the online recipe, Jena left out the anise extract and used white sugar instead of brown sugar, to match our grandmother's recipe. I further updated to use table salt and omit the white pepper, to match our grandma's recipe. Jena has given me permission to share this updated recipe.

Special Prep/Equipment
Cookie sheets with parchment paper
Butter sticks, at room temperature

2 sticks (1 cup) unsalted butter, room temperature	2 teaspoons baking soda
1½ cups sugar	¼ teaspoon cloves
2 large eggs	1½ teaspoons cinnamon
5 tablespoons molasses (more depending on your taste)	1 teaspoon ginger
	1 teaspoon ground cardamom
¼ teaspoon salt	3½ cups flour

1. Cream butter and sugar until well blended. Add eggs, molasses, salt, baking soda, cloves, cinnamon, ginger, and cardamom until mixed together. Add flour and blend until incorporated.

2. Press dough to 1" thick, cover in plastic wrap, and refrigerate for at least 30 minutes.

3. Preheat the oven to 350°. Cut dough into 16 pieces. Roll each piece into a thick rope about ½" thick. Cut rope into small bite size pieces and place on cookie sheets with parchment paper.

4. Bake for 6 minutes. Bake longer if you want them a little darker and crisper. Store in an airtight container.

Yields 12 cups of tiny cookies

TANTE FINI'S SUGAR COOKIES
∽ Heidi Stubner

I am a violinist on Broadway, and for orchestras both domestic and international, as well as an entrepreneur, Dean and mentor/educator/career coach in music, art, and special creative projects. I am a Medical Musician in the field of ICU and Hospice Care.

This recipe has been in my family for generations. Tasty and so easy to make!

Special Prep/Equipment
Mixing bowl, spatula/wooden spoon, measuring cup, wax paper, cutting board or smooth non-stick surface

Before baking, cookie dough needs time in the fridge.

1 stick butter, softened

1 raw egg yolk

1 hard-boiled egg yolk

1 cup sugar

2 cups flour

Note: For adults you can add 1 tablespoon rum and you can also add finely ground nuts, but they need to be almost pulverized, or the texture changes.

1. Combine all the ingredients together in one bowl, adding one at a time. Mix, preferably by hand, until blended together and smooth in consistency.

2. Once finished, take the dough and roll it into a long tube, like a cardboard paper towel roll. You can divide it into two rolls if you'd like. Take each roll and wrap it in wax paper and place it in the refrigerator for about 2 hours. Overnight is fine, too.

3. When ready to bake, preheat oven to 350°. Take rolls out of the refrigerator and on a cutting board cut quarter-inch thick slices and place on a baking sheet.

4. Bake in preheated oven until cookies are brown on the bottom and slightly brown on top. About 8-10 minutes.

Yields about 24 cookies, depending on how thick or thin you made your roll.

GRANDMA HAZEL'S REFRIGERATOR COOKIES

 Kathleen Thomson

I've been playing violin for decades in NYC with my amazing 802 colleagues.

Grandma Hazel was my biggest fan, and after any little performance she would smile her loving smile and tell me how sweet my violin sounded. These cookies remind me of her loving devotion to her grandchildren ... and I usually keep a roll or two of this cookie dough frozen in our freezer, ready to slice and bake at a moment's notice. My kids' friends all love these. I hope you will enjoy them, too!

Special Prep/Equipment
Cookie sheets

2 cups white sugar

1 cup shortening (Crisco)

½ cup molasses

2 eggs, beaten

1 teaspoon baking soda dissolved in 1 tablespoon hot water

1 teaspoon ginger

1 teaspoon cinnamon

¼ teaspoon salt

4½ cups flour

1. Preheat oven to 350°.

2. Cream the sugar and shortening, in an electric mixer if you have one. Add molasses, ooh and ah as the colors mix together. Add liquids, mix. Add the dry ingredients slowly, and don't worry if the dough gets pretty thick.

3. On a lightly floured surface, roll the dough into logs, wrap in wax paper and chill. How long to chill, you ask? If baking today, then refrigerate for at least 1 hour, or more. But this recipe is awesome; you can also freeze the dough. Just be sure to wrap it tightly before freezing.

4. Either way, slice the dough, place on a cookie sheet, and bake in a preheated oven. How long? Grandma Hazel used to say to just watch them, take them out when they are done. Usually I bake for 8 - 10 minutes, but if you like crispy cookies you might bake them a little longer.

Yields 3 - 4 dozen cookies

GRAMA DOROTHY'S ALMOND ROCA

 Erin Gustafson

I am an oboe and English horn freelancer. I play in orchestras and subbed on several Broadway shows. Most recently I have been Acting Second Oboe with the New York City Ballet.

Every Christmas, my Grama Dorothy would make batch after batch of this simple, yet delicious treat. She would give it out to everyone she knew, from friends and family to the ice cream delivery guy. The recipe works best in its low-brow form. No need for expensive chocolate and flaky sea salt. The only modification I made is to use salted butter instead of sweet cream.

1 pound salted butter (can also use unsalted)

3 cups granulated sugar

½ pound whole blanched almonds

18 - 20 ounces Hershey's chocolate bars, broken in pieces

One can (about 14 ounces) walnuts, chopped

Special Prep/Equipment
Candy thermometer, 11 x 16" jelly roll pan, strong wooden spoon for stirring

1. In a tall-sided stockpot (to control splatter) melt the butter and sugar. Cook, stirring constantly, for 5 minutes.

2. Add almonds and cook until thermometer reaches 300°, again stirring constantly. Keep the mixture at 300° for a bit to make sure it reaches the "hard crack" stage.

3. Spread hot mixture in jelly roll pan and when it sets a bit (2 - 3 minutes) lay one half of the broken chocolate on top to melt. When melted, spread it around with an offset spatula or the back of a spoon and cover with half of the chopped walnuts.

4. Let stand until completely cold (I usually leave it overnight in the refrigerator).

5. The next day, or when cold, turn the brick out onto wax paper. Melt the other half of the chocolate in a double boiler. Spread the chocolate onto the "clean" side and sprinkle with the last of the walnuts. You may have extra walnuts that you can save for another recipe.

6. When cold again, break into pieces and enjoy!

> **Note**
> All I can say is stir like you've never stirred before! I also keep oven mitts on my hands to avoid burns and splatter. Also, it really helps to have everything ready to go before you start because once it's ready you don't have time to wait to chop nuts or unwrap chocolate.

This recipe makes a lot of candy.

EASY, NEVER-FAIL COCOA BROWNIES
Judy Kahn

I play flute and piccolo, in chamber music and the Goldman Memorial Band.

I have adapted this from Hershey's Cocoa. It never fails, and is NOT messy like those other recipes using melted chocolate. I've been using this recipe for over 50 years, to everyone's delight.

½ cup dry powdered, unsweetened cocoa	1 cup sugar
¾ cup flour	2 eggs
½ teaspoon baking powder	1 teaspoon vanilla
½ teaspoon salt	½ cup broken walnuts or raisins (my choice, always)
½ cup shortening or soft butter (butter is best)	

Special Prep/Equipment
8" square pan

1. Preheat oven to 350°. Grease an 8" square pan.

2. Sift the first 4 ingredients together with a whisk in a large bowl.

3. In another, medium bowl, cream the butter and sugar, then add eggs and vanilla and mix thoroughly.

4. Add these wet ingredients into large bowl with the cocoa (carefully so as to avoid dust cloud) and stir till well-mixed.

5. Add nuts or raisins, as desired and mix in well.

6. Spread the mixture in the greased pan and bake for 25 minutes, or until done (use toothpick trick).

7. Remove from oven, place on wire rack to cool, cut into desired size. Enjoy!

Yields 16 (2 inch) brownies. Serves 4 people if you eat ¼ of the pan each, or more reasonably 8!

ITALIAN PIGNOLI COOKIES
∽ Mary Lamont

I am a singer/songwriter, who has been called the "Queen of Long Island Country" by Newsday, and the first American country band to tour Mainland China. *www.MaryLamont.com*

I got this great recipe from my late mother-in-law, Mary Marchese. Not sure where she got it. I am blessed to have many recipes from this great lady.

Special Prep/Equipment
Cookie sheet(s) and parchment paper
Electric mixer is helpful

1 pound almond paste

1⅛ cups sugar

1 tablespoon honey

⅛ teaspoon cinnamon

¼ teaspoon lemon flavor (lemon extract)

½ teaspoon vanilla

4 egg whites

Powdered sugar

Pignoli nuts (pine nuts), 4 ounce package is just enough

1. Preheat oven to 300°. Soften the almond paste, by placing in microwave for 30 seconds (or more, depending on your microwave).

2. In large bowl, mix softened almond paste and sugar. Mix in honey, cinnamon, lemon extract, and vanilla. Add egg whites and beat (I use an electric mixer). Mixture will be sticky.

3. Line a cookie sheet with parchment paper. Spoon mixture out in rounds the size of a half dollar onto wax paper. Leave about an inch between rounds. Press some pignoli nuts onto each cookie. Generously sift some powdered sugar over the cookies.

4. Bake 300° for about 15 minutes. (Do not overcook – the edges should be a LIGHT brown.) Remove from oven and let cool for a few minutes before removing from parchment paper with a spatula.

5. Store covered.

Yields approximately 50 cookies

CHOCOLATE WAFERS
∽ Kathy Taylor

I am a clarinetist and bass clarinetist in New York and Connecticut.

These are a favorite with family and friends and the most requested recipe I have. They make perfect Christmas trees, hearts, stars...so delicious and not too sweet.

Special Prep/Equipment
Silpat pan liners work very well in this recipe

1½ cups sifted all-purpose flour

1¼ teaspoons double-acting baking powder

⅛ teaspoon salt

6 ounces unsalted butter, at room temperature

1¼ cup sugar

1 egg

½ teaspoon vanilla

¾ cup strained powdered, unsweetened Dutch process cocoa

Milk

1. Sift flour, baking powder, and salt. Set aside.

2. Cream butter and gradually add sugar. Beat for 1-2 minutes. Beat in egg and vanilla.

3. On low speed, beat in cocoa, scrape bowl and add flour mixture. Beat gently until smooth.

4. Wrap dough in plastic wrap, flatten lightly and refrigerate for at least one hour.

5. Preheat oven to 400° and adjust rack to top position in oven.

6. Flour a rolling pin and pastry cloth. Work with ⅓ of the dough at a time, and keep the rest chilled. Roll the dough to a scant ⅛" thickness. Cut into shapes with desired cookie cutter.

7. Place cookie shapes on the baking sheets and brush cookie tops with milk.

8. Bake on top rack in oven for a total of 8-10 minutes, reversing position of cookie sheets after 3-4 minutes for even baking. Watch carefully and do not let edges burn.

9. Cool on a rack. They will crisp as they cool.

> **Note**
> Don't use too much flour on pastry cloth or when rerolling scraps.

Yields about 36 cookies

STORMIN' NORMAN'S BLONDIES
∾ Norman Weiss

I am the Keyboard/Assistant Conductor at *The Phantom of the Opera.*

I often offered these at the Saturday matinee intermission. Musicians, actors, stage crew, wardrobe, hair, etc. were all welcome! So I cut them into 48 pieces.

1. Preheat oven to 350°.

2. Butter bottom and sides of the baking pan. Add parchment paper to bottom of pan and butter the paper.

3. In a large bowl, combine flour, baking powder, and salt. Whisk to combine.

4. In a large mixing bowl, cream the butter and brown sugar until light and fluffy. Beat in eggs, one at a time until well blended. Add vanilla and beat.

5. Stir in the flour mixture until blended.

6. Fold in dark and white chocolate chunks (or morsels).

7. Spread batter evenly in pan.

8. Bake for 24-28 minutes (rotating pan halfway through baking) until the top springs back when lightly tapped with fingers. Toothpick should come out relatively clean.

9. Cool completely in the pan on a wire rack. When cooled, cut into desired pieces.

Yields 12-48 blondies, depending on size

Special Prep/Equipment
9 x 13" baking pan, parchment paper
Stand mixer or hand mixer is helpful.

> 2 cups all purpose flour
>
> 1 teaspoon baking powder
>
> ¼ teaspoon salt
>
> 2 sticks unsalted, room temperature, softened butter
>
> 1¾ cups firmly packed light brown sugar
>
> 2 large eggs, room temperature
>
> 2 teaspoons pure vanilla extract
>
> 1 cup chopped bittersweet chocolate (or dark chocolate morsels)
>
> 1 cup chopped white chocolate (or morsels)

> *Note:* If wrapped tightly in plastic wrap after completely cooled, they will last in the fridge for several days, or in the freezer for much longer.

ENID'S CHOCOLATE CHIP COOKIES
(WITH OATMEAL)
Enid Blount Press

I am a freelance clarinetist who loves improvisation, chamber music, playing solo recitals and in orchestra, teaching, and learning new things in many areas of life.

Teaching in beautiful Oneonta, NY in the summers at a music festival for 10 years involved loads of musicians' parties. I made cookies often and developed this recipe there. It is my go-to cookie recipe always.

Special Prep/Equipment
Stand mixer is handy, but not necessary.

2 sticks butter (cold is fine, if using stand mixer; room temp if not)

1 cup firmly packed brown sugar

Skimpy ¼ cup granulated sugar

2½ teaspoons pure vanilla extract

2 large eggs

¾ cup whole wheat flour

1 cup all-purpose flour

¾ teaspoon baking soda

¾ teaspoon baking powder

½ teaspoon salt

3½ cups oats

2 cups high quality chocolate chips, semi-sweet

1. Preheat Oven to 375°.

2. In a stand mixer or large bowl, cream together the butter and sugars until smooth. Beat in the vanilla and eggs, one at a time.

3. Whisk the dry ingredients together (flours, baking powder, baking soda, and salt). Blend into the batter.

4. Add oats, stirring minimally, and chocolate chips. This is a thick dough that may require hand mixing at the end unless you have a powerful mixer.

5. Drop by heaping tablespoons onto ungreased cookie sheet, silicone mat, or parchment paper. Bake until slightly golden on top, or to your liking, around 10-12 minutes.

6. Lay cookies on a rack to cool.

> **Note**
> To make Enid's Decadent Chocolate Chocolate Chip Cookies, add ½ cup extra granulated sugar, 1 extra egg, and ⅓ cup high quality cocoa, sifted in with the flours.

Yields approximately 50 cookies, enough for a party or a couple of families.

VEGAN HAMENTASHEN

∿ Jessie Reagan Mann

I'm a freelance cellist who performs in a variety of genres including Rock, Pop, Broadway, World, Liturgical, and music for Dance. Also a member of the Indian/Jewish Om Shalom Trio, my left hand technique book, *60 Seconds to Excellence* is published by Ovation Press. *www.cellochic.com*

Hamentashen are delicious triangle cookies that tie into the festive holiday of Purim where you dress up and make lots of noise. This has become a family tradition. It's a lot of fun to make with kids or friends!

Special Prep/Equipment
Cookie sheets, electric mixer or beat by hand
This cookie dough needs to chill overnight.

4 cups flour (pastry is best, unbleached all-purpose is fine, can also make them using gluten free flour)

4¾ teaspoon baking powder

¼ teaspoon salt

1 cup margarine at room temperature (I use Earth Balance)

1¾ cups granulated sugar

½ cup water

2 teaspoon vanilla extract

Filling: Pie filling is fine, I prefer fruit preserves/jam (apricot, raspberry, poppy seed, etc. get creative!)

1. In a large bowl, with a mixer set on medium, or by hand, beat all ingredients (except the filling). Add a small amount of additional water if necessary to smooth. (I add close to ½ cup more water, depending on the flour.)

2. CHILL OVERNIGHT.

3. Take dough out of fridge while preparing the next steps.

4. Preheat oven to 375°. Lightly grease 2-3 cookie sheets. Clear table or counter surface.

5. Flour your counter or table and roll a handful of dough to ¼" thickness. Cut out (roughly) 3" circles with the top of an upside down glass. (pint glass/wide ball jar) Smaller circles just make smaller hamentashen. You could also use circle cookie cutters. Make sure the dough will not stick to the surface, if it does, flour it and roll again.

6. Place about ¼ -½ teaspoon of desired filling into the center of each circle and fold into triangular shape. Roll up the bottom to make a flat edge, then the sides and pinch the corners. Warning: space them out in the pan — they expand quite a bit!

7. Bake for 10-20 minutes or until slightly browned. Remove from cookie sheets and cool on wire racks. Baking time may vary depending on your oven.

8. Enjoy warm or cool and store in an airtight container.

Yields 15-20 (depending on their size)

SWEET THINGS

"ROBERTA'S SWEET ENOUGH" CHOCOLATE-ORANGE ICE CREAM

Roberta Piket

I am a jazz pianist, organist, occasional vocalist, arranger and composer living in the New York area. *RobertaJazz.com.* When I lived in Brooklyn there was an ice cream parlor named Pete's on Atlantic Avenue that sold chocolate orange ice cream. It was sad when they went out of business, so when I started making my own ice cream, chocolate orange was one of the first flavors I tried.

For this recipe I use an inexpensive Cuisinart ice cream maker. You can get them online for about $25. It doesn't require any ice and the machine does the churning.

I adapted this recipe from the basic chocolate ice cream recipe that comes with my Cuisinart machine. In addition to the orange flavorings that I've added, I have reduced the amount of sugar and increased the amount of chocolate. One good thing about ice cream recipes is that you can get an idea of the flavor before the point of no return, so feel free to adjust it to taste before you chill it in the refrigerator.

Special Prep/Equipment

Ice cream maker

Plan ahead! The freezer bowl needs to be in the freezer for at least 24 hours before churning.

1 cup high quality cocoa powder	2 cups cream
⅓ cup granulated sugar	½ tablespoon real vanilla extract
¼ cup packed dark brown sugar	3 tablespoons orange juice
Dash of salt	1 teaspoon real orange extract
1 cup whole milk	

1. In a medium bowl, combine the cocoa, sugars, salt, and mix well.

2. Mix in the milk using either a hand mixer on low or a whisk. Make sure the dry ingredients are dissolved.

3. Stir in the cream. Whisk well until completely blended and smooth.

4. Stir in the vanilla, orange juice and orange extract. Use a spatula to stir in anything coating the sides of the bowl so it's all well blended.

5. Refrigerate for at least an hour. You can leave the mixture in the refrigerator overnight if you prefer.

6. Turn on your ice cream maker and pour the mixture into the pre-frozen freezer bowl. Let is churn until it becomes thickened and airy, about 15-20 minutes. The ice cream will have a soft, creamy texture and be much "bigger" when done.

7. Move the ice cream to an airtight container and place it in the freezer for at least 2 hours. Thaw slightly before serving for best flavor.

Yields about 5 cups of ice cream

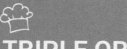

TRIPLE ORANGE CAKE

〜 Reva Youngstein

I am a flutist in various freelance orchestras in and around NYC, and I teach flute at the Brearley School in Manhattan.

This is an absolutely delicious, moist upside-down cake that looks really pretty. The flavors are perfectly balanced. If you give someone this cake as a gift, they'll know you appreciate and love them. I have given this cake to many musician friends at holiday time, and everyone enjoys it so much! I found the recipe in a magazine, and have renamed it, and changed it quite a bit, to increase the orange flavor, and shorten the prep time. It might look hard to make, but it's not...and so completely worth the effort!

Special Prep/Equipment

9 x 9" square baking pan

⅔ cup light brown sugar

¼ cup melted butter

2 tablespoons water

2-4 oranges of three different varieties, like naval, clementines, tangelos, etc

1 cup flour

1 teaspoon baking powder

¼ teaspoon salt

¼ teaspoon ground cardamom

2 eggs

¾ cup sugar

¼ cup milk

¼ cup orange juice

Zest of one large orange

2 tablespoons butter, cut into bits

½ teaspoon orange extract

½ teaspoon vanilla extract

⅓-½ cup orange liqueur, like Cointreau or Triple Sec, optional, but recommended

1. Preheat your oven to 350°.

2. In a small bowl, combine brown sugar, melted butter, and water. Mix well, and spread evenly, over your baking pan. Peel, and thinly slice, crosswise, all of your oranges. Place slices in a pretty, overlapping design, covering all the brown sugar/butter in pan bottom. Set aside.

4. In a large measuring cup, stir together your flour, baking powder, salt, and cardamom.

5. In a large mixing bowl, using an electric mixer, beat the eggs on high speed for about 3-4 minutes. Then, reduce the speed to medium, and gradually add the ¾ cup sugar, beating an additional 3 minutes until light and fluffy.

6. In a small pan, heat milk, orange juice and zest and the chopped 2 tablespoons butter. Heat just until butter melts, then pour into batter and stir. Lastly, quickly stir in your two extracts (but NOT the liqueur, save it for later!)

7. Place in hot oven and bake for 35-40 minutes, until toothpick inserted in center comes out clean.

8. Cool on a wire rack for 15 minutes. Run a knife around the edges to loosen sides, and invert onto your serving plate. If there's any brown sugar remaining in pan, carefully spread over the fruit.

9. For the finishing touch, poke cake in numerous places with your toothpick, and then brush or sprinkle your orange liqueur over the whole cake top.

10. Enjoy while all your guests savor each bite, and shower you with praise and "hhmms".

Serves 8-9

POACHED PEARS WITH HONEY RICOTTA

∿ Sarah Elizabeth Haines

I am a string doubler (violin/viola) and a singer/songwriter. Most recently, I was on the road with the *Hamilton* tour, and I put out an album of my own music last year.

I have always loved poached pears, because they feel like a special occasion dessert while still being pretty easy to make (as long as you have the time to let them sit!) I really love this recipe because it's versatile and you can adjust it easily based on what you have around and what you like; to that point, this recipe is one that I modified to my own taste from the Flavor Bender's "Red Wine Poached Pears" recipe. Instead of an apple in the poaching liquid, you can use berries or even pomegranate seeds, and you can adjust the warming spices if you don't have or like, say, star anise. It makes the whole house smell amazing while the pears are poaching, which is especially comforting on a cold winter evening. You can use mascarpone instead of ricotta, but for some reason I sort of like the grainier texture of the ricotta with the pears.

3-5 Bosc pears (avoid Bartletts—they'll fall apart!)	6 whole cloves	1 teaspoon vanilla extract
500-750 ml red wine	1 whole star anise pod	1 cup ricotta cheese
1 small apple, cut into large chunks	Approximately 1" fresh ginger	2 tablespoons honey
1-2 cinnamon sticks	3¾" strips orange peel	Ground cinnamon, ground ginger, pinch of nutmeg, to taste
	¼ cup apple cider	

Special Prep/Equipment

The pears will sit several hours in the saucepan before serving.

1. Peel your pears whole, leaving the stem intact. Slice off the bottom of the pears so they sit upright in a saucepan with just enough room to be covered with the lid of the pan. Try to select a saucepan where the pears will fit snugly together (I used a 2 quart saucepan for 5 pears), or you will need more wine to cover the pears.

2. With the pears in the saucepan, pour the wine in until the pears are covered all the way to just below the stem. Add the apple, cinnamon stick, cloves, star anise, fresh ginger, orange peel, apple cider and vanilla extract and bring to a simmer.

3. Once simmering, cover and continue to simmer for 30-45 minutes. This will vary depending on how large your pears are — you are looking for the pears to be soft when tested with a fork without being mushy.

4. When the pears are soft, remove from heat and let them soak in the poaching liquid for at least 4 hours. These can be made a day ahead, as they keep well in the fridge.

5. To make the ricotta complement, put 1 cup of ricotta in a small mixing bowl and with a hand mixer whip in the honey, nutmeg, cinnamon, and ground ginger to taste — I would do slightly more cinnamon than ginger, and be careful not to overdo the nutmeg — a little goes a long way!

6. Before serving, remove the pears from the poaching liquid and strain the liquid into a small saucepan. Bring the poaching liquid back to a simmer and reduce until it reaches a syrupy consistency (it should get to around ¼ of the amount of liquid you started with, or even less). Place one whole pear on each plate, and serve with a dollop of the ricotta and a drizzle of syrup.

Serves 3-5 (1 pear per serving)

CRANBERRY WALNUT UPSIDE DOWN CAKE
Adrienne Ostrander

I am a timpanist/percussionist and I freelance in the tri-state area. I perform with symphony orchestras and musical theater productions. I also work for the New Jersey Youth Symphony.

This is a great Thanksgiving dessert but can be eaten anytime! My sister Stephanie served this on Thanksgiving and I have adapted it, making it my own!

Special Prep/Equipment
Cast iron frying pan
(approximately 10-11" diameter)

For the topping:
½ stick of unsalted butter

¾ cup packed light or dark brown sugar

¾ cup chopped walnuts

1¾ cups cranberries

For the cake:
1½ cups flour

1 teaspoon baking soda

1½ teaspoons baking powder

½ teaspoon salt

1 stick unsalted butter, at room temperature

¾ cup granulated sugar

2 eggs

½ teaspoon vanilla extract

¾ cup buttermilk, well shaken

1. Preheat the oven to 350°.

2. *Make the topping:* melt the butter in the skillet over moderate heat. Add in the brown sugar and stir until the sugar is dissolved. Sprinkle in the walnuts and cranberries and remove from heat.

3. *Make the cake:* in a bowl, whisk together the flour, baking soda, baking powder, and salt. In a separate bowl, combine the butter and sugar, and beat until light and fluffy. Add the eggs and vanilla to the butter and sugar.

4. Alternately add the dry ingredients and the buttermilk to egg mixture, stirring until just combined. Don't over mix.

5. Heat the topping in the skillet at moderately high heat until it starts to bubble. Gently spoon the cake batter over the topping and transfer to the oven.

6. Bake 25-30 minutes in preheated oven.

7. Cool in the skillet for 15 minutes, then invert the skillet, turning the cake out onto a serving plate.

Serves 8

NANA'S CHOCOLATE M&M CAKE
Rebecca Young

I am Associate Principal Violist, New York Philharmonic.

This is the recipe my mother used for our birthday cakes since I can remember. My own kids usually insisted I decorate it the way she did - vanilla frosting inside, chocolate outside and M&M's all over. I've made this recipe for wedding cakes, with a thin layer of a simple raspberry sauce on each layer, under the buttercream. To die for! My other favorite way to make this is simply in a bundt pan, with a little powdered sugar sifted over top. Easy and DEEEELICIOUS! You're welcome!!

Special Prep/Equipment
Two 8" or 9" pans (or 1 bundt pan)

1. Preheat oven to 350 °.

2. Grease and flour the pans (or bundt pan).

3. In a large bowl, mix first 6 ingredients until combined. I use a handheld mixer.

4. Mix in chocolate chips.

5. Transfer to prepared pans. Bake for 50 minutes.

6. Allow to cool for at least 10 minutes before removing from pans.

7. Cool completely.

8. Decorate and serve.

> *Notes:*
> I've taken to baking at 325° for a little longer. No matter which temperature you choose, <u>always</u> start checking for doneness about ten minutes before the recipe calls for. In a pinch, use canned frosting.

¼ cup vegetable oil	½ pint sour cream
½ cup water	1 box Duncan Hines Devil's Food Cake Mix, or similar
2 eggs	
1 package instant chocolate pudding	12 ounces semi-sweet chocolate chips

Optional Raspberry Sauce:
Heat the contents of a big jar of seedless raspberry jam with 2 or 3 tablespoons of Chambord for a few minutes over low heat, whisking constantly. Allow to cool. You'll want to put a ring of buttercream, a "dam," around the edge of each layer of the cake so that the sauce doesn't pour over the edge. Omg! So good! Using this sauce elevates the cake enough so that you'll want to use a good buttercream from scratch, not the canned kind!

Serves 12-20

I know of no more admirable occupation than eating, that is really eating. Appetite is for the stomach what love is for the heart. The stomach is the conductor, who rules the grand orchestra of our passions, and rouses it to action. The bassoon or the piccolo, grumbling its discontent or shrilling its longing, personify the empty stomach for me. The stomach, replete, on the other hand, is the triangle of enjoyment or the kettledrum of joy. As for love, I regard her as the prima donna par excellence, the goddess who sings cavatinas to the brain, intoxicates the ear, and delights the heart. Eating, loving, singing and digesting are, in truth, the four acts of the comic opera known as life, and they pass like the bubbles of a bottle of champagne. Whoever lets them break without having enjoyed them is a complete fool.

～ Gioachino Rossini

BEST CHOCOLATE MOUSSE
～ Katherine Hannauer

I've been a freelance violinist for decades. I've played everything from Beethoven to Broadway. These days I'm working toward my next act: becoming an occupational therapist.

This is my mom's recipe; she served it at dinner parties when I was growing up. It's delicious, and if you serve it in beautiful glass dishes it looks so fancy that you'd never guess it's ridiculously easy to make.

Special Prep/Equipment
Pretty glass bowl, or 6-8 martini glasses

1 (12 ounce) package Nestle (or similar) chocolate morsels	5 egg whites
	½ cup sugar
2 egg yolks	
Pinch of salt	*Optional:*
1 cup whole milk	1 tablespoon of rum, brandy, or bourbon

1. Put the chocolate morsels in a blender along with egg yolks and a pinch of salt (add the optional booze if you're using it).

2. In a saucepan, heat milk to just below boiling, then pour it over the chocolate. Blend until smooth.

3. In a large bowl, beat the egg whites until stiff, then beat the sugar into the egg whites (slowly).

4. Pour the chocolate mixture over the egg white mixture *gently, so as not to collapse the egg whites!* and fold it all together with a spatula.

5. Pour into your prettiest glass bowl (or 6-8 individual ones. I like to use martini glasses) and refrigerate until set, about 5 hours.

6. Serve as is, or top with whipped cream and/or fresh berries. I like to put a couple of fancy little cookies on the plate, too, sometimes.

Very important message from my mom:
Use real chocolate. If you use "chocolate flavored" morsels, apparently the mousse will not set properly! I usually use Nestle brand because they're readily available (and it's what Mom always used) but I made it with Ghirardelli one time and that worked great.

Serves 6-8

APPLE CRISP
～ Peter Sanders

I am Artistic Director of the Central Vermont Chamber Music Festival *(cvcmf.org)* and am a member of the cello section for the NYC Ballet Orchestra.

This is a recipe that I remember my mother making as a child, the addition of the Farina in the crisp might (or might not!) have been mine. It is delicious right out of the oven or can be microwaved after being refrigerated. Careful, you will eat it faster than you think!

Special Prep/Equipment
Pyrex loaf pan
Zester for the lemon

1 stick of unsalted butter cut into ½" pads

1 or 1¼ cups flour,

½ cup dark brown sugar

⅛ cup farina

Pinch of salt

Approximately 8-10 Macintosh apples, peeled and cut into small pieces

Juice and zest of 1 lemon

1. Preheat oven to 350°.

2. *For making the crisp:* mix by hand the butter, flour, brown sugar, farina, and salt in a metal mixing bowl. You want it to be chunky so that pieces of the crisp sit on top of the apples.

3. Put the mixture aside and prepare the apples, placing directly into the pyrex pan. When the pan is full to the top with apples, zest the entire lemon onto the apples, and then squeeze the juice onto them as well.

4. Then, carefully cover the apples with the crisp mixture and bake in a preheated oven for 50 - 60 minutes until the crisp is a golden brown and the apples have reduced.

5. Eat hot out of the oven! It is delicious by itself but you can be decadent and add a small bit of vanilla ice cream.

Serves 4-6 as a dinner dessert, but it depends on who is eating it!

BANANA BREAD
April Johnson

I am a violinist, performer and teacher.

This recipe was adapted from "Standing Ovations" a cookbook written in my Iowa hometown in 1979 by the board of the Tri-City (now named Quad-City) Symphony.

Special Prep/Equipment
2.2 quart Pyrex square pan, large mixing bowl, sifter or wire mesh strainer

½ cup canola oil

¾ cup white sugar

2 eggs, beaten

3 very ripe bananas

2 cups all-purpose flour

1 teaspoon baking soda

½ teaspoon salt

¼ cup walnuts

¾ cup chocolate chips

1. Preheat oven to 350°.

2. With oil or cooking spray lightly coat a square 2.2 quart baking dish then sprinkle with flour. Gently tap sides to evenly spread flour, and then discard excess flour.

3. In a large mixing bowl cream oil and sugar, add eggs and mash in the bananas until well blended.

4. Sift flour, baking soda, and salt, and stir into the banana mixture, only until moistened. Stir in nuts and chocolate, just to mix.

5. Bake for 38 - 42 minutes. To check for doneness insert a toothpick in the center. If it comes out clean the bread is done.

Yields 12-16 pieces

CARROT PUMPKIN LOAF CAKE
∾ Shelby Yamin

I am a violinist on historical and modern violin. I am also a teacher.

I haven't managed to mess this one up, so it must be a pretty good recipe!

Special Prep/Equipment
8 x 11" baking dish

1. Preheat oven to 350°. Grease your baking dish.

2. Sift together the flour, baking soda, baking powder, cinnamon, and salt.

3. In a separate bowl, mix together vegetable oil, sugar and egg. Add to flour mixture.

2 cups flour

2 teaspoons baking soda

2 teaspoons baking powder

2 teaspoons cinnamon

1 teaspoon salt (omit salt for low sodium version)

⅔ cups vegetable oil

1½ cups sugar (just 1 cup works, too!)

1 egg (substitute 2 egg whites for low fat version)

2 cups grated carrots

1 (15 ounce) can pumpkin puree

1 cup raisins

12 ounces cream cheese

⅔ cups powdered sugar

1½ teaspoons vanilla

4. Add grated carrots, pumpkin puree, and raisins. Mix until combined.

5. Bake in prepared pan 45 - 60 minutes, until toothpick comes out clean.

6. *Make icing:* Mix cream cheese, powdered sugar and vanilla in food processor or by hand. Set aside.

7. Once cake has cooled, spread icing on top.

Serves about 10

CRANBERRY CRISP
∾ Avery Yurman

I am a winds doubler (with a specialization in double reeds and saxophone) vocalist, keys player, composer, orchestrator, and actress. In addition to performing in all genres and contexts, I also love being a public school and private studio music educator.

This recipe is one that my parents and grandparents developed, and it became a family holiday tradition. Though it can be enjoyed year-round, we made it our tradition to bake it together on Thanksgiving while watching the Macy's Day Parade on TV. Oftentimes, we would make it again for the winter holidays. Our family hopes that you can make this recipe and enjoy some sweetness and coziness — especially during this very trying time. We send our love to you all, and our warmest wintry wishes to the whole world for a better, healthier, and brighter 2021.

Special Prep/Equipment
Medium/large baking dish - covered (cover or foil)

2 bags cranberries, washed and drained

1 scant cup white sugar

1 cup rolled oats

About 1 cup oat bran

½ cup brown sugar

6-8 tablespoons butter, melted (use enough butter to moisten the topping)

You can substitute out the melted butter with vegan balance (such as Earth Balance) or vegetable oil (½ cup)

1. Preheat the oven to 350°

2. Wash and drain the cranberries, and place them into the baking dish. Mix in the white sugar.

3. In a separate mixing bowl, prepare the topping: mix together the rolled oats, oat bran, brown sugar, and melted butter.

4. Place the topping on top of the cranberries in the baking dish.

5. Bake, covered, in preheated oven, for 35 minutes.

6. If you prefer the top to be more browned, uncover and bake for an additional 5 minutes.

7. Let cool, and then enjoy!

8. You might even enjoy it with ice cream. Can be served hot or cold (as yummy leftovers!). It also makes a great yogurt topping.

Serves about 10

ALMOND TORTE (a.k.a. SHAKE DOWN PIE)
Andrew Adelson

I play English horn and oboe in the New Jersey Symphony Orchestra and I'm an Adjunct Professor at Rutgers University.

This recipe is from Susan, who got it from Sherrie (who got it from Elizabeth's mother) who brought it to Eliza's valentines-making gathering on February 7, 1999, in Tenants Harbor, Maine.

Special Prep/Equipment
Straight sided 8" pan or a pie plate

1 stick butter, softened	1 teaspoon vanilla extract
1 cup brown sugar	2 teaspoon almond extract
1 cup sifted flour	
Pinch of salt	Slivered almonds, for the top
1 egg, beaten	

1. Preheat oven to 350°. Grease a straight sided 8" pan, or pie plate.

2. Mush all but the last three ingredients together into a cookie dough.

3. Add the vanilla and almond extracts and mix well.

4. Press the dough (wet fingers work best) into your prepared baking pan or dish. Press on slivered almonds.

5. Bake for 20 minutes at 350°. Take out of oven and bang on counter twice (to minimize rising).

6. Put back in the oven and bake 10 minutes more. Remove from oven.

7. Let cool before cutting into wedges.

> **Note**
> The finished torte ages well, and freezes well.

Serves 3 - 6 depending on how much of a sweet tooth you have!

GRANDMA'S PIEROGI WITH CHERRIES
∿ Dr. Irena Portenko

I am a concert pianist, teacher with 30 years of experience, and founder and director of the international festival *Music in the Alps*.

This is a family recipe, although I realize there are also another thousand families who can claim it as their inheritance. Pierogi with any stuffing usually raises brows, causes commotion, and stirs emotions. However, these tender, sweet, yummy creations covered with a bit of sour cream are irresistible. It takes much longer to make, than to devour it. Usually a few hours to a few minutes. Those who know what it is anticipate it eagerly; for those, who try it for the first time – it is a great discovery and eternal craving with no point of return.

Special Prep/Equipment
Board
Wooden rolling pin
A glass to cut circles out

2 cups of flour

2 yolks

1 cup of warm water

Pinch of salt

Marinated cherries

Sugar, to taste

Sour cream or yogurt

1. Combine flour, yolks, water and salt in a bowl. Knead on your board for a good 30 - 45 minutes. Throw the dough against the counter for about 50 times (the more the better) for a fluffier result. Cover with a bowl and rest for a few hours.

2. Using a wooden rolling pin, make a thin layer of dough. Turn a glass upside down and cut circles out of the dough. Fill each circle with cherries to fit, a bit of sugar, and flour. Close up each one by bringing edges together and pressing them one against the other. Continue until the dough and cherries are gone.

3. Boil water in a pot with a bit of salt. Carefully put one portion of pierogi at a time in a boiling water, cook for 7-8 minutes.

4. Enjoy with sour cream or yogurt.

Serves 3-4

ROLAND'S BIRTHDAY CAKE
∿ Karen Bogardus

When the pandemic hit I was the flutist on the *Les Miz* National Tour. I am principal flutist with the Binghamton Philharmonic, Berkshire Festival Opera and Martina Arroyo Opera Orchestra. Currently during the pandemic I teach 6 to 8 hours per week on Zoom, otherwise am unemployed. Before the pandemic, I was extremely busy teaching, and performing and traveling weekends to play out of town concerts. Since the pandemic, I have played 2 outdoor concerts, 2 streamed concerts and recorded a track for a CD. I spend a lot of my abundant free time cooking now.

This is a Bogardus family recipe. Roland was my grandmother, Margaret Bogardus' brother. This is our family's birthday cake recipe. When I was younger my mother always made angel food cake for our birthdays, but by the time I was about 12 she started making this family birthday cake. I guess she thought our palettes were sophisticated enough at that age to eat the walnut cake. We loved it! She gave the recipe to a restaurant that we were regulars at and they added it to their menu for a while. Their version did not come out nearly as well because they finely ground the nuts. Both my mother and I were very disappointed when we tried it.

Special Prep/Equipment
9" springform pan – this recipe will not work in a regular cake pan, so be sure to use a springform pan.

1. Preheat oven 325°.
2. Lightly butter your springform pan.
3. Cream butter and sugar, add flour, baking powder, salt, and ground nuts. Fold in egg whites and add lemon juice or buttermilk.
4. Put batter in pan.
5. Bake for 1 hour. Let cool before removing and icing.

Serves 8-10 slices

Cake:
1 cup butter, room temperature

1½ cups sugar

2 cups sifted cake flour

2 teaspoons baking powder

½ teaspoon salt

1 pound ground walnuts or pecans – do not over grind, they should be quite chunky (my grandmother used pecans)

6 egg whites, stiffly beaten

2 tablespoons lemon juice or buttermilk

Icing:
¾ cup confectioners sugar mixed with enough lemon juice (1 tablespoon or slightly more) to make it liquid enough to drizzle over the cake top.

JEWISH APPLE CAKE
 Suzy Perelman

I'm a Broadway violinist!

It's called "Jewish" because instead of milk, orange juice is used so that observant Jews can eat the cake immediately following a meat meal, thereby adhering to the laws of kashrut (keeping kosher).

Special Prep/Equipment
Bundt pan

1. Preheat oven to 350°. Grease the bundt pan.
2. Combine the sliced apples with the cinnamon and the sugar. Set aside.
3. In a large bowl, mix together the oil, sugar, and the eggs. Mix in the orange juice and vanilla.
4. In a separate bowl, combine your dry ingredients: flour, salt, and baking powder.

5. Mix together the wet and dry ingredients, and then stir in the apple mixture. Place all ingredients into a greased bundt pan.
6. Bake in hot oven for 75 minutes.

Serves 8-10

5 or 6 apples, peeled and sliced

1 teaspoon cinnamon

5 tablespoon sugar

1 cup oil

2 cups sugar

4 eggs

¼ cup orange juice

2½ teaspoons vanilla extract

3 cups flour

1 teaspoon salt

3 teaspoon baking powder

CRÊPES SUZETTE

Isaac ben Ayala

I am a pianist and conductor. I was music director for many musicals and I played mostly jazz piano and for religious services.

My father used to make this for me growing up. I have since gotten some of the techniques for making it from Chefs Julia Child and Jacques Pépin. I also ate it once again when I was on tour with Quincy Jones in Paris on July 4, 2000. Then, I had it again the next time I was in France, this time in Juan-Les-Pins playing with my jazz trio.

Special Prep/Equipment
Small non-stick frying pan, whisk

1. Make the crêpe batter. Gradually whisk all ingredients together until a very thin batter is created.

2. Pour a very thin layer of batter on half of a small nonstick frying pan and turn pan until a very thin disc pancake is created. Use a fork and fingers to flip over pancakes to cook on both sides. Set finished pancakes on a plate.

3. Make the Orange-Cognac Sauce. Using a thin grater, remove the zest from the outside of the orange. Cut oranges in half and squeeze the juice out of the center of the orange and retain the pulp (minus the seeds).

4. In a pan, melt the 2 tablespoons butter and whisk in sugar, zest, pulp, and juice from oranges. Let caramelize and reduce for several minutes.

5. Add crêpes pancakes to pan with Orange-Cognac Sauce, coating fully and folding twice in half until quarter sized crêpes are created.

Crêpes:
½ cup flour

1 cup milk

½ stick melted butter

1 egg

¼ teaspoon salt

2 teaspoons sugar

Orange-Cognac Sauce:
2 large oranges (zested, juiced and pits removed)

2 tablespoons butter

1½ tablespoons sugar

2 tablespoons Cognac

2 tablespoons Grand Marnier

BE VERY CAREFUL DURING THIS PART:

6. Make sure your face and anything flammable is far from the pan during this part of the recipe!

7. Continue to cook in pan for several minutes then add the Cognac and Grand Marnier. Turn the pan slightly to the side allowing the flames to set the alcohol on fire in the pan. If you have an electric stove simply use a long handle lighter to set the mixture ablaze. (Again, keep your face and all flammable things well away from pan when doing this!!!). After the alcohol is burned off, your Crêpes Suzette is ready to serve.

Serves 2-3

One of the greatest pieces of advice my father ever gave me: "If you're looking to really impress someone, particularly a girl, flambeéd crêpes suzette is a good way to go."

Hugh Jackman

SNEEZE CAKE
~ Kathleen Nester

I am a flutist in the New Jersey Symphony Orchestra, the Stamford Symphony Orchestra and am on the music faculty of NYU.

Melissa Clarke's *Sweet Comfort Crumb Cake* printed in the New York Times at the beginning of the pandemic has provided lots of distraction and comfort for me and my family. Clarke's recipe provided many variation options depending on what ingredients were available to the baker. I've adapted and revised, changing many of the ingredient quantities, and adding dried fruit, chocolate chips or nuts until I reached my own favorite version. This was recently modified once again when a family member accidentally sneezed on the cooling cake. I immediately put the cake into a 425° oven (where vegetables were roasting) which resulted in a crumbly crumb topping with a crispy crunch!

Special Prep/Equipment
A mortar and pestle, to freshly grind whole spices
9" circular cake pan and parchment paper

1. Preheat the oven to 350°.

2. Make the topping: combine flour, oats, brown sugar, salt, and spices. Add to melted butter and coat all crumbs. Set aside.

3. Line the bottom of cake pan with parchment paper and grease with a little butter.

4. Make the cake: cream butter, sugar, eggs, buttermilk, and vanilla.

5. Separately, combine flour, baking powder, baking soda, and salt.

6. Fold dry ingredients into wet ingredients, using as few strokes as possible.

7. Pour batter into cake pan. Scatter pineapple randomly over the top and then sprinkle the chopped pecans over the fruit. Sprinkle the crumb topping over the pecans.

8. Bake for 45 minutes in preheated oven.

9. Allow the cake to cool.

10. Have a family member sneeze on top of the cake.

11. Put the cake into a 425° oven for 5-7 minutes to make a crunchier top.

12. Serve warm.

Cut the cake into 8 even wedges and eat them all!

Cake:
½ cup unsalted butter, room temperature

½ cup granulated sugar

2 large eggs

⅔ cup buttermilk

2 teaspoons vanilla extract

1½ cups all-purpose flour

1 teaspoon baking powder

¼ teaspoon baking soda

½ teaspoon salt (I use kosher salt)

2 teaspoons lemon zest

1 cup of fresh pineapple pieces

¼ cup pecans, chopped

Topping:
¼ cup flour

¼ cup rolled oats

½ cup brown sugar

½ teaspoon salt

1½ - 2 total combined spices: cinnamon, ground cardamom seeds, and allspice – to taste

4 tablespoons melted butter

FRUIT TORTE
Bruce Adolphe

I am a composer, author, the Piano Puzzler on Performance Today, Director of Family Concerts and Resident Lecturer for the Chamber Music Society of Lincoln Center, and Artistic Director of Off the Hook Arts Festival.

This Fruit Torte recipe was created by Marija Stroke, my wife, inspired by her paternal grandmother Edith's recipes. Grandma Edith became a cook and pastry chef in order to help her family survive during their flight from the Nazis. She fled her home country of Yugoslavia through France and Spain, escaping Europe in 1943 via South Africa, Mozambique, and Palestine, bringing her skills and secret recipes to New York finally in the 1950s, where she worked for decades in private homes, cooking and baking for violinist Mischa Elman, among others.

Marija created the current recipe specifically to make a delicious gluten-free dessert that our daughter, Katja, who had just been diagnosed with celiac disease at age 9, could eat, particularly when we were visiting people who did not make gluten-free desserts. While this recipe need not be gluten-free, all-purpose gluten-free flour can be used in place of wheat flour; almond meal is the primary flour in this recipe.

Following a recipe is a performance that reflects the personality of the chef-artist. A concert pianist, Marija provides suggested timings rather than strict metronome markings, as well as practical guidelines that allow the performer of the recipe to use intuition and artistry appropriately to bring the cake to…fruition.

Special Prep/Equipment
10½" diameter springform cake pan

For crust:
18 tablespoons unsalted butter

1⅛ cup sugar

3 eggs

1.85 cup almond flour

1½ cup all-purpose flour
(wheat or gluten-free)

½ teaspoon ground cloves

1 teaspoon cinnamon

Pinch salt

Notes: I would suggest that if you are using gluten-free flour, Bob's Red Mill all-purpose baking flour is excellent.

For custard:
3 egg yolks, plus 1 whole egg

½ cup sugar

½ cup + 1 tablespoon flour
(wheat or gluten-free)

½ - 1 tablespoon milk or soymilk

1 teaspoon vanilla

Choose 1 fruit, or a combo:
9-12 ounces blueberries, washed, drained;
or 3-4 apples: washed, dried, cored, sliced thin;
or 8 plums, washed, pitted, sliced thin;
or 8 apricots, washed, pitted, sliced thin

Fruits: There are many fruits that will be delicious in this Torte. We love it with blueberries or apples or Italian oval plums or ripe apricots, or a combination of different fruits.

1. Preheat oven to 350° and generously grease your springform pan. You can additionally cut a circle of parchment for the bottom of the pan into which you can rub some vegetable oil so that the cake is easier to serve later.

2. Make the crust. Melt butter on very low flame and pour into Mixing Bowl #1. Add sugar and mix.

3. Beat eggs in little bowl with fork and add to Mixing Bowl #1. Mix.

4. In Mixing Bowl #2, mix dry ingredients: almond flour, all-purpose flour, cloves, cinnamon, and pinch of salt.

5. Combine wet and dry ingredients in mixing bowl #1, and mix all together.

6. Spread batter in springform pan evenly on the bottom and up an inch on the sides. (You can use a layer of plastic wrap on top of batter to help you spread the batter evenly without it all sticking to your fingers.)

7. Put in preheated oven for 10-15 minutes to partially bake while making custard.

8. Make the custard. Separate 3 eggs, putting only the yolks in the mixing bowl. Add the 1 whole egg to the 3 egg yolks and beat.

9. Add sugar, flour, milk (or soy milk), and vanilla being sure to mix in between each new addition.

Final Assembly:

10. Remove pan with partially baked crust from oven (it has baked for 10-15 minutes). If the sides have melted down, this is your chance to press the sides back up with a plastic spatula now that the crust is a little more solid.

11. Pour the custard mixture into crust and spread evenly with plastic spatula.

12. Arrange your prepared fruit on top of the custard. We start from the outside, placing the fruit (overlapping) in concentric circles. If you prefer the fruit raw or barely baked (if using berries or other fruits which taste good raw on a tart), you can delay adding the fruit until the cake is almost done or done.

13. Put back in oven until crust is golden brown, and custard is cooked, approximately 30 minutes.

14. Cool on rack for 10 minutes and serve. Or cool to room temperature and refrigerate. Torte is nice either warm, or at room temperature.

Yields 16-20 pieces

SOUTHERN PECAN PIE
 Gary Hamme

I'm a freelance oboist in the NYC metropolitan area.

This was a family recipe handed down from previous generations. True for most southern desserts, it is quite sweet!

Special Prep/Equipment
Pretty glass bowl, or 6-8 martini glasses

1. Preheat oven 375°.

2. Mix together the sugars and flour.

3. Beat in the eggs, milk, vanilla, and melted butter. Fold in the chopped pecans.

4. Pour into an 8" unbaked pie shell. Bake in preheated oven for 40-50 minutes.

1 cup brown sugar

½ cup white sugar

1 tablespoon flour

2 eggs

2 tablespoon milk

1 teaspoon vanilla

½ cup melted butter

1 cup chopped pecans

8" pie shell, unbaked

Serves 8

MARTHA'S KEY LIME PIE
William Moersch

I play marimba, timpani, percussion, and hammered dulcimer. I was a free-lance musician in NYC for 22 years and then Professor of Percussion at the University of Illinois at Urbana-Champaign for another 23 years (and counting).

Martha, my mother, was from a farm in deep south Georgia, yet I never heard her speak with a Southern accent. She maintained that a "real" Key lime pie should never include condensed milk!

Special Prep/Equipment
Double boiler, mixer or whisk

1. Beat egg yolks. Add ¼ cup sugar, lime juice, and salt.

2. Cook in double boiler until mixture coats a spoon, about 10 minutes.

3. While the mixture is cooking, dissolve gelatin in cold water. Remove mixture from heat and add dissolved gelatin and lime rind. Mix well.

4. Chill in ice box until mixture begins to thicken, about 15 minutes.

3 eggs, separated

½ cup sugar, divided

½ cup Key lime juice (about 6 Key limes or bottled)

¼ teaspoon salt

1 tablespoon gelatin (1 envelope)

½ cup cold water

1 teaspoon grated (or minced) lime rind (about 1 Key lime or ½ Persian lime)

1 10" graham cracker pie crust

5. While mixture is chilling, beat egg whites with remaining ¼ cup sugar until they stand in peaks. Fold beaten whites into chilled yolk mixture.

6. Pour into graham cracker crust. Chill in refrigerator for several hours.

Serves 6-8

BONVISSUTO FAMILY RICOTTA CHEESESCAKE
Susan Lorentsen

I have been a violinist at Radio City Music Hall for 32 years, and I've performed in 35+ Broadway shows, classical freelance orchestras, etc.

My husband, trombone player, Bruce Bonvissuto's mother made this and it was always his favorite, so I learned to make it early in our marriage! I love how much lighter this is than a NY style cheesecake. I added the zest to brighten up the flavor a bit!

3 pounds ricotta cheese (full fat)

9 eggs

1½ cups granulated sugar

3 tablespoons cornstarch

2 teaspoons vanilla

Zest of 1 lemon or orange

Combine next 3 ingredients for optional crust:
1½ cups graham cracker crumbs

5 tablespoons unsalted melted butter

¼ cup granulated sugar

Fresh berries or raspberry sauce for serving

Special Prep/Equipment
9" springform pan, electric mixer

1. Preheat oven to 325°

2. Make crust if desired & spread on bottom of springform pan.

3. Place all of the ricotta in a mixing bowl. Using an electric mixer, add eggs one at a time incorporating well after each addition.

4. Mix in sugar, cornstarch, vanilla, and lemon (or orange) zest, and pour into prepared pan.

5. Bake in preheated oven for 1½-2 hours — the cheesecake will not be totally firm, but should not be "jiggly" in the middle. It may crack as it cools and falls in the middle.

6. Serve with raspberry sauce or fresh berries, if desired.

> **Note**
> You can make a traditional American graham cracker crust or make it with no crust. Or you could use crushed biscotti or Amaretti cookies (yummy!!). I can't eat gluten so I usually make it without a crust, but it's helpful to grease the pan with butter and sprinkle with flour (or the crushed cookies) so the cake won't stick.

Serves 10-12

VEGAN COCONUT BERRY MOUSSE
(QUICK & HEALTHY)
Claudia Schaer

I am a violinist, recitalist, and teacher.

I made this once for a family get-together; this year, I finally visited my parents after a year away. My mother is not in great health, and is very picky about what she likes to eat. I made this mousse for Christmas Eve ... the rest of us had a cupful, and she had the rest of the bowl ... and I've been making it since! It's quick, easy, fresh, and very yummy! I think the lemons are the best part (and I remember when I was a kid I tried lemon sorbet in Europe and thought it was the best thing ever, long before it was available where I grew up!)

Special Prep/Equipment
Blender

1. Put everything in the blender. Blend until smooth, approx 2-3 minutes. Enjoy!

Serves 8-10 (or 4, plus my mom)

I use all organic ingredients:

2 (13½ ounce) cans of coconut milk

2 bananas

2 lemons, peeled, pits removed

2-3 cups of frozen raspberries (or strawberries, or blueberries – choose your favorite!)

1-2 tablespoons of honey, sweeten to taste

Note:
You can substitute maple syrup or agave nectar if you avoid honey for ethical or other reasons.

CHOCOLATE-PEANUT BUTTER CUPCAKES

⌒ Louise Owen

I'm a violinist who wears a variety of musical hats in NYC. I'm an Associate Musician in the Metropolitan Opera Orchestra, I'm concertmaster for Harry Connick Jr., and I've held chairs in several Broadway shows over the years, including *Anastasia*, *The King and I*, *South Pacific*, and *The Producers*.

These cupcakes are inspired by a swoon-worthy chocolate cake with peanut butter frosting from *Sky High: Irresistible Triple-Layer Cakes* by Alisa Huntsman and Peter Wynne. These intensely chocolate cupcakes are not overly sweet, and the combination of neutral oil and whole milk ensures that the cake doesn't dry out. A decadent peanut butter frosting puts these over the top.

These cupcakes were a particular favorite of the *Anastasia* orchestra, the last Broadway show I played. My delightful bandmates were always up for being festive at intermission, whether it was someone's birthday, a particular anniversary, or simply celebrating the reality that we were all there playing a beautiful show together. We had several bakers in our midst who regularly brought in treats, but I was always on birthday cupcake duty. These chocolate-peanut butter beauties were the most frequent request from my kitchen.

Special Prep/Equipment
2 standard-sized 12-cup muffin tins
Electric hand-mixer (for the frosting)

For the chocolate cupcakes:
1⅓ cup granulated sugar

1 cup all-purpose flour

⅔ cup unsweetened cocoa powder, preferably Dutch process

1 teaspoon kosher salt (use a little less if using regular table salt or fine sea salt)

1 teaspoon baking powder

1 teaspoon baking soda

1 large egg

1 large egg yolk

⅔ cup whole milk

1 tablespoon vanilla

4 tablespoons neutral-flavored oil (such as vegetable or canola)

½ cup boiling water

For the peanut butter frosting:
6 tablespoons (¾ stick) unsalted butter, at room temperature

6 ounces cream cheese, at room temperature

2-3 cups powdered sugar, sifted if lumpy

⅔ cup smooth peanut butter

A big pinch of kosher salt

For garnish (optional):
2 ounce bar of semisweet or bittersweet chocolate

1. Make the cupcakes: Preheat oven to 350°. Line two standard-sized 12-cup muffin tins with 8 paper liners each. (This recipe makes 16 cupcakes.)

2. In a large bowl, whisk together all of the dry ingredients till well-combined. In a separate, medium-sized bowl, whisk together the egg, egg yolk, milk, vanilla, and oil. Add this mixture to the dry ingredients, and stir to combine. Whisk in the boiling water. The batter will be very thin.

3. Spoon the batter evenly between the 16 prepared muffin cups, filling each only about halfway. This will prevent the batter from spilling over the sides or sinking.

4. Bake for 18-20 minutes. If your oven is small and your pans won't fit on the same rack, switch the position of the pans halfway through the baking time so the cupcakes bake evenly. Begin checking for doneness at 18 minutes; the cupcakes are done when a toothpick inserted into the center comes out clean.

5. Let the cupcakes cool in the pans for 10 minutes, then turn them out onto a wire rack to cool completely.

6. Make the frosting: Put the softened butter and cream cheese in a large mixing bowl, and beat with an electric mixer until light and fluffy. Gradually add the powdered sugar, 1 cup at a time, mixing thoroughly and scraping down the sides of the bowl with a spatula. (Note: I usually add just 2 cups of sugar, but some people like their frosting sweeter, so add the additional cup to suit your taste.) Continue to beat on medium speed till light and fluffy, another 3 to 4 minutes. Add the peanut butter and the salt, and beat until thoroughly blended.

7. When the cupcakes have cooled completely, frost each cupcake as desired. I use an ice cream scoop to portion out a generous amount of frosting on top of each cupcake, and then I use a butter knife to spread it evenly. If I have a bar of bittersweet chocolate handy, I often grate a bit of chocolate directly over the frosted cupcake using a Microplane zester, or I might use a vegetable peeler to make a few small chocolate shavings, just for a little visual interest. (But it's totally not necessary!)

8. The cupcakes taste best within a day or two. Store any leftovers covered in the refrigerator.

> **Note**
> I love Valrhona cocoa powder for its velvety deep chocolate flavor, but use the best cocoa powder you can. I always use Smuckers Natural Creamy Peanut Butter for the frosting, since I don't like the taste of commercial hydrogenated peanut butters. (But use whatever smooth PB you like best!)

Makes 16 generously frosted cupcakes. You may have a little frosting leftover, but I don't think you'll mind having extra once you taste this heavenly peanut butter goodness!

Haydn left Vienna in the late 1780's to go work in Hungary and did not like the food there. He writes to a noblewomen back in Vienna: "Here in Estoras no one asks me: Would you like some chocolate, with milk or without? Will you take some coffee, black, or with cream? What may I offer you, my dear Haydn? Would you like a vanilla or a pine-apple ice?"

OSGOOD PIE
~ Tish Edens

I am a cellist and part-time freelancer.

This pie is from my mother's side of the family. We always had this for dessert at Christmas dinner. It is chock full of pecans and raisins and is similar to a chess pie.

1. Preheat oven to 350°.
2. Mix well together all of the ingredients, except for the egg whites. Fold in beaten egg whites and pour into the unbaked pie shells.
3. Bake for about 45 minutes.
4. Cool completely before serving.

Yields 2 pies

2 cups brown sugar, tightly packed	1 cup of raisins
4 egg yolks	1 teaspoon of cinnamon
3 tablespoons cider vinegar	¼ teaspoon of cloves
Pinch of salt	¼ teaspoon of nutmeg
5 tablespoons of butter, melted	¼ teaspoon of allspice
2 cups of pecan halves	4 egg whites, beaten until stiff
	2 unbaked 9" pie shells

NOODLE KUGEL
~ Diane Lesser

I am a freelance oboist who plays Principal Oboe in the New York Pops, Oratorio Society, Musica Sacra, Voices of Ascension, and other groups.

This was my mother's classic kugel recipe, and lots of Local 802 members ate this (and many other delicious dishes) in her kitchen for decades!

1 pound extra-wide egg noodles	1 package (8 ounce) cream cheese	2 tablespoons sugar
1 stick (½ cup) unsalted butter, melted	1 cup milk	1 tablespoon cinnamon (or more if you prefer)
½ cup sugar	6 large eggs, lightly beaten	
½ teaspoon salt	1 (1 pound) container small curd cottage cheese (4% fat)	*Note:* From time to time, my mother added ½ cup raisins and/or crushed pineapple — her kugel was always better than mine!
1 (1 pound) container sour cream	*Topping:* ½ cup crushed cornflakes	

Special Prep/Equipment
You can use a Cuisinart or electric mixer to mix all
ingredients (besides the noodles) or whisk them all
by hand.

1. Preheat the oven to 350°. Butter a 9 x 13 x 2" (3-quart) baking dish.

2. Bring a large pot of water to a boil and cook the noodles according to the package directions until al dente. Drain and transfer the noodles to the prepared pan. Add the stick of melted butter to the noodles and mix well.

3. In an electric mixer, Cuisinart or by hand, beat together the sugar, salt, sour cream, cream cheese, and milk until smooth.

4. Add the eggs and beat until well mixed. Blend in the cottage cheese.

5. Pour mixture from all blended ingredients over the noodles and stir until incorporated.

6. In separate bowl, stir together the topping ingredients: cornflakes, sugar, and cinnamon. Sprinkle topping mixture evenly over the kugel.

7. Bake 1-1¼ hours or until lightly browned and slightly bubbly near the edges.

8. Cool, slice and eat warm or at room temperature.

Serves 8-10

CRANBERRY PIE/CAKE
∽ Orin O'Brien

My instrument is double bass. I am in the New York Philharmonic, and I was in the New York City Ballet Orchestra before that. I also teach at Manhattan School of Music and Mannes.

My mother loved cranberries and she gave me this recipe. I don't know if it was original with her, but I made it for her whenever she visited NY.

Special Prep/Equipment
9 x 13" baking dish. If you use a smaller, deeper pan or dish, it comes out more "gooey".

2 cups fresh cranberries

½ cup sugar

½ cup chopped walnuts or pecans

2 eggs

1 cup sugar

1 cup flour

½ cup butter and ½ cup vegetable oil, melted together. You can use canola or any light oil. (Olive oil is too heavy)

1. Preheat oven to 325°.

2. Grease (or Pam) baking dish. Spread cranberries on bottom of pan and sprinkle with the ½ cup sugar and the walnuts or pecans.

3. Beat eggs well and add the 1 cup of sugar gradually. Beat. Add flour, melted butter and oil, and beat well. Pour over berries.

4. Bake in preheated oven for 45-60 minutes.

Makes 4-6 small portions

Sweet Things 237

NAOMI'S HOMEMADE APPLESAUCE
∾ Naomi Youngstein

I am a violinist in the New Jersey Symphony Orchestra since 1987, and coach/leader in the New Jersey Symphony Orchestra Academy Youth Orchestra Program.

I grew up near two orchards, so there was always applesauce freshly made in my mom's kitchen during apple season. Now I like to go apple-picking, first with my kids, now with my nieces, and maybe someday with my grandchildren! This applesauce is delicious served warm! It's good for dessert, as well as an accompaniment to pork or latkes. It freezes well, too.

Special Prep/Equipment
A large pot is needed.

1. Peel, core, and seed apples. Be sure to cut out the tough seed membrane, as well.

2. Cut apples into 1-1 ½" chunks, and place in your large pot. Add juice and spices to apples and mix.

3. Place over medium-low heat and bring to a simmer. Cover pot and stir frequently so fruit does not stick to pot bottom.

4. Once apples get mushy, taste and adjust spices. I add no sugar, but if you prefer your applesauce sweeter, you can add honey or brown sugar, a tablespoon at a time.

5. Approximately 20-30 minutes of simmering and your apples will be ready to mash. I use a potato masher because I like chunky sauce, but an immersion blender could be used if you prefer a smooth sauce.

Makes at least 3 quarts of sauce

10-12 small McIntosh apples

6 large Rome apples

4-6 sweet eating apples, such as Gala or Honeycrisp

¾-1 cup orange, apple or cranberry juice (add more if it seems dry after cooking 10-15 minutes)

1 tablespoon cinnamon, or to taste

½-1 teaspoon nutmeg, cloves, allspice or a combination, to taste

LEMON CURD (a.k.a. LEMON CUSTARD)
Sarah Davol

I have had the good fortune to play oboe and English horn with 14 Broadway shows including long running productions like *Les Miserables* and *Mary Poppins* as well as the short runs of *Little Women, Bombay Dreams, Finian's Rainbow, Titanic* and others. Playing ten wind instruments for *Bernarda Alba,* the off-Broadway flamenco show at Lincoln Center was memorable, too.

This recipe was inspired by the abundant Meyer lemon tree in our friend's yard in the San Francisco Bay area. I ended up making this recipe several times and it reminds me not only of that glorious lemon tree but also of wonderful time spent with friends in the California sunshine.

Special Prep/Equipment
This recipe takes about 12 minutes of assembling and cooking. It will require a lot of whisking. You'll want time for the curd to cool and set in the fridge after cooking.

1 cup white sugar

6 lemons, medium to large sized (2 must be organic)

6 egg yolks

½ cup salted butter, cold (1 stick)

Nilla Wafers for dipping

Note: Set the 6 separated out egg whites in bowl in fridge. You can make meringues or an egg white omelette with them, but they have to be used up pronto, within a couple of days.

1. Measure the one cup of sugar into a bowl. Zest the two organic lemons (or if you don't have a zester, cut into really tiny bits) onto a plate or wax paper. Add zest to bowl with sugar and stir; a bullet or food processor helps to incorporate, but you can stir by hand.

2. Squeeze lemons into a strainer over a separate bowl: you will need ½ cup of fresh squeezed lemon juice. (If you are using Meyer lemons, make ⅔ cup of juice.) Check to be sure there are no seeds in the juice. Pour the ½ cup strained lemon juice into sugar and whisk.

3. Into a separate bowl, separate out 6 egg yolks from 6 egg whites (If you get a broken yolk, it's okay if there is a little bit of white with the yolks.) Add the 6 egg yolks to the bowl with sugar, lemon zest and lemon juice and whisk for about a full minute. Whisking is important to make sure the curd is silky.

4. Pour mixture into a pan on LOW, gentle heat and WHISK CONSTANTLY. You have to keep whisking – no going away to practice or make reeds.

5. Once you see the curd begin to thicken and it's bubbling a little, turn off the heat. The curd should be thick enough to coat and stick to a spatula or wooden spoon.

6. Cut up the cold butter into big chunks and add to the curd. Keep stirring until the butter is incorporated into the mixture.

7. Pour curd through a strainer into a bowl. Spoon strained curd into a jar or cover in bowl with plastic wrap directly on the curd's sturface, so a skin doesn't form. Put jar or bowl into the fridge to cool.

8. Once cooled, spoon curd into small bowls and put out Nilla Wafers on a plate for dipping. Also good as a spread on scones, cupcakes, and more!

9. Stores in fridge for about a week.

Serves 4

VIENNESE SACHERTORTE
~ Barli Nugent

As the flutist and founding member of the Naumburg Award-winning Aspen Wind Quintet, I toured the world for 20 years. And, about to note my 20th year at the Juilliard School, I am now serving as Assistant Dean, Director of Chamber Music, Executive Director of the Mentoring Program and member of the Graduate Studies faculty.

A family recipe, we all remember its origin! My Czech grandmother married my Russian grandfather when they met in Vienna, and they raised their family there. She was an excellent cook and her Sachertorte recipe is far tastier than anything sold in Vienna, either at the Sacher Hotel or Demels.

Special Prep/Equipment
Three 8" round cake pans

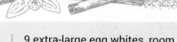

For the cake:
¾ cup unsalted butter, softened

1 cup confectioner's sugar

6 ounces Baker's sweet chocolate, melted*

9 extra-large egg yolks, room temperature

Scant ¼ teaspoon lemon rind, finely grated (avoid the pith)

⅜ teaspoon ground cloves

¾ teaspoon ground cinnamon

1¾ cup, scant toasted fine bread crumbs

9 extra-large egg whites, room temperature

Pinch of salt

For the frosting:
1 cup evaporated milk or heavy cream, depending on which taste you prefer

1¾ cup sugar, or a bit less

8 ounces unsweetened chocolate, NOT melted

½ cup plus 2 tablespoons unsalted butter, cold

1½ teaspoon vanilla

For the filling:
10-14 ounces top-quality apricot preserves**

1 quart of heavy whipping cream

*French Callebaut bittersweet chocolate is also wonderful, usually found at Fairway.

**I prefer St. Dalfour 100% fruit, with no added sugar, made in France – always available at Zabar's.

1. *Cake:* Preheat the oven to 325°. Butter and flour three 8" round cake pans; set aside.

2. In large mixing bowl, beat the ¾ cup butter and add confectioner's sugar. Add slightly cooled melted chocolate and blend well. Add egg yolks, one at a time, then add lemon rind, cloves, cinnamon, and bread crumbs.

3. In another very large and immaculate bowl, whip the egg whites with salt just until stiff BUT NOT DRY and fold into chocolate batter. Pour into the prepared cake pans and carefully smooth top of batter lightly so that each top is flat. Bake for 20 minutes. Do not overcook or cakes will become dry. Insert cake tester to check – they're perfectly done if tester comes out moist, but not with raw batter clinging to it. If you see raw batter, put the pans back for a few more minutes. Cakes will be thin and flat. Cool.

4. If you're not putting it together that day, wrap each layer tightly with plastic wrap and leave at room temperature, and put it together the next day. Layers can also be frozen, tightly wrapped until used, but fresh is best.

5. *Frosting:* Bring evaporated milk or cream and sugar carefully to a boil, reduce heat and simmer with bubbling for 7 minutes. You really need to keep an eye on this – it can burn or boil over pretty easily – so do not walk away! After 7 minutes of consistent simmering, remove from heat, add unsweetened chocolate and stir until completely melted. The mixture should begin to look thicker at this point. Then add cold butter and vanilla and stir until completely melted. Let sit at room temperature and stir occasionally until completely cool.

6. The icing will be quite thick by now, the consistency of sour cream. If it isn't, refrigerate for 15 minutes or so until it is. If it gets too stiff in the refrigerator, stir it vigorously until it softens up. This recipe generally makes too much frosting for the cake, but the leftover frosting is my kids' favorite hot fudge sauce over vanilla ice cream.

7. *Putting together:* Place one cake on a very flat platter. Spread with a decent layer of apricot preserves (not thick; not thin), almost all the way to the edge of the cake. Place the next cake on top; spread with more preserves. Place top layer over. If you have time, cover the cake with plastic wrap and refrigerate for an hour to set the preserves. Next, spread a very thin layer of the cooled frosting completely over the sides of the cake, sealing in the apricot preserves and covering the cake completely. Do the top last. There should be no drips of icing running down the side.

8. Put cake in the refrigerator (uncovered) for an hour, allowing this thin layer of frosting to harden. Then frost a second time, this time a thicker layer, leaving a smooth, glossy surface. Again, allow to harden for an hour in fridge. Then frost a third time for complete coverage. Using a cooling rack is a good idea so the excess can ooze off. Refrigerate overnight to "ripen." An hour or so before serving, remove from refrigerator, as it is ideal to serve this cake at room temperature.

9. *To serve:* The Austrian way, according to my Viennese mother, pianist Irene Schneidmann: whip the heavy cream until it's the consistency of sour cream (but not stiffer), then barely sweeten to taste with a spoonful or two or confectioner's sugar and a light splash of vanilla. Each slice should be covered with a ridiculous amount of this whipped cream, called "schlag" in German. You now have Viennese Sacher Torte mit Schlag. Yum!

Serves 16-20 (this is a very large torte)

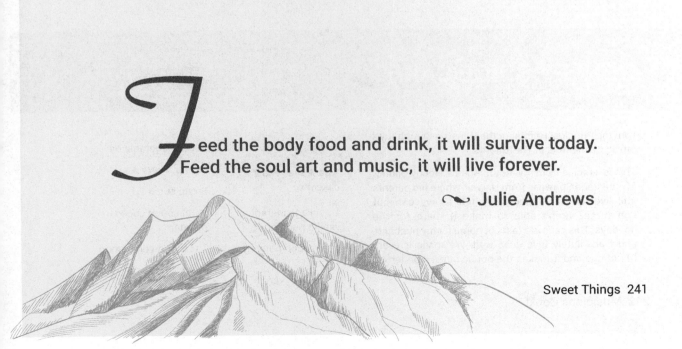

*F*eed the body food and drink, it will survive today. Feed the soul art and music, it will live forever.

∿ Julie Andrews

SOUR CREAM COFFEE CAKE
~ Keve Wilson

I am an oboist with the Broadway revival, *Company,* and teaching artist for the 92Y and Bridge Arts Ensemble. I am married to Kerry Farrell and the owner of Bugsy, the Portuguese Water Dog.

I grew up eating this lovely cake on Sundays baked by my southern Mom. It's perfect with a glass of milk or cup of coffee.

Special Prep/Equipment
9 or 10" tube (bundt) pan

1 cup (2 sticks) butter, softened	2 cups flour
1 ½ cup granulated sugar	¼ teaspoon salt
2 eggs	1 teaspoon baking powder
1 teaspoon vanilla	½ cup crumbled walnuts
1 cup sour cream	6 tablespoons brown sugar
	1 teaspoon cinnamon

1. Preheat oven to 350°.

2. Combine butter and sugar in a large bowl. Add eggs and beat all together. Add vanilla and sour cream. Mix well.

3. In a separate bowl, combine flour, salt and baking powder. Fold this into wet mixture.

4. In a small separate bowl, mix nuts, brown sugar, and cinnamon. Sprinkle half of this mixture in the bottom of tube pan. Add half of the cake mix, remainder of nut/cinnamon mix, and top with the rest of cake mix.

5. Bake in preheated oven for 50 minutes to 1 hour, or until a toothpick inserted in center comes out clean.

> *Note:* You can also make this without the nut/brown sugar/cinnamon mixture.

Serves 8 at least

CONLEY SPICE CAKE
~ Megan Conley

I am the Principal Harpist of the Houston Symphony. I am also a member of The Knights.

This is a recipe from my mother-in-law, Nancy Conley. My husband Shawn is from Hawaii, where his parents still live. We visit them as often as we can but sometimes aren't able to make it there for the holidays. This cake is a taste of home for my husband, and I absolutely love it as well. We make it every Christmas and it makes the house smell wonderful.

4 eggs, beaten	½ cup vegetable oil
1 package yellow cake mix	¾ cup sherry
1 package instant vanilla pudding	⅓ cup sugar
1 teaspoon nutmeg	½ teaspoon cocoa powder
	1 teaspoon cinnamon

Special Prep/Equipment

Bundt pan

1. Preheat oven to 350°.

2. Beat 4 eggs in large bowl.

3. Combine in another bowl (not with the eggs): the packages of yellow cake mix and instant vanilla pudding, and then the teaspoon nutmeg.

4. Beat these dry ingredients (cake mix, pudding, nutmeg) into the beaten eggs, alternately with vegetable oil, and sherry.

5. Combine in a separate, small bowl: sugar, cocoa powder, and cinnamon. Put aside.

6. Spoon the batter into the Bundt pan alternately with the sugar/cocoa powder mixture (cake batter first, then ½ of the sugar, then cake batter, other ½ of the sugar, rest of batter. Make sure to leave enough batter for top layer.) Swirl the sugar layer by pulling a knife through the batter.

7. Bake for 50 minutes in preheated oven. Test to see if it's done with a toothpick or knife. Toothpick should come out clean.

> **Note**
> You may need to change the vegetable oil quantity; check the cake mix box and adjust accordingly.

Serves 8

CARROT CAKE
∾ David Evans

I am the Associate Conductor/Keyboard at *Wicked* on Broadway for 16 years.

I got this recipe from my sister, and she can't remember where she got it, but we've been making it forever.

Special Prep/Equipment

Two 9" cake pans

1. Preheat oven to 350°. Grease two cake pans.

2. Mix dry cake ingredients.

3. Add wet cake ingredients and carrots, and mix.

4. Pour into prepared cake pans

5. Bake in preheated oven for about 30 minutes.

6. Let cool. Remove cake from pans.

7. Make the icing. In a stand mixer or by hand, blend together the butter and cream cheese. (Easiest if each is first sliced into sections.) Then mix in the sugar, vanilla, coconut and walnuts.

8. Frost between layers and then over the whole cake.

Serves 12

Cake:	
2 cups flour (1 cup white, 1 cup whole wheat)	1 ¼ cups oil
	4 eggs
2 cups brown sugar	3 cups grated carrots
2 teaspoons baking soda	
3 teaspoons baking powder	*Icing:*
	1 stick butter
1 teaspoon salt	1 8 ounce box cream cheese
1 teaspoon cinnamon	1 box confectioners sugar
½ teaspoon nutmeg	2 tablespoons vanilla
¼ teaspoon allspice	1 cup flaked coconut
¼ teaspoon ground cloves	1 cup chopped walnuts

BLACK BOTTOM CUPCAKE
~ Carolyn Douthat

I'm a NYC trumpet player, freelancer and current student at Manhattan School of Music (BM '22)!

This recipe can also make mini cupcakes — reduce the oven temperature to 325°, and bake for about 12-15 minutes. For the cake, a devil's food cake mix can also be used, with 1½ x the filling. These cupcakes go great with a chocolate ganache icing, but they're also plenty decadent all on their own!

Special Prep/Equipment
Electric hand mixer or stand mixer is preferred, but if you don't have one, you'll just have to do a bit more stirring!

Filling:
12 ounces cream cheese (or neufchâtel)

1 egg, beaten

1 tablespoon oil

⅔ cup sugar

⅛ teaspoon salt

9 ounces chocolate chips

Cake:
1½ cups flour

1 cup sugar

¼ cup cocoa

1 teaspoon baking soda

½ teaspoon salt

1 cup water

⅓ cup oil

1 tablespoon vinegar

1 teaspoon vanilla extract

1. Preheat oven to 350°.
2. Combine and beat filling ingredients, except chips; then, stir in chips. Put aside.
3. In a separate bowl combine cake ingredients, and beat.
4. Place paper or foil cupcake liners into cupcake tin.
5. Fill cupcake wrappers about ½ - ⅔ full with cake batter.
6. Spoon in filling to near full.
7. Bake 20 - 25 minutes in preheated oven.

> **Note**
> I've used this recipe both with and without paper cupcake cups, and it's worked great either way! Just be sure to grease the pan with a non-stick cooking or baking spray if you don't use the cups.

Yields 12-16 cupcakes (or about 48 mini cupcakes)

MOM'S PINEAPPLE CHEESECAKE

~ Deborah Assael-Migliore

I'm a freelance cellist in NY for the past 30 years. Most recently I was a member of the pit at *Frozen*. I've held the chairs at *The Little Mermaid, Newsies, War Paint, Bright Star, Into The Woods* and others. I'm also a member of the New York Pops and very active on the NYC freelance scene.

This recipe was handed down to me by my mother-in-law, Rose Migliore. It was a family favorite of my husband Mike Migliore (who was also a musician) while he was growing up and it continues to be the most requested dessert recipe from my kids, Lana and Mikey. Besides being delicious, my favorite thing about this recipe is that it is baked in a sheet pan. So, instead of a 5-inch high cheesecake, you are able to cut this cake into small bite size pieces.

Special Prep/Equipment
9 x 13" deep sheet pan is needed, as well as a mixer.

1. Grease your sheet pan. Melt the stick of butter.

2. Make your crust. Pour graham cracker crumbs into a bowl. Add 3 tablespoons sugar and mix. Add melted butter to bowl, and mix (a spatula is fine but I end up using my hands). The mixture will be crumbly, not solid like dough.

3. Pour crumb mixture into greased sheet pan and spread evenly, pressing it down into the pan. Refrigerate while you assemble the cheesecake filling.

4. Make your filling. Preheat oven to 325°.

5. Using a mixer (stand or hand held) beat eggs well. Add 1½ cups sugar and mix well until fully combined. Gradually add smaller pieces of cream cheese. Mix very well till smooth. Add 1 teaspoon vanilla.

6. Pour onto crust; it will probably come up to the top of the sheet pan.

7. Bake in preheated oven for 25 minutes or till set (I put a piece of aluminum foil under the pan in case any spills over) Remove and let cool.

8. When cool, top with drained crushed pineapple.

9. Now, preheat oven to 450°.

10. Add 3 tablespoons sugar to 1 pint sour cream and mix. Spread over crushed pineapple.

11. Bake cheesecake at 450° for 10 minutes. Remove from oven, let cool and cut into 2" squares.

Serves 6-8

For the crust:
2 cups graham cracker crumbs

3 tablespoons sugar

½ cup butter (one stick)

For the filling:
4 eggs

1½ cups sugar

3 (8 ounce) packs of cream cheese (you can substitute low fat cream cheese for 1 or 2 of the packs)

1 teaspoon vanilla

1 (20 ounce) can crushed pineapple, drained

1 pint sour cream

3 tablespoons sugar

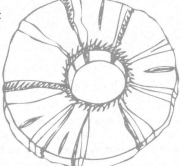

GRANDMA'S ORANGE JELLO SALAD
Keith Hermann

I was the first pianist of the original Broadway show *Cats,* and later went on to serve as its conductor. As a composer, I received a Tony Award nomination for creating the score to Broadway's *Romance/Romance.*

My son, AJ, who now works for the YES Network, began his sports journalism career at Boston University, where he oversaw a weekly radio program at which sports, and much more, was discussed with listeners. I was tuned in one week and was astonished to hear him disparage his grandmother's jello salad, which had been served faithfully for generations to enjoy on Thanksgiving. When I heard "yucky combo of fruit and who knows what" I had to call in. I straightened him out on air, and got an apology for grandma. As I am still paying for that college education, I continue to force a few fruity bites down him every Thanksgiving.

Special Prep/Equipment
9 x 13" casserole dish

1 large box of orange Jell-O

2 cans crushed pineapple

2 cans apricots

1 cup (or more) mini-marshmallows

3 tablespoons butter

3 tablespoons flour

¾ cup of reserved pineapple and apricot juice (drained from cans)

¼ cup sugar

½ tub (regular size) of Cool Whip

Shredded cheddar cheese, as desired

1. Prepare Jell-O per box instructions in large 9 x 13" casserole dish. (You can use the quick method.) Put into refrigerator until partially set.

2. Drain fruit and put into a colander, saving the juice. Cut the apricots and mix together with the pineapples.

3. Once Jell-O is partially set, mix the fruit into the Jell-O until all are combined. Cover top of Jell-O mixture with mini-marshmallows and return to fridge to set completely.

4. Over medium low heat, melt butter and add flour, to create a roux. Add combined ¾ cup fruit juices, sugar, and stir until very thick. Remove from heat to cool.

5. After thickened fruit juice mixture is cooled, combine with the Cool Whip and then spread over Jell-O mixture.

6. Top with oodles of shredded cheddar cheese and dig in!

Serves 8-10

GRANDMA GLADYS' WALNUT COFFEE CAKE
Carlo Pellettieri

I am a cellist who plays on Broadway and in several regional orchestras such as the Greenwich Symphony, Ridgefield Symphony and Northeastern Pennsylvania Philharmonic.

I unearthed this handwritten recipe from the bottom of a kitchen drawer. It was in my grandmother's handwriting and addressed to me. I remember I first made it when I was 11 years old and a student at the Cathedral School on the Upper West Side. The occasion was a cake baking contest at the annual school fair. The judges were Jerry Stiller and Anne Meara. I remember Jerry saying he enjoyed my entry very much. Sadly I didn't win, but I did get honorable mention.

Special Prep/Equipment

Tube pan, electric mixer is helpful

1. Preheat oven to 350°. Grease your tube pan.

2. In a mixing bowl combine butter, sugar, eggs, baking powder, salt and baking soda. Mix with an electric mixer until smooth.

3. Add the flour, sour cream, vanilla, and mix again.

4. In a small bowl combine the topping ingredients: sugar, cinnamon, and walnut pieces. Stir together with a spoon.

5. Pour half of the batter into a greased tube pan. Sprinkle half the topping onto the batter in the pan. Now add the rest of the batter on top of that. Sprinkle with the remaining topping.

6. Bake in preheated oven for 45 minutes.

Serves 4-6

1 stick of butter, softened

1 cup sugar

2 eggs

1 teaspoon baking powder

¼ teaspoon salt

1 teaspoon baking soda

2 cups flour

1 cup sour cream

1 teaspoon vanilla

Topping:

¼ cup sugar

1 teaspoon cinnamon

½ cup chopped walnuts

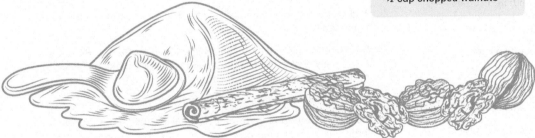

*M*usic is one of those things that is constantly going on in my head all the time. It's sort of like the evolution and creation of doing food, or my philosophy about wine. It's always beating in my head, so it keeps the spirit moving.

～ Emeril Lagasse

LUSCIOUS LEMON PUDDING

~ Suzanne Mueller

I'm a freelance cellist. I primarily perform as a member of CROSS ISLAND, but also appear with the McCarron Bros. jazz quartet and folk duo Hungrytown.

This is very easy to prepare and the interesting thing about this dessert is that it separates into 2 sections: the top ⅔ is cake consistency and the bottom is pudding. It's very refreshing and always very popular! Inspired by a recipe from the Food Network.

Special Prep/Equipment

8" (2 L) square or round glass baking dish (or 6 ramekins)

Large, shallow roasting pan

½ cup granulated sugar (reduced from 1 cup - I don't like things too sweet)

3 tablespoons all purpose flour

3 eggs - separated

¼ cup unsalted butter melted

1 tablespoon finely grated lemon zest*

½ cup fresh lemon juice* (You can also substitute orange for lemon, if you prefer.)

1½ cups 2% milk

1. Preheat oven to 350°.

2. Butter your baking dish, or ramekins.

3. In bowl, sift together sugar and flour; set aside.

4. Place egg whites in large bowl. Beat for 4 to 5 minutes or until stiff peaks form. Transfer whites to another bowl.

5. Add egg yolks to same bowl and beat on until yolks are thick and lightened in color.

6. Add melted butter, lemon zest, and juice; beat for 1 more minute. Alternately beat in flour/sugar mixture and milk, making 5 additions of flour and 4 of milk. Fold in egg whites.

7. Heat several cups of water until very hot.

8. Transfer lemon mixture to prepared baking dish(es). Place dish in large shallow roasting pan. Add hot water to half way up side of baking dish.

9. Bake in center of oven for 50 to 55 minutes. Cool for 5 minutes.

10. Top two-thirds will be cake consistency and bottom third will be pudding consistency.

Serves 6

GREAT GRANNY'S OLD-FASHIONED PEACH PIE FROM SWEDISH ROOTS

~ Rhonni Hallman

I am a violinist. I am a member of the Hudson Valley Philharmonic, a freelance studio musician and an orchestral and chamber music player active in Ballet, Opera and teaching.

This recipe has been handed down from several generations in the Elmquist family. It is so delicious with just a few ingredients. The big secret is you must use good peaches! A simple crust dough or thawed frozen is fine and quicker! The stars should be the peaches!

Special Prep/Equipment

9" pie plate
Pot with water for blanching peaches

1 pie crust for a 9" pie

6 large freestone peaches
(eat any that don't fit)

1 cup sugar

½ cup flour

¼ cup butter

½ cup cream

1. Heat oven to 450°.

2. Thaw 1 pie crust 40 minutes or make dough for 1 crust.

3. Put water into pot large enough to hold peaches. Bring to boil. Cut an "X" on bottom of each peach. Blanch in boiling water 40 seconds. Remove from water. Let cool until touchable. Pull skins off starting from the "X" on bottoms.

4. Halve and pit peaches.

5. Put crust into pie plate. Place peach halves in plate, cut side up.

6. Fill in spaces with any leftover peaches.

7. Combine sugar and flour. Sprinkle over all letting it fall into cracks.

8. Dot <u>generously</u> with butter. Use extra if necessary.

9. Pour cream into each pit hole.

10. Place pie in oven and let bake for 10 minutes.

11. Then, turn temperature down to 300° and bake 45 minutes longer.

12. Serve warm or room temperature.

> *Note:*
> This pie is great served warm
> with a good vanilla ice cream.

Yields 1 pie

PROFITEROLES
~ Diane Lesser

I am a freelance oboist who plays Principal Oboe in the New York Pops, Oratorio Society, Musica Sacra, Voices of Ascension, and other groups.

This is one of my family's favorite desserts, and you can use the pâte à choux recipe for just about every filling you like, sweet and savory! My mother made them as cream puffs for decades, and she filled them with a combination of vanilla custard mixed with whipped cream. I use vanilla ice cream as an alternative.

Special Prep/Equipment
Double boiler, electric mixer, piping bag with ½" tip

2 baking sheets and parchment paper

Pâte à choux:
1 stick unsalted butter

½ cup whole or 2% milk

½ cups water

2 teaspoons sugar

¼ teaspoon salt

1 cup flour

3 or 4 large eggs, beaten

Egg wash: 1 beaten egg plus 1 tablespoon milk or water

Filling:
Häagen-Dazs vanilla ice cream or a mixture of vanilla pudding and whipped cream

Chocolate Ganache Topping:
4 ounces heavy cream

4 ounces fine semi-sweet or bittersweet chocolate, chopped

Note:
I use Callebaut chocolate but use whatever you prefer.

1. Preheat oven to 400°. Line 2 baking sheets with parchment paper.

2. Combine butter, milk, water, sugar and salt in a saucepan and bring to a simmer. Reduce heat to low. Add all the flour and stir briskly with a wooden spoon until the dough becomes tight and pulls away from the side of the pan, approx. 2 minutes. Mash the dough ball against the pan to cook the flour. Remove from heat.

3. Place the dough in an electric mixer, and on low speed, slowly add 3 eggs one at a time, until the eggs are completely incorporated and the dough is smooth. The dough will be glossy and fall from the spoon in ribbons. If dough appears dull, not glossy, then beat in the 4th egg.

4. Fill a piping bag with the dough, using a ½" plain tip. Pipe the choux onto the baking sheets, making each about 2-3" in size, and leaving 1" between them. Gently brush the egg wash onto each choux.

5. Bake for 20 minutes, reduce heat to 350° and continue to bake until they are golden brown, approx. 10-15 minutes more. Allow to cool completely before filling. Slice each and add filling.

Filling: I fill them with Häagen-Dazs vanilla ice cream or a mixture of vanilla pudding and whipped cream.

Chocolate Ganache Topping: melt cream and chocolate together in the top of a double boiler and mix until smooth. You can add ½ teaspoon vanilla and 1 tablespoon butter, if you like.

Yields 6-8 portions

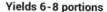

MOST DECADENT BANANA PUDDING
John Bronston

I am a pianist and musical theatre conductor and I also dabble in NYC piano bars as a singing pianist!

I tried to figure out how to improve all of the elements of banana pudding from the wafers to the flavor of the bananas and the texture of the actual pudding. This recipe makes a large amount so I often serve it during tech to the band (or double it and include the cast)!

Special Prep/Equipment

Mixer

Large disposable casserole pan (I use the deep foil disposable pans that are 20 X 13")

1 pound (4 sticks) butter (divided)	5 cups whole milk (divided)
½ cup solid vegetable shortening (I prefer Crisco in the stick form) plus extra for pan	1 teaspoon vanilla extract
	6-8 bananas, sliced
2 cups sugar	1 shot of bourbon or whiskey
2 cups brown sugar (divided)	2 containers Cool Whip (I prefer extra creamy)
5 eggs	1 package cream cheese, at room temperature
½ teaspoon salt plus a generous dash (divided)	3 small or 2 large boxes of instant vanilla pudding
½ teaspoon baking powder	
3 cups all-purpose flour, plus more for pan	2 cups heavy or whipping cream

1. Preheat oven to 350°. Grease and flour your casserole pan.

2. Your first step is making a cake base for the pudding. With a mixer, cream 2 sticks of butter and shortening together. Gradually add 2 cups of sugar, 1 cup of brown sugar, mixing in, a little at a time.

3. Add eggs, 1 at a time, beating after each addition. Add ½ teaspoon of salt and baking powder to the bowl and then add flour, alternating with 1 cup of milk, starting and ending with the flour. Stir in vanilla.

4. Pour into prepared casserole pan and bake for 1 -1 ½ hours, until a toothpick inserted in the center comes out clean. The cake will be deeply golden brown. Let cool completely (preferably overnight). If you want your pudding base to be crispy you can slice half of it into strips approximately ¾" wide and leave out to dry overnight or lightly toast in the oven before continuing. (You will only use half of the cake in the pudding. The other half of the cake is great with coffee all week long!)

5. Lay cake strips out on the bottom of a large casserole pan. I generally use the same size pan for the pudding as I did for the cake. Top with sliced bananas.

6. Melt at least 1 cup of brown sugar and 2 sticks of butter in a saucepan. Stir until this comes to a boil and is well combined. You may need to play with the amounts here - you want it to look like smooth caramel but should still retain a little grit from the brown sugar. Remove from heat and add a generous dash of salt and a shot of bourbon or whisky (you can sub vanilla here if you like) and stir until bubbling from bourbon stops. Pour over bananas and cake.

7. Mix together one container of cool whip and the package of cream cheese with an electric mixer. Add the boxes of vanilla pudding, and best until well combined. Add remaining 4 cups of cold milk and 2 cups of heavy cream and beat until combined and begins to look set and fluffy. Pour over bananas and cake. Chill, covered in plastic wrap to keep skin from forming. When set, top with more whipped cream or cool whip.

Serves 12-16

RASPBERRY OR BLACKBERRY DUMPLINGS
Clarissa Nolde

I am a flutist and band director at McKinley Community School and Woodrow Wilson School in New Brunswick, NJ.

This family recipe for raspberry dumplings came from Aunt Dot. Since I grow lots of blackberries in my yard in New Jersey, I like to make this with either fresh or frozen blackberries all year long. Lemon zest and lemon juice can be used for either berry, but I prefer orange zest and orange juice with the blackberry version.

Special Prep/Equipment
Large pot or pan with a heavy bottom

1. Place the berries, water, sugar, salt, cinnamon, zest and juice of lemon or orange in the large pan or pot.

2. Boil for 4-5 minutes.

3. While the berries are cooking, blend dry ingredients in a small bowl with a fork. Cream softened butter into dry ingredients until the mixture resembles coarse crumbs. Mix in milk until just blended. Do not beat.

4. Drop the dumpling mixture onto the boiling berries by the heaping tablespoon. You should have enough for about 6-7 dumplings. Cover and simmer on very low heat for 20 minutes. Do not lift cover while cooking.

5. Uncover and cool before serving with either whipped cream or vanilla ice cream.

Serves 6-7

For the berries:	For the dumplings:
2 cups berries (raspberries or blackberries, fresh or frozen)	1 cup flour
2 cups water	½ cup sugar
1 cup sugar	2 teaspoons baking powder
Pinch of kosher salt	
1 teaspoon cinnamon	Pinch of kosher salt
The juice and zest of either a large lemon or orange. (Lemon works best with raspberries and orange is best with blackberries)	3 tablespoons unsalted butter (softened)
	½ cup milk

STOLLEN
Alexis Gerlach

I'm a cellist from New York City. I've mostly been playing chamber music here and around the country for most of my life!

This is a stollen that my grandmother baked for my family every Christmastime when I was growing up. She'd mail the giant loaf to us in New York City, filling up any extra space in the package with pine boughs cut from the trees in my grandparents' yard. The cake gets even better as it ages, so if you can, make it at least a few days ahead, keeping it in the fridge until you're ready to eat it.

Special Prep/Equipment
Baking sheet

1. Dissolve yeast in warm water. Add sugar, salt, eggs, 1 cup of butter and half of the flour. Beat 10 minutes at medium speed. Blend in remaining flour. Fold in almonds, citron, raisins, and lemon zest. Put a damp kitchen towel over the bowl, and allow to rise in a warm place for 1½ hours.

2. Preheat oven to 375°. Cover your baking sheet with parchment paper, or grease it. Using a wooden spoon, stir down the dough with 25 strokes. Turn out dough on a well-floured surface and shape it into a 12 X 18" oval. Spread over it the remaining 2 tablespoons softened butter. Fold over one long side towards the center, then the other, and finally, fold the short ends over a few inches. Transfer to your prepared baking sheet and bake for 45 minutes.

3. While the stollen cools for 5-10 minutes on a cooling rack, mix glaze ingredients in a small bowl until smooth.

4. After the cake cools slightly, pour glaze over the top and allow to cool completely.

Serves about 12 (one large loaf)

1 package dry yeast	1 cup slivered almonds
¾ cup warm water	½ cup chopped glazed citron
½ cup sugar	½ cup raisins
½ teaspoon salt	1 tablespoon lemon zest
3 eggs	
1 cup + 2 tablespoons unsalted butter, softened	*Glaze:*
	2 tablespoons hot water
3½ cups unsifted all-purpose flour	1 cup powdered sugar
	4 tablespoons butter, melted

wo things you can't fake are good food and good music.

〜 *Etta James*

BANANA BREAD WITH CHOCOLATE GANACHE
~ Virgina Mayhew

I am a tenor saxophonist and I have been part of the NYC jazz scene for over 30 years.

My friend, professional chef Rima Mazzeo Crow introduced me to the idea of adding a layer of chocolate ganache to banana bread.

Special Prep/Equipment
An 8 x 4" loaf pan is needed.

Ganache:
½ cup 75% dark chocolate chips (4 ounces)

½ cup heavy whipping cream

Cooking spray or soft butter, to grease pan

Batter:
2 cups all-purpose flour

¾ cup granulated sugar

2 teaspoons baking powder

½ teaspoon baking soda

¼ teaspoons salt

4 or 5 medium-size ripe bananas (or overripe)

¼ cup milk

¼ cup unsalted butter, melted

1 large egg

2 teaspoons vanilla extract

Chopped nuts of your choice (I like pieces of raw walnuts and pecans)

1. Preheat the oven to 350°. Coat your loaf pan with cooking spray or soft butter.

2. Make the ganache. In a small bowl, combine the chocolate chips and the cream. Microwave on high for 30 seconds. Stir. Microwave on high for another 30 seconds, or until the chocolate melts. Whisk until smooth and glossy, and set aside. May take longer to melt.

3. Make the batter. In a medium bowl, combine the flour, sugar, baking powder, baking soda, and salt. Mix with a fork and set aside.

4. Place the bananas in a large mixing bowl or food processor and mix or process until the bananas are well mashed.

5. Add the milk, melted butter, egg, and vanilla. Mix or process until blended.

6. Add the flour mixture and mix or process until just blended. Don't over-mix; stop when the flour is just incorporated. Fold in the chopped nuts.

7. Spoon half of the batter into the prepared pan and smooth the surface. Pour the chocolate ganache over the first layer, level with spatula. I like it when the chocolate is about ⅜" thick, a real layer of chocolate.

8. Top with the remaining batter and smooth surface.

9. Bake for 50-60 minutes, until a wooden toothpick comes out clean, or with little moist bits clinging to it (time may vary)

10. Cool on a wire rack for at least 10 minutes before removing the bread from the pan.

Makes 1 loaf (about 6-8 servings)

NONNA'S TIRAMISU
~ Sarah Pratt-Parsamian

I play violin; I am a member of New York City Opera, and perform regularly with the New York City Ballet, and as a sub with the New York Philharmonic. I teach privately at home, and at a studio in Manhattan. My students perform regularly on concerts at various venues that I organize and produce.

It's been a very tough year for all of us in the arts; we saw our jobs evaporate, our enthusiastic audiences disappear into isolation, and our concert stages shuttered overnight, as a pandemic, the likes of which we have not seen in 100 years, swept around the globe. We all dealt with the hardship in different ways. An avid performer, teacher, and outdoor girl myself, I poured my pent-up energy into many avenues: learning to use Zoom so my violin students would be able to continue their lessons; learning solo repertoire I had been meaning to learn for years but had never found the time; performing socially distant chamber music (isn't that an oxymoron right there?) in a mask for live video broadcasts; homeschooling my two kids; running more miles than ever before on park trails near my Queens apartment…AND cooking for my family. Sometimes, there is nothing more satisfying than preparing and presenting a beautiful home-cooked meal…or just a really, really good dessert! Here is one of my best recipes, passed down from the Sicilian side of my family. Tiramisu literally means "pick-me-up" – and we surely can all use one!

Love to you all – we will play together again!

Special Prep/Equipment
Electric mixer, 9 x 13" baking pan
Before serving, this tiramisu
needs several hours in the fridge.

1. Beat the egg whites with an electric mixer until hard. In a separate bowl, beat egg yolks, and sugar with a fork; add the mascarpone to the yolks, mix with a spatula, then fold in the egg whites. Mix espresso, Kahlúa, and Anisette (or Grand Marnier) in a bowl, and set aside.

2. Assemble the tiramisu. In the baking pan, start with a thin layer of the mascarpone mixture on the bottom. Dip the lady fingers in the espresso mixture, and arrange them neatly to form one layer, filling the space of the pan. Cover this with another thin layer of mascarpone. Add another layer of soaked lady fingers; cover with a thick layer of mascarpone. Sift powdered cocoa to dust the top of the tiramisu.

3. Refrigerate for at least 4-6 hours before serving.

4 eggs – separate whites from yolks

4 teaspoon white sugar

1+ cups espresso coffee

1 shot Kahlúa liqueur

1 shot Anisette, or Grand Marnier liqueur

1 (475 gram) tub mascarpone

1 package ladyfinger cookies

½ cup unsweetened cocoa powder

Serves 8

FOR OUR PETS

SIMPLE DOG TREATS
～ Katherine Cherbas

I work as a cellist in Broadway shows, several NYC-area freelance orchestras and whatever chamber music opportunities I can find.

My son has many food allergies, and has also suffered allergic skin reactions when licked by a dog who has recently eaten. My parents went on a quest to find a recipe for dog treats that would not include anything to which my son would react. This recipe is adapted from *cleanfingerslaynie.com.* The original recipe uses gluten-free oats, peanut butter, and a banana but we substitute soy nut butter for the peanut butter.

1½ cups gluten-free oats

½ cup soy nut butter

1 large ripe banana

Special Prep/Equipment
Food processor or blender
Rolling pin

1. Grind the oats in a food processor or blender to a fine texture. In a large bowl, mash the banana with a fork until smooth, then add the soy nut butter and ground oats. Mix until a tacky dough forms. Adjust the texture of the dough by adding a little more ground oats if the dough is too sticky, or a little bit more soy nut butter if the dough is too dry.

2. Preheat oven to 350°.

3. Line your work surface with parchment paper and roll out the dough into a circle about ¼" thick. Cut the dough into the desired shapes – you can use bone-shaped cookie cutters or just use a knife to make squares or rectangles. Transfer the dough onto a baking sheet that has been lined with parchment paper.

4. Bake in preheated oven for 12-15 minutes, or until the bottoms are golden brown. If you overcook them, they will become dry and brittle and fall apart. Let the cooked treats cool for at least 15 minutes before serving. They can then be stored in the refrigerator for up to two weeks, or frozen for up to one month.

Yields 3-6 dozen treats, depending on size

THE BEST HOMEMADE CAT FOOD
~ Judith Hirschman

I am a percussionist, timpanist, and opera contractor.

I wanted to give my fur baby the very best diet! I modified this from a recipe from *The Cat Lady* YouTube channel. I like to use a blender for making the food (rather than a grinder) because it's less messy, the liver and hearts are less processed, and the vitamins are better dispersed. In my recipe I don't use any commercial calcium supplements.

Special Prep/Equipment
Blender

21 ounce mix of chicken livers/hearts

4 egg yolks

8 ounces water

2000 mg taurine

4000 mg salmon oil

200 mg vitamin B complex

200 IU vitamin E

1 teaspoon salt

5 pounds chicken (approx 2 medium chickens plus 2 breasts- boned and with only half the skin)

2 ¼ teaspoons eggshell powder

1. Place the chicken liver/hearts, egg yolks, water, and vitamins (shake powder or squeeze oil from the capsules. Do not include the capsule casing) in the blender to liquify - this takes less than a minute. Remove to a separate bowl. Set aside.

2. Place chicken and skin in the now empty blender and grind.

3. Sprinkle eggshell powder over ground chicken; combine organ meat/ vitamin mixture with chicken in the bowl.

4. Freeze in small containers, enough in each for 2- 3 days, and thaw as needed.

Makes a month's supply for a medium (12-14 pounds) cat.

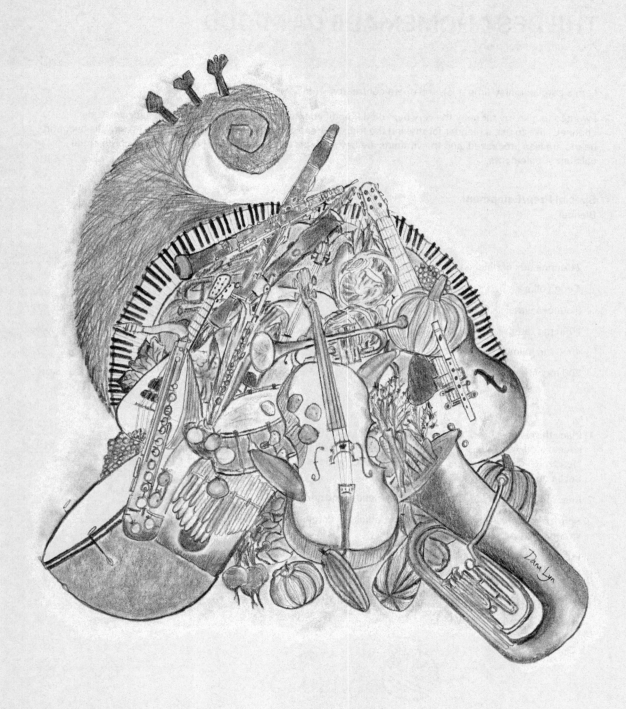

Recipe Index

C

D

H

I

SOUP? Sounds good!

Recipe Notes

Recipe Notes

Made in the USA
Columbia, SC
08 July 2021